the rocks near the large boul water and stopped and stood sniffing the air like a hunting dog trying to point out the prey to its master. It dropped down again and headed for the water's edge and then stopped and stood up again. Vidan's skin started to crawl, the fear was welling up inside his chest as the dragon smell got closer. Then he realized it wasn't because the venti got closer, it was because of the huge black shape flying overhead. It was Mortes! His mind was again in a state of panic, not from the smell, but because the book lay so far away from him under that rock. A venti was standing so close to where it lay hidden, and now Mortes was coming and he would be paralyzed by dragon fear again. He could handle a single venti that wandered a little too far, but he still could not get control of his fear when Mortes was near.

The giant, black dragon circled twice and then landed a little awkwardly on the shore. The dragon was too big for the slanted shoreline scattered with boulders. She cramped herself between the tall pine trees and the waterline. Her mouth opened in a shrieking bellow, but over the sound of the waterfall, he could barely hear it. Vidan also found that he couldn't smell that awful smell that had him cowering in her presence. Then he saw something he had never seen before. Mortes bent her head toward the ground almost to lay her neck flat, and a human shape slid off of what looked like a saddle, onto the ground.

How could a human be so close to her? Why wasn't he writhing in fear? Mortes straightened her head up and then looked towards the dismounted human. It almost seemed as though they were talking. Vidan needed to know what they were saying. He touched his wand to both of his ears and then said "esculti" and pointed the wand towards the dragon. Suddenly the deafening sound of the waterfall became quiet and he could hear the raspy, breathy, unnatural voice of Mortes,

"Where is he? Where is the Book?" she snapped.

"I grow impatient with the two of you and your weak hunting skills. Do you need to be punished?"

Another voice answered in a deep, calm, unfeeling voice, "My queen, I know you are tired of waiting but this wizard is tiring. Soon his magic will die, and he will die with it!"

Vidan knew immediately that this was the voice of the human. His voice was smooth and sounded as it should, except there was a hollow sound to it, an unfeeling sound. It sent shivers up his spine.

The next voice he heard was a higher pitched voice yet matched its mother's raspy tone.

"Mother, I can smell him so clearly. He must have been here just moments before I arrived," hissed the venti.

At that, Mortes drew her head up high and looked around the edges of the water and looked to where it started flowing down stream again. He could see her red glowing eyes. They looked hot like there was a furnace burning behind them. They were piercing and evil. It was like she could see through everything.

"Have you searched the edges of the water?" she said annoyed.

"No mother, you arrived just as I started to work my way to where the scent is strongest," said the venti.

She let out a scream and smashed her front legs into the shore, "Get back to searching, you useless bag of scales!" As she did she sent boulders crashing into the water in her fit of rage. She was now restlessly clawing at the stone beneath her.

Instantly the venti dropped back to its hunting dog stance and began sniffing the ground and rocks. Vidan's mind was racing.

What should I do? I can't fight my way out of this. I am too weak to cast any meaningful spells.

"My queen," he heard the human speak again.

"Yes?" she hissed.

"What if he were using the water to hide his scent? We could be wasting precious time here as he floats further and further down the river."

"You are right," she said as she turned her head back to the mouth of the river heading off downstream. She had thought of this earlier, and now it was confirmed. They must move down river now. It was getting late, and with every passing second it grew darker. Soon she would not be able to see well enough to find him, especially with his scent being covered up by the water. "Come," she commanded and lowered her head again. The human climbed back into his position and in a quick pounce, the black dragon was airborne once again.

Vidan could not believe his luck. She is gone. Now his concern returned to the single venti that was crawling around the rocks looking for him. He hadn't been paying attention to the venti once it had gone back to its search. He had been so focused on his mother, that he had hardly noticed it. He didn't see it at first. The night was getting darker, so it was difficult to spot its' black scales in the moonlight. Then he heard a noise directly below him. The venti had worked its way over to the falls and was sniffing at the end of his trail. Vidan dropped his hooded head against the cold wet rock ledge and hoped it would not see him. Then he heard, as clear as could be, a low screeching intake of breath. It sounded like the venti had propped itself up on its hind legs and was sniffing into the ledge where he lay hidden. Then he realized that he had not released his hearing spell. He was still hearing what the venti was doing. He slowly raised his head again to see what was happening. To his surprise the venti had turned back around and was headed back to the place he entered the water. This time it went with a purpose. Instead of turning back to the water's edge, it turned towards the Book. Its steps became purposeful.

Vidan knew it could now smell his scent on the Book. He had to act quickly, or it would call his mother back. Vidan pushed himself to his knees and yelled out "Incendi" as he wrenched his wand in a slashing motion towards the venti. With a sizzle and a crack, brilliant streaks of lightning shot from Vidan's wand. The sound of scorching flesh and the venti's cry of pain rang clearly in his ears. He mindlessly pointed the wand to his ears and said "termi". The roar of the waterfall returned.

He was now more tired than ever. He had to use his levitation spell to get down from the ledge he was on. When he hit the ground, he stumbled toward the Book, anxious to place it safely back in his robes. He stepped over the pile of smoldering reptile, the pungent smell much better than the normal dragon scent he detested. He pulled the rocks out of the way and quickly placed the Book back into his robes.

Just as he did he felt his hair stand on end again.

"She saw the light you fool!" he spoke out loud.

His only instinct was to run back to the ledge. As he did he heard a piercing screech and the night sky lit up with blazing red and yellow flame. Mortes had seen the white light and had heard the cry of her child. She wanted this human dead. She wanted the book he held destroyed, and she wanted it destroyed now.

Vidan jumped behind the curtain of falling water as the dragon landed with a crash on the shore. She breathed flames into the falling water with a vengeance. Vidan could feel the unbearable heat, but it was not enough to scorch him. The immense amount of water constantly falling from above was stopping the flames and turning into an enormous cloud of steam. It became the perfect cover. Vidan let out a blood curdling scream as though he had caught fire and dove headfirst into the flowing waterfall. As he did he swung his wand in an arc and said "impervio, fundo, levito".

He shot like a stone slung from a catapult straight into the depths of the water, an invisible bubble keeping him dry and allowing him to breath. The only problem was he could not see a thing. He shot forward until he hit the bottom of the river. He looked back up toward what he thought was dry land. It must have been, because he could see an eerie red light from the flames glowing overhead. He looked back down stream only to see blackness. He motioned his wand forward and the spell moved him in the same direction, but this time it was slower and more controlled. Suddenly, he crashed into something in the darkness. Was it a boulder? Maybe this was not such a good idea. Then he felt it. He had done too much. He had pushed himself too far. He was too weak. At least Mortes did not have the Book. His vision blurred, and he lost consciousness.

Vidan came to, cold and wet. He could feel the current pulling at his feet and legs. He was face down in the mud. He was coughing up water and his lungs hurt. His whole body hurt. It was still dark. He pulled at the mud and sand trying to get out of the water. It was no use. He collapsed with his face turned to the side, so he could breath. Mortes had to be out there somewhere looking for him. He knew that she would be combing the river trying to catch the faintest trace of his scent. It would not be long now.

As he lay there in the cold mud, he found himself caressing the binding of the book. His thoughts went to his sister, her husband, and their awful fate. He thought of their two children, Vidian and Rhen, the two beautiful children that had to suffer because their uncle could not protect their family. The uncle who had been entrusted with all the power to protect them, yet had failed to do so. The guilt he felt was overwhelming. His throat hurt, and his eyes began to well with tears.

"Enough," he said out loud. "It will not end this way! I will not go down in tales as the coward."

He pushed himself up again and pulled at the mud and sand. It hurt, but he was determined. Slowly but surely, he pulled himself up the muddy shore. Then he noticed the mud started to get warmer and he could smell sulfur. As he crawled, he noticed there was a warm stream of water running across him. He knew where he was. He had washed up on the sand bar along the big bend in the river where the mineral hot springs were. He couldn't wait to soak his sore body in one of these warm pools.

Then he thought, *Are you crazy? She will be out there searching. You don't have time for that.*

He didn't exactly know where the thought came from next, but he was glad it came. *I need to rest if I want to survive.* The smell of sulfur that came from these hot springs would cover what little scent he would have after he had climbed all the way in. If he could make himself comfortable and somewhat hidden here, he might just get a much-needed chance to rest.

As he slopped around in the greasy mud, he was very careful to keep track of the temperature. Some of these *pots* got so hot they would boil you alive, but others were very enjoyable to lounge in. He finally reached the side of one. He could faintly make it out in the moonlight. It was nestled right up against an embankment, offering at least some shelter. The temperature was excellent. Then he realized it wasn't exactly water. It was a big pool of mud.

He was too tired to search any more for a different pool, so he climbed in. It was so warm and comfortable. It was just what his aching body needed. Vidan pulled himself to the far side of the pool near the embankment. The mud only came up to about his hips at the deepest part. He worked himself into a comfortable position under the embankment near the edge where it was much shallower. The soft mud under him made the most comfortable bed. He relaxed for the first time in a month. There was no sign of the dragon. He could not smell her, nor did he think he could smell her over the sulfur. This was also comforting.

If I can't smell her, then she will not be able to smell me. He was so tired. He just wanted to sleep.

Before he dared to sleep, there was something he had to do. He couldn't take the chance that his slightest scent could escape while he slept. Just to be sure, he began to smear the mud into his hair and beard. He filled his hands with the warm creamy, sulfur filled mud and smeared it all over his face and every part that might poke out of the mud hole. All he could smell was the sulfur. He closed his eyes and drifted into a calm, much needed sleep.

When he opened his eyes again he was blinded by the white-hot sun peering straight down on him. From what he could tell it was just after midday. He had slept the entire night and half of the next day! He couldn't believe how rested he felt. He also noticed how warm he felt. His entire body was deeply relaxed. After a while he decided to sit up and take bearings on his surroundings. Just as he had predicted the night before, he was at the bend in the river where the steaming mineral springs bubbled into the river. He sat in a creamy brown mud that bubbled around him. The smell of sulfur almost smothered him now.

He couldn't believe the amount of time he had been hidden from the dragon. He had never been able to stay hidden for longer than a few hours. *This is progress*, he thought. He was certain that the smell of the sulfur and the mud mask had been able to shield him from Mortes's senses for the night. *Why had he never thought of this before?* How nice it would have been to have slept all those nights. It didn't matter now. He found a deep peace knowing that this would be where he would spend his nights from now on. He knew that he would now be able to get sleep at night. The smell did not matter. He could regain much of the rest he needed to be at his full strength.

He sat lounging in the mud and his head seemed clear for the first time in weeks. He started to focus on what he was going to do. He needed a plan. He started to think about the Book and all the spells that he had studied over the years. Spells like the levitation spell that had helped him hide last night at the waterfall, the illumination spell he had used so many times to find his way through the dark caves in the mountains, and the protection spells that his master had made him work on so feverishly to get right. He never did get the protection spell right. He was able to make a shield that would protect him from small objects. It would at least stop flying arrows, but the objects would always hit him leaving a bruise, or a small cut.

What a great sorcerer he had turned out to be. If he would have perfected this spell, it would have given him some protection from the fires of the dragon. As he had grown older, he thought this spell no longer had much significance, as his only worries had been the people bickering about who owned what property and the other trivial worries of his government. He had never imagined that dragons really existed. He had thought they were just old tales to frighten little children. Just then, a thought crossed his mind. *If the dragons were real, then maybe some of the other legends were real as well!*

Before he knew what, he was doing, Vidan found himself scrambling out of the mud hole. He headed for the cool river waters. He pulled the Book from his muddy robes and dipped it into the clean water. He quickly brushed his hands over the cover and spine under the water. When he pulled it free of the slow-moving current, it was clean and dry, even though it had been soaking in the mud all night long and he had just pulled it from the river. He set it down only long enough to rinse his arms and hands. He then set off into the cover of the brush and trees along the side of the river.

He found an inviting rock and sat down next to it. It was perfect to lean his shoulders against. He rapidly slid through the pages searching for something. Then he stopped abruptly. On the open page in front of him was the title "Portal to Cana". He started to read. It was the legend of the great and powerful keeper named Brac. He too had met with a dragon and fought many fierce battles. The dragon had been injured, but it could still fight. Brac had also been injured and could barely crawl. He knew that the dragon now had the upper hand. His only thoughts were now to find a way to keep the Book safe from the dragon. While the dragon looked over its wounds and caught its breath, Brac cast the spell known as the Portal to Cana. Before the dragon knew what was happening an arch of white smoke appeared next to the keeper and he rolled into the glimmer of the portal. With a loud crack the portal closed, and the dragon screeched in fury to find its prey was gone.

The legend spoke of another world of humans that were warring between themselves. Brac described it as "a land of death, war and of lost morals." It was an unpleasant place, but Brac was able to stay hidden for weeks there. He regained his health and eventually returned and defeated the dragon. If it had not been for the portal, the Book would have been destroyed and the people enslaved.

At the end of the writing were the instructions for the spell. Vidan had seen this part of the Book many times but thought it had just been a story for entertaining children. He had even read this to Vidian and Rhen many times. How they loved to imagine that their uncle was the same heroic keeper. They would roll through the doorway and pretend to go to another world only to return through another doorway jumping onto their uncle's back yelling, "Die dragon!"

This was the plan that he had been waiting for. He could learn this new spell and escape to Cana and practice his spells. Mortes would not know he had left and would continue to hunt for him. He could return with a well thought out plan of attack. Who knows, he could maybe even find something in this other world that might help him defeat the dragon. Either way, it would give him at least some time to focus without the fear that the Book would be lost to Mortes while he came up with a better plan. He started to read through the spell's instructions. It seemed simple. Just a flick of his wrist and a thrust of the point of his wand with the words "Apellum Di Cana." He sat there in the bushes flicking his wrist and pointing his wand at the air. He tried different inflections in his voice, but nothing seemed to work.

At one point he saw a slight ring of white smoke and his heart began to beat rapidly. At the same moment a chill went up his spine as he felt a large dark shadow flicker over where he sat. He flinched as he looked to the sky. Sure enough, he caught the glimpse of a shimmering black-scaled body shoot overhead. He should have been watching more closely. He had grown accustomed to smelling the dragon before it even got close. He must not be able to smell her through the sulfur. At least he had his wits about him still.

He closed the Book and tucked it into his robes. He turned instinctively to the mud where he had spent the night before. It didn't matter that his hands were all wrinkled and soggy from the night before, he must go back in. Grabbing the base of a shrub, he slipped over the embankment and dropped into the mud. He quickly covered his entire body with the smelly, smooth cream and tucked himself in with his head partially hidden by a small bush that hung over the embankment. He hunkered down in the mud so that his nostrils and eyes were above mud level with the rest of his body below the surface. This was his only hope. She was so fast. If she even caught a touch of his scent she would be there in a twitch of her tail.

That is when he noticed the mud in the pool beginning to tremble. He could feel the solid ground beneath him tremble, and then he could smell her. It was not as strong, but her powerful smell of fear drifted through the sulfur and made him want to wretch.

His hands began to quiver, but he found that he did not lose control for the first time. A black muzzle dripping with black ooze slipped over the embankment directly above him. He could see every detail of the underside of her jaw. Large patches of missing scales were covered with what seemed to be scars. Just then a large glop of the black ooze dripped into the pool next to him. The stench was powerful. It was not the stench of death to which he was accustomed. It was more like rotten food. The smell that drifted from the refuse pile beyond the north castle wall, but intensified one-hundred times. He could see the translucent, razor-sharp teeth of her upper jaw as her mouth gaped open, tasting the air. He had to admit, she was an amazing creature. She was the perfect killing machine.

The ground trembled again as she pulled her body over the embankment. Large pieces of dirt crumbled off the edge and rolled into the pool of mud where he tried to stay hidden. One of them just missed him and he flinched, pulling his body to the far side of the pool and making a gurgling noise. The dragon stopped instantly and swung her head to the side so that her eye could focus on the pool, near the embankment. Vidan closed his eyes and lay motionless.

"What is it?" the calm human voice asked.

"I can smell the slightest hint of him," she hissed, "but I can't tell if it is fresh".

Her head swung back towards the river and she finished crawling over the bank. Her tail landed directly on Vidan as it cleared the bank. It forced him under the mud completely. He didn't dare to move until her tail slid free. Luckily it did so just before he could not go without air any longer. He surfaced and snuck a breath as quietly as he could.

He slipped a hand to his eyes to clear the mud. He needed to see what was going on. The dragon had stopped at the shore and was looking at the ground. Vidan had a shot of cold realization wash over him. He knew what she saw. That was where he had exited the river. He realized that he would have left a trail in the mud. A trail that would lead her right to where he lay. Now real fear was welling inside of him along with the fear that came from her scent. He knew he still had the advantage and he must act quickly if he wanted to live.

He pulled his wand from his robes and sat up. "Inferno, Incendi" he cried at full voice!

A large ball of fire encompassed by streaks of crackling lightning, shot from the tip of his wand and struck both the dragon's rider and the dragon in the back. The human had no chance. He fell writhing in the mud with the bones of his back charred and exposed. Almost simultaneously, a bolt of white lightning like the one from the night before, but much more powerful struck the dragon in the back of the head. She screeched in pain and fury as her body convulsed and thrashed on the beach. Her tail came crashing along the shore and hit Vidan mid body. It threw him almost ten cart lengths into a rock wall along the river's shore and he fell on all four in the warm soupy mud.

He propped himself up on his hands, trying to get his wind back. His eyes were blurry, but could still see Mortes thrashing on the beach. As he got to his feet, he realized that he was trapped against the rock wall. The dragon was slowly getting to its feet as well.

Mortes let out a scream that almost burst his ear drums. She wheeled about to face him. Her eyes were just small slits now that were full of rage and vengeance. Vidan quickly cried "levito" and motioned to a boulder on the shore. He then swung his wand towards the head of the dragon. The boulder flew towards Mortes. Not even looking away from Vidan, the dragon raised her front claw and batted the boulder away like a toy. He cried "Incendi" and a bolt of lightning flashed directly at her chest. She reared up on her hind legs and the bolt hit the large protective scales and made a sizzling sound. It made no mark and she began to rumble with deep laughter.

"You should have finished me while you had the chance!" she snickered. "Your magic is no match for my fully armored front side. It is impervious to even my own fire. This has gone on too long human. Now give me the Book!" she commanded.

He could not run, he knew she would burn him to ashes. He could not defeat her. This was his last chance. Suddenly, he could see the face of his niece and nephew. He could hear their voices crying "Hooray for Uncle Vidan." A tear dropped from the corner of his eye. His wand sent a tingling feeling up his arm. In an instant, he felt courage like he had never felt in his lifetime, and he knew what to do.

He pulled the Book from his robes and held it in front of him. The dragon's eyes became large again as it caught sight of the black-bound book. But something odd was happening. The silver ivy that encircled the book was glowing. Vidan had never seen this before, but there was no time to waste.

As the dragon took just a moment to focus on the Book, Vidan flicked his wrist and said "Apellum Di Cana". The ivy around the book flashed and an arch of smoke appeared to Vidan's side. The dragon lurched towards Vidan. As it did he blurted the only spell that came to mind. "Vidian" he blurted. Red hot sparks issued from the end of his wand and a sparkling butterfly shot toward the dragon's head. It had bought him the time he needed. The dragon saw the butterfly shooting towards her head and flinched. As the butterfly started circling into the air, the dragon reared up on her hind legs again in defense. Her face was full of confusion wondering what terrible end would come from a sparkling butterfly.

As the dragon's attention was drawn away from him for a split second, Vidan dove into the portal. He sloshed in the mud as he slid through.

To Vidan's surprise he lay in the end of a brightly lit hall, in what seemed to be a palace. Mud had splashed in along with him, covering the floor. It was made from the most brilliantly colored and polished granite that he had ever seen. There were people standing at the end of the hall, looking at him astonished. They wore odd looking clothing in a fashion he had never seen before. A roar from the dragon behind him and the look of horror from the people in the hall, brought Vidan's attention to the Book.

To his left he saw a door open against the wall. He quickly pulled it toward him and stuffed the book and wand behind it and pushed the door to the wall again. Pressing both hands onto the door and said "Protego." A magical blue glow illuminated the door for just a moment, and then Vidan felt the end. He had not closed the portal. He felt the most unbearable heat searing his skin. The last thing he saw was the skin on his hand catching fire. The last thing he heard was the screams of the people in the hall. Their screams were mingled with what sounded like his own scream. Then it was dark.

Chapter 3

Nick Channing

It was a usual day. The wind was blowing slightly, and a few white clouds drifted through the October morning sky. But, Evanston, Wyoming was far from usual. Nick was used to deep, green lawns and neatly fenced yards. It seemed so foreign to him that people really lived in the middle of nowhere like this. There were more homes on just one street of his old neighborhood than in this whole zip code.

He had never even been in a mobile home before they moved here. Evanston was full of them. His dad had tried to explain that Evanston was remote and that mobile homes were the most affordable way to get a house there. He really didn't care. He was just annoyed it wasn't like the home he knew.

This morning he was rudely pulled from his deep slumber by the sound a neighbor's dog barking. When sleep left him, he realized that he wasn't dreaming and that he really was living in a double-wide trailer in Evanston. As the realization hit him, he sat up abruptly in his bed. He began to panic. *Am I late?* He looked at the clock. It was five o'clock. He had two hours.

This was his first day of school at Evanston High. He had been dreading it. Not only was he a sophomore, but he was a sophomore in a new school. He had spent years in his old schools, chipping away at the granite barriers between himself and the popular crowd. It seemed like he had finally broken through and that the warm light from the other side was peeking out at him, when the news of the move doused the light and any hope of finally fitting in with the cool kids.

He knew that he was in an awkward stage. It seemed like all his clothes were getting too small, and his aunt was always joking with his mother about how she must not feed him enough, because he was getting taller and skinnier every time she saw him. He had never had overwhelming amounts of self-esteem, and this didn't seem to help his situation. He was a sharp-looking kid for a boy entering puberty. His hair was a sun-bleached blonde with the slightest natural wave to it. He had let it get longer this last summer. He had a thing for the "Seventies" look. He had a nice tan from spending time at the beach and mowing the lawn. The tan took away a little of the awkwardness, but did not completely remove it.

His mother always made sure he had some nicer clothes, but he had just been growing so much this year that she didn't want to spend as much with fear he would just grow out of them. At the start of the summer he had been only 5'7". He was now 5'9" and it had been only a few months. With his less expensive clothes and the fact that he was feeling so awkward, he worried even more about fitting in at his new school.

Nick was sick to think that he knew no one. He would have to start from scratch. It made things worse to know that the other kids at school had been in class since August. It was now the first of October and he would be behind. He was going to need to catch up to the class. That meant loads of homework.

Back home in Maine, he had fit in just great. He had four friends that he had known since the first day of kindergarten: Chris Weston, Matt Evertson, Jesse Rinker, and Ryan Gilling. They were inseparable. He couldn't remember a single day growing up that he wasn't hanging out with at least two of them, except for holidays and family vacations. Even then, mom let one of them come occasionally. He had so much fun on the trip to South Dakota when Jesse came, that he didn't even consider that a "family trip." It was more like a week-long sleepover. They had gone to Flintstone Village and Mount Rushmore. There wasn't any particular thing that stuck out from the trip. He just remembered laughing and joking with his best friend all day, every day. They never got tired of each other. It was enjoyable.

Today was no trip to South Dakota. Today was a nightmare. So was the last year of his life. Nick had never known life any different than the life he had in Maine. He lived in the same yellow, wood-sided house his whole life. Their home was nestled between giant shade trees that had been there since the pilgrims landed, for all he knew. It was an older home, but Nick's parents had made it a very comfortable place to live. His mother loved to decorate, not to mention keep things neat and tidy. Nick's dad loved to work outside in the yard, and so the outside was as beautiful and homey as the inside. There were mature, nicely trimmed bushes and immaculately cut grass framing the cute little house. They had a dog, a fence, and even a hill for sledding in the winter. He had a younger brother named Shaun and a baby sister named Vanessa. Everything had been so perfect it seemed, except for when he tracked mud in the house or forgot to get home before his curfew. He had to admit now, that was his own fault.

His room had been the same room from when it was a nursery until the day they had slung all the memories into boxes and left. Nick's father was an engineer for AFC, The Augusta Fuel Company. They supplied heating oil to the homes in Maine and were one of the best at doing it. During the last few years, people had been turning to alternative fuels and his company had been slow making the necessary market adjustments. Nick felt very bitter towards the company. Their short sightedness had cost him his life. They started to lay off workers and cut costs. Nick's dad had been one of the more tenured engineers, but they let him go. His father had always said they were looking for "Young blood" and were weeding out the "Old thinkers."

Nick's life was changed forever that day. His father and mother called them all together as a family and told them that their father had lost his job. They proceeded to tell them that they had been looking for anything else in the area, and even in the state but could find nothing. AFC had been kind enough to make arrangements with one of their fuel suppliers and had landed him a job in Evanston, Wyoming.

Nick could remember how he felt the blood leave his head, like someone had pulled a plug in his toes. He had felt the tingling, as the blood emptied onto the kitchen floor through his feet. Then someone plugged the hole and the blood rushed back to his head. His face felt like it would explode as he begged and pleaded that there was something else they could do. He was panic-stricken. He couldn't leave his friends. He couldn't leave this house. He couldn't leave his life. Secretly, he couldn't imagine leaving Alyssa Gooden. Alyssa had been his secret crush since the 2nd grade. He had never met a girl that could be so beautiful and fun at the same time. They had been good friends their whole lives. Just friends, but he wanted it to be more. He had always been too scared to ruin a good thing, and now August Oil was making that choice for him. It wasn't fair!

He had so many vivid memories of this house, the people and the town of Augusta. He could remember the Christmas plays at the elementary, waiting in the hallway off the gymnasium with his reindeer horns made from construction paper before going on stage. He could remember stringing popcorn for the school tree. He could remember all the Christmas eves that he had spent trying to fall asleep. He remembered how afraid he was that he would still be awake when Santa flew in with his presents and that he wouldn't get anything because he wasn't asleep. He remembered all the autumns when the leaves had fallen on their lawn. They always piled them up and would run and jump into them. Only the cool night air and the smell of mom's fresh bread could lure them away. He remembered how secure it felt to sit at the counter and eat the bread with jam, and then to weasel a spot on the couch between mom and dad to watch the Monday night football games.

He remembered going to the cemetery on Memorial Day to leave flowers on his Grandparents graves. He remembered how dad would smile and tell the stories of his parents with a smile on his face. It almost felt like they came alive again on those days. There was a magic here. He could not explain it, but his heart was glued to this town and this home. He was sure that it would kill him if they tried to pull him away. He was sure that when they left, his heart would stay attached to his home. He was sure as they took him away his heart would stay in Augusta. He wouldn't be able to feel anything again.

All of his life experience came from living in that home, and he did not want those feelings to disappear. Nick's Mom and Dad had reassured him there was nothing they could do. They had already been checking for employment locally and there was nothing available for his dad. The other companies were doing the same things, "Downsizing."

They kept telling Nick, "Remember Nick, it's not the house that makes a home. We still have each other!" that just made him angrier.

It was weeks before Nick could speak to his mother and father. He spent every minute with his friends. He spent time at his old elementary, his junior high, and even went to his old future high school. Every minute that passed just left him with one less minute to soak it all up. He felt as though it were harder to breath each day. Finally, it came. The house had been purchased by the Chezeck family from Jersey. The contract gave them a date that they had to be out. It was on a Tuesday. It was the worst Tuesday of Nick's life. He had spent the night before going through all his old things. He had slowly peeled all of his posters from the walls and boxed up the last of his personal items. That left him with only a black duffle bag full of clean underwear, pants, shirts, and socks. At least he had his hand held Q5 in there to keep him entertained on the drive in the U-Haul truck.

When the last poster was down and the last box was loaded onto the truck, he sat down on the carpet, overwhelmed by the emptiness of the room.

"This isn't fair!" he said to himself. "Why is this happening to me?"

Overcome with self-pity, Nick turned off the light. He sat down on the sleeping bag in the corner of the room and looked out at "his yard" and "his fence". He stared up into the crescent moon and realized that this was the last time he would ever look at it from here. He climbed into the sleeping bag and slept for the last time in "his room". He fell asleep thinking about every birthday he had had, every Easter, and every moment from his childhood. As he did, he had to keep wiping the tears that kept welling in his eyes. After he had fallen asleep, his mother came into the moonlit room and knelt by his side. She reached out her hand and brushed away the last tears that had put him to sleep. Nick never saw her body shudder as she wept silently. He never knew her heart was hurting as bad as his. He didn't realize the hardest thing for his parents was to see his life upturned and ripped away from him like this. He never thought of their lives being torn from them. He couldn't understand how much they wished they could continue to provide him with what he wanted. They felt helpless. If he had, things might have been a little different when they got to Evanston.

Chapter 4

Evanston, Wyoming

Nick sat straight up in his bed staring at the wood paneled walls of his new cell. It was 6:15am and there was no way he could sleep any more. In his reminiscing, he had fallen back to sleep. The dog that woke him up was still barking. It was Rambus, the neighbor's Doberman. He hated that stupid dog. Once it started to bark it wouldn't shut up. It was like the Jones never even noticed how loud and obnoxious the stupid animal was.

It was in their yard! How could they sleep through that? Nick thought.

He had already been feeling miserable enough the night before, but now he was in an even worse mood if possible. The bus wouldn't be here until 7:30am and it only took him 10 minutes to get ready for school. He could have slept in another hour if it weren't for that stupid dog.

Nick slipped his legs over the side of the bed and touched them down on the old, multicolored carpet. His eyes stopped for a moment on the carpet. He was amazed that anyone would even buy a carpet made up of brown, orange and green strands. After his wondering, he pushed himself to his feet and towards the bathroom in the center of the trailer.

Nick's mind continued to wander as the hot shower careened over his skin. Soon the small bathroom was full of hot steam. He kept going over all the injustices that had come upon him over the last few months to keep his mind off of going to school for the first time. Every time he thought about catching the bus, his stomach turned, and he was sure he was going to be sick. So, he did everything he could to keep his mind off it. It really didn't work though. A giant knot was forming in both his throat and his stomach. How was he going to pull this off? He didn't know anyone. At least the school wasn't as big as the one he was used to in Maine. His old junior high was made up of 2,000 students. Evanston only had just over 300.

Begrudgingly he climbed out of the shower and grabbed a clean towel from the loose towel rack. The towel rack that seemed like it would fall off the wall every time he touched it. He couldn't believe how "junky" this house seemed to be compared to what he had been used to. He couldn't believe that his mom or his dad would even consider buying a house like this after the beautiful home that he had grown up in. He remembered the day they looked through town with the realtor. They hadn't seen anything better, at least not anything that was in "Dad's" price range. Every time they headed for a new home he would get excited just to be let down as they pulled into the driveway of another run-down trailer home with yellow weed filled grass and an old, gray, chain-link fence. There were hardly any trees, and the ones that had trees (if you could call them trees) looked as if the trees were begging for water and a good pruning with a chainsaw.

His mother had smiled at him when they decided on this trailer and said, again, "It isn't the house that makes a home Nick, it is the family inside." That is when Nick spat out the venomous words that seared his mother's heart, "It will be hard to feel love in a junk hole like this!" Nick's father had never been physical with him before, but that day was a first for many things. "You take that back!" his father spoke strongly as he grabbed him by his arms and forced him to look into his face. Out of the corner of his eye he saw his mother turn her head and wipe a tear from her eyes, as his father shook him. "I will not put up with your attitude any more Nick! You have been acting like a baby for the last two months. I have put up with it because I knew you were hurting inside, but not anymore. Can't you see this is difficult for us too?"

Nick found more words filled with malice pouring from his mouth. He could only remember saying was, "You have no idea what I am feeling," and the most dreadful thing, "You can't even take care of me, look at this house!" and that is when he ended up on the ground on his back. He remembered the confused look on his father's face that he had never seen before. It was a fierce look, his face was fiery red, and his eyes were angrily fixed on his face, but his jaw line seemed broken and quivering. His eyes were welling up with tears. Just then Nick's mother stepped between them. Her eyes were red, but she was now working up a smile. She said "Stop!" and went on to tell his father how happy she was with the house. In her usual way, pointed out the fun she could have whipping it into shape. That was his mother. She was always focusing on the positives.

Nick remembered how miserable he had felt after saying those things to his dad. He could never imagine saying them to someone he loved so much. It seemed to worsen the rift between them. Just two months ago they had such a great relationship, just like they had always had. As soon as the news broke of the move, Nick had closed up. It wasn't on purpose, but he just didn't feel happy, and he didn't want to talk to anyone. No matter what they said, they couldn't change a thing. They couldn't buy his house back. They couldn't give his father his job back. He was going to Evanston High School, whether he wanted to or not.

Nick just wished he could erase those cruel things that he had let slip out in frustration. That day he felt like a terrible son. He already felt bad. When he was around his dad, he didn't feel like he could look him in the eye. He wanted to ask for his forgiveness and take it back, but he felt so selfish and that made him angrier. More than anything, he just wanted to hug his dad, he hoped his dad would just reach out to him, but he didn't. They just tried to avoid each other from that point on. Nick could tell that this just made his mother even more miserable.

Nick was brought back from these terrible memories with a knock on the bathroom door. "Nick, come on buddy, I need to get ready for work!" said his dad with a little anger in his voice. Nick realized that he was staring at himself in the mirror with a mouth full of toothpaste when his father had jolted him from his thoughts. He quickly spit and rinsed and said "Okay, okay. I am almost done." He wrapped the towel around his waist and opened the door. His father was overrun by the thick steam that poured out of the small bathroom as Nick slipped by down the hall. All the steam made it easy to avoid eye contact.

Once in his room, he swung the door closed and started slipping into the best set of clothes that he could find. As he looked into the mirror his stomach tightened again as he noted how the clothes didn't fit quite right. They were his cloths from last year and he had grown. They were just small enough to make him feel uncomfortable. He clenched his teeth as he felt overcome with a wave of anger again. He grabbed his backpack and his phone and headed for the kitchen.

When he sat down at the kitchen table, he realized that mom wasn't home. It was Monday. On Mondays his mom left at five and headed to her new job stocking shelves at the grocery store. Nick's mother had never worked, that he could remember, until now. This reminded him again of how hard things had become since they had sold their home. Dad and Mom had hoped they would get more for the old house and that they would be able to cover all the moving expenses from Maine to Evanston. It didn't happen, and they had been completely strapped ever since. Dad's new job was a job in the field he was used to, but the pay was half of what he had been used to at Augusta Fuel. Nick couldn't believe how much he had taken for granted.

He pushed himself up from the table and headed to the cupboards to get a bowl and some "Marshmallow Crunch". *I could definitely use something sweet today,* he thought to himself. He sat back down after he had poured a bowl with some milk and found himself focusing on the activities on the back of the box. After his third bowl, he headed out of the house without a word goodbye to his dad. He noticed that the bus wouldn't be here for another twenty minutes, but he didn't want to get stuck in the house in an awkward conversation with his dad.

He made his way out to the paved road and headed for the stop sign where the bus would stop. It was a warm day already, and he couldn't see a cloud in the sky. The sun hadn't come over the horizon yet, but he could see the line of sunlight working its way across the landscape. It would be peaking its head over the horizon very soon.

He sat down on a big rock that was just off to the side of the road. It was surrounded by 3-foot-tall weeds. He plugged in his headphones and flicked through his playlist. After finding one of his favorite songs, he let the music numb his thoughts. So numb that he didn't notice the other person sit down next to him 10 minutes later. It was another sophomore just like Nick. He had spiked jet-black hair. His clothes were much more "hip" than Nick's. He had almond eyes and the perfect smooth complexion that his Korean family roots had given him. He himself was second generation and living in Evanston. He was as "American" as the farmer down the street.

Nick was startled when a song ended, and he heard a cough. The sound was so close and unexpected that it startled Nick and he jumped.

"Calm down, I am not going to jump you," said a reassuring voice. Nick turned to see who was sitting next to him. The boy was smiling an infectious smile. "I am Joe" he said with his hand outstretched. "You must be the Channing kid," Joe said.

"Yeah, Nick. How did you know that?" Nick asked.

Joe smiled even bigger, "Are you kidding me? In a small town like this you get to know everybody, and everybody knows you. You are the only face I don't recognize, and tourists don't catch the school bus. I figured you had to be the new kid."

There was something very likeable about Joe. Nick couldn't pin it down, but there was something familiar about him. Joe was definitely a talker. He just kept going on. He asked question after question about who he was and about Augusta Maine. Nick even lost himself for a moment and forgot that he was completely miserable. He even smiled a few times as he heard Joe complain about how little there was to do in town.

"So how did you end up here?" Nick asked. Joe raised his eyebrows and sighed.

"Well unfortunately for me, my dad landed a good job with Mountain Fuel about 3 years ago. We packed up and moved here from Salt Lake City. I have been bored out of my mind ever since. Living out here on the edge of town doesn't help. It would be better if I had a car! I did hear that your parents had bought the place next door and it gave me some hope when they said they had a son who was a sophomore too."

Nick seemed to warm even a little more. "So, we might have some classes together?" Nick asked.

"Sure thing" said Joe, "There are only 25 new sophomores this year, so I bet we have almost all of our classes together. No doubt that we will have English, Math and Gym together." Joe assured him.

"Good, at least I can talk to you, well that is if you will let me," Nick said sheepishly.

"I will save you a seat in every class I can. I could use a good friend."

It was like Nick had known this kid for a few years. Something about him didn't scream small town at all. He was very fun, laid back, and likeable. It made the whole morning more bearable. Slowly but surely five other students slowly showed up. None of them really showed much interest in Nick, and only barely noticed Joe.

"What is up with them?" asked Nick.

"Oh, they are full timers. They are juniors and seniors and all of them have been serving a life sentence here in town. Don't expect them to notice you for a while. It took two years before any of them would pay me any attention. They are good people, don't get me wrong, but they live for the horse races and rodeo, and that isn't my thing. So we don't have a lot in common," Joe explained.

A few minutes later the bus rounded the corner and they were on their way to school. The day had started off way better than he could expect. He had even made a friend with a pretty cool kid. He was happy he wouldn't be alone the whole day. Who knew, he might even do okay hanging around Joe. It didn't take more than three hours to change his mind.

It all started after second period. His first class was English, and sure enough he sat with Joe. It was nice. He didn't feel too bad about things. Second period wasn't too bad either because it was art. The teacher seemed nice, but Joe wasn't an "artist", so he had to go it alone. After second he had "first lunch." He spent the whole time looking for Joe, and when he couldn't find him, he finally got in a line and ended up with only five minutes to eat. He quickly sat down at the first open table he came to and started to dig in. Not moments later he heard all six chairs around him jerked out and saw very large figures sitting down.

"What are we going to do to him?" said a deep manly voice.

"Let's take him to the locker room, pants him and duct tape him to the flagpole!" said another.

"Naw, let's just push him out into the parking lot stark naked and leave him a map to the office to fetch his clothes," laughed another voice.

Nick stopped chewing. He even stopped breathing. He had heard of this before. He had seen the hazing back in Maine, but had never been in the line of fire before. Nick struggled to keep his hand that was holding his fork steady. He could feel the lump in his throat and stomach from this morning return twice as strong. He couldn't look up. He just stared at his plate of food wishing this were all a dream.

"You know, I think I would like to just make a good example of him in the parking lot after school. Sophomores don't ever get privileges at this school. I think I will enjoy kicking him around out there," said the first voice.

Nick felt his eyes welling with tears. He couldn't really see his plate clearly, all he could see were dark shapes around him at the table and the fuzzy shape of his plate in front of him. The tears managed to distort everything into a crazy dreamland, but he knew this was really happening.

Right as he was sure that he was going home with a broken body and as the school papers new headline, he heard the one chair directly across from him get pulled out.

As he heard it slide out he heard a reprimanding voice say, "You guys get lost, and leave the poor kid alone."

He could hear nothing else but chairs moving, not another word for at least 30 seconds. Nick's face was still glued to the same spot on the table, his head was lowered so that he didn't have to look at anyone. Just then a strong hand grabbed his.

"Look at me. Hey, look at me!" the voice commanded.

Nick slowly looked towards the voice across the table. As he tilted his head up, the water brimming in his eyes was pulled free by the gravity. He quickly swept his free hand to catch them before anyone else could see. There on the other side of the table, was a senior that looked more like a man. He had short dark hair and a physique like the incredible hulk.

"What is your name kid?" the new voice asked with compassion.

"Nick," he said softly.

"Well Nick, of all of the open places in the lunchroom, you picked the absolute worst place to sit. This is the senior's table. Only seniors sit here," said the voice.

The tears seemed to dry up and Nick could focus enough to get a clear view of the person talking to him. He had genuine concern on his face, and Nick had a feeling for just a second that he wasn't alone. Even though he had no idea who this person was, he had a savior, a hero. He just wanted to throw his arms around this guy and hug him for saving his life. (At least that is what it felt like to him.) Nick didn't though. He was still frozen to his chair. The hulk-like figure rose from the chair and patted Nick on the shoulder.

"Nick, everything will be ok. Just don't sit at this table!"

By the time Nick could find his voice, his hero had left. Leaving Nick alone in his chair at a table he wasn't supposed to be sitting at. His thank you went unheard, but Nick Channing was changed forever. He could not believe what had just happened. His day was ruined, but at the same time he had just had a new experience that left him speechless.

He couldn't stop thinking about how grateful he was to this mystery person. He found himself wondering about how many other people wandering the busy halls were having these terrible experiences like him. He wondered how many of them were as miserable as he was. As Nick wandered into 3rd hour class late, he decided that he would be like his new hero. He would stick his neck out for others. He was going to try as hard as he could to make others feel better too.

Third period was history. The teacher was a no-nonsense man named Mr. Carson. He was older, with graying hair and wrinkles deeply cut into his leathery skin. His voice was different than his demeanor though. It had an interesting tone to it that caught you up and helped you hear the excitement he had for what he was teaching. It wasn't until halfway through his lecture on "Pearl Harbor", that Nick realized that Joe was sitting in the back of this class. It wasn't long and the bell was ringing, and he was quickly making his way to Joe's side.

"So, what do you think of Evanston High so far?" Joe asked.

"Not my favorite place in the world," Nick said with sincerity.

Joe just smiled and said, "You don't have to tell me."

For some reason this was comforting to Nick. It was nice to have someone around that thought like he did. The last few months had been very lonely, and he liked saying things out loud to someone who could appreciate them. Nick was happy to know that on "A" days he would have three of four classes with Joe.

They headed off to Biology for the last class of the day. To make things a little better there was a pep-assembly in the gym for the football game that night. This meant less class and more time to talk.

During the assembly, Nick found out the name of his new hero. It was Kirk Lancaster. He wasn't only the Incredible Hulk's twin, but was also the captain of the football team and starting middle linebacker. Nick couldn't believe it. He also picked out a few of the guys that had swarmed the table as fellow football players. Nick realized that if Kirk hadn't shown up when he had, he would have been in for it. The thing he couldn't believe was that someone so big and popular, would take time out to help a scrawny little sophomore with pants that were too short. He could tell from the speech that he made that he was a sincere person who really cared, and by the reaction of the senior girls, he could tell that he rated well with the ladies.

On the way home from school, Joe filled Nick's ears with all the up to date information of the different cliques at the high school. Nick never mentioned the incident at lunch. He felt too stupid. But his face reddened a little when Joe mentioned not ever sitting at the front tables in the lunchroom. He also let him know about senior hall and all the other parts of the school he should avoid. Nick was irritated that all this information hadn't been disclosed to him earlier, but he didn't say anything.

Joe also mentioned that he would love to hang out, but that he had to go into Salt Lake with his Mother to visit his Grandfather in the hospital. Nick asked if he would come over the next night to hang out at his house and made sure to let Joe know about his new gaming console and flat screen in his room. Joe said he would love to come over the next day after school.

Chapter 5

Bubbled Glass

The next day at school was uneventful. Nick chose to steer clear of the lunchroom all together. Instead it was to the vending machines and off to the cubby in the hall by his locker. Classes seemed to drag on forever. The only one that seemed worthwhile was P.E. and that was because Joe was in this class with him.

"I have a good idea for after school!" Joe said. "Do you like scary stories?"

"Of course I do," Nick replied. "What do you have in mind?"

"Well, I thought instead of vegging in your room we could go down to the abandoned part of town and I can show you the town legend," Joe said dramatically.

"Show me the Legend?" Nick said with a smile.

"You'll see," replied Joe.

The last 20 minutes flew by as they chased a soccer ball around the football practice field. Nick liked PE just because it was a chance to do something physical. It seemed like he didn't spend much time playing sports like he had in Augusta. It was amazing how much better he felt after he had run up and down the field a few times. When the warning bell rang, Nick was covered in sweat and was feeling excited about the adventure Joe had planned for them.

Before he knew it, he was jumping off the bus and running for the shower. He was still all sweaty from playing soccer. He only had fifteen minutes before Joe would be banging on his door, ready to go to the abandoned part of town. He took the quickest shower he could. He climbed into some old clothes, as Joe had said to wear something he didn't mind getting dirty. He couldn't wait to see the town legend. He hoped it would be something worth seeing. He grabbed a few granola bars and inhaled a quick bowl of cereal.

Nick jumped up when he heard a loud knock on the front door. He snatched up his old shoes from the laundry room and headed for the door. When he pulled it back, there stood Joe in Black clothes, head to foot.

"Going to a funeral?" mocked Nick.

"Wait and see. You better grab your bike though, we have a little bit of a ride," replied Joe.

Nick's mountain bike wasn't the best-looking bike, but it got him anywhere he needed to go. He had had it for two years now, and he had ridden it hard back in Maine. He pulled it free from the lawn mower and hoses that had it trapped in the old tin shed in the back yard.

"Woooow, that baby has seen the road hasn't it!" Joe couldn't help letting out when he saw the bike for the first time.

"It works just fine," Nick shot back as soon as Joe had finished his sentence.

They both jumped on their bikes, and Joe pushed down on his pedal and yelled "Follow me!"

They headed for the main part of town. Just before they reached the bridge that went over the river, they headed out a road that Nick had never noticed before. The road didn't even have lines painted on it. It curled around a couple of warehouses, and then it disappeared behind one of the bigger ones. As they turned around the corner leading behind the larger of the two buildings, Nick became aware of the strange feeling surrounding this place. Behind the warehouse was a street lined on both sides with old commercial stores, but not a sign of life. They were very old buildings, but in great condition. They seemed like buildings that should have been prime real estate. It was a haunting feeling. He felt as though these streets should be bustling with shoppers, cars and along with that, the sounds of motors, bells (from shop doors), and all the other sounds of a bustling street.

All that was here now was a deep silence. The buildings and trees behind them seemed to muffle all the sound from the rest of Main Street and the surrounding area. He started to notice that each window was boarded up with weathered plywood. It almost looked like someone had prepared for a hurricane many years before and just never came back after the storm.

"I had no idea this was even here!" Nick gasped.

"Most people don't. Not unless your family has lived here for a long time. No one really talks about it anymore either," Joe said quietly.

"Well, let me hear it!" Nick said, with more enthusiasm than he had felt in the last four months.

"Not just yet, I have to take you to where it all happened. It is right down there in toward the middle of the street. Do you see that three-story building?" Joe asked Nick.

Nick strained his eyes a little but did notice the one building that was taller than the rest. It became clearer as the two walked toward it, pushing their bikes. Soon they were standing directly in front of the building Joe was talking about. It seemed odd to Nick that this beautiful building was not being used. It stood three stories, with an ornate crown piece directly over the center of the building making it an additional 10 feet tall. It was made of granite and carved with great precision. It depicted a king being tended to by his servants and an inscription was below it in Latin that Nick didn't understand. As he looked over the building one thing stood out to him. The windows on this building were not covered with plywood. They were intact, but they were a darkened color. He also noticed that at the corners of the windows he saw some black stains running up the sides of the window.

When they were standing directly in front of the grand marble stairs that led up to the front door, Nick realized he could see bubbles in the glass. That is when it hit him.

"There was a fire in this building!" he said out loud.

"The game is a foot Watson!" joked Joe. "You should have been a detective with a mind like that."

Nick didn't say anything back as he walked up the ornate stairs to the front door and started to run his hands along the granite stones under the window sill. It was amazing how beautiful it was on the outside even though he could tell the inside must be ravished by the fire that had melted the windows. He couldn't see anything through the rippled, dark glass except darkness.

It was obviously a very fancy hotel. It must have been around for a long time as well judging by the style. Joe was walking around to the side of the building to what looked like the guest check in area. It had a small pull through drive right up to a pair of brass doors. Joe put his bike up against the wall and motioned to Nick to do the same.

"You have to leave your bike here. The front is all chained up, but there is a way in around back," Joe whispered.

"Why are you whispering?" Nick said back.

"We aren't supposed to be in here, so I don't want to draw any attention," Joe said through tight lips. "Just follow me and be quiet. Once we are in we can talk all we want."

The two slipped around to the back of the building to what looked like the loading dock. Joe climbed up onto the dock and hurried over to an old garbage bin on wheels. He bent over and pushed his shoulder into it and it slowly moved over about two feet. Nick could see what he was doing now. Right behind the garbage bin was a two-foot by three-foot opening. Nick recognized it as an old coal chute. He saw a lot of these back in Maine. People used to purchase coal from the local heating company who would deliver it through the coal chute. The old door was missing, just leaving a big hole in the side of the building. It was black inside and Nick didn't quite know if he was going to be squeezing into that hole anytime soon.

Without warning Joe disappeared into the hole feet first. Nick could see him drop out of sight and could hear the sound of his feet hitting some type of floor below.

"Hurry up," came an echoing voice.

So, Nick got down on all fours and peered into the dark space below.

"Don't come head-first, slip your feet in and drop down," Joe ordered.

Nick did just as he had been told and slid his feet into the darkness and dropped in. The floor was further down than he thought and so when he hit, he couldn't keep his balance and sprawled out on his belly. Nick could hear Joe laughing and then realized a bright light was shining in his face. Joe had turned on his flashlight only after he had landed to see what had happened.

"Thanks for turning that on after I jumped!" Nick snapped at Joe. Nick noticed that he was in what had to be an old boiler room, from what he could see in the light of Joe's flashlight. Old pipes were running all over and there was a big black shape against the far wall. From what he could see, everything, including the walls and floor were black.

"Is this where the fire started?' Nick asked.

"No one really knows?" Joe said, "But I'm not saying anything until we get upstairs. Follow me."

Joe led the way with his flashlight. There were some stairs in the far corner. They followed them up the black stairwell to the main floor. Nick couldn't explain why, but his hair started to stand on end, and he had goosebumps everywhere. He could now see some light coming from the windows in the front of the building, but the light was distorted by the melted blackened glass.

When they reached what must have been the main lobby, Joe piped up "Have a seat. I can tell you the story right here where they found thirty of their charred bodies," Joe said creepily. Another shiver went up Nick's spine. Something just didn't feel right about this place.

Nick sat down on the floor eager to hear the story now. He was interested to hear what had happened here. When he sat down Joe turned off his light. All he could see now was the soft gloomy glow coming from the windows and the shape of Joe's head in the darkness.

"Well, let's see, hmmmm, how did it all start? Oh yeah. It was in the fall almost 10 years ago. This used to be the nicest Hotel in town. It was always very busy, filled with all the fancy 'big wigs' from the different gas companies, horse racers, and travelers who were stopping through. The hotel was nearly sold out. The lobby was completely full of guests. This street used to be the place where all the best dining and entertainment was."

Nick could imagine the streets busy just as he had been thinking. He was imagining to himself that the hotel lobby where they now sat was completely full of people, checking into the hotel and just lounging in lobby chairs. As his eyes had adjusted, he noticed that by the blackened remains of what had to be the registration desk, there was what looked like an old-fashioned bar. Behind it he could make out misshapen bottles that were still in their original place when they had been heated until the glass had softened and allowed the necks to droop. He could imagine that no one expected a thing, and the guests were all just enjoying themselves at the time.

"Was it an explosion?" asked Nick.

"Well, that is where the legend comes in. It was about 8:30 PM and just getting dark. Witnesses from neighboring businesses say that it was the most shocking thing they had ever seen. Suddenly there was a flash of bright yellow light that glared from the windows, and the front doors blew wide open and billowing flames blew out into the street like a flame thrower. The heat was so extreme that people standing on the other side of the street were severely burned. There were people standing on the stairs, and a few cars directly in front of the door. The cars were burned so badly that the paint was completely removed, and all the glass melted into puddles inside and around the cars. They say that the people on the stairs didn't even have time to let out a scream. When we leave I will have to show you where the cars were at."

"Anyway, the odd thing was that not a single window was broken, but the fire had blown the doors wide open. Everyone in the entire hotel was killed. The only screams that were heard were from the top floor of the hotel."

"They figured that the fire had come from the basement from the coal piled up in the boiler room where we came in. Some say that the natural gas lines that run behind the hotel must have been leaking and somehow filled the entire hotel with gas without anyone noticing it. They think that when the maintenance man was shoveling coal into the boiler, a spark must have fallen into the coal storage and started the whole load on fire. When the fire got big enough and the gas had reached a point just right for it to catch fire, the whole place ignited in a gleaming fireworks display. Most of the people from town figure it different."

"There was a huge investigation to see if the gas company was the cause of the fire. They shut down the entire street and it went on for months. They counted over two-hundred and fifty burnt bodies. Some were found in the shower charred with the water still running. In the boiler room they found metal rivets from someone's pants, a belt buckle and charred bones and teeth of what they expect were those of the maintenance man. They figure that the heat from the coal completely consumed anything in the room that would burn."

"Upstairs on the third floor was the most gruesome sight of all. This is the only floor that the windows did not melt. Most all the furnishings were still intact, but scorched. There were signs that the fire was not as strong in these areas. The heat from below was so intense that it had bubbled the people's skin and flash roasted them according to the autopsies. Their bodies were intact and some of them were found draped over the radiators under the windows with their hands stuck to the metal window frames. They figure that they were struggling to get the windows open but died in their frantic attempt to open the windows."

"After five months, one day the investigation was over. Everything was packed up and they left. The gas company was never named as the culprit and they never had an official cause. It was all a mystery. They reported that the only thing that could have happened was a gas leak from inside the hotel and that the burning coal would have added to the problem. It left everyone asking, why, if it was a gas fire, there wasn't a massive explosion when it was ignited. How did the windows melt without getting blown into the street below?"

"That is when the rumors started to fly. People were saying it was a terrorist attack. Others were claiming a cult was responsible and others were blaming the whole thing on a naturalist group that wants to shut down the gas company for ruining the wilderness areas where they run their pipelines. The oddest claim of all is that some locals believe it was a curse. A curse because the hotel was built on an old Indian burial ground. They believed that it was the power of their ancestors, 'Dark Magic'.

As Joe said this his voice faltered a little and Nick felt his hair stand on end again.

"The store owners had been unable to run their businesses because the investigation had shut the entire area down for safety. They didn't want to endanger anyone else until they could figure out the problem. With hopes that the gas company would have to pay retribution for the damage and loss of business many of the store owners waited to see the outcome. When there was no one to blame, they had already lost too much money to be able to start up business again. The popularity of the street had turned to that of horror and everyone started to avoid coming here. Most of the businesses that had insurance to cover their losses relocated to Main Street. John Croft moved his Pharmacy and grocery store first, and everyone else followed. The city boarded up the empty shops when JP Commercial couldn't pay the loan they had on the buildings they owned. A few of the property owners that were insured could, but the others just declared bankruptcy. The city purchased the property at the auction in hopes of reviving the area, like I said there is a lot of history here, but no one has ever done anything with it."

"So, the question is, what really happened? For some reason, I don't think it was old Indian magic, but every time I come here, I get the feeling that something isn't right."

For a few moments it was deathly silent. Nick had to wonder if he were sitting where someone had died 10 years before. Suddenly Nick broke the silence. "I can feel it too! It's weird, hard to explain, but real creepy."

Joe snapped out of his trance and said, "Let me show you around." Nick looked at Joe hesitantly. He had come in here willingly, but after hearing about the two hundred and fifty people who had died, he felt as though he were in a tomb. The building still had the smell of an incinerator from a crematory. "Aww c'mon, they removed all the dead people during the search, and they are buried in the city where their families were from. You won't be running into anything too scary." Joe poked at him.

"I'm not scared, let's look around." Nick said loudly, trying to convince himself.

Joe led him upstairs and turned off his flashlight. Now Nick saw why he was in black. He wanted to scare him. All Nick could see was some pale form of Joe's head floating off the ground at what looked like the correct height. They walked up to the second floor, and as Nick rounded the staircase that headed up to the third, he couldn't find Joe anywhere.

"Joe, where are you?" Nick asked loudly.

He could hear a muffled laugh that he thought came from up the staircase. He hurried up the stairs and noticed that as he got to the landing halfway up that it was getting lighter. This added to his courage and sped his steps upward.

"Joe?" he called again but this time he heard nothing.

As he entered the hallway from the stairs on the third floor, Nick noticed what Joe had said about the heat from below. The once white walls were black at the bottom but turned into a dark brown that went to a dirty tan to an eggshell color at the very top of the walls and ceiling. He noticed that the floor must have been covered with fancy carpet, but all there was now was black stubbly fingers as though it had all melted under tremendous heat. He could see where all the light was coming from, a door in the hall was opened into one of the guest rooms and light from outside was pouring out into the dark hall.

Nick cautiously walked toward the room. It seemed like the closer he got to the room the more eerie this building seemed. He finally reached the door and slowly edged his way in. All the furnishings were still in the room. They were not their original colors and were singed. The carpet was melted just like in the hall. The bottom of the bed posts were completely black. The finish was completely bubbled on every piece of woodwork left in the room. The wallpaper in this room was charred and hanging in pieces all over the room.

Nick walked over to the window remembering what Joe had just been saying about the people who were found with their hands stuck to the metal frames. He looked down at the frame just above the silll. He could see two marks with something black stuck to the frame about shoulders width apart. He wondered if this was where someone had fought for their last searing breath trying to escape the unbearable heat. Although the windows weren't melted, they were coated with black and dust. Nick could barely see the outlines of the street below.

Just then he heard something. It was a breathy low whisper, "Help me."

Although his first thought was that it was Joe, He couldn't keep the shiver from going deeper into his soul than ever before.

"Joe!" he shouted a little frustrated but tinted with worry.

He heard it again but louder this time. "Please, help me!"

It sounded like it was coming, from what he assumed, was the bathroom.

"Joe, serious, I'm not an idiot!"

Nick couldn't help but move closer and closer to the door. Just as he got to the door he heard it again, "Helllpp meeee!" It was coming from behind a blackened linen shower curtain. Before he knew what was happening, the shower curtain was pulled back and a gruesome face was jumping towards him and all he could hear was a haunting scream. Every part of his body jumped, and he felt like he couldn't breathe. He fell backwards onto the blackened floor. Instinctively he pushed himself towards the door with both of his feet trying to stand back up. As he got to his feet he heard the unmistakable laughter of Joe. He turned his head back toward the gruesome face that had just come for him and realized it was hunched over and shaking in rhythm with Joe's laughter.

"You jerk!!" shouted Nick, as he punched Joe in the shoulder.

"I, wish…I caught that…on video," Joe barely managed to push out between his fits of laughter.

Nick was just getting his breath back, but his hands were still shaking. For a moment he felt as though the rubber Halloween mask was real. He thought that a victim from the fire had somehow survived or a ghost had stayed to haunt the old hotel. Either way he had never been so scared in his entire life. Joe was still laughing to himself as they walked down the third-floor hall towards the other staircase.

Even though it was lighter on this floor than the others, it wasn't by much. It felt so weird, like a bad dream that you might have. Everything was black or at least darkened by the fire. It just left a haunting feeling in his stomach. Something just wasn't right about this place, and he couldn't figure it out. With every step toward the other staircase, the darker it started to get. Joe's head started to "float" again. Joe started to laugh again and that was it. Nick broke the silence.

"Stop laughing, Joe it isn't that funny."

"Oh yes, it is!" Joe managed to get out before he started into another fit of laughter.

"You're dead!" yelled Nick just before he started for Joe.

At that, the laughter stopped, and Joe started to run down the dark stairs. Nick hurled himself into the dark towards Joe. They rounded the landing on the second floor and started down into the dark of the main floor. Nick was so close to Joe's floating head now. He reached out to try and grab his shirt and lost his footing on the stairs. He caught Joe, but not like he had planned. He crashed down on top of him pushing Joe down the stairs face first. Luckily Joe got his hands under him as he came crashing down the stairs with Nick on his back. They both crashed into something as they fell, and it was coming down the stairs with them. Everything sounded twice as loud in the dark of the burned-out hotel. The two came to a halt when they hit the main floor.

For a moment it was quiet, then "Are you okay Joe? Sorry, I didn't mean…"

Laughter split the air. Joe was laughing even harder than before. This time Nick joined in. They both laughed until they thought they were done, and then one of them would make a small noise and it would start again, even louder than the time before. After what seemed like a good twenty minutes the two finally got themselves together. They were still sprawled out on the floor where they had landed.

"What did we break?" Joe asked.

"I have no idea," replied Nick, forgetting how angry he had just been with his new friend.

The darkness was finally broken by Joe's flashlight shining back up the stairs they had just fallen down. It was blinding at first. Nick hadn't realized how his eyes had adjusted to the dark.

Joe whirled the light around to where they were. Pieces of what was left of an old burnt grandfather clock lie all over the floor. By the looks of it, it had already been destroyed by the fire, but it must have been standing when the two crashed into it on the landing between floors. Blackened gears and other metal pieces were all over the place. As they looked through the pieces of clock all over the black floor, something caught Nick's eye. There was something white running along a door that sat right near the bottom of the stairs. Nick grabbed Joe's arm and forced the light over to the door.

"That is weird." Nick said.

"Wooaaao" Joe let out.

They walked closer to get a better look. There in the middle of a fire ravaged building, was bright white paint. It seemed so out of place. It looked as though it had just been painted that morning it was so clean. A piece of the main clock face lay at the foot of the door.

"I swear on my life, I have been in here a hundred times, and I have never seen this. That piece of clock must have nudged the door away from the wall," Joe said quietly.

Nick reached out his hand and pulled the door away from the wall. They both took in a deep breath when the back of the door caught the light. While the front of the door looked as if it were turning into charcoal, the back side was clean and crisp just like it was brand new. It was a fine walnut with a perfect finish. It was clean and smooth just like it had barely been installed. Nick broke the baffled silence.

"How in the world?"

"This is really weird," said Joe. "I have been in here so many times and I have never seen this."

"You just said that Joe," Nick reminded him.

"Yah I did, it's just so weird," Joe said again.

Nick swung the door all the way open. Just as he did, he noticed something down by the base board. A black book was leaned against the wall right below where the hinges were. It was about seven inches by nine inches. There was one handprint that wrapped around the spine of the book. It looked like someone had grabbed the book with a muddy hand. Nick leaned over and picked it up. It looked very, very old, but it was in good shape. The cover was made of black leather. Arching across the front in fading, silver calligraphy it read "ODD FELLOW". The edges of the book were laced with fading silver ivy. The back cover had been made with extra leather so that it could wrap around to the front and protect the contents. It had a clasp made from what looked like white polished bone that was pushed through a slit in the leather from the back to hold it shut. Even though it looked very old, it had an elegant appearance.

"What is that?" Joe moved in closer with the flashlight.

"I am not really sure." Nick said as he slumped to the floor with his back against the bright, white paint.

He slid his hand over the cover. There was not even a speck of dust on it. He moved his hand to the clasp and opened the book. He noticed immediately that the pages were yellowing with age. The edges looked worn, like the book had been well used. Even with all the signs of use, the book was in incredible shape for something that seemed to be so old. He started to turn the pages and noticed that even though they looked old, they were not brittle, and he had no fear of damaging the book. He started to read some of the titles out loud.

"Morte", "Ilumino", "Natura"... "these look like spells or something," Nick said with awe in his voice.

"Gimmie a break," said Joe. "That is the dumbest thing I have heard in a long time."

It was quiet for a moment as the two read the instructions below the title. *Hold your wand high in the air and bring it down in a zig-zag motion....Make Eye contact with the person you want to control and say in a commanding voice "Iussus."*

Nick looked back at Joe and said, "Maybe this is just some person's book that is way into fantasy."

Joe looked at Nick for a moment, and then said, "That doesn't explain why the door and wall aren't burnt."

As this slipped from his lips, they both felt shivers running through their body-- not the cold chills that you feel when you are scared, but the shivers you feel when you witness something inspiring.

Nick continued through the book until he came to a portion in the very back where the pages went blank. He quickly turned back a few pages and read, "I do not know exactly the amount of time I have been running from her now, but I do know time is growing shorter each day for me to find a solution. It seems I have less and less time before she finds me now. Sleep is so precious, yet I get so little of it."

"If you are reading these pages, it means I did not make it. You must now keep this book. You must protect it from her. She can't have it, or she will destroy it. The things within this book are so precious. It is the only way that man can survive. Remember she calls herself Mortes and you will never forget the first time you smell her stench."

"What is this nonsense?" Nick said out loud.

"You got me," Joe replied.

"This is all just too odd for me," Nick said.

He put the clasp back through the slit of leather and set the book down. He walked back over to the door to inspect it.

"Can you shine that light over here?" he asked Joe.

The light jumped from where they had been reading to the nicely finished door. "How could everything else in here burn, but not the wall and back side of this door?"

Nick slid his hand over the nice finish and just stood there thinking. As he thought his eyes wandered to the floor. He noticed that on the floor there was a triangle wedge the length of the door. It was not black like the rest of the floor. He could see brown on the floor. Nick bent down and touched the brown surface. It was dried mud. He brushed his hand back and forth and it revealed the most beautiful marble he had seen. It was dirty, but it wasn't blackened like everything else in the building. He started to brush his hands back and forth on the floor. As he did he realized that all around the closet there were ripples on the floor. He looked up at Joe.

"This closet was full of mud when the fire happened," he said excitedly.

"How do you know that?" asked Joe.

"Well, look at the floor. Look at these ripples. They are hard, but look what happens when I push on them with my thumbnail."

Sure enough, he pushed down with his thumb nail and the ripples would break off in big chips, revealing more of the marble finish underneath.

"Help me for a second," ordered Nick.

Joe dropped to all fours with Nick. They were breaking up chips of baked mud and revealing a beautiful marble floor. In the next twenty minutes they were able to clear a four-foot semicircle on the floor in front of this closet. Then they started to hit the end of the baked mud. The floor turned black again and nothing would come off. They both stood back up and backed away for a better look. Joe picked up the flashlight and pointed it right to where they had just been brushing away the dirt.

"Look," Joe said, "Is it me, or are those handprints at the edge."

"You're right," said Nick.

Just along the edge of where they had been clearing the black from the floor, were two clear handprints. It looked as though someone had been struggling toward the door. Nick checked the back of the door, and sure enough there was part of a muddy handprint towards the bottom of the door on the unburned side. It was obvious that this had all been here from the time of the fire because the mud was blackened on the top. You had to break through the top to get down into the original color of the mud. Nick was amazed at how well preserved the marble was that had been under the mud.

Nick's head was running at a million miles an hour. Why was there mud on the floor? Why was it just in this area? Whose handprints were these? Was it the same handprint that was on the book? If it was, why would they be trying to protect this silly book of imaginary spells?

He grabbed Joe and pushed him towards the next closest door.

"I need to see over here," he said to Joe.

He reached out and pulled the door away from the wall. The door was charred on both sides. The entire wall was black. They checked every door on the whole floor. Every door was the same. They found themselves standing in front of the closet door again. Nick knelt again and reached inside the closet. The floor was black and there was no mud. He rubbed his hands along the floor between the mud and the closet floor. A perfectly straight line appeared as he rubbed.

"Where did this mud come from, and how come there is a perfectly straight line right here?" he asked out loud.

"No idea," said Joe.

Nick walked back over to where the book lay. He sat down again and started thumbing through the pages again.

As he did, Joe put the light right in his face. He turned his head quickly away as the light temporarily blinded him. When he opened his eyes again, he saw something he hadn't noticed before. There was something dark and slim leaning up against the first hinge of the door. Nick slid his hand over to it and grabbed it. He felt as though he had just grabbed a pin cushion. He dropped whatever it was to the ground. Joe looked at him surprised.

"What is it?" he asked.

"I don't know, but it hurt. I need your light again," said Nick.

As the light shone on the object, Nick realized what it was supposed be. It was a magic wand. Not the kind that you would see in a professional magic show with the white tip, but a strange, ancient-looking wand. It had a handle that was carved from the wood from which it was made. In the handle were odd looking markings that wrapped around the wand in swirls to make up the grip. A small ridge made an end to the handle and then it tapered down to a point at the end. The wood was dark, almost black like the book. Nick was drawn to it again. He reached out his hand and picked it up. This time the feeling of pins shot into his hand again, but he did not drop it. The feeling subsided and he felt a tingle run up his arm and down his back to his feet.

He couldn't tell if it was really happening or just in his head. He swished it back and forth in a trance. Nothing happened. For a moment he realized he almost had expected something to happen.

"I'm going crazy!" Nick said to Joe.

"You didn't expect it to be magic, did you?" Joe mocked.

"To be honest, for a moment, I did," Nick came clean.

"Okay then…we better get going," Joe replied uncomfortably.

Nick couldn't put his finger on it exactly, but he felt different since he had found the book and the wand. His thinking was suddenly more open, and he wasn't really embarrassed to say what he was thinking. He almost wanted magic to be real. He wanted an escape from normal life. He just wanted an escape.

"Bring your light over here one last time," Nick said, "I want to see if there is anything in the closet."

"Fine," said Joe walking back towards the closet.

Nick took a step towards the closet with the book and wand in hand. As he drew nearer, he could make out the blackened remains of a typical janitor's closet. There was an old mop sink on the floor. Nick wanted to get a better look at something he could see glimmering out of the blackened sink. He stepped through the door and suddenly felt funny. He turned to look at Joe.

Joe was staring back at Nick with wide eyes of disbelief. Nick was trying to figure out what was going on. Nick's vision was suddenly getting blurry, and his feet started tingling. Joe stood looking at the Closet looking back at Nick, blinking to see if this were really happening. What looked like smoke had appeared in an arch in the door that Nick had just walked through. He could see Nick, but he his image was wavering like he was a reflection in a pond. Nick suddenly looked at Joe concerned and frightened.

"Joe, are you all right? I am feeling weird!"

Joe couldn't get a word out. He just stood there with wide eyes and his mouth opening and closing like he was trying to say something.

Nick took a quick step back through the doorway, as he did, he felt as though he were falling. As he fell, he could see Joe in front of him wavering like a reflection on water, and then all he could see was black. His head was swimming and spinning. Then he lost consciousness.

***

Joe saw Nick step back towards him and directly under the newly formed arch. As Nick's foot hit the plane of the arch, it disappeared inch by inch as he stepped forward. This slowly happened with all of Nick until finally his whole body disappeared as he walked himself into nothingness.

The moment he was gone completely, the smoke arch vanished. Nick was gone, and the only thing that Joe had heard was the sound of rushing wind.

Joe stood looking at where Nick had been. He blinked again and called out in a question.

"Nnnniiiick?"

When all he heard back was his own voice bouncing off the walls, Joe found himself running back to the boiler room. He wasted no time climbing back up and out through the coal chute. In a blink he was on his bike pedaling for home. His hands were shaking. He couldn't explain what just happened. What was he going to say to Nick's parents? He decided to go to the police station instead. He would just tell them they were checking out the place and they got separated. He would tell them Nick didn't have a flashlight and he was worried because he hadn't seen him since they got separated. It was half true.

As Joe rounded the old warehouses, Nick's bike slipped from the wall where it was leaning and fell to the ground.

***

Chapter 6

Cold and Alone

When Nick came to, he was lying on his back. He noticed that he was shivering and cold. He also noticed that something wasn't right. He could feel things poking him in the back, and he felt cool air all over his body. More of his body than he should. Nick sat up quickly and opened his eyes. He was outside. Not only was he outside, but he was not wearing any clothes! He instinctively covered himself and looked around.

He was in a pine forest. The floor was covered in ferns. The pine needles he was sitting on were poking him everywhere. He jumped to his feet and started to brush off the needles that stuck to him, while trying to protect his decency. He closed his eyes and pinched himself. "This must be a dream!" he heard himself say. His eyes flew back open at the sound of his own voice. He noticed that it was dusk. He must have been out for only a few minutes. Long enough to catch a good chill in the cold air of the forest.

There was only one possible answer in his mind. "Joe?" he called, "What is going on? Where are my clothes? This isn't funny! This is actually pretty sick!" he yelled full of anger. He looked all around under the trees for signs of Joe hunched over laughing at his best prank ever.

There was no reply, just the sound of an animal scurrying off at the sound of his angry voice. Nick focused on his surroundings. He could see tall pine trees all around where he stood. He could see orange light peeking into the forest from the autumn sky. The forest floor was covered with ferns, grass and pine needles. To his right on the ground lay the strange black book and the wand, but there was a new item that Nick didn't recognize, but welcomed. It was a pile of black material. He picked up the silky black cloth that lay with the book and saw that it was some type of a robe. He quickly slipped into it to cover his body. He was surprised that for as thin as it seemed, it was very comfortable, and he immediately felt warmer. He felt less self-conscious having covered himself up. He was still shivering, so he sat down again next to the book and wand, and wrapped his arms around his knees to try and get warm.

He continued to look out under the trees into the forest. Wherever he was, he didn't recognize any of it as Evanston. *Where did that jerk take me?* he wondered to himself.

The last thing I remember was walking into the closet and then everything went fuzzy and black. Nick wondered if he had used some type of chloroform or ether to make him lose consciousness. He had heard that either one could knock you out if you were to inhale enough. Either way, it was getting dark and he had no idea where he was. By the look of things, he was all alone, lost in the woods.

After a few minutes of thinking to himself, Nick decided that he better get moving. "Sitting here will get me nowhere," Nick said out loud. He stood up, scooped up the wand, and grabbed the black book. After contemplating which direction to go, he finally headed out in the direction of the setting sun. He remembered that there were trees up the Mirror Lake Highway to the Southeast of town. He guessed that this is where Joe had brought him, stripped him and left him for a good laugh. If he headed to the West, he should come to the Highway and at least then he could follow the road back into town.

Nick decided then that Joe was no longer his friend and that he would never speak with him again after pulling something like this. "What a jerk!" he mumbled.

Nick made his way very slowly through the trees. It was painful to walk through the forest with no shoes. Some areas were just smooth dirt, while other areas were covered in pine needles, broken branches, and sharp rocks. Nick started to worry when he realized that it would be completely dark soon and he would have an extremely hard time finding his way around, especially with no shoes. He wondered how cold it would get tonight and if he would be able to stay warm. He might be out here all night.

He started to watch for pieces of wood. He wondered if he could start a fire without matches. He had just watched a reality survival show last night. The contestant had used a stick and another piece of wood to create a hot ember and started some dry grass on fire. He decided it was worth a try. He looked for a spot with a comfortable looking tree trunk and some soft dirt to sit on where he could wait out the night. He found one of the larger pine trees in the forest that had some very large roots bulging out of the dirt around it. It had a space between two of the roots that looked like a king's throne. He figured if he sat between them he could lean his back against the trunk and rest his arms upon the large roots for armrests. He would start the fire just a few feet beyond to keep him warm. He felt good as he looked over the campsite. It seemed like the perfect spot. It even had other trees lined up in sort of a circle to give it a safe, secluded feeling.

Nick collected some dry wood and placed it by the tree. He also looked around for some rocks to make a fire pit to keep the fire from spreading to the forest floor and trees around him. He remembered from his time in scouts that he should clear the area around the fire of dry grass and anything that would burn. He began clearing the dirt of all debris that might catch fire. It was getting dark quickly and he needed to hurry.

Nick grabbed some dry grass and made it into the shape of a bird's nest. He broke up some small pieces of wood for tinder and placed them near the ring. The hard part would be making a flame. He grabbed two pieces of wood. One was skinny and long, the other was short and wide with no bark. He grabbed the skinny piece with both hands and began to rub it against the other piece.

Nick's hands were aching now. He could feel the sting of blisters forming on the palms of his hands. Sweat was running into his eyes, and he could only smell a hint of scorched wood. It was getting very cold and it was completely dark. He knew if he didn't keep trying that he could get hypothermia or even freeze to death. Nick forced his arms to move.

They burned with every motion and the stinging in his hands got worse. He had no idea how long he had been trying to make this fire, but he was sure that it was more than an hour. He continued to stare into the blackness where the wood should be clutched in his hands and pushed harder and harder. Suddenly he thought he saw something glow red. He stopped but saw nothing. He quickly started again. He saw the red but did not stop. He saw it grow brighter. His heart jumped from his chest as he stopped, and he could still see a soft red glow. He reached for the small bird's nest he had made. He gently tipped the ember into the dry grass and blew softly into it. The grass crackled and started to smoke. His hands trembled with excitement as he saw yellow flames licking out at his face. He moved the burning grass into the fire pit with the tinder and started to stoke his precious fire.

A few moments later, Nick sat by a warm fire. He was examining his bleeding hands. The man on the show had made it seem so simple. He decided that it was worth the pain as he felt the heat warming his body. He felt a sense of pride as he gazed into the flames that he had made. The light of the fire contrasted vividly against the dark blackness of the forest. For the first time, Nick felt a chill of fear creep up his neck as he realized he could see the fire, the tree trunk that he was leaning against, and a few feet all around the fire. What brought the chill was the brief thought of what else was out there in the forest watching him. What was out just beyond the light of the fire?

At least he had the fire between him and the darkness. To his back and sides were the trunk of the tree and the two large roots that he was sitting between. At least this gave him a little comfort.

Nick got up enough courage to get up from his spot by the fire when he looked at his firewood. He had not gathered enough firewood to keep the fire going. He realized that the fire would die out soon if he didn't venture out to find some more wood. He noticed that the further he got from the light of the fire, the better he could see the forest around him. He could also see his fire and the area he was sitting in like it was highlighted by a spotlight. This made him feel uneasy again as he thought whatever else was out in the forest would know exactly where he was and what he was doing.

After a few minutes searching around, Nick had made a small stack of good-sized branches. He loaded as many as he could into his arms and headed back to the fire. After a few trips, he thought he had enough wood to last through the night.

The forest was quiet. Very quiet. This made him feel even more alone and worried about staying the night here. The chill went up his back once again, and Nick hurried back to his fire. He quickly added some of the larger pieces of wood he had just gathered. The fire grew larger, reaching its long yellow fingers closer to the sky. The bigger it grew, the better Nick felt about being alone in the woods. He would just have to stay up and keep the fire roaring. He settled back against the tree trunk. It was warm on his back from being exposed to the fire while he collected wood. All was dark except for the fire and the small area that it lit up. The only sound that could be heard was the popping and crackling of the fire.

Nick held the book in his hands and flipped through its pages. The light of the fire wasn't enough to let him read it, but it was enough light that he could see detailed diagrams and very elegant writing. As he flipped through the pages it seemed that they went on forever. It seemed odd. The book was only about three inches thick, yet it seemed as though it was much thicker as he flipped through the pages again. The feel of the leather against his hands was smooth and cool. The corners were contoured and soft, but not tattered.

There was something different about it. He could almost feel a current in it. A current that resembled a pulse of something living like blood pulsing through veins. It was the only thing he could liken it to. Then he noticed the pulse seemed to match his own through his hands.

You're going crazy! He thought to himself.

He had noticed a pocket on the outside of his robe earlier and decided it would be a good place for the book. He slipped it into the perfectly sized pocket. When he did, he was amazed. He could feel the book with his hand, but he couldn't feel the book against his body on the inside of the robe.

"Now I know I'm going crazy," he said out loud and nestled back into the trunk of the tree.

The fire felt so good, it was the perfect distance from the tree, and it was warming him to his core. Nick investigated the flames and thought of his warm bed that sat empty tonight. The longer he stared at the red-hot coals, the harder it was to keep his eyes open. He leaned his head back against the tree trunk and let his eyes close halfway. He opened them again and they pushed back as though they had weights tied to them. He fought back one more time and then gave in. Sleep tightened around him like a boa constrictor, rendering him helpless.

Chapter 7

One Big Party

Nick was at home on a Saturday morning. He didn't have to get up, so he just lay there thinking about what he would eat when he got out of his warm bed. He couldn't remember his bed being more comfortable and inviting. It seemed to cling to him, keeping him from lifting a single part of his body, so that is where he would stay. Oddly enough, his sheets began to get cold, very cold. They were cold enough that he began to shiver. His bed wasn't comfortable any more. It was hard and started to tip up as though to dump him out on the floor. That is when his eyes flew open.

He was very confused for a minute or two. Still waiting between consciousness and his dream world, he couldn't focus on what was happening or where he was. Finally, his eyes focused on the gray and red coals at his feet. Then he woke fully with a jerk, as though someone had just slapped him across the face with their hand.

He knew exactly where he was, and he wished he were back in his dream basking in the comfort of his bed. He lay against the tree beside the red coals of the fire he had made. He was shivering from the cold night air that had snuck in as soon as the fire had died out. His first thought was to reach for more wood, but he heard something that made his heart jump. He had heard someone yelling. He then noticed more than one voice yelling. It sounded like someone was having a really good time.

Nick sat up from the tree and looked around. To the right of where he sat, he could see light coming from off in the woods. As he leaned to look towards the light, he could make out more voices coming from this area of the forest. He could also see the light flickering as if it were a candle. His heart began to beat a little faster. He was excited to know someone was out here that could take him back home. The loneliness he had felt, was quickly replaced by excitement.

He stood up and started towards the light and voices. He rubbed his hands over each of his arms as he walked, trying to warm himself up again. The orange and yellow light jumped back and forth behind the trees as he walked. As he got closer, he could start making out the voices a little more clearly. They were yelling more than talking. Occasionally, there would be a loud cheer, followed by laughter.

The fire was much further away than he had first thought. By the sound of the voices, he thought it was only a few hundred yards away. As he got closer, he realized how loud this group was. The fire was not just a campfire, it was a huge bonfire. Nick was just on the tree line near the huge fire. He could feel the heat from fifty feet away. Not enough to warm his body, but enough to give him goose bumps. He could see the shadowy figures laughing near the fire with their backs to him. He could also see the faces and clothing of those that were facing him. They were turned so the light lit them up like a spotlight.

"They must be part of one of those medieval groups," Nick whispered to himself.

The 10 or 15 he could see all had their heads shaven. Most of them were shirtless, their skin covered in black tattoos. Some had grizzly beards that looked like that of a homeless man. Others wore what looked like leather armor covered in metal studs shaped like diamonds. At the shoulder, it ended and what looked like chain mail sleeves ran down to mid forearm. He noticed that large swords and axes lie against trees and knees. He realized it wasn't hot chocolate that they were drinking in those mugs either. A few were gathered around a large, wooden barrel tipped on its side. One of them staggered back and forth and grabbed on to the others to keep himself upright. The others just laughed.

Great, all I need is to catch a ride home with a bunch of drunken men who think they are Knights of the Round Table. At least I will fit right in with my wizard's robe! Nick thought to himself.

Just then there was a huge commotion at the side of the fire and a lot of yelling. At the same time, something collided with Nick, knocking him off his feet and onto the ground. He was hit so hard it knocked the wind right out of him. He realized that it wasn't just one person, but two people on top of him, and one of them had a dirty, rough, scratchy hand covering his mouth. The other had their head by his ear.

Then he heard a whisper in a quiet feminine voice, "Keep quiet if you want to live!" The voice was so full of emotion that Nick instantly began to be fearful.

Nick's senses heightened, and he could hear what was going on by the fire.

A strange, unfeeling voice called out "What is going on here?!"

"Master, we found these boys crawling around in the shadows of our fire."

"Good, we could use some entertainment. Are there any others?" said the strange raspy voice.

"We are looking as we speak," said the other.

Nick felt chills run through his body at this and suddenly felt an urge to run. He tried to turn his head towards the fire, but the hand, held his head firmly in place. He strained his eyes to the side and could make out the shadowed figure looking their direction out through the trees. He could also see two boys about his same age. They were wearing tattered old rags for clothing. It looked like they fit right into this medieval celebration, but something made his blood go cold. He could see stringy, greasy ropes, tied around their hands. He could make out a thin line of what looked like blood running from the place where the ropes were tied. One of the boys had a bloody lip and the other's eye looked like it was swollen shut.

"Master, what shall we do with these?" the other voice interrupted.

"Let's have a game of course," he yelled.

The entire group around the fire erupted into yells of excitement.

"We will let them go and give them a small head start. Then whoever catches them can kill them!" he said.

Nick felt real fear for the first time in his life. Real solid, keep yourself alive fear.

He felt the body on top of him slide to the side and heard the voice to the side of him whisper "Follow us now and keep quiet."

Nick rolled to his hands and knees and crawled after the dark shapes of these two strangers.

"Enjoy the last few moments of your lives!" cried the raspy voice. "I will give you a count of forty!"

The hair on Nick's neck stood up as he ran blindly after the black shapes that he assumed were new friends. At least they had stopped him from walking right up to these men and becoming the "main event". It didn't really matter though, because they would soon be running after whatever moved in the forest, and by the sound of it they wouldn't care what they got a hold of. Just then, Nick tripped over something in the forest. He went crashing through some brush and landed on some rocks. They caught him right across the shins. *Classic Nick*, he thought to himself.

The strong hand that had been covering his mouth minutes before pulled him from the ground and a gruff voice said "You want to get us all killed? That is just giving them an idea of where we are. Follow me. It isn't about how fast we go, but how careful we go. We have an advantage here. It is dark, and we have a head start. If we don't make more noise than they do, we can get out of here alive." His words were so numbing. He knew that they were in danger, but it just seemed so unreal.

About ten minutes later, Nick's lungs were aching. He could taste blood in the back of his throat, and he could feel it starting to sting. Way behind him he could see what looked like five or more torches winding through the trees.

"We are almost there," he heard the female say. Her voice then turned to Nick, "Can you swim?" she asked.

"Are you joking?" asked Nick back.

"I need to know now," she said impatient. Nick could feel her eyes narrowing by the sound of her voice.

"Yes, I can swim, but can I get warm afterword?" Nick replied.

"You will be much colder dead," she said very matter of fact.

The next thing he knew, they were pushing him into what looked like a hot air balloon basket. He couldn't tell in the dark. That is when the moon lit up the water moving by below, very far below.

"Won't it be obvious where we have gone when they see the rope and this basket at the bottom?" Nick asked.

"Shut up and help pull on the rope," the gruff voice said.

Nick did as he was told but was very uneasy with the idea of what they were going to do. As the three of them pulled on the rope, the basket lifted into the air toward the tree branch the rope was thrown over. Once they were in the air, the basket swung out over the cliff directly under where the rope had been wound. The weight was too much to hold, and it slid from all their hands. Nick's stomach jumped into his throat and he couldn't even make a sound. The basket was plummeting towards the water. It didn't fall as fast as normal, because of the long rope that had been wrapped over the branch twice. They still fell and fell quick.

They landed with the basket upright, the weight of their bodies crushed them to the floor as it hit. The freezing water came rushing over their heads. Nick swam for the surface, panicked. The cold water was already making his hands and legs tingle. He wouldn't be able to swim far. As he surfaced, he looked for the shore.

He heard the voice of the woman again, "Swim to the far shore. We will meet there."

Nick did as he was told again and worked his cramping muscles, forcing them to slowly pull him across the river. He climbed up the rocks on the shore and made his way to the tree line. He looked back up to see how far he had fallen. He couldn't believe it. It seemed to be about a seventy-foot drop. He couldn't tell in the dark, but it was high. A torch appeared at the top of the cliff, and a bearded figure peered out over the edge. Nick shrank back into a bush. Two more torches appeared, and then a cliffside of torches showered light onto the trees at the edge of the cliff. He couldn't hear what they were saying, but saw them all turn and start moving along the cliff's edge for about fifty feet. Then the torches disappeared as quickly as they had appeared.

His two new friends came out of the water much further downstream, and so Nick worked his way their direction. When he got to them, he noticed why they were so far down stream. They had come to shore with the rope to the basket and had pulled it in as well.

"What are you doing?" Nick asked.

"We don't want them to find this. It will just give them somewhere to start looking again. Who knows if it would have caught up somewhere nearby," said the male voice.

"How did you know it was here?" Nick asked.

"We put it there," he replied.

After they had hidden the basket and very long rope in the trees and bushes, they started off in the same direction they had been going when they got to the cliff. They were no longer running, but they were walking fast. After what seemed like a few hours, they came to the end of the trees. Nick was confused again. Before him under the moonlight, was a barren landscape. It was open flat land with no vegetation whatsoever. Off in the distance he could see large clumps of what looked like rock. They seemed to get bigger and bigger the further you looked. This didn't look familiar at all. Where was he?

For the first time, it was light enough to roughly see what these two people looked like. The man was about 5 inches taller than Nick, but he was much bigger. His shoulders looked square, like one of the football players that had heckled him at school. The woman was about his height, but very slender. Both wore old clothes that resembled those of the other two boys that had been tied up at the fire. He still couldn't see their faces because they were wrapped up in some type of scarf. He could only see the glimmer of the moon in their eyes when they turned just right.

"Rhen, we need to rest!" the woman said.

"I know Vi, but not until we get behind the first hill of rock. We need a fire to get dry, and we can't chance one until we have that hill to hide it. You know they won't follow us out here," Rhen said.

"Hurry, by the way his teeth are chattering, I think he needs a fire, and then we get our answers," Vi responded.

Nick hadn't noticed how much he was shivering until Rhen had said this. His teeth really were chattering.

Nick could see the first hill in the distance. It was a sharp silhouette against the star filled sky. The sound of a warm fire got Nick moving even before the other two had told him which way. As they walked toward the mass of rock in the darkness, Nick realized what Rhen had just said, "then we get our answers." This hung in Nick's mind with the hint of distaste he could hear in Rhen's voice. *What did they want? What were they looking for?* Nick didn't even know where he was, let alone anything about these two.

It only took a few minutes to reach the rock they were walking towards. It took just as long to walk around it to the back side. The moonlight seemed like it was getting brighter as everything became more visible. Nick realized that his eyes were just getting used to the darkness. It had taken a few minutes, after having the bright light of the fire and the torches all around them. They were in the middle of a sand dune, from what it looked like. The sand was a pale white from what he could tell. The rocks that he had seen scattered sporadically around the flat landscape towered over them when they got close.

The rocks, or hill, they were behind now was the size of a college basketball stadium. On the back side of this rock there was an opening that allowed them to walk back into the rocks. There was a large overhang that sheltered them from about ten feet above.

The one he called Vi lit a torch and light sprung to life. Nick looked around and realized that these two had been here before. A swath of black covered the overhang and worked its way down the wall to a fire ring made of rocks. A pile of chopped firewood was neatly stacked against the rock wall. A large canvas was stuffed full of something with the top cinched shut with some rope.

Vi quickly set the torch in the fire ring and started to add kindling. Within moments the fire was raising its curling fingers towards the overhang. Before he knew what he had unconsciously done, he was standing with his hands stretched over the warm fire.

Chapter 8

Answers

Nick was just getting warm when the girl started to unravel her scarf from around her face. As she did, it revealed beautiful tan skin with the most beautiful blonde curls he had ever seen. It seemed that her hair had been spun from the finest silver and gold. It wasn't natural. Then his gaze was drawn to her eyes. They were the most stunning green with flecks of yellow. He had never seen eyes like these before. His eyes were trapped on her and he couldn't look away. He suddenly realized she was staring back annoyed.

"What are you staring at?" she said.

"Sorry," Nick said quietly as he realized what he was doing.

"Now we get our answers," Rhen said as he sat down by the fire. "First of all, where did you get that robe?" Rhen asked.

"Well, I don't really know who left it. I guess that Joe left it for me after they dumped me naked in the woods," Nick said angrily. "Why do you care?" Nick asked.

"We haven't seen those robes in years. They were worn by the Keeper of Secrets, our beloved Uncle Vidan. He went missing ten years ago when Mortes appeared. We have not seen him since…" Vidian paused for a moment "..since our parents died."

"I am sorry." Nick apologized, though it was no fault of his.

"Where are you from?" Rhen continued with the questions.

"Well I just recently moved here from Augusta Maine." "Augusta?" puzzled Rhen.

"Yes, Augusta. Have you heard of it?" asked Nick.

"No, we haven't. How far is Augusta from Ashton?" asked Vidian.

"Where is Ashton from Evanston?" Nick asked

"Evanstown, I have never heard of Evanstown, either," said Vidian.

"Evanston, not Evanstown," Nick replied.

"Why do I have the feeling that I am nowhere near Evanston? Where am I?" said Nick.

"Currently you are with us in the forbidden sands," Rhen announced clearly.

"Forbidden Sands? What are the forbidden sands, and where are they? And by the look of all the crazy stuff going on at the fire and cliff jumping, I think I have some questions of my own. None of this seems normal to me. I have never been chased by adults like we were tonight," Nick rambled. The reality was just setting in that he had just been running for his life. He wasn't feeling good. Something was wrong, really wrong.

"Have you been hiding out in a cave somewhere?" replied Rhen. "Those 'Adults' were the headhunters of Mortes, we call them the 'Dead Ones'. They have been taking all the children for months now. They put them to work in the mines as slaves. Those boys that you saw at the fire were slaves that had tried to escape from the mine. The 'Dead Ones' hunt them for sport, to make an example of them," Rhen explained.

"Dead Ones, children slaves, and hunting children for sport, what are you playing at? You really expect me to believe this?" Nick asked.

It wasn't what Vidian said, but the way she said it that made Nick feel dizzy. "This is not a joke. Those boys are probably dead, or worse, they are being tortured. We call them the Dead Ones because they are dead to any feeling. They are dead to any sense of the normal. When they make the oath to the dragon, something changes, and they change. They do things that no human would ever do to another," Vidian's eyes fell to the fire as she said this, and he could hear her sniffle.

Nick looked over at Rhen. "Dragon? What are …" His mind was racing.

He was seeing all of the last few hours in his mind in fast forward. He didn't recognize any of the landscape at all. As a matter of fact, something looked odd about some of the plants. He felt sick to his stomach. His knees were giving way, and the next thing he knew, he was kneeling away from the fire throwing up whatever might be in his stomach. After a few minutes of this, Nick felt weak. He rolled onto his back. The stars got fuzzy and he passed out.

"Boy!" Nick heard muffled in his mind. "Can you hear me?" he heard a little more clearly.

Then something cold and wet washed over his face and he felt energy surge through every bone in his body as he sat up and took a deep breath.

"Are you feeling okay?" the girl asked him.

"Not really. I feel like I am dreaming. The last thing I heard you say was Dead Ones and Dragon," Nick said. "There are no such things as Dragons!" Nick shouted.

"Oh, how we all wish that were true. We thought that Dragons were just old tales that our Uncle Vidan used to entertain us for bedtime stories. I can assure you, this dragon is real. Very real. Here is proof." Rhen thrust his hand into a leather pouch and pulled out something shiny and black. It looked like an enormous bird's claw, and had a small patch that looked like black snakeskin, but the scales were huge.

Vidian, the girl, reached into another bag and pulled out a black, rounded object. Nick swore he could see florescent-green flecks in the fires light.

"Is that an egg?" Nick asked.

"Yes, and this is the claw and scales of the one that was unfortunate to be protecting it," Rhen answered. "Luckily it was just a baby, but even so, it was very dangerous."

"Are there more than one of them?" Nick still wasn't sure he believed any of this, but there was something so real in their voices. They spoke as if the words brought back painful memories.

Nick did not notice that Vidian had sat down next to him. She reached her hand out and rested it on his back.

"We are telling you the truth. There is a dragon trying to enslave all humans. She has destroyed our cities, enslaved our people and killed our parents. She will not stop. Her greed grows each day. She has made the King's castle her nest and continues to build her armies of Dead Ones. The castle is swarming with venti doing her bidding.

"What is a venti?" Nick asked.

It seemed like it had been hours. Nick had continued to ask questions. Rhen and Vidian had continued to answer them. They had plenty of questions of their own.

"…and that is when I found this," Nick pulled the leather-bound book from the hiding spot in his robes.

As he did, he realized that the leather was completely dry. The pages were completely dry, not a trace of water from the river he had been swimming in just hours before.

Nick heard a gasp from both siblings at the sight of the book. Nick saw tears streaming down Vidian's dirt-covered cheek. Rhen's head fell into his hands. Nick barely could hear what escaped Rhen's lips.

"All is lost. Terran is doomed to misery."

It was awkwardly quiet for what seemed like forever. Nick could hear the soft sobs from the girl. He didn't quite understand why the book would evoke such a reaction. He had been very clear in his explanation that this could not be his world. This all had to be a dream, or they were just two sick people trying to put Nick in a mental institution.

From the sound of their story, they were living in the dark ages of humanity. They had never heard of a car, or furnace. They didn't even know what a watch was. When they saw the book, it all became so real to him. His knees were getting weak again. His head was spinning.

"I think I better lie down again," Nick said as he lay down on the sand.

"Not only was the robe our uncle's, but the book was as well. It was his duty to guard it, and to use it. His was a great responsibility, and the book never left his possession. The fact that you have his book is evidence of his passing. We have feared for his life all this time, but now we know the truth. He must be dead," Rhen said.

Vidian picked up where he had trailed off. "He was the Keeper of Secrets, our only hope against the Dragon. No one else knows the power of the Book. No one else has been apprenticed in the way of the Keeper," she said through sniffles. Nick had sat up again as she was speaking.

"Can I see it?" She asked.

"Sure," Nick said as she reached out for it.

She caressed the leather like it was a long-lost friend. Nick could see the memories flooding her mind as her eyes welled with tears again.

"Oh Uncle!" she exclaimed through a soft sob.

"We need you!" she said, desperately sobbing.

Nick's stomach turned. He must be getting close to passing out again. He could see what looked like stars swirling around Vidian.

Nick heard a quick intake of breath again, and heard Rhen's voice full of awe, "Vidian, look!"

Vidian looked up from the book to see what had caught Rhen's attention. Nick realized that they all could see what he had thought were stars. He could see them more clearly now. They looked like perfect ghostly tear drops floating through the air. They were glowing faintly as they fell.

"Uncle?" Rhen shouted and looked around the fire.

"Uncle Vidan!" called Vidian but there was no answer, just the soft crackle of the fire.

The ghostly white tear drops began to swirl into one large ball of light, and then shot toward Nick. It happened so quick Nick was only able to let out a small yelp before he was enveloped by an excruciating burning sensation and the light. The last thing he realized was that his left hand felt like someone was etching something into his skin with a knife, and then he lost consciousness once more.

Chapter 9

The Mark

When he could focus again, Nick did not see the fire, Rhen or Vidian. All he could see was white light and he could feel the rush of wind against his skin, yet he could hear no noise. Suddenly, he could see the shape of a man in front of him. He was dressed in a white robe like the one he wore. The only hint of color was the silver ivy that wound around the edges of the sleeves and edges of the robe. He had a beard that was white, so white it was impossible to make out an individual hair, they all just blended into the brilliant shape of a beard. His skin was perfect and flawless. His eyes were kind, full of care, and Nick felt no fear, only comfort.

Then he heard his voice, but his lips didn't move.

"I am Vidan Oddfellow. I am the last Keeper of Secrets of Terran. I was trained by my father, Oren. I thought that I had failed my people, but I have not. The Book must have survived when I didn't, and you are the proof. What is your name?"

"Nick Channing," Nick said.

"Nick Channing? Well, Nick Channing, you have inherited a heavy and important errand. You are now responsible for the well-being of the people of Terran, my people. You are responsible for keeping the balance of good and evil in check. You are responsible for banishing the Dragon Mortes from our land. You are to be the hope of my people, or all is lost and only misery will be found in the land."

"This isn't real, this is a bad dream. I will wake up and be back in my home. I will be back with my parents, back with my brother and sister," Nick said out loud.

There was a thunderous clap, and Nick felt it shake him to his core.

"This is not a dream. I assure you," he heard in his head.

"This is real, all too real. Mortes the dragon is not a thing of your imagination. Her jaws are death, her breath is the very fires of hell. She feels no pity or sorrow, and if she finds out you exist, she will stop at nothing to destroy you and the Book," said the voice in his head.

He had trouble seeing the man through all the bright light, but his eyes bored into his soul. He could see and feel the intensity of his emotions.

"I thought I was a good Keeper until the day she appeared. I learned, then, how unprepared I really was. If the Book would have come into her grasp, she would have destroyed it and all hope with it. I was able to open the portal of Cana and protected the Book before I died. The question I have, is how did you come by the Book and return it to Terran?"

"I was with my friend looking through the old hotel. We fell down the stairs and there it sat behind the door. All I did was pick it up and walk through the door. My hands started to disappear, and my friend as well. The next thing I remember, I was lying in the forest with no clothes and this book and these black robes were lying beside me," answered Nick.

"I see," said Vidan. "That must be it. I died before I could end the spell. It must have left the portal open from your side. When you picked up the Book, it opened the portal to my world, and since I had passed on, you became my replacement as the new Keeper. The book would have taken you to a place that would ensure your safety. "

Nick's head was swimming now. He could feel how dire his situation was, and was beginning to feel the weight of it.

"How could this happen?" Nick said rhetorically. "I am just a kid. I have no way to kill a dragon. I can barely get myself to school on time. Mom just barely started to leave me with my sister on date night."

His throat was constricting now, and it was getting hard to speak. "I am not responsible. I can't save anyone…" his voice trailed off and tears began to stream down his face as he felt the full weight of what he had just been told.

"Nick, you must listen, and quickly. I feel the power fading and we will soon lose contact. You must study the Book. It is full of history of my people, but it is also full of spells and the art of magic. I wasted my time as Keeper with trivial spells, and did not push myself as I should have. You must push yourself. You must learn all that you can. You must perfect the most difficult ones and make them habit, if you have any hope of defeating her…. there is no other that can use the Book now. You are bound to it, and it to you."

Vidan's voice was growing faint as if someone were slowly turning down the volume on Nick's radio. He noticed that the brightness of the light was growing dim, and his vision got blurry like when he stood up too fast.

"You must learn to fight Nick. You are the Keeper now. Please do what I couldn't. Protect Vidian and my people. Please, tell her that her uncle is sorry...."

There was more that Vidan said, he was sure, but the voice had gotten too quiet and the vision of the man had faded into blackness. The next thing Nick remembered, he was sitting up gasping for air. Water dripped from his hair and his robe was sopping wet. Vidian knelt beside him with a hand on his shoulder. Rhen towered over him with an empty water skin. The fire had died down to coals.

"Are you ok?" Vidian asked.

Nick couldn't even answer because of the emotion he was feeling. He just sat there staring at the ground. He couldn't explain what had just happened, but he knew it was real. He knew he was no longer on "Earth" as he knew it. He was in some different land, "Terran" is what they had called it. He could feel in his soul that he really was responsible now, but he also knew that he was not capable of what these people would need. Nick was crippled by fear and he could not say a word.

Even though Nick didn't respond, Vidian continued to talk to Nick and tried to care for him in his stupor. Only two hours later did she leave his side and sit whispering to her brother in the shadows of the cave. That is when Nick finally found his voice.

"Vidian?" he asked in a hoarse voice. "What did you say your uncle's name was?"

"It was Vidan," she replied. Her face screwed up into a confused state.

"He says he is sorry…."

Nick felt the hair on his arms stand on end as he spoke. It was deathly quiet for a long time after this, and he wished someone would speak. He knew these were words spoken from the grave, and he was the intermediary. In the ensuing awkward silence, Nick stood by the fire drying his wet hair and clothes. The flames no longer gave him warmth, and his companions kept their distance.

That is when he discovered it for the first time. Even though he couldn't see it, he could feel the pain as he ran his finger over the back of his left hand, just behind his index finger. Right where he had felt the burning sensation on his hand before he saw the lights, he could feel raw skin as if he had burned himself badly. He leaned over near the light of the last red coals, so he could see his hand. Sure enough, on the back was a very small, but distinct symbol as though he had been branded with a miniature branding iron. It was the shape of the letter S, with a line extending from the right bottom. While he looked at it, Nick couldn't help but notice a change inside himself. He couldn't pinpoint exactly what it was, but something was different.

Since no one spoke, Nick laid back down on the ground, and curled into a ball on his side. He eventually managed to fall asleep.

Chapter 10

House in the Rocks

Nick woke up to the pleasant smell of something cooking over the fire. When he was able to open his eyes, he could see Vidian reaching out to turn something on a rock. The smell reminded him of fresh biscuits or pancakes. As he sat up, he also noticed the light of day streamed in around the corner of the cave. Yet it was still faint. He also noticed that Rhen was not there.

Vidian was the first to speak when she noticed he was sitting up.

"Last night," she paused "what happened to you?"

Nick was a little surprised at first. She almost seemed frightened of him today.

"Well, uh, I was hoping you could tell me," he said.

Just then, she pulled whatever it was she had been cooking off the rocks and slipped them into a piece of clean cloth. She slid over next to Nick and sat down, extending the warm cloth in his direction. He opened it to find four small biscuit-like cakes. She indicated they were all for him and that he should eat.

The cakes were still warm and surprisingly delicious. They had a flavor of honey, yet a hint of saltiness as well. He expected his mouth to stick together like when he ate his mother's biscuits for breakfast, but these cakes were very moist and soft. He liked them a lot.

"What we saw in the air just before your, well, your fit, was my uncle's spell. I am sure of it. After we saw it, you fell to the ground screaming. Your body was flailing around, and you sounded like you were in pain. Then it stopped and you were still. We couldn't tell if you were even breathing, and Rhen could not hear or feel your heart. Rhen believed you were dead, but I could see the color in your cheeks by the light of the fire. We waited, forever it seemed, and still nothing. Rhen decided to pour the water on you after he had shaken you and yelled at you. We weren't sure what to do. By the time he poured the water on you, we were sure you were dead...."

Nick suddenly understood the awkward silence from the night before. First, he had shown up wearing their dead uncle's robes, then they had seen a sign of their uncle they hadn't seen in years. According to Vidian, he had collapsed screaming like a possessed man before coming too. Then he only broke the silence to speak to her with words from the dead.

"I am sorry if I scared you last night. I had no control over what was happening. I have never experienced anything like it before. My hand burned and I fell to the ground. When I could see again, I was surrounded by bright light, and a man stood before me…."

Nick went on to tell Vidian everything that he had seen and heard. He told her again that her uncle was sorry. This time her reaction was much different. Tears welled in her eyes and she fell forward into Nick's chest and sobbed.

Nick felt out of place and wasn't sure what he should do, so he finally just patted her on the back. For a moment, he almost enjoyed being so close to her. He did find her very attractive, and his heart went out to her. After she was able to gain her composure, she sat back and started to smile. Nick was very confused again. He didn't know how someone could go from sobbing to a giddy smile in just a matter of minutes.

"Do you know what this means?" she yelled out, standing and then twirling around.

"No, not really," Nick answered.

"This means we should celebrate!" she said excitedly. We lost all hope when our uncle never returned. We knew something terrible had happened to him, but not exactly what. Without a Keeper we had lost all hope. The tides have turned, and now there is hope. We have a Keeper. We have a way to vanquish the dragon and return things to the way they were. It might take you some time to learn, but there is hope." Nick thought he almost heard a giggle in this last phrase she was so giddy.

"I hope you aren't getting so excited over me. This is all a big mistake. That book was meant for someone else. I am just a young boy. Do I look like a dragon slayer? Do I look like someone that could really be a hero?" he asked sarcastically.

His sour reply didn't dampen her spirits at all. She continued to bounce around the fire and smile at the thoughts that ran through her head. Nick found himself thinking that this could not be the same girl that had saved him from the fire last night. That girl was solemn and angry. This girl was giddy and well, a girl.

She kept smiling and quietly talking to herself as she gathered the few things that Rhen had been carrying the night before. As she did, Nick found himself smiling too as he watched her for the next few minutes. He forgot about all that was happening for a brief moment and lost himself in those beautiful eyes. He had thought they were beautiful the night before, but the happiness that she was showing worked like a spell of its own. He was lost and motionless for a few minutes, just taking her in.

"What are you staring at?" Rhen said in a gruff voice.

Nick jumped startled as he came out of the trance he had been in. He realized that Rhen was just repeating this for the second time.

"Nothing, it's just, look at how odd she is acting…" he said feeling a little stupid for staring the way he was.

Rhen then turned to Vidian and started to explain how he was able to cover their tracks from the night before and that, from what he could tell, there were no signs of the Dead Ones anywhere nearby. Vidian in turn went into full detail of what Nick had explained to her about the night before. After she had finished, even Rhen turned and looked Nick over briefly. There was a gentler look on his face, and almost a smile.

Nick felt the weight from the night before start to come back again. The look of hope on their faces was too much and he started toward the entrance of the cave.

"Wait," warned Rhen "you can't go stomping around in those robes. We need to keep your identity hidden. If Mortes or the Dead Ones were to get word of a Keeper, there would be trouble fast. Put these on."

He held out a pair of tan trousers with a leather strap, and a linen shirt with an open neck. Nick gladly slipped the trousers under the breezy robe and then slipped the robe off and the shirt on. He felt a little better having some pants on after all the adventure.

He folded up the robe and Vidian offered to put it in Rhen's small pack. He handed it over without a question and she tucked it away.

Within the hour, they were headed out though the cave entrance. The sun was high in the sky and very hot. Nick was able to see the landscape for the first time in daylight. He could see the slight impression of green trees back from the way they had come. They were completely surrounded by sand and dirt. Large rock hills pushed themselves out of the ground, and you could see the occasional sprig of bright green desert weeds trying to spring towards the sun.

Nick wished he had a hat, or something to cover his head and neck. Rhen pushed them on all afternoon. He continued to say that they needed to get "there" before night fall, or it would not be safe. Nick kept asking where they were going, but Rhen wouldn't say.

By the late afternoon, Nick felt as though he was getting to know Vidian a little better. She walked beside him as Rhen lead the way in the burning sun. Vidian was very different today and kept smiling. She had found a desire to talk about her uncle and what he was like. She had gone on and on about the kingdom of Detre and how wonderful it was. Nick was very interested in her description and was excited by the prospect of seeing a functioning castle. His hopes came crashing down as she explained how the dragon had ravaged the castle and made it her own blackened lair. He decided that the castle was off his list of things to see.

As it was growing dark, Rhen called back to them, "Just over this ridge!"

It seemed like Nick's legs were made of lead. All the walking they had done was taking its toll. His mouth was dry, and lips were chapped. All he could think of was cool water. He was so thirsty.

As they climbed the last sandy, dusty ridge they could see Rhen stooping under a rock ledge and then he disappeared. "That's it," said Vidian. "That's our home."

Nick was confused again. He was looking up into the shadow of a very large cliff and rock mountain. There wasn't a sign of green life anywhere on it. It was the most unappealing place he had ever seen. The thoughts of living in a hole in this huge mass of rock seemed so discouraging and uncomfortable to Nick. They were still out in the middle of a dusty, sandy, rock wasteland. All he could see for miles were gray rocks and dirt. "How could this be their home? Why would you live under a ledge in the middle of nowhere?" He thought to himself.

When they finished walking and sliding down the hill they slipped under the rock ledge themselves. Just a few feet under the ledge was a small opening about 3 feet wide and 2 feet tall.

"Follow me," said Vidian as she slipped her feet into the opening and disappeared inside. Nick could hear her slide on the stones' surface.

Nick slipped his feet into the opening and the next thing he knew he was sliding down into a dark hole very quickly. When he hit the bottom, he couldn't see the floor and his knees slammed into his chin as he fell face-forward onto a dirt covered cave floor. There was light flickering from a torch, and it took a second for his eyes to focus. When he could see, he was startled at the sight.

It was a cave, but it looked like a home. There was a wooden table in the middle of the room with animal skins draped over a bench on both sides of the table. There was a flat rock ledge with a pile of animal skins and what looked like blankets and pillows. It was the most comfortable looking bed and all he wanted to do was to crawl in. There was a second bed across the room in a smaller cubby that must have been Vidian's.

Near the table was a makeshift counter. It was made from a pine tree that had been cut horizontally to make a flat surface. It was resting on flat stacked stones that held it in place waist high. On the counter were plates, cups and eating utensils. There were ceramic jars that Nick assumed held flour and other cooking ingredients. Under the counter were handmade baskets with different items that Nick couldn't make out in the dark shadow of the counter above.

Rhen was hunched over by the right side of the counter with a small torch in his hand, trying to light a small fire. Nick was amazed that the fire he was lighting was in a small fireplace cut right into the stone. There was a mantle and hearth just like a fireplace you would expect to see in a Christmas painting, but it was all made of the natural stone from the cave wall. The smoke was curling up and disappearing into what must be a chimney carved into the rock. Nick found himself drawn to Rhen's side running his hands over what he realized was flawless stone work. The oddest thing was that it seemed to be about half the size it should be.

"Did you build all of this?" Nick asked Rhen his eyes wide with amazement.

"Oh this?" He waved his hand. "We found this little place while running from the Dead Ones. The fireplace was already here, and these bunks were here, but it had been vacant for a very long time. We found cobwebs as thick as willow branches hanging everywhere. We realized it was the perfect place to call home, so we cleaned it up and made it our own. I made the table and benches and the counter. Vidian made the blankets and pillows. All the rest we rummaged up from our little treks. If you think this is impressive, come see this!"

Rhen led him to the far-left side of the cave. There was a small arched doorway that they both had to stoop to get through. Rhen held up his torch and Nick peered around the small room. He couldn't believe what he was seeing.

The stone room was perfectly square. Crown molding carved into the stone. What looked like a small pedestal sink carved out of stone and then a stone bench next to an area with a recessed floor. Next to the sink was a chain with a polished stone handle hanging from the wall and a stone spout carved right out of the wall pointing into the sink. Rhen pulled the handle next to the sink and water trickled out. Then Rhen stepped into the recessed floor. When he did Nick could see the floor drop about a quarter of an inch. When it did, water began to sprinkle out of the ceiling in the corner of the small room.

Nick couldn't believe what he was seeing. The craftsmanship was exquisite. He had never seen anything like it. He couldn't imagine how many hours it would have taken to build this room. "How in the ...." Nick started, and then couldn't find the words.

"I know, that is exactly how we reacted. It has sure been nice. The water is sweet and clean. You can drink it right from the spout. It must filter down through the large rocks above the cave somehow. I don't understand it, but it has been a life saver," Rhen said with a grin.

"I can see why you made this place home. It is a shame it is all about half the size you would expect though," replied Nick.

"Well, if you were the one carving this all, I bet you would want to reduce the size as well. I can only imagine the time that went into this place. This is the only finished room. They must have started on the living room and quit, because not much had been done in there," Rhen said pushing a thumb out toward the other part of the cave.

As they stood there, Nick felt the pains of thirst and effects of the sun return.

"May I?" Nick asked.

"Of course," replied Rhen.

Nick pushed his mouth under the spout and pulled the handle. Cool water rushed out and splashed refreshingly into his mouth and soothed his dry lips. He drank and drank, as long as he could without taking a breath. Rhen was right, the water was cool and sweet, as though it was coming directly from a fresh spring.

When he felt it would make him sick to drink any more, Nick released the handle and straightened up. Rhen motioned to him to follow him back into the other room.

"Let's make a bed for you before it gets too late. You can't be sleeping on the floor." He turned and yelled into the other room, "Vidian, make us something to eat. I'm starving."

It took Nick and Rhen only a few minutes to clear some things off one of the rock ledges that seemed flat. Then they piled some animal furs, a few blankets and a pillow on it.

"Go on then, test it out," Rhen said smiling.

Nick didn't think twice. He climbed in and felt his body almost collapse into the soft furs beneath him. It was so wonderful. He didn't want to move a muscle.

Nick woke a few hours later as Vidian was gently shaking his arm and calling his name.

"Nick, come and eat some supper. It will be cold if you wait any longer."

His body felt so heavy. *My hands must have weights tied to them*, he thought. He sat up and the smell of food brought him back to life. He slid himself over the edge of the rock ledge he had been sleeping on and slowly walked to the table.

Rhen had his head down and elbows spread resting on the table shoveling whatever was on his plate into his mouth. Vidian pointed to a full plate lying on the table that was apparently for Nick. He swung a leg over the bench and sat down. Looking at his plate, he could now see what it was. There was some type of delicious smelling meat and a mush of some sort filling the rest of the plate.

Nick picked up the three-tined fork that was setting next to his plate and took a hesitant bite. He couldn't make out what he was eating. He couldn't decide if it was a mashed potato or some type of cracked wheat or maybe both, but it tasted good and was filling. He decided the meat must be deer. It was a good flavor but had a slightly wild taste to it.

It was very quiet as they all ate. Nick hadn't noticed how hungry he was. He was so thirsty walking through the heat. It was so intense and that was all he had thought about on the journey.

As Nick scraped up the last of the mush on his plate, Rhen startled him by speaking up "We need to go to the mines tonight! I can't just sit here and let them hurt people." Vidian's countenance changed immediately. Her eyes seemed to darken, and her forehead wrinkled.

"It's too dangerous!" she said forcefully with a waver in her voice. "The Dead Ones are everywhere, and if they caught us…"

"We will not get caught," Rhen fired back. "I'm not that stupid. I just need to see who has been caught, and if there is any easy way to free someone, I will. Imagine if it were you down there again. I don't even like to think about it." He shook his head.

"I didn't say you were stupid, I just said it was dangerous. I don't have any desire to even see the Dead Ones. They will do anything to you. It scares me to even see their unfeeling eyes, even if they aren't looking at me. I can't imagine being face to face with one again." Vidian shuddered involuntarily.

Nick could feel her tangible fear. Vidian was rattled by these "Dead Ones".

Nick couldn't help but ask "Who are the Dead Ones?"

It was quiet for a long moment and then Rhen turned his head to look at Nick.

"They are almost indescribable. They are in the service of her, the dragon. Normal men cower in fear at the hint of her awful smell. They lose all ability to think clearly and can't move. They are completely frozen with fear and await their destruction. It is a built-in hunting mechanism for the dragon. It isn't fair, but it is the way men react."

"The Dead Ones are men who have pledged themselves to the dragon. Somehow, she can change them. They become dead to her smell. They become dead to humanity and they become dead to all emotion. They fear nothing. They care for nothing but themselves and wealth and stature. And they carry out her will at all cost. They do things that no sane human would do to another human. Death follows them everywhere. The blank cold look in their eyes will make you sick and send chills up your spine."

"Each one of them shaves their head as they enter her service, and they mark their bodies with black ink that is etched into their skin. Each has his own markings, but all have her mark on the back of their skull. You will know it when you see it. Do not fight them if you are caught. They will snap your spine without even a thought," Rhen finished.

Nick was speechless. He had thought that the drunken men they had been chased by were scary enough, but this description gave him a new respect for how dangerous they really were. It reminded him of the most heinous criminals, which had done unspeakable things to captives. It reminded him of horror stories that he had heard from the older kids around the campfire. He thought of his video games on his Q5 at home, and the Zombies that attacked with no feeling and no thought or guilt.

A terrible feeling came over him. A dark, evil, hopeless feeling. The sound of Rhen's voice had been so matter of fact and serious that Nick didn't doubt the evil he described. He knew that these men were real and that he was in a very dangerous and evil new world. He could only imagine what Mortes was like. They had described her massive size-- the impenetrable scales that covered her body. They described her powerful claws and legs. The thing that scared him the most wasn't just the power, or the flames, but the evil way that she slaughtered thousands with no remorse.

"Nick are you alright?"

It was Vidian. Nick shook his head realizing that as he had listened to Rhen, his head had dropped, and he was staring into the dirt and stone floor.

"Yes, I'm ok, but these men you are describing sound terrible. I have no desire to see one," Nick said quietly.

"Nor should you want to," said Rhen. "They run the mines and drive the slaves. They do a great job because there is no question in the slaves mind that if they do not do as they are told, they will be tortured or killed in brutal ways," he finished.

"What are they mining?" Nick asked.

"They are mining gold and silver. The dragon has no need of it but lusts after as much of it as possible. They pull it from the mines and take it to her at the castle. They also take steel from the mines to make swords and shields for her Dead Ones. Her armies are growing every day. Only the most evil and selfish people choose to join her. They give their life to her, in service, but lose all of what it means to be human. Sure, they are alive, but at what cost? All that surrounds her is death and destruction. My life is worth more than that."

It was silent for a moment and then Vidian spoke up.

"That is why Rhen wants to go to the mines. There are honest good people suffering there. We were there. We have dear friends that are there. There is no doubt that they are suffering. It is horrible..." she broke off, as she hid her head and turned around.

"I'll be honest, I'm afraid, but if people are suffering I want to help," said Nick. "I don't know what I can do, but I will help."

After another long discussion, the three decided it would be best to wait until the next night to travel to the mines. They had traveled far and hard to escape capture, and if others would need their help, then they needed to be rested. One mistake because someone was tired would put their lives in jeopardy. This reasoning made the decision simple for the three of them.

Later that evening after they had climbed into their beds, Nick lay examining the black robe and the book. He slid the book back into the pocket and marveled at how the robe stayed limp and foldable even with the book in the pocket. He folded the robe and folded it again. He couldn't believe it. It was now the size of a handkerchief, but the book had been placed inside. He unfolded the robe again and reached into the pocket. There he found the soft cool leather of the black book.

He now believed in magic. He couldn't believe how strange this all was. He decided that, to keep it safe, this was the best way to hide the book. He would fold it up and place it in his back pants pocket like a handkerchief and button the wooden button. No one would ever know it was there.

With this decided in his mind, he settled back into the soft blanket and furs of his bed and stared into the flames licking at the air in the fireplace. His eyes grew heavy and he couldn't fight it any longer. Nick tumbled into a comforting sleep. Warm, relaxed, and safe, for now.

Chapter 11

The Mines

Nick woke to the delicious smell of bacon. Vidian was cooking breakfast and Rhen was nowhere to be found. Nick jumped quickly out of bed and offered to help Vidian. She declined his help with a smile and told him he could wash up in the washroom.

Nick did just that. He slipped into the room that Rhen had shown him yesterday. He quickly disrobed and stepped into the recessed floor and the water started to flow. When he stepped under the flowing water, it took a moment to catch his breath. The water was not freezing like the water out of your house in the winter, but it was not warm either. It felt so good to get clean. He found a strip of linen that he assumed was to be used to towel off. He snuck a long drink from the spout in the stone sink and slipped back into his clothes.

When he returned to the living area, Rhen had returned from wherever he had been. He was sitting at the table and raised his eyes and hand to Nick.

"Morning," Rhen forced out through a mouthful of fluffy biscuit.

Vidian motioned to Nick to sit down on the other side of the table and he did. Sitting in front of him was a plate full of the same fluffy biscuits that Rhen was eating, covered in a white gravy with a small pile of bacon. Nick was in heaven. He loved bacon anyway, but the white gravy and biscuits were delicious.

Nick really was starting to like Vidian. Not only was she beautiful, but she had been so respectful and kind to Nick. She was taking care of him. Ever since he held her that night as she sobbed, he could feel something growing inside of him. He wanted to get to know her more.

After breakfast was done and they had all eaten, Nick helped Vidian clean the dishes and put everything away while Rhen sat by the fire. Nick had notice that Rhen wanted nothing to do with the cooking or cleaning at each meal. He assumed it was a cultural stereotype. Nick was more than happy to help. He had always pitched in at home. He had plenty of good memories talking with his mom and dad about school with his hands soaked in suds at the kitchen sink. Several times he ended up with bubbles on his head and in his ears for starting a kitchen water fight with his dad.

Suddenly, Nick felt a painful lump in his throat and tears welling in his eyes. Luckily no one was looking at him. *Will I ever see them again?* he thought. *What if I don't make it back?* Things felt way too real for a moment and Nick lost himself in the fear of loss.

The sound of Rhen clearing his throat brought Nick back to the kitchen table with Rhen.

Rhen looked up thoughtfully at Nick, "I think I found a way to free a group of prisoners this morning. There is a small creek bed that twists and turns its way down the mountainside to the entrance of the mine. I got up early this morning while it was still dark and worked my way slowly down it. It is unguarded and comes out about nine cart lengths from the tunnel that leads to the cells. I think we can sneak in and down to free a small group of them when night falls. We just need to wait until it is late. Wait until the guards are asleep. There will be only a few watching the entrances. The night watch only has three Dead Ones that rotate through the mines at night. The mines are too big for three people to keep an eye on. This will give us plenty of time to get down the tunnel and free the first cell we come to. The key will be to keep them quiet and not alert the guards. The cells are close enough to the main cavern that any noise will echo loudly."

"There are only three guards?" Nick asked.

"Yes, but they are Dead Ones. Three Dead Ones are more than enough if they find us. The other twenty to thirty guards will be sleeping in the quarters about eleven cart lengths in the other direction of the entrance. If they are alerted, we will be cut off trying to get to the creek bed and out of the mines," replied Rhen.

"Do you think it will be hard to keep the miners quiet?" asked Nick.

"No, they will do anything to get out of that place. But if we are caught, the punishment will be terrible," answered Rhen.

"Then we won't get caught," said Nick resolutely.

They spent the rest of the day going over and over their plan and looking at all the possible outcomes and scenarios. At last, the sun started to sink into its soft pink bed and they felt confident they would change someone's life for the better that night. Nick started to feel nervous. He had butterflies in his stomach. He had never done anything that could get him killed if he were caught.

They put together a small pack with some food and water and Rhen handed a knife to each of them. When he saw the knife in his hand, he realized things were much more serious than he had thought before. This knife was more of a small sword. It had a hilt like a sword and a small leather scabbard with a belt to strap around his waist.

Nick realized he needed to get his mind straight. This knife was to hurt someone that might try to kill him, no would kill him. *Am I really willing to kill someone if I have to?* he asked himself. He wasn't sure what the answer was, but he knew if he wasn't, he would be the one that would die. The knots in his stomach seemed to grow tighter. The only thing that made him feel better was thinking of the people that were suffering in the mine. The stories that Rhen and Vidian had shared were terrible and he knew something needed to be done.

As they climbed out of the entrance to Rhen and Vidian's home, the sunset was almost turning to a night sky. They worked their way to the North and eventually found steeper terrain with trees and brush. Nick couldn't see at all in the dark, but he could smell the sweet smell of pine and juniper in the air. The steep slope of rocks and trees came to a more gradual incline and eventually flattened out.

"This way," Rhen whispered from up ahead.

A hand reached out in the dark and grabbed Nick by the collar of his shirt just as his right foot slipped on some loose dirt and he started to fall to his right.

"Are you ok?" asked Rhen.

It was his strong hand that had caught him. Nick didn't answer out of embarrassment. Rhen stopped Nick and asked him to look out to his right.

"Can you see where you almost went?" Rhen asked.

"You almost fell down there. It would have made quite a noise."

Nick squinted into the dark. After a moment he realized what Rhen had meant. Out in the blackness Nick could make out some yellow lights below. Nick had almost slipped off a ledge that dropped down about three hundred feet. As Nick squinted at the lights he realized they were ten or twelve torches spread across the area below him. He could only see a circle shape near each torch that also gave off a faint light.

"I see the torches, but what is the other light?" Nick asked quietly.

"They are the tunnels into the mines. The tunnels are lined with torches every fifty feet," Rhen responded.

"Now no more talking. Once we enter the creek bed ahead, you will need watch your step. A loose rock rolling will alert them we are coming," said Rhen, much more serious than before.

Just then the moon's light started to radiate over the mountain peak and Nick could see a little better. The ledge he had almost stepped off dropped straight into the area where the small torches dotted across the small valley floor. From what he could tell, they were high in a mountain area. The mines were nestled between two mountain peaks. Nick could make out the creek bed ahead that they would enter. He could make out a few turns before it started into some taller trees.

After a few minutes they had made their way into the creek bed and worked their way over a few fallen trees that lay across the creek. As Nick straddled one of the logs he heard a cry that froze his blood cold. It was a loud screeching noise. It made the hair on his arms and neck stand on end.

Rhen held his hand out toward them to stop and hold still. Nick felt so vulnerable with his leg swung over the dead tree and his chest and arms wrapped around it to let him down onto the other side. Rhen was looking about to see where the sound had come from. Just then they knew. They saw the light of a torch coming from where they had been just moments ago when Nick had almost plunged into the valley below.

Nick could make out the shape of a man with a shorn head holding the torch high and looking around on the ground. He saw him lean his head back and arch his back as he made the same screeching sound again. That is when he saw one for the first time. The man was holding onto what seemed to be a rope. When Nick heard the noise, he knew it was a chain. Something was chained to the end of it. All Nick saw was a large black shape about the size of a small female lion. The torch light reflected off the creature's glistening skin. Just then it reared back on its hind legs and extended its black wings. It curled its head toward the sky and let out a loud screech of its own. It was bone chilling. Nick knew it was a venti. The sound was indescribable. The knots in his stomach had now paralyzed him with fear.

The creature was excited and smelling the ground. It was obvious that it could smell something. The man holding onto the chain reached out to its neck and Nick heard the chain drop to the ground. His heart froze in his chest and he held his breath. He clenched his eyes shut bracing for what was coming next.

Just a few days ago, Nick would have never dreamed such an animal existed. He was having a hard time dealing with it as a reality after seeing the scales and claw. Now he knew they were real, and he was about to be killed by one.

The venti bolted into the tree line and a moment later there was a human scream. Nick had opened his eyes and looked in the direction of the scream. The partial moon had crested over the mountain peak now. There was enough light to give more detail to what was happening just a short way up the hill. He could see the pale light of the moon reflecting off the creatures glistening skin. It was dragging something almost as large as itself. Then Nick could see. It was a young woman. It had her leg in its jaws and was dragging her limp body out of the trees.

The creature's master stroked its head and put the chain back on it. He pulled something from a bag at his waste and tossed it on the ground for the animal. It quickly snatched up whatever it was and lifted its head back as it chewed and swallowed. Nick was disgusted at the strange sounds that the creature made as it swallowed its prize.

A few moments later the man seemed to survey the area. His gaze stopped and held in their direction for a moment. Nick could faintly make out a scowling face covered in black tattoos. The man was shirtless with a leather strap that crossed over his left breast. He could see two large pouches tied at his waist to a leather belt. As he turned to his left Nick saw, hanging across his back was what looked like a battle ax.

The man pulled on the chain of the venti and they started to disappear toward the mine. As they descended, Nick realized that there was a crude trail with wooden railings leading to the dark valley below.

Rhen, Vidian and Nick all held very still for what seemed like forever. No one dared make a sound with that creature around. Eventually when Rhen felt it was safe, he motioned everyone to gather close together.

"I thought we were done for," said Rhen. "Had that venti picked up our scent, we would have had no chance of escape. They track humans better than a hound."

Nick was still in shock from what had just happened. His heart was still pounding, and he didn't feel safe at all.

"You did really good," Rhen complimented Nick as he patted him on the back. "I was worried you might try to run and draw attention to us, but you played it perfect."

Nick wanted them to think he was just playing it cool and didn't mention anything about being frozen with fear. Nick was sure he couldn't have moved even if he wanted to.

"That poor girl must have tried to escape," said Vidian.

"She must have gone missing today, because that venti was not here yesterday. I bet she went missing and they sent for one to track her and bring her back," Rhen added.

"Do you think she is still alive?" Nick asked.

"Yes, she is alive. They wouldn't kill a perfectly good slave unless they must. I can't say that she isn't hurt. By the way it was dragging her in its mouth, I am sure it will take a while for her to be up and about. I would have done something, but there is no way we could take on a venti and a Dead One. The whole mine would have been alerted and we would be captive," said Rhen.

"We all know what to do, so let's get this done and get back home," said Vidian grimly.

Vidian didn't seem so confident with her last statement. She seemed shook up with the introduction of the venti into the plan. Nick was really having second thoughts about the whole thing now. His confidence had left completely, and he realized that he had no experience in such serious circumstances. His life was truly at risk.

The knots seemed to get worse and worse, as they started to work their way down the creek bed. The trek to the bottom seemed to take forever as they slowly moved over the rocks. Each time someone would stumble or snap a stick, they would hold completely still and listen for signs that someone had heard. Eventually the creek bed leveled out and they could see the light from the tunnel torches where the people were being held.

They could see a clump of bushes and rock where the creek bed opened to the small valley floor. Rhen motioned them all to take cover behind the rock. They silently slipped into position to watch the open area in front of the tunnel entrance. They watched the Dead One enter the mine with his prisoner. The venti was not with him. After he went in, the only sign of life was the flickering of a few torches spread out through the open space. Nick could see the jagged mouth of the tunnel now. He felt panicked thinking about going down the tunnel and getting trapped inside.

After waiting and watching for guards, the three slowly crept out of their hiding place and headed into the tunnel. The walls were jagged and cold. The floor dropped at a very steep incline. Some areas were steep enough that steps had been carved into the rock to make it passable. Torches were lit every fifty feet, giving light to the path.

The deeper they went into the mine, the damper it became. Soon the walls became wet and the trail became slick. There were no sounds coming from within the mine. The only thing Nick could hear was his own breathing and their own light footsteps. Occasionally, one of them might slip and make enough noise for Rhen to stop and scowl at them.

Nick had no idea of how far they had descended into the mine, but he imagined it had to be at least four-hundred to five-hundred feet. The walls of the tunnel started to narrow, and Nick started to feel claustrophobic. Suddenly Rhen threw his hand up for them to stop and pointed to his ear with a finger to his lips.

Nick strained to listen. He heard nothing at first. Then he heard an unnerving laugh. It wasn't a light-hearted fun laugh, but a man's gruff voice. It was the laughter of someone up to no good and laughing at the expense of someone else.

Rhen began to move forward slowly. The tunnel turned sharp to the left just in front of them. As they worked their way around the corner, the laughter got louder. The tunnel opened into a small cave where four other tunnels all converged. There was no sign of anyone else but now they could hear mumbling and laughter. Whoever it was, they were close.

Rhen reached up and took the torch from the wall in the small cave. He dug it around in the dirt on the floor of the cave until he was able to smother its light. The cave went dark and the far-left tunnel entrance seemed to light up as the torch went out. There was no question of where the voice was coming from now.

Nick was impressed at the way Rhen just seemed to know what to do. He was not much older than him, but had obviously had enough life experience to handle about any situation. It almost made Nick feel bad for him. He had to grow up so quickly to survive and protect his sister. Nick realized how sheltered he had been his whole life in comparison.

Rhen slipped silently to the mouth of the tunnel to see what he could see. The other two followed him. At the mouth of the tunnel they could hear clearly now.

"Oh, the pain I'm going to cause you missy," said the horrible voice.

The tunnel dropped down about five feet, very steep, and then opened into a wider room. They could see bars in front a large dark opening. Nick assumed it was where the slaves were kept. He could only see one man up against the bars. His arm was reaching through in the direction of the woman on the ground. Tears were running down his black and dirty face. The pain in his eyes was terrible to see. They were full of horror, longing, and hatred all at the same time.

The tear-stricken man cried out, "Stop, please stop!" Spit shot from his lips in his desperate and intent plea to stop the man.

"Quiet!" the evil looking man yelled, and then spit in the direction of the bars.

He hovered over the woman on the ground, pacing in a circle. A terrible grin as though he were thinking to himself about the fun he was about to have.

The woman on the ground was conscious, but she had a deep gash on her upper thigh on the front and on the back. Blood was coagulating but still freely flowing into the dirt. She was wearing tattered and dirty brown trousers with a shirt that seemed to be made of a white or tan linen that had long been blackened by working in the mines.

"Try to escape on my watch will you? Had I not caught you, I would have paid dearly when she found out. I am going to have to teach everyone a lesson through you!"

The man grinned an evil grin. His voice was hollow and eerie. His appearance was frightening. His eyes did not seem normal. The pupils were clouded and almost gray. The whites were yellowed, and his skin color was pale with a hint of green. Nick could see immediately why they were called the Dead Ones. There were scars all over his uncovered torso. Some looked like burns, some were long cuts and the one that was most disturbing was what looked like a huge bite mark over his right shoulder that went down into his chest area. What wasn't covered in scars was covered in black, cryptic looking tattoos.

He reached down and grabbed the woman by the hair. The woman let out a gasp. He then took his knife to the back of her shirt and tore it in half. The woman, in her feeble state, did all she could to keep herself covered with the torn shirt.

The man inside the bars sobbed. Both his hands outstretched.

"Kyra, I'm so sorry. I love you...."

His head dropped forward toward the floor along with his tears. The Dead One let out an ear-piercing cackle of delight as he grabbed a leather whip from his belt. It had five straps of leather with jagged pieces of bone woven into them. It was obvious what it would do to this poor woman.

The woman was weak and had no way to fight back. She just did her best to cling to the torn pieces of her shirt with her back exposed to the Dead One. Nick was so appalled at what was happening. Rage was building deep in his chest. His vision was filling with red. All that was good inside of him cried for justice, and cried for this man to be dealt with at whatever cost. Just as he was moving his foot forward, Rhen bolted down the tunnel at the man. He heard Rhen but by the time he had turned and looked up Rhen was plunging his knife deep into the man's shoulder. His eyes never flinched. He turned and swung his knife at Rhen. Rhen managed to barely dodge the blade, but didn't see the man's left hand coming from the other side. It collided with his cheek and mouth with a sickening thud that sent Rhen staggering backward. He tripped and sat back on one knee as the man rushed at him.

Rhen felt loose dirt under his hand and threw it into the gray eyes of his attacker. His eyelids blinked but it didn't seem to faze him. With an angry bellow, the Dead One grabbed him by the throat and started to hit him in the face over and over. Nick knew he would kill him. Before he realized what he had done, Nick jumped down the tunnel and drove his knife into the back of the Dead One's neck, just below his skull. As he did his force drove the man's limp body into the wall of the cave cushioning Nick's fall.

The Dead One lay still, and all was quiet except for the soft sobbing of the woman.

Nick quickly stood up. He had blood all over his hand that had held the knife. It wasn't the red blood that Nick was used to seeing from a nosebleed. It was blue-black unnatural looking blood. As soon as the surprise of the color had worn off, he wiped his hands in the dirt and rubbed his hands together to clean it off. His head began to spin.

"I just killed a man!" he said quietly to himself.

He dropped to one knee as Vidian ran into the light to check on her brother, who was lying groaning on the ground.

"He will be ok. He just needs a minute," said Vidian after examining her brother.

Nick stood up and walked over to the woman Kyra.

He knelt and asked, "Are you ok mam?"

Her lips moved but Nick couldn't hear what she said as Vidian was busy tending to Rhen and helping him sit up.

Nick leaned in over her head and asked, "What was that?"

He then felt her arms weakly wrap around his neck, and he heard "Thank you!" as tears sprung from the corner of her eyes.

He put his hand to the side of her cheek and said, "You're welcome."

He didn't know why but as the words came out, his throat constricted, and tears formed in his own eyes. He was glad her tormenter had been stopped before she had been hurt any more.

"Unlock the cell," came a voice urgently. It was the man who had called Kyra by name.

He looked to be in his twenties. He was tall and thin with dark hair. His eyes were shallow and his cheek bones prominent as though he hadn't eaten right in months.

"How?" Nick asked

"The key on his belt," the man was pointing to the Dead One.

Nick scurried over to the dead body and pulled the key ring from his leather belt. There was only one key, so it was easy to unlock the old, worn padlock that held the cell bars closed. As he unlocked the cage, Nick noticed the murmuring of other voices and started to make out other people moving forward to get out. In all, Nick counted ten other people. He was sickened when he realized four of them were children that must have been no older than eight. They had sad eyes and were filthy.

"We need to move quickly," came a strained voice. It was Rhen. He had regained consciousness. "Be quick but quiet. Follow me," said Rhen.

Nick noticed that his face was swollen badly. He could barely recognize him except for his hair and his voice. Blood was still running from his nose which he chose to ignore except for an occasional wipe with his shirt sleeve.

He is tough, I'll give him that, Nick thought to himself.

Just then the tall skinny man walked up to Rhen.

"Rhen, your timing couldn't have been better. I owe you my life. Kyra tried to escape earlier today. They had put her on trail duty. I thought she had made it as she had been gone most of the day and night. We were all asleep until that Dead One came dragging her back to us. You know how they are with trying to make examples out of everyone. When I saw her again my heart was broken. I did not want her life to end this way…" he broke into a sob and couldn't continue.

"I'm glad we came when we did. You have always been a good friend John. I would do anything for you. I had no idea this was happening, but very glad to have helped."

Rhen introduced John and Nick. He told John that Nick was new to these parts and from a town called Evanstown, in the east. John thanked Nick for coming along and helping them escape.

As they lined up to leave the tunnel, there was little to no talking. These prisoners seemed to fear the noise. Nick thought that this would be a plus to get them out. Nick walked up to Vidian and Rhen at the head of the line.

Vidian threw her arms around him. "Thank you so much. I thought he was going to die. You saved his life." Her tone was matter of fact and grateful.

He wrapped his arms around her and hugged her back. It felt good. His cheeks filled with blood and turned red.

Nick muttered "You're welcome." He felt awkward. "I couldn't just stand there and let him die."

"Well, thank you," said Rhen.

"You were the courageous one," said Nick. "I just killed a man from behind."

"That was not a man, he was a Dead One. There is a big difference. The Dead Ones feel less pain and do not care for anything. They are not human. Not after the change. Even their blood is no longer like ours. You seem like a good person Nick. Don't feel guilty for what you just did. We saved Kyra from a horrible event that would have ended her life after she had suffered terribly. You saved my life for certain as well. It was him painlessly, or the two of us as painfully as possible," said Rhen.

Nick was silent and wanted it to be that easy. His mind was swimming with thoughts of guilt and shame. He had always been taught that you never took another person's life. He never imagined he would be put in a position to do so, or that he would have to do so. He didn't have time to think about this now. They needed to get to a safe place.

Rhen had a plan. As they worked their way back up the tunnel. Rhen had the last prisoners put out the torches. They carried a pail of drinking water from the cell and used it to quickly dip the torch to smother it. As they moved up the tunnel, they left the previous section dark. Rhen explained it would be easier to see someone coming from below if they saw a new light behind them. It made sense.

Soon they were back at the entrance. As they put out the last torch, they were surrounded by darkness. It made Nick feel much more comfortable to know that if anyone was out there they could not see them with the torches out. They scanned the darkness outside the tunnel and could find no sign of Dead Ones. Slowly but surely, they sent one prisoner at a time to the creek bed.

Things were going as well as they could hope for. They hadn't accounted for the Dead One, but it had worked in their favor. Now there were only two on watch. They just had to work up the creek bed quietly and over the pass at the top before disappearing into the forest below. Just one thing hung in the back of Nick's head. They had brought in that creature to track the girl. Why wouldn't it be able to track them?

It was Nick's turn to cross to the creek. Rhen was motioning to join the group. He looked to the right and all was clear. Just as he was ready to run for it, he looked the other way and heard voices. All the way across the clearing, the other two Dead Ones were talking under one of the torches. They were too far away for Nick to hear what was being said. They had just walked out of the entrance to another tunnel.

Nick motioned for the group to go and pointed back toward the problem. Rhen quickly understood and started moving the group out before the guards came within earshot of the escaping prisoners. Nick sat motionless in the darkened tunnel entrance.

Nick watched as Rhen and Vidian moved the prisoners up the creek bed and out of sight. Nick was impressed at how silent they were moving. He kept a watchful eye on the guards. They were still standing near the cave entrance where they had been before. As Nick was ready to look back to where the prisoners had disappeared, he heard what must have been a rock crash onto another, high up in the creek bed. Someone must have knocked it loose in their push up the creek. Nick saw the two Dead Ones turn their heads in the direction of the sound. It hadn't been too loud. Nick hoped they would dismiss it as an animal.

The two guards slowly started to move his way. He saw one of them pull a sword from its sheath at his side. Nick's heart started to race. They were coming right towards him but looking up towards the creek bed. If they found the escaping prisoners and his new friends, he couldn't imagine what would happen. He didn't want to imagine.

Nick made up his mind. He spun back around and felt his way along the black tunnel walls into the darkness. By the time the two crossed over to the creek bed, he figured he would be deep inside the tunnels again. After a good minute into the tunnel, Nick let out a yell. He tried to make it sound like a warrior's battle cry.

"Eeeyaaaaaaaaaaawww!!" he yelled back towards the opening from where he had come.

Nick was trying to draw the Dead Ones in after him. The others would be able to escape if he could draw them back into the mine.

As Nick thought this through, he realized what he had done. *They will follow me in!* His heart started to race, and his hands started to sweat. He quickly turned and started moving down towards the cells. He could faintly make out a little light. He turned his head back and realized he could see light growing from the other direction. That meant the Dead Ones had heard his yell and were coming down the tunnel with their torch.

"All of the torches have been put out and left on floor," said a gruff low voice.

"Someone is up to no good," replied another.

"I will be up to no good once I catch them," said the first voice.

Nick was moving as quickly as he could without making too much noise. The cave finally opened to the larger opening with the four different tunnels. Nick could see the light from the torch pouring from the tunnel on the far left. He decided to head to one of the darkened tunnels. He chose the one on the far right.

Just as he crouched down against the wall inside the mouth of the far-right tunnel, the room lit up with the bright light of a torch. Nick had his back against the near side of the tunnel. He sat listening, hunched down in the black shadow from the light of the torch.

"This way," said one of the voices. "Let's check on the prisoners in cell one."

As the light faded from the torch, Nick started moving deeper into the dark unknown tunnel he was now in. He knew he needed to distance himself from the Dead Ones. He felt his hands along the walls and looked forward into the darkness. He saw faint light ahead. As he crept forward he started to make out the huge cavern of the mine. He could barely see the dark lines of rigging and a hand hoist to lower people and equipment into the mine. Then he saw where the light was coming from. It was multiple torches that were burning down inside the mine. When he realized what they were, he could see how enormous the mine was.

Nick's vision was adjusting slowly to the light. He was standing on a large, rocky overhang that butted up against the wooden platform of the hoist. It was big enough to fit four or five people on at a time. There was a large rope running up through the middle of the platform that ran through two huge pulleys and then back down below the platform. A large wooden lever was attached to the platform that looked to be some type of braking system.

To Nick's left was a pile of wooden barrels. He quickly slipped behind the barrels and saw a smaller ledge that was in the shadows. It was just big enough for him to slip out of sight. Just then, the mark on his hand began to burn.

"Ouch," he said quietly as he reached for his hand.

He heard a yell coming from the direction of the cells. "They have escaped!"

Nick wasn't sure what to do, but was sure the two Dead Ones were headed back to the surface. *They will be caught for sure*, Nick thought. He needed to buy them more time.

Nick thought about his first day at school just the other day. He remembered how Kirk had stopped his torture. He remembered committing himself to helping others. By the look of the group of prisoners, they had suffered plenty. Nick did the only thing he could think of. He pushed his shoulder into one of the stacked barrels. He pushed into it until it fell from the ledge. It was quiet for a moment, and then Nick heard it crash to the floor.

Nick quickly slid back behind the barrels to hide on the small ledge. He knelt, making himself as small as possible in the shadows. Within moments, Nick could hear footfall coming down the tunnel. The platform lit up with bright torch light and he could see the back of one of the Dead One's heads. They were peering over the edge.

"They are trying to release the others," said one of the unfeeling voices.

"I don't care if we have to replace all of them. Someone will pay for this tonight," said an angry voice.

Nick's blood was cold. He felt short of breath. He didn't dare move a muscle. He couldn't move a muscle.

The two guards stepped onto the platform and pulled up the lever. Nick realized that it must have a counterweight system, as the platform dropped out of sight at a smooth, controlled rate. Soon the only sound he could hear was the rope running through the pulleys and the light was gone from the torch they had held. Nick slipped back out from behind the barrels and back to the ledge.

As he looked down at the Dead Ones below, he could see them working their way across the mine to the other side. From what he could see from their torch, the mine bottom was not clear and flat, it was uneven and piles of rock and dirt, almost fifty feet high blocked a direct route across the mine. Walkways were winding back and forth between the piles and in some areas the walkways dropped into crevices that wound back and forth. The Dead Ones were in one of these crevices in the middle of the mine. Nick couldn't see them, but he could see their shadows on the other side of the crevice where they were being projected by the torch they held.

Just as Nick thought it would be safe to head back out of the tunnels and to the surface, he heard a shuffle from the tunnel he was thinking of heading up. He jumped towards the barrels but was too slow to react. A large square shouldered figure appeared out of the darkness. Nick winced as it burst from the tunnel.

"Rhen?" Nick gasped, as he realized it was his new friend.

"Nick, are you ok?" Rhen paused as he looked Nick up and down to find no sign of harm.

"Yes, they haven't seen me," Nick replied.

"Good! That was perfect. They are on their way to our home now. Vidian is leading them there and will make sure they cover their tracks and scent. They should be safe. We don't have much time though. The guards all know we are here. The Dead Ones sounded the alarm before you came back into the mine screaming your war cry. Once they were inside, I knew I had to come after you. I yelled to the barracks that someone was trying to free the prisoners in the mine and sent everyone to help. I had to make sure the others could get free," Rhen blurted out as quickly as he could.

Looking around, Rhen asked "Do you still have the cell key?"

Nick felt in his pocket and felt the cold metal key. "Yes, I do. Why?" Nick asked.

"I have an idea that just might work. We have to move fast-follow me."

Then Rhen gathered himself and leapt off the ledge they were standing on. He grabbed one of the ropes easily with his hands and wrapped his legs around it. Then he started to slide down the rope to the floor below.

Nick's heart was beating rapidly now, and his hands got sweaty. He could hear men's voices in the tunnels above. He knew he had no choice. The rope looked so far away, even though it was only about five feet from the ledge. The mark on his hand started to burn again and instinctively Nick jumped to the rope. To his surprise he easily caught it with both hands and grabbed on tightly. Just like Rhen had done, he wrapped the rope around his right leg and pinned the rope between his legs. He was surprised how easy it was to lower himself down. He went as quickly as he could without losing control of his descent. The rope was heating his hands from the friction, but the bottom of the mines was getting closer.

Once on the ground, Nick followed Rhen through the maze on the bottom of the mine floor. They were almost running now. Nick glanced up and could see torches filling the upper sides of the mine and could hear men yelling to cover entrances and to take positions. It was obvious that there was no way out. These men knew every nook and cranny of their prison and would not be letting anyone escape. Nick just hoped that Rhen knew what to do. He realized they weren't heading to where the Dead Ones had gone. They were heading to the right side of the mine.

"In here," whispered Rhen.

They ducked into a four-foot opening in the rock. It led into a tunnel that was small enough that they had to get on their hands and knees and crawl. They crawled for what seemed like fifty feet and then it opened into a larger tunnel that was lined with torches. The floor dropped in a curving arch to the left and they ran down in circles until the tunnel flattened out again into a large opening. Against the far wall Nick could see another cell.

We must be recruiting some soldier to try and break out of here, Nick thought. Rhen ran to the cell door and held his hand out for the key. Nick quickly handed it to him, and he unlocked the door.

Before Nick could ask any questions Rhen pulled the door open and said, "Get in quick."

Nick did as he was told and stepped into the cell. Rhen followed him in and quickly closed the door behind them. He reached through the bars and locked the door and removed the key. They were now prisoners. Nick finally understood what they were doing. They weren't going to fight. They were becoming prisoners to save their own lives.

Chapter 12

Prisoners

The rest of that night was stressful. Yelling men ran through the mines looking for the prisoners. They never even thought to open the cells. Why would anyone trying to escape lock themselves back up? Nick and Rhen seemed to tense up every time a guard would come through the cell area. Rhen's face was bruised and swollen from the encounter with the Dead One earlier in the night. Nick wasn't worried that they would recognize Rhen. His face had been seen by the guards before so he wouldn't seem out of place. The swelling would conceal his identity to the guards, yet make him seem familiar. Nick was more worried about himself. He was a new face and he worried they would notice him.

They never thought to check the cells that night. Eventually, they posted guards at the front of the cell and Nick managed to get a few hours of sleep.

Some of the prisoners in the cell recognized Rhen through the swelling and half-closed eye. They were more than willing to try and hide them with their group. The guards never counted the prisoners because they were always under watch by two or three guards when they were working. Rhen had been a prisoner there before and figured that the guards would recognize him enough not to think twice. Even if they did question him, Rhen had escaped when they moved him to the mill in Ashton beside the old castle. He would just pretend like he had been sent back weeks before. They weren't sure what to do about Nick.

When morning came, Nick didn't wake to the light of the sun, but woke to the yelling of the guards.

"Eat up! It is time to get to work!"

They had slid three very large metal trays under the door. They were full of a wet cold mush. There were no utensils and the prisoners used their hands to scoop the food into their mouths. They were very organized and made sure each person got their share. Nick was impressed at how they seemed to be bonded together like a family. He could tell they were looking out for each other. No one said a word, but quickly got in line and ate their share. Nick passed on the food at first, but Rhen urged him to eat.

"You won't make it through the day if you don't. This day will not be pleasant," he said.

Nick scooped up his share and slipped to the corner. The texture was that of cracked wheat. The flavor was very stale and had a metallic taste. It was cold and slimy. Nick would have spit it out if it weren't for Rhen's encouragement. He realized Rhen was right. They were prisoners and he was in for a terrible day. It would be a lot worse with nothing to eat and no strength. Soon the cell door was opened, and the prisoners lined up to head out. Rhen whispered to Nick to get behind him and to do as he did.

They lined up and headed out the door. At the mouth of the door, a guard stood with a pail of water. He poured it out into the cupped hands of the prisoner as he walked up. Each eagerly drank as much as they could before it ran through their fingers and then hurried up the tunnel with the rest. The man holding the bucket must not have been a Dead One, as he had no markings and had a top knot of hair that hung to his mid shoulder. The rest of his head was shaven. Pieces of splintered bone were stuck through the gnarled hair that dangled down. He was filthy like he hadn't bathed in months. When Nick drew near he kept his head down and hands out. He feverishly slurped at the water to make it appear that he was as desperate as the others. He almost gagged at the terrible smell of the man holding the pail. Then he managed to quickly slip after the others. The man hadn't even paid attention to him.

The guards pushed them up the tunnel and out onto the mine floor. The mine was alight with hundreds of torches and Nick was taken back at what he saw. The cavern he was in was enormous. It was obvious to him that all the stone had been removed by hand. He could see four other groups of prisoners with guards leading them to their working places. He could see scaffolding made of wood lining the far sides of the mines and several lifts like the one Nick had seen last night. He realized that each lift must lead to an exit from the mine.

That must be how they get the gold and silver out, Nick thought to himself.

The guards led them to a large tunnel entrance. It was to the far right of where they had come out of their cells. They sent the prisoners in without a word and stood guard at the entrance of the tunnel. Nick realized that there was not an exit the way they were going. Torches lined the walls, and at the back of the large tunnel were shovels, picks, makeshift wheelbarrows, large canvas bags with two rope loops attached to them and a few movable oil lanterns. Nick could see large hammers and metal chisels lying on the ground.

The prisoners all took places as though they were picking up from the day before. Luckily for Nick and Rhen there was an extra bag and pick. Rhen grabbed the pick and motioned for Nick to bring the bag. Rhen went to work on the side of the tunnel. The sound of the picks, hammers and chisels were almost deafening. The ping of ringing metal bounced off the walls and dust started to fill the tunnel.

Nick's job was simple. He was to pick up the rocks, as Rhen broke them from the mine walls. He would fill his bag until it was half full, and then Rhen would help him shoulder the canvas bags like a backpack. Nick would then carry it out past the soldiers and dump it onto one of the lifts. The lift would then carry the load as three prisoners pulled on the ropes hand over hand until they reached the top. When it reached the top, they would load the rocks into a wooden cart that was pulled by mules. From there Nick couldn't see where it went.

While loading the rocks, Nick saw a glimmer and his eyes lit up. He reached out and picked up what looked like a small piece of gold. Rhen nodded to him that it was gold but pushed Nick's hand to the bag with it. Nick realized it must be for his own safety. The guards would not want to see one of the prisoners hanging onto the prize they were working for. Besides, what good would it be down here?

The day dragged on and on. After what seemed like hours, the guards handed a bucket of water to one of the other prisoners carrying rocks to the platform. This must have been the signal it was time for a short break. The prisoners all gathered around on the floor of the tunnel. There were a few low whispers but not much talking. Nick was amazed at how quiet it had been as they worked. When he tried to talk to Rhen, Rhen had held his finger to his lips to tell him to keep quiet. It made the work even more painful with no conversation.

Nick's hands were getting raw and his shoulders were hurting from the ropes and the weight of the rocks he was carrying to the platform. When he thought he couldn't go on, the guards stopped them for a break. The break was just enough to give him some hope of making it through the day. His legs were getting weak and he was extremely hungry. Nick was very glad that Rhen had urged him to eat the gray sludge from this morning. He could only imagine how hungry he would have been.

It was hard to tell what time it was, since everything was lit by torch light. Nick had no way to know if they were close to being done for the day or not. He also had no idea how late the guards would make them work. The tunnel they were working in looked completely different now. Nick had been counting how many trips he had made to the lift, to give him something to think about. This load would make forty-nine. He tried to imagine the size of the pile that all of these loads would make. Then he looked at Rhen. He was tired, and he was taking short breaks between each swing. Nick realized he should have offered to switch him a long time before.

"Let me switch with you Rhen," Nick said.

Rhen looked up as if to protest, then gave in and handed the heavy pick to Nick. "Thanks," he said.

Nick started to swing the pick awkwardly. At first it bounced of the rock at funny angles, but soon he learned to aim for a small crack or to hit the same area over and over until the rock gave way and crumbled.

A few minutes later, Nick was glad he had relieved Rhen. One of the Dead Ones came into the tunnel to inspect the work they were doing. Everyone seemed to pick up their pace when he did. The rhythm of the hammers and picks hastened. All except for one. A short thin man with a beard seemed to be struggling with his pick. He was only able to get it up to chest level and drop it. He tried to do it with a quicker pace, but it was obvious he didn't have the strength left.

"Lift it over your head!" screamed the Dead One.

The man brought it up to chest level and his arms shook as he tried to raise it higher. He couldn't do it and the pick came down on the rock.

With a scream of rage, the Dead One hit the man upside the head with his fist. The man dropped to the ground in a heap. The Dead One's hand went straight to his belt. He pulled a whip free and started to lash out at the man. Nick could hear his screams filling the air.

Rhen's voice brought him to, "Keep working or you will be next."

Nick realized he had been staring at the commotion and everyone else was working as though nothing was happening.

The whipping went on for an eternity it seemed like to Nick.

"That will be a reminder to you all. If you can't work, you will pay the price," the Dead One yelled when he was finished.

The man hardly moved on the ground. His body was covered in blood and his tattered clothes had been shredded in the places the whip had lashed him.

No one moved to help him. The hammers and picks continued to ring out. When a few minutes had passed, and they were sure the Dead One was not returning, two of the prisoners loading bags and wheelbarrows (including Rhen) ran to the man's side to tend to him. They propped his head up and tried to make him comfortable. The only good thing that had come of it was that the man rested there until the shift was done.

When the guards came back into the tunnels, they ordered them to clean up and dump the last load. Then they pointed to the two people closest to the man who had been whipped and told them to help him back to the cell. Nick was glad that they only had to deal with one Dead One today. The other guards were cruel, but nothing like the Dead Ones. It seemed like they wanted to hurt people-- lived for hurting people. He couldn't stand their white, cloudy eyes and odd, corpse colored skin. It made him ill just to be near one.

The prisoners were soon winding back down the tunnel into their cell. When the door was closed the guards pushed six large trays like the ones from this morning under the door. They were full of moldy bread and cooked potatoes that had long been cold. The food had no flavor except for mold. The fact it was cold brought no comfort like a home cooked meal, but Nick welcomed it to sooth the hunger he was feeling after the hard day's work.

His hands were sore and starting to blister. His shoulders hurt from carrying rocks, and his arms felt weak. Nick started to feel overwhelmed thinking that this was his lot every day. There were no beds to sleep on, just hard cold floor. There were no blankets, no pillows. There were no bathrooms, just two dirty buckets in the dark corner. No wonder these people looked like they did. Ragged and worn, skinny and tired. There was no hope in their eyes. Just pain and sadness.

The door opened to the cell and the guards brought in three buckets of water. Nick could see another set of guards dragging two chairs and a small wooden table into the cavern opposite of the bars. After getting them into position they headed back up the tunnel.

"Looks like we will have company tonight. They must be upset about the escape from last night. They don't want to chance another escape," said Rhen.

Nick's stomach turned. He was looking forward to being able to ask questions and talk quietly with Rhen during the evening, but this would definitely be a problem now.

"You worked hard today," Rhen said to Nick. "It is exhausting work. Mind numbing with the silence. Eventually everyone breaks down after a few weeks. I was worried about you today, but you are a good worker. Just keep doing like you did today and we will be okay until we figure out a plan."

"Do you still have the key?" asked Nick.

"Yes, I do." Rhen whispered back. "I hid it in a crack in the cell wall where we slept last night. It will be safe there until we need it. I covered it with that nasty food from this morning to hide it in the crack at the bottom of the wall. They will never know it is there."

It was so good to hear a person's voice. So good to talk to someone after the silence all day. Nick did notice that his ears were still ringing from all the noise from the clanging tools, but they seemed to be eased at the sound of Rhen's voice.

Rhen motioned to Nick to move back to the place where they had slept the night before. It was a small area in the front left corner of the cell. It was a small nook in the cave that bent back slightly out of sight from where the guards had placed the table. A set of bars lined the side of the nook, and the light of the torch filtered in from the side. The opening of the bars was only about two and a half feet tall. And then above that was solid rock. It was the perfect spot for Rhen and Nick to hide away from the guards but would also let them see what was going on outside the cell.

Nick and Rhen slid back into their private cubby and quietly discussed the day's events. They even tried to come up with some escape plans, but none of them seemed to be even remotely possible. For a moment Rhen got a concerned look on his face.

"Where is the book?" he whispered into Nick's ear.

Nick pulled the black piece of cloth from his pocket and showed it to Rhen. Rhen hadn't seen Nick fold up the robe after like he had. Nick unfolded the piece of cloth. He was amazed again, as he did, how the robe seemed to get larger than it seemed to be when it was all folded up. When the pocket was exposed, Nick reached inside and, sure enough he could feel the smooth leather under his fingers. He pulled a corner out and Rhen broke into a smile.

"How does it do that? Do you have the wand?" Rhen asked.

Nick pulled it part way out of the spine so that Rhen could see its hand carved handle and then slipped it back into place.

"In all of the commotion I forgot all about it. I just had a moment of panic. You have to keep it hidden. They can't know it still exists," Rhen said. Nick nodded. "At the same time, we have to find time to read it. If you can learn just something simple it could get us out of here."

Rhen had stated the last sentence so matter-of-fact, that it surprised Nick. He hadn't really thought about learning anything new that could help them. He hadn't thought about the man that had spoken to him when he had passed out. He had said that he was the only hope for the people of Terran. He had told him he must learn to be the keeper now. With all the running and hiding and work in the mines, Nick had not even given any of this real thought until just now. He didn't know if he really believed it. He had seen things like the robe and the book and ending up here, but he still couldn't believe that he could control some magic power.

"We will have to watch the guards. When it gets late, and they fall asleep or when they are not here, you will need to study and read. These people need you, Nick. I need you," Rhen said seriously.

"I'll try, but I have no idea how to do this. Don't get too excited," Nick whispered back.

"Then open it now, read what you can, and I'll let you know when they are coming to put it away," Rhen replied.

Nick did as he had been asked. He scooted into the cubby a little farther and pulled the book out, turning it to the side, so he could read the words on the page. He started from the front page. It was a title page of sorts. It was written in a calligraphy "Odd Fellow Book of Secrets." The next page was a warning to the reader that within the book were the family secrets of the Odd Fellow family. It explained how they were to be entrusted from father to son and passed on forever. The parent was to teach the child as an apprentice. A warning was included that if the person learning from the book was to use the power for evil, or their own personal gain, they would be struck down and cursed under the oath of the keeper.

The next page was the oath of the keeper, with instructions to read it out loud and to insert the new keeper's own name. He felt silly, but he whispered the oath as he held the wand in his hand.

"I, Nick Channing give my life to fulfill the role of Keeper. I accept the responsibility that comes with this great honor and will be held accountable for my actions. I will fight for honor and good. I will serve the people of Terran and defend their ways and legacy. I will give my life if required…" Nick paused as he thought about this and then continued "I will serve the people with the powers I now take upon me. This is my oath and my bond."

As he finished, Nick felt a surge of energy emanate from the book and rush through his hands and arms, spreading throughout his whole body. It was a real feeling of power.

He could not describe it with words, but his doubts about himself seemed to be diminished for a moment as he knew he couldn't deny what he had just felt.

The weight of the oath he had just made seemed just as real. He felt a nervous feeling and reread the commitment he had just made over and over. After he felt he truly understood what he had read, he looked up at Rhen. He was frozen with a look of awe on his face staring at Nick.

"I could feel that," Rhen said quietly. "I was always with my uncle and saw him do magic tricks for us, but never did I witness anything like that."

There was a reverence in Rhen's voice. The look on his face told Nick that he truly believed that Nick was the new Keeper.

"Keep studying, I'll keep an eye out for you," Rhen said, and turned towards the bars again.

Nick read for at least another hour. The first pages of the book helped to explain that with the Oath in place, the book would bestow all the rights and privileges of keeper to the new keeper. It went on to explain how this power was always there, but that his body would not be able to physically keep up with the power it held. If too much power were to be used before the keeper had properly trained and built up the required magical stamina, the power would weaken his body and kill him. The book warned the user not to do too much, too fast. Nick got the idea. He now had a powerful force inside of him, but if he did not train carefully and consistently it would be dangerous to use.

The first spell that it led him to was a simple light spell. It instructed him to hold the wand handle and to say "Illumino". Nick tried this over and over. He could feel a stirring inside, but there was no light. The book warned him not to go on until he could master this spell. Frustrated, Nick continued to try. He knew it was there; he could feel it. He just couldn't get the result. According to the book, the end of his wand would glow a soft white. He would be able to control the light by how hard he would squeeze the wand. Just then, Rhen was tapping his shoulder. Nick looked up to see a fur-booted leg swinging by the bars in front of him. In a moment, Nick had the wand pushed back into the spine and the robe folded back into a small handkerchief. They could hear the chairs scrape slightly on the ground and then the muffled echoes of two guards muttering to each other.

This was Nick's cue. It was time to go to sleep. He lay down on the hard floor and laid his head on his arm for a pillow. He now realized how tired he was. His shoulders still ached and his whole body seemed to complain. He knew it wasn't comfortable, but he was so tired. Soon he was drifting off to sleep.

The next morning it was depressing to wake up to the same thing. Trays full of gray slop and a handful of water to drink on the way back to the mine. They worked in the same tunnel as they had the day before. Nick had found out from Rhen that the name of the man who had been whipped the day before was Alex. Lucky for Alex, the guards left him in the cell to recover from his beating. Two of the prisoners helped him eat his breakfast and made him as comfortable as they could before leaving the cell.

The day was just as exhausting as the day before. At least no one was beaten or whipped. Nick found himself lost in thought all day. The excitement of being the new keeper had his mind racing. After going over all that had happened and feeling what he had last night, he knew he was the keeper. There was no denying the new power he felt. He was overwhelmed with the responsibility that it brought, but excited to search this new power. He couldn't wait for the shift to be done and to get back to his private spot in the cell. He just hoped that the guards would leave them again for a while before taking their watch. The work was wearing him out physically, but he was in good spirits.

At the end of the shift, Nick was almost running to help get everything cleaned up to leave for the night.

"What has gotten into you?" Rhen asked. "The guards are going to want to punish you just because you have too much energy," he finished.

"Oh yeah," Nick replied.

He realized he might be a little too excited for someone who just finished a grueling day's work in the mines. Nick didn't want to draw any unnecessary attention to himself. He immediately reeled himself in.

When they got back into their cells, he ate his moldy bread and cold potatoes as quickly as he could and slipped back into his spot by the bars. This was his new routine, day after day. Rhen had noticed the change in him and had mentioned it several times. Nick now had a purpose. He had hope of getting out of the mine. All it would take is some time and attention to this new power. He knew would find a spell that would help them escape. He just had to master this first lesson. He could feel the power, but he couldn't control it.

A week later his excitement was starting to fade. His frustration started to take over. He had tried to do the light spell over and over. He could feel a stirring from within, but he could never transfer it to the tip of the wand. That night he sat with the book turned toward the torch light and the wand in his hand. He quietly said the word "Illumino". It didn't work again. In his frustration his mind went to a painful place. He thought of how he missed his mother and family. He thought of how he would never see them again unless he figured this out. He wanted his life back. He couldn't believe it, but he wanted to live in Evanston again. As these powerful emotions built up, he saw Alex lying on the floor. He hadn't walked since his beating by the guard. Nick wanted to help him.

Nick held the wand up again and, staring at the tip, confidently said "Illumino." He felt all of the feelings intensify and mix with the power he had felt from the book on the first day in the mine. It rushed down his hand holding the wand and then a soft white light began to glow. He was so excited. The feeling of accomplishment was amazing. *This is just the start!* he thought. He squeezed the wand tighter and the light grew around him. He quickly released the pressure and the light dimmed. Just to test it out, he dropped the wand. It continued to glow. He didn't even need to hold it.

"Finally," came Rhen's quiet voice.

Nick looked up to see his face lit up by the pale white light.

"Now turn that out before you draw attention to yourself," said Rhen.

Rhen was right. They couldn't risk any of their cell mates knowing too much. They were good people but knowing the truth about Nick could put them in danger.

"I don't know how," Nick responded, as he hid the lit wand under his robe.

"My uncle said…what was it…oh…apago."

Nick tried it. "Apago," he said, and sure enough the light went out.

Nick excitedly pulled the book back out and turned to the next page anxious to find what the next lesson would be. He read for a few more minutes until Rhen was tapping his shoulder and told him that the guards were returning.

He quickly put the book and wand away, but he couldn't stop smiling.

Chapter 13

Out and About

Nick didn't believe it when Rhen had told him they had been in the mine for forty-three days. Rhen had been making marks on the cave wall where he slept each night before he went to sleep. When Nick didn't believe him, he showed him the marks. Sure enough, there were forty-three marks on the wall.

Nick had noticed that all the hard work was affecting him differently than the rest of the prisoners. Instead of looking frail and weak, Nick noticed his arms were getting thicker and his legs were getting bigger. He was getting more muscular by the day. He could see his muscle tissue banded under his skin. All the hard work with the meager food was making him cut like one of the football players from school.

He had continued his studies each night when he could, but the guards were still staying in the tunnels at night. They were still concerned about the prisoners. This told

Nick and Rhen that Vi and the others hadn't been caught. Rhen had been right. She knew exactly what to do to lose the venti. Nick had worried that they would be caught and used to teach the others a lesson. Nick had no desire to see them beaten and whipped.

Alex had finally recovered after the others decided they should all sacrifice a little of their meals for him to get his strength back. It had worked. The extra food seemed to help him recover. The guards didn't wait for him to get fully healthy of course. They put him back to work as soon as he could stand. The others pitched in and let him rest in the tunnel until the guards would come. Alex then had the strength to keep up since he hadn't been working. Nick had taken as many turns as possible doing Alex's work. By doing this Alex began to admire Nick and they became close friends.

Nick's enthusiasm was becoming contagious among the group. He noticed more smiles among the prisoners. They seemed more eager to help one another. It made Nick feel good that he might be part of a little joy in such a miserable place.

Nick had mastered the light spell and had also been able to lift small objects with a levitation spell. He was surprised how it seemed to drain him of so much physical energy. When he lifted a small stone just four feet, he felt exhausted immediately and the stone wavered and fell to the ground. So far this was his favorite. He had always wanted to be able to will objects to fly. He just never thought it was a possibility. He was now working on an invisibility spell. He couldn't wait to master this one.

This spell didn't require him to say anything out loud. It was just a series of wand movements and thoughts. It started by touching the ground in front of his feet and then swirling the wand upward and turning in a circle with the wand above his head and then arching it back to the ground in front of him. When he would try, he could feel the stir of power inside of him, but he wasn't sure when to think the words in his head.

Finally, after three nights his feet disappeared. The drain on his energy was noticeable and immediate. He quickly undid the spell by waving the wand back and forth as to erase the spell. Sure enough, his feet reappeared. He was so excited. He had always wanted to be able to move around invisible.

Luckily Nick and Rhen had moved to the other corner of the cell where there were some shadows. He had memorized the instructions from the book, so he didn't need to stay hidden to rehearse it. He was sure if anyone looked his way and could even see some of him, they would think they were crazy. Rhen tried to draw away any unwanted attention by standing in front of Nick in the light and leaning against the wall. It must have been enough, because no one seemed to look their way. He was so motivated to get this right that he stayed up in the dark corner quietly working on it after the guards came back and everyone was fast asleep. It was easy because there were no words to say. The best he could do was the bottom half of his body.

A few nights later, he was able to get it to work.

Rhen let out a low whistle. "Now we are getting somewhere."

Nick was only able to stay invisible for about twenty seconds and then he would start to flicker back into view. His head would start hurting and he would collapse to the floor weak and tired. He could only practice the spell a few times a night but after a few more weeks he could stay invisible for quite some time.

Nick was ready for some action. He asked Rhen to give him the key to the cell. He was sure he could stay hidden from the guards now. He was able to cast the spell without thinking too much about it now.

"You can't stay invisible the whole time you are out there," Rhen protested.

"I don't plan on it," Nick said back "I can use it when guards are coming and then slip by them. When I can get a good hiding spot I can release the spell, so I don't get too tired. I will be fine."

Before the guards came back for the night Nick and Rhen decided it was time. They pulled all the prisoners in the cell together and explained who Nick was and what he was about to do.

"So, he will start looking for a way for us to get out. Until then, he might find some things to make our lives a little more bearable," Rhen finished.

"What if he is caught?" said Ellen a woman with red, matted hair and freckles.

"Then he will be punished. We will say that he disappeared during the shift and no one had noticed him missing. I think it is worth the beating we could receive. As a matter of fact, I am willing to take that beating myself," Rhen replied.

This answer seemed to calm everyone's concerns.

"Show them," Rhen said looking to Nick.

Nick pulled the wand from behind his back, and touching the ground in front of him while swirling it up his body and turning and arching the wand back to the ground. When he did, he vanished. There was a sharp intake of breath by all. They were looking to where Nick had been, but there was no sign of him. Large smiles broke onto all their faces and Nick saw the hope return in their eyes.

"Like I said, I will take the beating, but I won't have to. He just won't get caught," said Rhen with a large smile.

Nick had fun with his cell mates for a moment as he wandered between them and tapped on their shoulders and whispered in their ears. They giggled and laughed as he did. The look of wonder on their faces was priceless. When he reappeared, the admiration on their faces was noticeable. Nick had gone from helpful cell mate to a source of true hope in those few moments.

It had been decided. The next night he would leave the cell. The plan was to do it when the guards had left after they got back from their work in the mines. Nick was nervous and excited at the same time. He tried to save his energy during the day so that he would have plenty of it that evening. The others were happy to shoulder some of his workload with hopes that he might find some way for them to escape.

Soon the day was over, and they were locked back into the cell. Rhen waited for the guards to leave and then used a small stone to break the hardened dry slop that he had covered the key with. He used his pinky to break the key free from the little crevice and they hurried to the door. They listened for signs of guards, but could hear nothing. Rhen carefully reached through the bars of the cell, inserted the key, and turned it. With a crisp click, the padlock clanked free. Rhen did his best to quiet the noise. He swung the creaky door open just enough to let Nick out. Nick slipped out and took the key from Rhen and slipped it in his pocket.

He locked the cell from the outside and said, "See you all later."

"Be careful," Rhen reminded him.

Nick disappeared up the tunnel.

It felt so good to be out of his prison and walking around freely, but he was very anxious. He wasn't sure where the guards went after the shifts. He knew he needed to find out where they were going each night so they could figure out an escape route. Nick worked his way up the tunnel the same way they went to the mine each day. That was the direction the guards would head each night after locking up. As Nick reached the end of the tunnel where it opened into the mine, he could hear voices. He quickly did the spell and crept to the entrance of the tunnel. There, by the opening, were the two guards that took them out to the mine each day and put them back into their cells.

Nick could hear them arguing about something. They were both upset and raising their voices.

"You told me that you would watch them tonight and then I would watch them tomorrow," one seethed.

"No, I said I would do it tomorrow, not tonight. You should listen better," he said as he pushed on the other's shoulder.

That was all it took. The next thing Nick saw was the two angry men punching and wrestling each other to the floor. He wasn't in the mood to watch this, so he crept by the two brawling on the floor. Nick barely dodged one of their legs as the man swung it around to get in a better position.

He hurried away and as he did, the sound of the scuffle slowly diminished. He decided he would head to the tunnel where they worked each day to break the spell and get a little rest. No one was anywhere near there at night. He was sure of it.

After he broke the spell, he sat near the entrance and looked across the mine. He could see five of the guards walking together toward a tunnel on the opposite side of the cavern. They disappeared inside. A few moments later one of their two guards hobbled across the mine alone brushing something from his lip. He headed toward the same tunnel. *This is worth it already*, Nick thought to himself. He now knew where they headed each night.

Nick rested long enough to feel comfortable using his spell again to get across the cavern. He wanted to find out what it was the guards did each night; not just where they went. Soon he was hurrying across the mine. It was an eerie feeling to be in such a large cavern all alone. The ceiling was almost black with darkness it was so high. The torches burned bright enough to give shapes to the out cropping of rocks and boulders. There was enough light to see across the mine but not enough to make out full details.

He hurried to the same tunnel the guards had gone into. He headed in and hurried as fast as he could to find another resting place. There was nowhere to hide that he could find. The tunnel just seemed to go up forever. He waved his wand back and forth and he saw his legs and arms reappear. He knew he couldn't afford to waste his strength. This tunnel was well lit. Torches seemed to be placed much closer together than the other tunnels. The rock was an orange-tan color. The floor was almost perfectly flat like a concrete walkway. He also noticed that there were some strange intricate carvings every so often along the walls.

As he worked his way up the tunnel, his attention was drawn to the torches. They weren't the same oil-dipped, wooden torches that were throughout the mine. They were ornate metal torches. The tops were shaped like licking flames with an opening where the fire was burning. Looking at one close, Nick realized that they were filled with an oil that was burning. The handles were decorated in bands of steel that formed lines and a thick triangle. It looked like something you would see in a castle. They seemed to be crafted by hand and each one was unique.

Nick's attention came quickly away from the torches as he heard voices coming from up ahead. As he drew nearer, he could hear it was mostly yelling and laughter. It was cruel laughter. It reminded Nick of the laughter by the bon fire. It made his skin crawl. He quickly performed the spell again and hurried forward.

The tunnel leveled off and opened into a huge room. The room was amazing. It had high arches carved into the ceiling cut straight from the stone. Nick recognized the detail of crown work and base work to look much like the stonework in Rhen and Vi's home. This room was impressive. Nothing was small scale about it. There were pillars carved into the walls and pillars every twenty feet throughout the room. They were carved from the same stone as the floor and the ceiling. It was as though some one had dug out the room, leaving only the stone for the pillars meticulously in the perfect spacing as though it had been carved and placed after the fact but there were no seams.

What was odd was how majestic this room was and yet it was filled with a group of ruckus pigs. They were strewn between the pillars on old wooden tables and chairs that clashed with the beautiful room before him. It was full of

Dead Ones with their shaven heads and black tattoos as well as the regular guards that drove the slaves in the mines. Even the regular guards, as terrible as they were, seemed uneasy around the dead ones, almost cautious.

They were eating and drinking. A large fat pig was roasting over the fire in the massive carved fireplace. The smell made his stomach hurt. He hadn't realized how good pork could smell. He hadn't eaten real food now for over a month and the smell of the meat made his mouth water. He wondered if he could sneak some of the meat without being noticed. He slipped to the fireplace avoiding the men. Finally, he stepped up to the pig and grabbed a hold of the steaming shank. It burned his hand, but he didn't care. He looked back and no one was near him or looking. Pulling hard and quick, the small shank popped off the pig and floated in midair for a moment and then disappeared. Nick had slipped it under his shirt, rolled it once, and made for the tunnel.

As Nick crossed the room a fight broke out over by the roasting pig.

"I called the shank. Who has taken it?" bellowed a terrible voice.

Nick couldn't hear the rest, as all he could hear was the sound of tables being overturned and men yelling.

He ran down the tunnel, excited to share the gift with the others. As he ran, his heart froze as he saw a man limping in his direction. It was the other guard that had been fighting down below. He had heard Nick's footsteps and was looking straight at him. He came to an instant stop, frozen. It took a moment for Nick to realize he was not able to see him, but it was obvious he had heard him. He had stopped and was looking around the tunnel.

"Anyone there?" called his nasty voice.

His face was a mess. Blood was running off a gash on his forehead and into his beard. It was now black, bloody, and matted. His left eye was swollen shut and he could barely see out of it.

He stood right in the middle of the tunnel. It was a narrower part of the tunnel and Nick knew he couldn't squeeze past without being noticed. He had an idea. There was a torch on the wall just in front of him. Nick reached out a finger and flicked the torch. It let out a metallic thud. The man's good eye went straight to the torch with an inquisitive look. He shuffled over to the torch to have a look. It had worked. The tunnel was wider here, and Nick barely slipped past. As he did, the man must have caught sent of the roast pig. His head turned about following the smell. Nick stepped away quietly and he saw the man shake his head and sniff towards the large hall and shuffle on. As he did, it seemed his heart started to beat again.

Nick moved down the tunnel and removed the spell again. He had to. He was feeling very tired and could feel his energy draining. He didn't run into any more guards on his way out of the tunnel. When he came to the mine, Nick couldn't see any sign of life and chanced being seen. He moved as quick as he could between the piles of stone and rock that were piled up. He slipped into every open trench or large crack that he could, just in case someone came into the cavern.

Nick finally reached the tunnel where they mined each day. He was relieved to slip into the shadows of the entrance. There were no burning torches here and it felt safe. There was no reason for the guards to pay attention to the actual mine sites. They were dead ends, and no one could escape going into one. That was his reasoning at least. It made him feel secure.

Nick sat down on a rock and pulled the pork shank from under his shirt. The piece he had pulled was the length of his forearm and as thick as his mid-thigh. It smelled so good. He peeled back the burnt skin and pulled a large piece of meat free. When he started to chew the meat, he found it hard not to let out a sound of delight at the flavor of the warm perfectly cooked pork. He hadn't eaten a real meal since staying at Rhen and Vi's home in the rocks.

For a few minutes he savored the delicious pork until he felt a pang of guilt. The others deserved some too. Nick got to his feet and wrapped the shank back under his shirt. He felt tired still but thought he might have enough energy to make it back to the cell. He did what he could to sneak back, but after he got about half way, he could hear voices echoing about the cavern.

The guards are coming back, he thought to himself.

Nick was forced to cast the spell and took off running for the cell. He held tightly to his precious gift, so it wouldn't fall out on the floor. When he got to the cell he didn't think to remove the spell, but just quickly unlocked it, swung it open and slipped in. He startled the prisoners who were sitting by the door. One of them let out a scream.

"Shhhhhhhh. It's me," Nick said as he removed the spell. "Quick, someone lock the door for me. The guards will be here in a few minutes," he said extending his hand with the key.

Rhen jumped up and locked the door.

"What do you have in your shirt?" Rhen asked looking at Nick.

There Nick stood with one hand holding his wrapped up shirt. His face broke into a broad smile.

"This," he replied as he pulled the roast pork out from under his shirt after he unrolled it.

There were murmurs of delight.

"Quickly now," Nick said. "Rhen hand this out and eat it before they come."

Rhen started tearing of pieces of meat and handing it around to the others. There were groans of delight as they got what must have been their first taste of meat in months. There was a sense of happiness in the dark dank prison cell, even if it was short lived. They had been given hope. More hope than these people had to cling to in a long time.

After the last of the meat was eaten, there was a large bone left over. Rhen realized this would be a problem if the guards discovered it.

"What should we do to hide this?" Rhen asked.

They all looked around the cell. There were not any cracks or crevices to hide something this big.

Then Alex spoke up. "Put it in the waste pail."

Nick looked over at the buckets that were left in the dark corner of the room for the slaves to relieve themselves into. They hadn't been dumped for two days and were more than half full. It was disgusting but perfect. Nick could hear voices coming down the tunnel. He reached out, grabbed the evidence, and ran to the corner with it. Holding the bone by the end, he pushed it deep into the waste to make sure it wasn't visible. Then he let it go and grabbed a small stone from the floor. He pushed the bone down about an inch to make sure it wouldn't be seen. The stench was almost unbearable, but it worked perfectly. There was no trace of the feast they had just shared. He dropped the rock and slipped back to his place in the cell to rest.

The guards wandered back to their spots at the table and Nick knew there would be no practice or study tonight. A few moments later, Nick heard a woman's whisper.

"Nick, thank you," It was Ellen.

"You are welcome!" he whispered back.

Chapter 14

The Prisoner is a Prisoner

Before Nick fell asleep that night, he couldn't help but smile and think about his new-found freedom. He wasn't free from the mines, but at least each night he would be able to do things for his friends that they couldn't do for themselves.

He did have a slight problem though. His shirt was greasy with pork grease and smelled like pork as well. He spent a good amount of time rubbing dry dirt on his shirt where the grease was to try and get the dirt to absorb some of it and break it up. He did notice that it had worked for the most part except now the one side of his shirt was forever dirty from the embedded dirt and grease. *Better that than getting caught for stealing the shank.* He thought.

The next day was a good one for their group. Everyone seemed to have more energy than ever, and smiles were exchanged as they worked. They were careful though not to let on to the guards that they were in good spirits. As the days passed, Nick continued his nightly explorations. He tried bringing extra food and water to the prisoners whenever possible. He was still tired at the end of the days, but he was always anxious for the next adventure.

Nick was getting to know the mine very well and feeling more and more comfortable being out on his own. The problem was he couldn't think of plan to help the prisoners escape. Rhen kept asking him questions about the other tunnels that led out of the mine and the habits of the guards each night. Rhen was frustrated because he couldn't come up with a plan without seeing things with his own eyes.

"Isn't there a way you can take me with you?" Rhen asked.

"There is, but I don't think I am strong enough yet," replied Nick. "There is an addition to the spell to hide others, but it warns about doubling the power strain to do it. I would have to dress in the robe according to the book, and you would hold on to the hem of the robe. I have to say an incantation with the wand movement and if you hold the robe you would be invisible along with me. If you let go, you would become visible again," Nick explained.

"Can we at least try it?" asked Rhen. "I can't stay here another day. I am worried about my sister. One wrong move by any of the prisoners she took with her and she could be captured or even worse dead," Rhen said his voice wavering.

Nick could feel the concern Rhen had for his sister. He just realized why Rhen had seemed on edge for the last three weeks. Rhen was worried his sister was going to be caught and or worse killed. All he wanted was to protect her and keep her safe, but in here he could do nothing but worry.

Nick agreed that they should try. He was worried about Vi as well. He had thought about her quite often during the days and nights in the mine. He didn't want to tell Rhen that though.

When the guards had left, and they had time. Nick pulled his robe out and slipped into it in the corner. He handed a hem to Rhen and uttered the spell and made the motions as before.

"Esconde di exo en di min." Nick felt the rush of the magic through his hands and out his wand. It fell upon them with a tingling sensation as he saw Rhen's face disappearing before him.

So that is what it looks like, Nick thought to himself as Rhen's face faded into nothingness.

Nick could feel the strain from his physical energy. It felt as though his arms and legs weighed twice as much. It made his head feel thick and his thoughts muddied. Nick didn't like the way it dulled his senses. After just 30 seconds, Nick waved the wand and ended the spell. He pulled the robe from his body and folded it up.

"What are you doing?" asked Rhen "That was great. I couldn't see any part of my body."

"It worked, but it was too much. I can't support magic like that for long. It drains too much from me," Nick said. "I can already feel the toll it took to hide you for just that long. We need to practice for just a little each night. I need to build up the strength for it. I would need to support it for much longer, if we are going to sneak around the mines," Nick explained a little angry.

"Hey, you don't have to be angry with me, I just wanted to give it a try," said Rhen.

"No, Rhen, I'm not mad at you. I am angry with myself. I wish I were more powerful. If I were, we could have been out of here already," Nick said back at Rhen.

Nick realized he was very concerned for Vi. They had not seen her since their capture in the mine. Just in the few days they had spent together, Nick had been intoxicated by her beautiful eyes and heavenly blonde curls. He realized he was worried just like Rhen.

He felt so frustrated that it was taking so long to learn new spells and to sustain them for a meaningful amount of time. Nick looked deeper into the book. He had seen more powerful spells that would char the guards to a crisp. Spells that would shield him from their weapons, but he remembered the warnings with each spell not to try the next page until he had mastered the page before it.

"It is ok. I understand. Thanks for trying. Don't get frustrated. This is a step in the right direction. You will just have to practice it some more and build up a tolerance. We only need to hide when the guards are close. You wouldn't need to hold the magic for long periods of time," said Rhen.

"I guess you are right," Nick said. "We can sneak through the tunnels unseen for the most part, and I am familiar with a few hiding places now that I have been out so many times. The guards seem to stick to the lighted tunnels, and we could hide you if we needed to."

The two agreed that this would be the most important part of his training. Nick promised he would work harder than ever to master this spell. The ability to have someone else sneaking through the tunnels with him brought him courage. He knew that Rhen didn't panic in the face of a problem and that would come in handy. He also knew that coming up with a plan to escape would come naturally to Rhen.

The next few weeks were uneventful besides the constant work in the mines. Nick was stronger than he could ever imagined. His arms were thicker and rounded. The weight of the rocks seemed light to him now. It was just part of the day. His hair was growing long and mangy. The clothing that Rhen and Vidian had given him was now well worn and filthy from all the work in the mine. Now and then the guards would show up unannounced with large buckets of water and drag the prisoners out into the tunnel one by one and soak them down to try and remove some of the dirt and stink, but it was never enough to get their clothes clean. If anything, it just embedded the dirt deeper into the fabric.

His late-night studies were paying off. He was getting stronger and stronger the more he practiced the invisibility spell. He could now keep Rhen hidden for a few minutes at a time without feeling his senses wane. The hard part now was getting Rhen to move in unison with him without speaking. They couldn't see one another while they were invisible, so they couldn't make hand signals or mouth words to each other. They had to resort to holding on to an arm and tapping signals with a finger. It was much harder than Nick would have thought. He didn't realize how much seeing someone helped with communication.

Tonight, was the night. Nick knew that when they finished in the mine, Rhen would go with him out to explore when the guards left them for dinner. The day dragged on again, but it was uneventful. For some reason the hair on his neck was standing on end and he had goose bumps all over. He had a weird feeling and couldn't explain it. It came and went all day long. Nick found himself turning to look over his shoulder several times to be met with the same feeling each time. At one point he swore he heard voices in the back of the cave they were tunneling in, but when he went back to investigate there were no voices and no one was there.

Rhen noticed Nick was acting strange. "What is it?" Rhen asked. "I have been watching you this morning and you keep looking over your shoulder," he finished.

"I'm not sure," said Nick. "I just feel like someone is there--like we are being watched. It just doesn't feel right. I've noticed it now for days, especially at night. Today it just won't go away. It is ... I don't know ... I guess, creepy."

About an hour later, Rhen came back over near Nick. "Ever since you mentioned it, I have noticed it as well. I can't pinpoint it, but I swear I heard voices whispering just a few minutes ago. The weird thing is that there was no one there to whisper," Rhen told Nick.

Just then they both felt it again. They saw it in each other's face. They instinctively moved back towards the group of miners.

Rhen and Nick finished out the day and were soon headed back across the mine to enter their cell. They both kept scanning the mine walls expecting to see someone or something. All they could see were dark shadows between the gray rocks. They saw the shadows jump from the flames of the torches but couldn't make out anything else.

As they entered the tunnel leading to the cell, the feeling became even stronger. Nick was sure that something or someone was watching them. When they got into their cell, Nick and Rhen climbed quickly into their spot in the corner and whispered to one another.

"Something is coming," Rhen said to Nick. "We need to go tonight!"

"We don't even have a plan," rebutted Nick.

"We will figure something out, as soon as they leave, we will leave with them," Rhen said.

With little argument the two came to an agreement that they needed to try something. The feeling was too strong. Nick even overheard the guards talking in the tunnel. They felt uneasy.

"…as if someone is watching us," Nick heard one say.

The guards were soon ready to leave, and so were Rhen and Nick. As the guards headed up the tunnel Nick pulled the book and robe out of their hiding places. He threw the robe on and Rhen grabbed the hem. With a flick of the wand they both disappeared. The lock clicked, and the door swung open.

The others were used to Nick sneaking out, and hardly noticed tonight. They slipped up the tunnel and as they approached the mine, Nick waved off the spell to plan with Rhen. Rhen seemed a little nervous to be in plain sight.

"Don't worry, I do this every night. I only stay hidden until I reach the mouth of each entrance. The torches usually burn deeper in the tunnels and we have these nice shadows to keep us hidden," Nick told him.

The uneasy look on Rhen's face told Nick that this hadn't helped much. They both clung to the dark shadows around the mouth of the tunnel. Looking out across the mine, they couldn't see any sign of movement except for the two guards that had left in front of them. They were making their way across the mine the same way they went every night to join the others for their dinner. They dropped out of sight as they followed the path behind a pile of rock and dirt. Nick knew the trail well as they walked it every day. The path slowly dropped down into a large crevice on the mine floor and worked back and forth a few times before coming back up on the other side of the mine. There was an intersection in the crevice with the trail that led to their worksite. It was after the second turn in the trail. This was where he wanted to go. He felt safe here at night. He reasoned with Rhen that the guards had no reason to check these areas since there was no exit, just tools and unmined ore.

After giving the guards plenty of time to have crossed the mine, Nick handed his robe hem to Rhen and waved the wand again. They silently moved down the trail keeping their eyes and ears open. There was no sound and no movement that they could see, yet the hair on Nick's neck was standing on end. He couldn't shake the feeling that someone was very close to him. Someone was following him.

They reached the intersection and hurried into the shadows of the work tunnels trail. Nick removed the spell again with relief as he could feel the energy draining him. He had built up a tolerance to the spell but that was sitting still in the cell. He hadn't expected it would make much of a difference walking around the mine, but it was making it much harder. He didn't mention anything to Rhen. He was worried enough as it was.

"Hurry, let's get down inside the tunnel," Rhen said uncomfortably and quiet.

Nick just nodded and followed him. He held out his wand as they entered the mouth of the cave and uttered "Illumino."

Bright white light sprang from the tip of his wand and lit the cave. It was a little too bright, so he relaxed his grip on the wand and the light diminished. It was just enough light to keep them from stumbling over rocks and not enough light to alert anyone out in the mines that there was someone down in the tunnel.

"Now what?" asked Rhen.

"I'm not sure, that's what I was trying to tell you," Nick replied. "We need to figure something out."

The two sat for a few minutes discussing their options, but nothing seemed to make sense. The only thing they could come up with was trying to sneak back up and out of the mine the way they had come in. Nick could make them invisible, but it would do no good to be invisible on a lift that wasn't. The only other way he could think of was out through the guard's dinner hall. The thought made Nick's skin crawl. In all the nights in the mines, the only place he had encountered the unfeeling Dead Ones was in the dinner hall. They would come in from the tunnel on the far side of the room. He never had seen regular guards go into that tunnel. He only saw the Dead Ones come and go through it. He hated their blank unfeeling stare. The other guards were always on edge when there was one around. They lashed out for no reason and the last time Nick had been trying to steal some food for his friends, he swore one of them was following him with its eyes. He felt cold chills come over him just thinking about it.

"We can't get out that way," Nick said. "I don't even know where that tunnel leads and there is no way I could cast the spell long enough to get us out."

"But what other options do we have?" Rhen asked.

"There are none. At least none that I can think of," Nick answered.

All at once a loud blare of a horn reached the tunnel where Nick and Rhen were hiding in. It was a low rumbling horn. One that Nick would have imagined would announce battle on a field of war. The sound made Nick's insides turn. Both of their bodies tensed.

"Something is not right," Nick said.

"Definitely not right!" Rhen echoed as he stood up and turned towards the entrance of the tunnel.

Rhen moved quickly further up the tunnel and up the zig zag trail that lead to the piles where they got rid of the extra dirt and rock at the platform. They slowed as they reached the top and peered out from behind a rock. The mine was full of motion and torch light. Nick could see guards running down trails with torches in their hand yelling. The horn sounded again. There was a group of guards heading across to the trails. Nick and Rhen could barely overhear what they were saying.

"...yes, two of them are unaccounted for. She said they are planning an escape. They weren't in their cell and the door was left unlocked," came one of the voices.

Rhen moved slowly back into the shadows of the zig zag trail and started making his way back to the bottom. Nick followed him down and back into the cave. The horn echoed once more through the cavern above.

"They are looking for us. I can't believe I did something so dumb. I forgot to lock the cell back up," Rhen said holding his head. "I can't blame the others; they had no choice but to tell. They would have been beaten for it," he muttered with his head down shaking it back and forth.

"We have to hide. I can't protect us. Where are we going to go?" Nick said nervously.

"We aren't going anywhere," Rhen seemed to come to his senses. "We will stay here in the back of this tunnel. If they come for us, you will hide us until they leave."

It seemed like it made sense. Nick knew they would never have a chance trying to escape now. The mine was crawling with guards and Dead Ones. He didn't have the strength to keep them hidden. It was the best thing to do. Once they checked this tunnel and found no one, they would set a guard at the intersection to make sure the prisoners wouldn't come down here. They would be safe for a little while.

Although they were not safe, it gave Nick some peace of mind that there was at least some sort of a plan.

"Up there," Rhen motioned to the back of the tunnel they had been mining. "We need to get up onto that ledge. If we stay at floor level, they might bump into us giving us away. We have to get up off the floor," Rhen said to Nick.

The ledge Rhen was pointing to was at the back left of the tunnel. It was a ledge about eight feet off the tunnel floor. It was just large enough for the two of them to fit onto. Nick realized that the torch hung on the wall just below the ledge and would give them a nice dark shadow to hide in even without the spell. The only problem was getting up to it. Rhen was a good climber, and it looked difficult for him to get up.

Rhen was hurrying over to the ledge. He was struggling to find a good hand and foot hold to work his way up. His foot kept slipping and his hands couldn't find anything to grab. Nick reached for his wand again and with a flick of his wrist and saying "Levito" tried the levitation spell he had started to work on. He pointed the wand at Rhen and slowly moved his wand toward the ledge.

Rhen's hands shot out and he gasped. He almost yelled out but caught himself. He was slowly floating into the air and onto the shelf of rock. Nick was amazed at the rush of magic that had shot through his arm and down the wand. It felt as though the wand was attached to Rhen physically and made it simple to move Rhen into his hiding spot. With the rush of magic, came a wave of exhaustion. Nick fell to one knee as he released the spell.

"Are you alright?" Rhen asked from his new perch?

"Yes, just tired," Nick replied.

"Don't do any more, I think I can help you up," Rhen said as he undid the leather strap that held his trousers up.

He dangled it over the ledge. "Wrap it around your wrist and then grab on," Rhen commanded.

Nick stumbled to his feet and over to the strap. As he wrapped the leather around his wrist he could hear loud shouting from up the tunnel. His heart jumped into his throat. He grabbed the leather with his other hand and Rhen started pulling him. He instinctively leaned back and pushed his feet against the wall. This seemed to help him take some of the weight off Rhen and to allow him to find rock footholds to move him up. Even being exhausted, the excitement seemed to allow him to do just enough to get over the edge and onto the ledge with Rhen. Just as he did, the voices grew louder, and they could see torch light filling the tunnel up ahead.

"Light all of the torches and leave them lit," came an angry raspy voice.

"No one sleeps tonight until we kill these two vermin," came the voice again.

Light was filling the whole tunnel as Nick and Rhen began to see the legs of four guards and a Dead One slowly grow into their bodies as they came down the tunnel. Only their heads were missing, as they hadn't come deep enough into the tunnel to expose them to Nick and Rhen.

Nick took this as his cue. He looked at Rhen to see he was already clutching at the hem of his robe. Nick gave the wand a quick wave, whispered the words, and could feel the spell take effect. They disappeared.

"Light the torches!" screeched the raspy voice.

A guard scurried into the back of the cave and lit the torch directly under Nick and Rhen. The others slowly walked into the cave along with the Dead One. They investigated every crevice and corner of the tunnel. Nick winced as the eyes of the Dead One crossed over the ledge where they were hidden and paused for a moment.

Nick's hands were sweating. He could feel the spell stealing his much-needed energy. He wasn't sure how much longer he would be able to keep them hidden. His hand was beginning to tremble, and his vision was full of stars.

"Keep searching the tunnels. They are here somewhere," yelled the Dead One.

Two of the guards hurried off and up the tunnel to continue their search. The other two stayed by the Dead One's side.

The Dead One was not moving from his spot and more than once he looked to the ledge where they were hiding. Nick felt uneasy as though he knew they were there.

Why isn't he leaving? Nick thought to himself.

Just then, Nick's vision became very blurry and he could hardly keep his hand up. He started to sway a little and then the spell broke. He could feel the flow of magic falter through his arm and sputter and die as it did. For just a moment, they were visible. Then Nick felt several strong, small, hands grab him from behind, covering his mouth and pulling him backwards. Nick thought he was delirious as he was pulled back into an opening that he was sure was not there.

He could no longer see the Dead One or his guards, he could see nothing but the black of a dark tunnel closing around him and then he passed out.

Chapter 15

The Heart of the Mountain

When Nick came to, he was confused. He had some type of a blindfold and gag tied around his head and in his mouth. It had a terrible, salty taste and was making it hard for him to breath. He was being dragged on some sort of stretcher through the dark. He could not make out the slightest hint of light. He could hear his captors' heavy breathing as they dragged him through the darkness.

Although he couldn't see who had captured him, he could smell them. It was a pungent body odor mixed with spices and the distinct smell of alcohol. He could hear their booted feet trudging along over the sound of the stretcher dragging on the tunnel floor. Occasionally, there was a sharp bump as they must be hitting into rocks or uneven surfaces in the tunnel floor.

Nick was amazed at the way they were able to move forward so rapidly into the darkness without bumping into the walls or falling. He couldn't see a thing himself, so how could they. They dragged them for what seemed forever to Nick.

Just then Nick heard a deep gruff voice with a thick accent. "It looks like he is awake."

Another voice answered, "Just in time to answer some questions. Velengar is curious. He must be very curious to expose us to this common folk."

Nick's heart was racing. He was realizing that he hadn't been hallucinating before, that someone had grabbed him from behind and dragged him into a tunnel that wasn't there just moments before. He wasn't sure if these were friends or if they were foes. He did know that someone wanted answers. These men had seen him use his new power and he was sure this would be the topic of his questioning.

Nick could feel the tunnel slant upward and the floor seemed to get very smooth. The litter they were being dragged on became much quieter and seemed to glide on the floor. The first hint of light started to creep into the tunnel and Nick thought he could faintly make out shapes to the walls as they were moving along. He couldn't wrench his head far enough around the side of the litter to see what was coming up but could tell the light was growing from up ahead.

The litter came to an abrupt halt without warning and it was dropped to the floor. Nick and Rhen crashed to the tunnel's surface along with it.

"Stand up you two!" commanded a different voice.

Nick did his best to get to his feet in the dim light with his hands bound. A strong, smaller hand grabbed his shirt and pulled him up.

Nick could see a bright, thin light coming from a crack in front of him. He heard the crack of shifting stone and a long groan as the light grew into a large doorway as a huge, stone door slid out of the way. Nick was speechless when he saw what lie on the other side in the light.

Hundreds of torches gave light to an enormous kingly hall. It was as bright as day. The room had a high ceiling, so high, that the light could not reach it, leaving it dark. Tall arches cut straight into the stone with highly detailed cornice and trim work covered the ceiling of the huge hall. The walls were adorned with the same intricate stonework and details. Everything seemed to have a shine to it. The stone had been flawlessly worked and then polished perfectly. The granite floor below their feet was the most brilliant of all. It had been polished more perfectly than he thought possible.

Without realizing it, Nick slid his foot back and forth and realized that the stone was raw and not waxed. He had never seen stone that had been worked like this before. It was stunning. The hall stretched out in front of them hundreds of feet. It was completely empty except for two guards in polished silver armor. Their helmets were open faced and allowed their thick braided beards to flow freely onto the silver Breast plate of their armor. They held what looked like battle axes across their chest towards one another.

His eyes were still adjusting to the bright light, but he could now see his captors. There were five short, stocky men with long, braided beards and leather armor that was different from the shiny armor of the guards across the room. Their faces were stoic and menacing. They glared up at Nick, watching their prisoner cautiously. He recognized them at once as dwarfs from his fantasy books. They looked nothing like the small people he had seen on television in the children's cartoons. These men were big boned and strong. They looked like they had spent their lives hard at work and eating hard to keep up with the work. There was an air of strength to their physique regardless of their short and round stature. If his hands weren't tied behind his back, he would have pinched himself to make sure he was really awake.

By the look on Rhen's face, Nick assumed he had never seen these men before. A look of bewilderment and wonder had placed him in a state of confusion. His mouth kept opening and closing as if he were about to say something but couldn't seem to find the words.

"What are you staring at smarty?!" said one looking up into Rhen's bewildered face.

Just then they heard the clatter of armor and a sharp stamp of feet as the doors across the hall began to open out into the hall. The two guards in front of the door had ceremoniously stepped away from the doors and come to attention. They stood with the handles of their long axes resting on the floor and their arm outstretched holding the handle just below the large blades. They looked forward at nothing, frozen in place.

A much larger version of the guards had pushed the doors open and was striding towards the rest of them across the large hall. Just then something cold and sharp pushed at Nick's back.

"Move to meet him," came a gruff command.

Both Rhen and Nick stumbled slowly forward to meet the giant dwarf moving toward them. His eyes were steely and cold. His gaze was fixed on the two of them as they worked their way toward him. His shorter legs traversed less ground, so even after starting later than the guard, they still met up about half way across the hall.

The dwarf reached his large hand out and grabbed Nick by the arm. He pushed him forward toward the door and pushed Rhen in the back giving them the clear impression to head for the open doors. Not a word was said. Nick had noticed that this dwarf must be older than the others. His hair was mostly silver and gray. There were still a few strands of dark brown hair intermixed, but the silver told the story of an old worn warrior. His hands were thick and callused, and his strong arms showed no sign of weakness. His armor was the same shining silver of the two guards in front of the doors, except this armor seemed to have much more fine detail worked into it. There was a large ridge of silver that rose up on his left shoulder from his armor just to the height of his mouth. It was on his shield-arm side, so

Nick assumed that it must be to protect his neck while in battle.

Nick began to feel uneasy. Were these new enemies? They must have seen him use his magic. They were going to want answers and he was not sure if they were someone he could give them to. Nick looked to Rhen as they were pushed through the door.

"Don't say anything!" Rhen cautioned Nick quietly.

Just then the dwarf smashed his forearm into Rhen's back.

"Do not speak until you have been spoken to!" he commanded.

The blow was surprisingly enough to knock Rhen onto the floor with his hands behind his back. He tried to catch himself by moving his feet under him quickly, but couldn't manage it and fell onto his side eventually hitting his face on the stone floor.

The dwarf grabbed him by his collar and dragged him back to his feet. Nick could see blood on his cheek where he had hit the floor. He pushed them forward toward their destination. Nick looked from Rhen's cheek to where the dwarf was pushing them.

A staircase carved and polished from the stone, rose up straight before them. The bottom was about 50 feet wide and slowly grew smaller as they climbed. They could see light coming over the landing at the top of the stairs but could not see past a decorative beam carved across the top of the roof. Stalactites hung from the ceiling and showed the natural form of the cavern they were in, and somehow brought majesty to the polished stone stairs.

They slowly worked their way up the large stairs. As they reached the top the light grew brighter and brighter. When they were able to see into the cavern where the light was coming from, they were amazed at the beauty. The walls were intricately carved with arching alcoves filled with shining, polished gold armor and battle axes. Large, beautifully crafted, gold Vases and jewelry hung displayed. The torch light glittered and bounced off the gold and silver treasures.

There in the center was a small set of stairs about four feet high, and on top of that was a golden throne. It was encrusted with hundreds of the biggest jewels Nick had ever seen. On both sides were two huge battle hammers carved out of stone. The hammers seamlessly came together with the golden throne. It seemed to Nick that everything that had been crafted within these walls was as close to perfection as he had ever seen. It was obvious this race worked with their hands and took great pride in their work.

Above the throne, the cavern ceiling had been carved back to reveal gems still embedded in the stone. There were thousands of them glittering. Nick was taken back by the natural beauty. He had never known a place that could be so rich in precious gems. Even such a simple task of exposing jewels from their hiding spot within the rock had been done in a way that required immense amounts of work. Fine designs had been carved in the stone surface between each of the exposed jewels and then each jewel was faceted in place, making the ceiling one giant work of art.

Sitting atop the throne was a weathered old dwarf. His hair was white and long. His beard was carefully woven and braided and fell majestically into his lap. His eyes were fixed on Nick and did not leave him as they approached the throne. It made Nick feel uneasy.

He was dressed in a robe of silky white. The robe had interesting designs of silver that trimmed it and gave it a feeling of importance. His rough knobby hands were covered in large golden rings with the same fine craftsmanship as the hall they were in. On top of his head was a silver and gold crown. The crown was smaller in the back and grew to a point in the front. The silver crown was trimmed with gold thorns twisted together in perfect detail. It was simple, yet extraordinary. There was only one jewel on the entire crown. It was a blood red ruby that was held in place by the twisting gold thorns right above the king's forehead.

His eyes were still fixed on Nick when he spoke.

"What is your name?" came a low, warm voice that did not match the demeanor of the man in front of him.

"Nick Channing," Nick stuttered.

"You have no need to fear me, Nick. From what I have heard, my men have just saved you and your friend from an ugly end," said the king.

"I am Velengar, king of the mountain dwarfs. We have been hiding in the shadows for the last thousand years. We are a people of legend to you, but as you can see we are very real," he paused and looked to his guards.

"Guards remove the ropes!" he shouted and waived his hand from the guards to Nick and Rhen.

"Why haven't you shown yourselves until now?" Rhen asked cautiously.

"Good question. What is your name?" asked the king.

"I am Rhen, son of Jon of Ashton," Rhen answered as the guards freed their hands and feet.

"Thank you for saving us from our situation!" he finished with true gratitude.

"You are very welcome. I feel it was very important to keep the two of you from harm. Especially from what has been reported to me Rhen son of Jon. I have been told that this one, Nick it is?" Nick nodded yes.

"Nick was seen at times and not seen at others. My men said that they saw him using a magic that has been missing from our world for more than five years. If I remember correctly, the last keeper we knew of was Vidan Oddfellow and you, Nick, are not Vidan."

"You knew my uncle?" blurted out Rhen immediately.

"Vidan was your uncle?" asked the king.

Rhen nodded.

"No, I did not know your uncle. Like I said we have been in the shadows, unknown to men for at least a thousand years. I did know of your uncle. Even though we have kept out of sight, we always need to know what is happening in the world outside. We keep watch to know what is happening in your world as it could affect ours as well. Once we heard of the dragon, we have been more alert and cautious than we have been in a long time. She has already taken over one of our mines. The one you were working in. We have been concerned at how close they are getting to uncovering more of our kingdom. When your uncle went missing, we grew even more concerned," Velengar said as his brows furrowed.

He continued, "We watched as the dragon destroyed the kingdom and enslaved many of the humans. We have not come out of the shadows in fear of what will come if we do."

"What do you mean?" Rhen asked.

"Dragons only have love for two things, riches and power. Our people love to unearth gold and gems and then craft them into the finest riches in the world. We take great pride in our craftsmanship. Our treasuries hold masses of wealth that humans have never imagined exist. If we expose ourselves to help the humans, the dragon would come to know of our people and eventually our craft and riches. The dragon would be consumed by its gold lust and would destroy our home and seek our kingdom and wealth as its own," Velengar said as he shook his head.

"How can you know that?!" Nick stated and asked at the same time. "There were people dying, they have been tortured, and the slaves' lives are miserable. You could have stepped in and helped us at any time." As Nick spoke the anger rose inside of him.

"You could have eliminated so much suffering!" Nick almost shouted at the king.

The guards stepped a half step towards Nick at this outrage.

"Leave him," the king waved off the guards. "I take no offense to this. You are correct in that we could have ended the suffering of many of your people, but at what cost to our loved ones? This is not the first time a dragon has come into this world. There has been one before, it is why our people went into hiding. The dragon discovered our people and our trade. She did not waste time in laying waste to our people. She did not spare our little ones. She showed no mercy to our women, and when we called to the other races for help, we received none. Our only hope was from a valiant keeper. He fought for all races, and he vanquished the dragon. Upon the dragon's defeat, we paid our respects to the keeper, but soon thereafter sealed up the mountain home to ourselves. We cut off the outside world for over one thousand years. We have been focused on keeping our people safe and so we have. For all this time we have avoided the wars of men, the haughtiness of the elves and the blood thirst of the goblins. We have been safe inside our mountain, and that, Nick, is how we know!" the king said resolutely.

"Elves? Goblins? My uncle read us stories of the dwarfs, elves and goblins, but we thought the stories were just legends. Is it true?" Rhen asked.

"Do you see my short legs and strong hands? Am I not much different than you Rhen?" Rhen looked at the king's legs and arms.

"Do you see this beautiful throne room? Have you ever seen this type of workmanship in the human realm above? We are dwarfs and we are real. The elves and the goblins are just as real. The dragon equally affected their people, and so they too have gone into hiding. A treaty was written between all races and signed after we hid in our mountain kingdom. They would all keep to their own and not interact

274

with the other races. It has been so for all of these years. We stay hidden here in our mountain while we keep watch on the outside world. The only communication we have had with the other races, has been with the elves. It has been limited as our races lose no love for each other. We communicate in agreement to never let the destruction surprise either people again. They are the ones that contacted us at the first signs of the dragon Mortes," Velengar finished.

"Are there more than the races you mentioned?" Nick asked.

"Oh yes, there are many races that lay hidden in the islands of the sea, the deep cracks in the earth and the dark forests of the North. We have record of many different types, but no contact with any but the elves since the closing of the mountain," Velengar answered.

"I am sure you have so many questions and must be hungry. We can provide clean clothes and a bath and then we will talk over a feast in your honor Keeper," the king said with reverence.

Nick was caught off guard by the reverence towards him. He felt awkward and the only thing he thought to do was to bow his head slightly in acknowledgement to the king.

"Thank you, King Velengar," Nick said along with the nod.

"Owengar, take these two to the guest quarters in town," said the king.

Two guards began to usher the two boys off to the left from the throne room through another pair of finely crafted wood doors. Torches and lanterns lit the corridors. The deeper they went into the mountain the more detailed every room became. The ceilings started to get taller as they walked and eventually they were led into a well-lit corridor with regular height walls but no ceiling. There was just darkness above the walls. Nick thought his eyes were playing tricks on him. He realized the further they walked that it opened up into a tremendous cavern above them.

The corridor led out into what seemed to be streets, lined with buildings carved right into the side of the rock walls. Lanterns hung out on huge posts extending from the building faces giving the ere of daylight to the cavern. Nick noticed high above he could see actual daylight streaming in from small archways high up in the cavern roof overhead. Rays of daylight fanned from these archways giving the cavern a regal and elegant touch. Nick could feel fresh air moving slightly in the cavern and assumed it was coming from the arched openings above.

He realized that the journey to the king must have taken all night. It was deep into the night when they had left the cell in the mines or at least he thought. Ever since they had entered the mines he just assumed they were working during the day.

Nick snuck a glance back towards the corridor they had just walked out of. It was an amazing sight. It looked like an exterior castle wall. They had just walked out of an archway and onto a polished stone drawbridge. Two huge metal chains were connected to the draw bridge and disappeared into two holes on the castle wall. The links to the chain were about six inches around and the link itself, was about a foot long. On both sides of the drawbridge were the stone carvings of two dwarven soldiers with their battle axes in hand. They were a perfect match to the dwarfs that had been guarding the double door they had seen before they entered the throne room. The castle wall was complete with battlements and soldiers standing watch.

The torches along the walls of the battlements lit more of the castle that was carved right from the stone inside the mountain. It was spectacular. Nick wished he could take a picture. The workmanship was flawless and unlike anything he had ever seen.

The two were led to a small home that was not far from the castle entrance. It was to the side of the street, carved from the stone like the rest of the city. It was detailed with mortar joints and even a flat roof line. It had three stories with windows only on the upper two floors and the lowest level was some type of farmers market full of fresh vegetables and fruit. There were some dwarven women looking at the items but now they were all just staring at the two human boys.

There was a door just to the side of the market that had stairs leading up to the second floor above. The guards gestured for Nick and Rhen to head up the stairs. At the top of the stairs there was a landing and another door into the house.

They were told that this would be their guest home for as long as they were to stay. Two guards were posted out front and they were warned that if they needed to go somewhere, that it had to be with their guards.

"It is for your own safety," said the guard.

Nick wasn't so sure about that, and by the look on Rhen's face, he felt the same way.

They were shown how to draw hot water from a pump into the tub in what was the washroom, and given towels and clothes to dress in.

"The king will be waiting for you at the feast, so do not take too long. It would be rude to keep the king waiting," said the guard named Owengar.

Owengar had a friendly face unlike the others. He seemed to look younger as well. His facial features were slimmer and more refined. His nose seemed more normal and not as bulbous as the others. He did not wear the ceremonious armor some of the others had worn, but wore a finely stitched jacket and leather belt. From the belt hung a small hand ax and a small, sheathed sword. His dark-brown hair was long like the others, but his beard was much shorter and clean cut. His hands and arms were very strong, but he seemed to be lighter on his feet and much trimmer than the others.

Nick and Rhen took turns in the washroom. Nick went first. He could not believe how wonderful it felt to take a bath with warm water. He wanted to spend the next hour soaking away the soreness in his muscles and the stench of the mine. The dwarfs even had bars of soap that reminded Nick of home. Home, he hadn't had much time to think of it. His eyes brimmed with tears as he remembered his mother and father's faces. The thought of his family brought a rush of emotion that he had been holding deep inside.

Nick found himself with his face in his hands sobbing when Rhen started to call his name through the door.

"Are you ok in there? We need to be quick. You heard what that guard said right?"

"Yeah, I'm just finishing up. I'll be right out. Sorry, it just feels so good to get clean," Nick answered as he wiped his hand across his eyes.

He jumped from the tub and dried off with a dwarven-made towel. As he dried off Nick, noticed how familiar this room seemed to him.

The home they were now in was much smaller than a human home, but it was elegant. It had detailed crown moldings and base trim all carved out of the beautiful gray stone of the cavern. Perfectly fashioned wood furniture and beautiful tapestries filled each room. Nick realized he had seen this work before.

"Rhen, this is just like your home in the rocks. I think the dwarfs must have built it," Nick told Rhen.

"That was exactly what I was just thinking. I always wondered about the detail and work that went into it. I wondered who would have taken on such a task. It just seems so odd that it is so far away from here and all by itself," Rhen answered back.

"I'm sure the king will know why it is there. We should ask him when we get a chance," Nick said to Rhen as they slipped past each other in the hall that led into the washroom.

Nick wandered into the main room of the home. There were windows that faced the street down below. Nick walked to one and pushed the shudders open. Bright light from the torches burst in from the streets. Nick gazed down to the street below. It had been quiet when they were led to the small arched door down below in the street, but it was now filling with curious dwarfs of all ages.

Nick smiled to himself as he looked at some of them. They all were so different. The children were smaller than normal children. Their faces were rounder than that of a human child. Their bodies were more round as well. They were the cutest thing Nick had ever seen. They weren't covered in beards like the men. They dressed in brown and tan trousers with white tunics. From the window, Nick could only tell the boys from the girls by their size.

Nick was surprised to find that the women dwarfs were much thinner than the men. Their hands still seemed to be stubby and thick for a woman, but their bodies were thinner. Yes, they were still short and brawny, but nothing like the men. They wore beautiful earth-tone dresses that had dark embroidery along the cuffs and sleeves.

The older dwarfs that were now out in the street used hooked canes to move slowly about. Their hair was white as the clouds with deep wrinkles cutting into their faces. The old men seemed to have beards that went down past their knees and their noses were much larger than they should be. The old women reminded Nick of his grandmother. They were much less wrinkled than the men with such sweet smiles on their faces.

A group of adults that had been talking slowly lifted their gaze to the window. They were all just staring back at

Nick. For a moment, it was quiet, and then there was a bunch of murmuring from the street below.

Nick quickly stepped back away from the window. The chatter was getting louder. He could hear only a few words.

"...a human?" "It is true..."

Nick realized that after all these years, he and Rhen were the first humans to enter the dwarven kingdom. Then he heard two voices.

"That is enough! Back to your homes!" said one.

"Clear the streets and back to your business! Order of the king!" Owengar called out.

They were very unsettled it was obvious. People had taken notice of the strangers in their city. Nick thought about what the guards had warned.

You must be with your guards at all times if you are to leave this home. It is for your own safety.

Nick felt uneasy. He realized that they were surrounded by a people who thought humans were selfish and there was a reason to keep them out.

Chapter 16

The Feast

After Rhen was clean and they had explored the little house for a moment, a knock came at the door.

"The feast is ready," Owengar called out.

Rhen opened the door and the two left with the guards back to the castle.

They entered across the draw bridge and followed their escorts to the main hall. The main hall had a very high ceiling and seemed to be the size of a football field. Just like the rest of the castle, everything was immaculate. A very long table surrounded by high-back chairs, was laid out with a deep-red, velvet tablecloth. Large candlestick holders were placed every five feet along the table. Silver platters and serving dishes filled the length of the table. They were filled with fruits, cooked vegetables, and all kinds of meats. The smell made Nick's stomach growl.

Owengar motioned to two chairs at the very far end of the table. Two dwarfs dressed in aprons and funny hats pulled the two chairs out as the two sat down. The table and chairs were smaller than the tables and chairs Nick and Rhen were used to. Nick felt a little too big for his chair as well as the table, but he was able to make himself comfortable.

As they sat down, the doors opened, and thirty dwarfs pushed their way to the table. Half were men in regal robes and the other half were obviously their wives dressed in elegant silk dresses. It was apparent that these men and women were important in the dwarven kingdom. Nick wondered who they were exactly.

As they approached, Nick pushed his chair back and bowed to them instinctively. Rhen did the same, following Nick's lead. This seemed to be the right thing to do if they were royalty. The response by the dwarfs seemed to reinforce that it was the right thing to do. They all looked toward Nick and Rhen and smiled and bowed back at them as they sat down in their seats.

Directly across the table from Nick and Rhen a very strong and weathered looking dwarf sat down with his wife. He had scars on his face and a red beard that was braided into five braids and then connected into one. He showed no signs of graying hair, but his wife's hair was streaked with silver. Her face didn't show the wrinkles of her husband, and her brown eyes glimmered in the candlelight.

"I am Ranthor and this is my beautiful wife Oakley," said the red bearded dwarf. "I am the general of war, responsible for defense of this great people."

Nick stood again and bowed to him, "I am Nick Channing, and this is my friend Rhen."

"A pleasure," said the two dwarfs, nodding in their direction.

Before they could be seated again, a horn was sounded, and two ornate doors near the head of the table swung open. Dwarf soldiers filed into the room in perfect military fashion creating a walkway between them, leading to the head of the table. A very fat dwarf with a brown beard walked through the path made by the soldiers and stopped at the head of the table. He was dressed in regal robes of his own. They were made from material that was green and gold.

He cleared his throat and then announced, "I present Velengar the Great, son of Rothgar the strong, heir to the realm of Delenthor and King of the mountain dwarfs."

At this announcement, all present pushed back their chairs and rose to their feet. Everything was quiet as the King entered. His crown was the same, but his clothes had been changed. In place of the silky white and silver robes he wore in the throne room, the King now wore a brown robe that was embroidered with gold. He wore a golden mail shirt beneath the robe. At the cuffs and neckline there was soft white wool. The robe had a long train that drug behind him as he walked along the clean polished floor of the main hall.

All present bowed a deep bow as the King walked to his chair. The King waived his hand towards the group and said, "Enough of the pleasantries, as you were."

The fat dwarf that had announced the King reached out and took the long robe from the King's shoulders and pulled out the large, throne-like chair for him to be seated. Once he was seated the rest of the group sat down.

Velengar smiled and announced, while hoisting the large mug in front of him "We are all here tonight to celebrate the return of the Keeper. This here at my left is Nick Channing, the new Keeper of Terran and our deliverance from the dragon Mortes. Let us all toast. Blessed be your head, Nick Channing. Here is to your future heroic acts that will keep our kingdom and people safe!" roared the king.

A loud rumble filled the main hall as all the dwarfs present raised their mugs into the air and cried "Health to the Keeper!"

At this Velengar resumed "Let the feast begin!"

Instantly the hall was filled with thirty more dwarfs bustling around the table dressed in the same white, cook hats they had seen the first dwarf wearing. They were carrying trays full of delicious-smelling foods that Nick didn't recognize. One of the dwarfs pushed in between Nick and Rhen and was piling food onto their plates. Nick brought the mug to his nose and smelled the liquid inside. It was an alcoholic mash of some sort. It had the smell of sour apples. Nick set it back down and asked the dwarf next to him if he could bring him a mug of water. With a nod, he hustled out of the room to do as he was asked.

For the next two hours, they ate and talked between themselves. Nick had been finished eating for a while and was only picking at some of the delicious deserts that had just been brought out. He and Rhen spent the evening learning all about the dwarven customs and history. The king had shared with them how his people had gone into hiding hundreds of years before when another dragon had infested the land. Her name was Seratis.

"She was pure evil, and like Mortes, had a lust for wealth," said the King.

"As the dwarfs mined gold and silver and every kind of gem, they became her main target. She started capturing the dwarven people one kingdom at a time. There were seven dwarven kingdoms when she came. She completely destroyed four of them in her quest for treasure."

"The dwarven people used to the walk the lands above freely, trading with the humans and the elves. After her arrival, we all went into the mines to hide until the dragon was defeated. After Seratis was destroyed, we went above ground one last time. My grandfather wanted to pay tribute to the Keeper. That was the last we were seen above ground, and very few saw us at that."

"Our kingdom here has been sealed shut ever since. During the reign of Seratis, we learned to reflect light into our caverns to be able to grow our gardens and crops. We raised our own hogs and cattle here within the mountain. If Seratis had any idea where we might have been hiding, she would have done anything to bring our mountain down to get to our jewels and gold."

"It was made know across the land when the mighty dragon fell. The rumors of a powerful keeper spread. Stories were told of how he was able to escape to another realm not in this world where he prepared to give the dragon battle one last time…." the King was silent for a moment.

"He returned and battled the dragon. He was victorious, but at great cost. One of the watchtowers reported back to my grandfather that they had seen the keeper with their own eyes. His skin was scarred from the flames of the dragon. His face resembled a skull with pink skin stretched tightly over it. His eyes were lidless, and he bore only one arm on the right side of his body, and the other was but a stump," the King paused again.

"My grandfather felt a deep gratitude for his selflessness. He went to him with the royal guard and payed him tribute with the utmost respect for saving our people and world. He fashioned the Keeper a mask of silver to hide his face and protect his lidless eyes. He made him an arm to match the mask that could be strapped on to his stump. The Keeper was able to enchant the silver hand and arm. It was as if he had never lost it. The Keeper welcomed the gifts and promised to protect our people by telling all that the dragon had destroyed the dwarven kingdom and its people. After this visit, my people were dead to the humans. We celebrated the victory here within our mountain home, but we chose to stay hidden. Things would be much safer if the world above believed that we had been destroyed by the dragon," he finished.

Nick could tell the King was a good man who took pride in his people and their legacy. He truly seemed to be excited to have Nick in his kingdom. Nick could tell by the reverence in his voice that he truly appreciated the Keeper that had rid the world of Seratis. When he spoke of him, his voice was quiet and pensive. Nick felt undeserving of the respect that Velengar was showing him.

"King, I am so grateful for this great feast you are having in my honor, but to be honest, I don't feel it is deserved. The Keeper that you speak of sacrificed so much and he is the one that deserves this honor. I have done nothing. I only found that I was the keeper just some short months ago. My powers are so meager. Please don't expect too much of me. I don't even know what I'm doing," Nick whispered as he leaned over to the king.

"I like your humility boy…don't you worry, I know a man that can help. Saer is his name. He was banished by his father Adamir the Keeper. He was the true heir to the Book of Secrets. He had trained his whole life to become the next Keeper, but he was young, arrogant and thought he knew best. His hunger for power drove him mad. He began to practice a darker side of magic and spells of his own making. I won't go into all the detail--it is not my place to tell--but I will tell you that his father fought with him to keep the Book of Secrets from him. His father stripped his power and transferred the right to his younger son. He then had him banished, as a prisoner, to the elven kingdom," Velengar finished.

"Did you say Saer?" asked Rhen surprised.

"Yes, do you know of him?" asked the King.

"My uncle was Vidan Oddfellow, Saer's younger brother. I have only heard his name a few times. I just knew

that he was unstable and was sent off to be helped by healers. Did my uncle know of the elves?" Rhen asked sincerely.

"He did not know of the elves. His father learned of them by accident while exploring and mapping the northern forests. The elven king recognized him for who he was and reluctantly showed himself to the Keeper, when his daughter was captured by one of his spells. She had found the human interesting and was watching him from the trees. She thought she had remained unseen. She did not know he had the power he did. He detected and captured her. Reluctantly, the elven king came forward to reveal himself to the Keeper to ensure the safety of his daughter."

"Once Saer was stripped of his powers, Adamir his father pled with the King to allow him to hide him away with the elves. His hope was that their peaceful demeanor would help his mind heal. Much has changed since the coming of Mortes and hopefully Saer has changed as well. We must get you to the elven kingdom. There you will be trained," said the King.

"I thought you said he was mad? Won't he try to take the book from me? Why would he train me?" Nick questioned.

"He is mad all right, mad with sorrow for what he has done. He has lost everything he held most dear, his family and the magic he loved. I don't know that Saer will help, but I believe that there is good in everyone. I believe that everyone deserves a chance to rise after they have fallen. If he won't help, then chances are greater that the dragon will eventually become unstoppable. Her armies grow, as does she. Eventually Terran will lose everything. We will be discovered, even destroyed, and this world will mourn its existence," said Velengar.

They spoke for another hour about the potential fall of the world to the dragon Mortes. They spoke of other options and plans if Saer would not help. The torches began to burn low in the great hall. Many of the dwarfs at the feast had drank and eaten themselves into a deep sleep. Their heads and arms rested on the tables. Others sat with their heads lolled back with their mouths a gape. The others were still picking at the food left on the tables. Gone was the loud laughter and boisterous singing that had been present at the beginning of the feast.

The King could see the two humans were tired and called for their guards to take them back to their quarters. Nick and Rhen bowed to the King and thanked him for the feast and his hospitality. Velengar smiled broadly. It was obvious he was pleased that they had enjoyed the evening. They wished each other a good night as Owengar came to their side. He escorted them together with four other guards back to their quarters and left two in the street to watch the entrance. Another two were stationed right outside the entry door and Owengar informed them that he would be sleeping inside in the great room. He assured them that he would give them their privacy.

Nick and Rhen didn't complain. Owengar had a very pleasant personality. He was very courteous and well spoken. Nick felt more comfortable around him than the other dwarfs. He had noticed at dinner that most of the other dwarfs had been very pushy and very self-centered. Many boasted about the great deeds their family was known for and some boasted of their own bravery and craftsmanship. Halfway through dinner Nick had whispered to Rhen asking him who the strongest and best might be.

Rhen was thinking the same thing because when he mentioned it, Rhen began to grin.

Owengar was different. He was reserved and humble. He was intelligent and quite handsome for a dwarf. He seemed much more kind and sincere than those that sat around the table at the feast. Nick had noticed that the other dwarfs seemed to ignore him and seemed to discount him. Nick and Rhen had found their interactions with him to be pleasant and felt at ease in his presence.

Just as the king had noticed, Nick and Rhen were exhausted. As soon as they returned, they slipped into the luxurious beds they had been given for the night. The last thing Nick heard in his head as he fell asleep was the ringing of plates and glasses and the loud voices he had heard at the feast.

Chapter 17

The Armory

Nick woke to the smell of fried eggs and fresh bread. He dressed himself and stumbled out into the great room. Owengar was moving about in the cooking area, placing plates and utensils at two place settings. Rhen was already seated at the table and eyeing a platter on the counter. Owengar motioned to Nick to sit down as he saw him enter the room.

Owengar served them up the fried eggs, ham, and fresh baked bread. There was the most delicious butter and fruit spread he had ever had to go with it. Nick thought he could get used to the way the dwarven people liked to eat.

"Why are there only two place settings?" Nick asked, "Won't you be eating as well?"

"Oh, no I must not. I am on guard duty," Owengar replied seriously.

"I would be offended if you didn't," Nick stated, "You have gone to all of this trouble and you have been away from your family all night."

"Are you sure? "Owengar asked tentatively.

"I am certain," said Nick.

Rhen nodded in the affirmative as well and pulled out the chair next to him.

"We would be honored," Rhen said though a mouth full of bread.

Rhen, Nick, and Owengar ate together and talked for the first part of the morning. Nick was still confused. He didn't understand how there was just torch light outside the window, yet he felt like it was early on a cold winter day. He didn't understand how a people could live inside the mountain like this without the warm sun on their skin. It made him yearn for a peek at the sky. The air in the room they were in seemed to be moist and stale. He couldn't stop thinking of fresh air and sunlight.

During their discussion at the table, Nick learned that Owengar was a new father. He had a wife named Keern. He glowed as he spoke of her beauty. The picture that he painted with his words was of a short mid-size dwarven woman with silky, red hair. He told them of her uncommonly pale, wrinkle-free skin and her stunning, green eyes. She had been a clothing maker for the royal family and had become accustomed to the finer fabrics and niceties of the King's family. She was always very particular about the way she was dressed and maintained her appearance. He was smitten the first time he saw her as an adult while on guard for the King's daughter. He knew of her when they were children but never had noticed her. She was offered an apprentice position with the Royal staff and took it at her parent's urging.

He had seen her and was smitten. After finding the right moment to speak with her in one of the castle corridors in private, he was able to get her to agree to court. She was shy and hardly looked him in the eye but over time this changed. It was from this romance that they were wed and now had a son together.

Nick could see the pride and excitement beaming from Owengar's eyes as he told them the details. They had given the boy the name of Rowen to honor his father. Nick couldn't help but feel a sharp pain as he thought of his father and how he had left their relationship. It made him wonder if he would ever get a chance to tell him how he truly felt. The feelings must have shown through his face as Owengar was silent for a moment.

"Are you alright Keeper?" Owengar asked.

"Yes, I am fine. You just reminded of my family, and please call me Nick, not Keeper," answered Nick.

Owengar couldn't help but ask Nick about his family. Nick found himself talking about his family and how he came to Terran. Owengar made a great audience. He sat on the edge of his seat as he listened to Nick explain his world.

"So, you came from a world of magic," stated Owengar as Nick finished explaining how an electric light worked.

"No not exactly," Nick replied.

He realized that Owengar did not grasp the idea of electricity. After their long conversation, Nick felt like Owengar was very sincere and he could be trusted.

After breakfast, they were taken before the king again. He had summoned them to come quickly. Owengar seemed tense and the guards fidgeted and looked side to side as they made their way back to the throne room. This made Nick uneasy. Something wasn't right. The dwarfs in the street all stopped to watch them pass and the streets would go quiet.

Once they entered the castle Nick expected things to settle down, but the guards seemed even more alert. When they came to the polished floors outside of the throne room, Owengar was almost pushing them towards the doors in a hurry.

When they entered the throne room, they could see the King dressed in his white robes sitting on his throne. A look of worry spread across his brow. When he spoke, he whispered quietly. He beckoned them to come near him to the throne.

"We must get you to safety. There is news from my royal guard that my people are restless and uneasy to have humans within our walls," the King said quietly.

"Aren't you the king?" asked Nick without thinking.

"Of course, I am!" shouted back the King red faced.

His lips quickly came back together, twitching, and a look of shame crossed his face. He returned to the quiet voice he had used before.

"I am sorry for the lack of control. I did not want to burden you with my problems," his voice was disturbed and uneven.

"There has been a group challenging my reign as King. They believe I do not honor those that came before me with my willingness to change the way we have done things for years. They want me removed from the throne and have been gaining political strength each day. Even now we have heard they are twisting this situation. They say bringing humans inside our walls is putting us all in danger and proves I am not fit for King."

"How is that hurting them?" Nick asked.

"My people are very concerned that you will tell others of our existence. Dwarfs are taught not to trust humans and so, the majority don't trust you. I am mostly concerned for your safety, not for retaining my throne," the King finished.

With that King Velengar beckoned a servant to his side and whispered something to him. The servant quickly ran out of the throne room through a side door in the shadows.

"We will get you to safety, but we need to sneak you out of here now. I have my most trusted men working on supplies and they will be here shortly. Owengar!" the King called to his guard, "I need you to escort these humans and show them the way to Irenthal. You must protect them with your life. I think the high pass will be the best way out undetected. Use the mine slides. No work has been done there for at least a year," said the King.

He then turned to Nick and Rhen. "Please do not judge my people for this. They mean well but are nervous. I expected a more pleasant reaction at the announcement of the new Keeper. I really thought it would give them hope and confidence. They just want to keep things as they have been. They want to be safe."

"I understand," Nick said and then thought to himself, *I guess we didn't impress anyone last night.*

Suddenly there was the sound of muffled shouting. It grew louder and louder.

"Make way!" cried a voice.

The sound of the guards bringing their axes together was heard outside the door. Then loud arguing.

"Step aside!" came a deep voice.

Soon there was pounding on the doors. Several voices called through the door.

"Open up Your Highness," called one.

"Where are the humans?" called the other.

A deep booming voice called out, "Let us in to see the King. We demand an audience with him!"

"It is Orthen!" said the guard closest to the door.

"I know my own brother's voice," the King snapped back. Just then the king's servant came scuttling back into the room.

"They are ready!" he said excitedly.

"Quick, this way!" the King motioned towards the stairs in front of the throne. The same grand stairs they had entered up when they were brought before the King.

Nick took in one more look at the ornately carved ceiling and all the glittering gems. He still couldn't believe how amazing it was. Then he was headed back down the polished stairs into the darkened doorway. At the bottom of the stairs were two strong-looking dwarfs. They held three bulging sacks over their shoulders that they handed to Owengar, Nick, and Rhen. Owengar whispered something to them both, and they headed up the stairs to the king. Owengar turned to face a beautifully carved, silver torch holder with a burning torch in it. He reached out and pulled it towards him. With a small crack and a pop, a seam appeared along the carved trim work on the wall and the wall swung back. It was a perfectly hidden door. Nick again was amazed at the craftsmanship of the dwarfs. The door was perfectly hidden to the naked eye until the trigger released the door.

As they walked through the doorway and it was swinging silently closed, they could hear the King saying with great irritation in his voice "What do you need so urgently brother?" And the door sealed shut behind them.

It was completely dark. Nick could see no sign of light, color, or shape.

"This way," called Owengar.

"I can't see," said Nick. "What way?"

"Oh, sorry, I forgot you can't see like we do in the dark," Owengar apologized.

Suddenly Nick saw in front of him sparks and then an oil dipped torch burst into flame.

Nick could now see the sides of the tunnel they were in. It was very crude compared to the other workmanship inside the dwarven kingdom. The floors were not the polished smooth floors he had seen throughout the kingdom. They were roughly cut, and the walls and ceiling were jagged. It reminded him more of the old mine tunnels he had seen in Park City. His family had taken a drive on a Saturday to visit the old mining town when they had first moved to Evanston.

"What is this tunnel for?" Nick said, "It doesn't seem like it fits here."

"This is exactly what Velengar had it built for, escaping. I know it is rough, but it is only for a situation just like this. He had it built in secret when he was first crowned King. Only ten of us know that it even exists and that is because we made it," said Owengar. "Now come quickly, we have a long way to go."

It seemed like they had been following the tunnel for hours when it finally came to an end at a clean carved door. Nick's hands and back were aching from carrying the bag that the two dwarfs had handed him when they left the throne room.

"We must do this in the darkness my friends. I am sorry. The floors on the other side of the doors will be the clean polished floors you saw before. It should be easy to follow me without tripping. We just can't risk the light drawing the attention of any of the passage guards. We aren't sure who is on the King's side and who is on Orthen's," said Owengar quietly.

"Here you can hold onto this and I will guide you through the dark. I will pull it to the side you need to walk on and then you pull it for him," Owengar said, pointing to Rhen. He pulled a five or six-foot-long rope out of the bag on his back and handed the end to Rhen and the middle to Nick.

Owengar put out the torch and all went black. Nick heard a click and then he could feel air rushing past him. He could see a faint light in the shape of an open doorway. He couldn't see anything else. They couldn't see, but they could hear muffled distant voices conversing.

Unable to see in the dark, Nick felt Owengar tug on the rope in the direction of the door. They slowly moved out through the doorway and to the right. Nick could feel the stone slant upward as they moved forward. He could feel a slight movement of cold air coming toward him down the tunnel. The air was cool and fresh. It did not have the pungent smell of mold and moss as the kingdom had down in the city streets. The air was dry. It was refreshing and eased his soul and lungs.

They continued winding through this new tunnel for a few minutes. As they moved forward, they could see more light with every step. Nick could almost make out the shape of Owengar in front of him, but still not enough to keep Nick from running into him when he stopped to whisper quietly to them.

"Sorry," Nick whispered.

"Please don't speak," Owengar answered in a very quiet voice. "We will reach the guards ahead. They are stationed at the overlook at the mountain pass. It will be very light there so you could easily be seen. There is a cave where they watch out over the pass below. This tunnel leads up to the cave and just off to the right side is a tunnel that leads to the back gate. When we get close, I will throw a rock down the tunnel to distract the guards. When they have turned to look down the tunnel you two will need to slip quietly into the tunnel to the right. Wait there in the darkness. I will present myself to the guards a few moments later. I will tell them that I am there to exit the gate on business for the king. At that point we can open the gate and leave without them knowing you are leaving with me. Do not make a sound!" Owengar commanded.

Owengar went silent and then tugged on the rope so that they knew to move forward. As they moved around the next bend, the light grew much stronger. Nick could now make out not just the shape of Owengar, but he could see him in the dim light. Up ahead Nick saw the backs of the two guards and could hear them talking. Nick felt relief when he could see the natural light from outside and feel the cool breeze on his face.

The guards were standing on a raised platform that had a wall around it. It was open to the outside of the mountain in the direction they faced. Nick could make out gray clouds framed by the parapet wall they were looking over. He could also see the finely carved walls of the tunnel behind them.

"I would love some Mutton with carrots and onions," said one of the guards.

"Don't talk about food when all I have are these dry ration crackers in my pocket," the other said irritably.

Owengar stopped against the wall about thirty feet from the guards. He pulled what looked like a small sling shot from his pocket. It was a stick with a "Y" in it with two stretchy straps and a leather strap to hold stones. He put a stone into the leather strap and aimed it down the tunnel past the guards. Before he let it fly he made sure Rhen and Nick were close at his side in the shadow of the tunnel.

When he was sure they were out of sight, Owengar let the stone fly. Nick was amazed at the speed and the accuracy of the shot. The stone shot straight ahead and down the center of the tunnel. The stone clacked against the floor a good thirty feet past the guards. Their heads turned toward the sound immediately.

"What was that?" asked one to the other.

"Duno? Go and see," said the other pushing his thumb down the tunnel.

Reluctantly, he walked down the three steps and turned down the tunnel. He lit a torch on the wall and started to walk in the direction of the sound.

"Who's there?" he called out.

As he did the other guard crouched on that side of the platform and looked down in the direction he was headed with the torch.

As the guard crouched Owengar gave Nick and Rhen the signal to move. Quickly and quietly, with his heart pounding in his throat, Nick slipped across the tunnel and turned right into the black tunnel as Owengar had instructed them. Rhen followed close at his side.

Just as they reached the dark shadow of the tunnel, they heard Owengar's voice boom through the tunnel with the light of a new torch surrounding him.

"Ensel, so good to see you again!"

"Is that you Owengar? How long has it been? Good to see you my cousin," said Ensel.

Once Ensel had turned around, Nick could make out his facial features. Ensel had a long face with a gray beard. His face was covered in deep wrinkles and two beady eyes. His nose was long and hooked. His eyes were full of sincere happiness to see his cousin Owengar. This made Nick feel much safer.

Owengar and Ensel exchanged pleasantries for a moment and then their attention was brought to the other guard coming back up the tunnel. He was holding the stone in his hand that Owengar had used to draw away their attention.

"The noise was this," said the other guard.

"Oh, that was me. I have to keep you on your toes you know," Owengar said with a broad smile at his cousin.

"I will admit, it did make me a little jumpy. We never have visitors at the back gate anymore. Speaking of that, what are you doing here?" Ensel asked his cousin.

Owengar made up an excuse that he was to communicate with the elven king information about Mortes and to collect information that they had regarding the outside world. The other two dwarfs didn't seem to question his duty at all. After a few more minutes of discussion, Owengar excused himself and gave his cousin a pat on the back.

Nick and Rhen pushed deeper into the tunnel as the light of Owengar's torch would expose them as he came closer. When they were around the next corner they stopped and waited for him. Owengar hurried past and waved to them to follow him.

The tunnel ahead slowly led downward to a grand staircase. The handrails were full of masterfully carved designs and the bottom of the polished stairs flared outward before two massive stone doors. The workmanship of the dwarfs continued to amaze Nick. Everything they did seemed to be overdone and extravagant. As they reached the doors at the bottom, Nick wondered how they would move such a massive, stone door. His question was answered as Owengar pulled a key from his pocket and slid it into the keyhole and gave it a turn. There was a mechanical sounding click and then the door slowly swung outward about four feet. Just enough for a person to pass single file. The light from outside came crashing through the opening and even though it was overcast, it seemed blinding to Nick and Rehn. Even Owengar held a hand up to his eyes as they stepped out through the door. Once they were out, Owengar turned back to the door and put the key back into the other side of the door. This side looked just like the cliff face it had opened from. The keyhole was hidden somehow in the cracks of the rock.

Owengar turned the key and the door swung back into place. As it fit back into its original position, the same mechanical click sounded, and the mountain was sealed shut. Nick stood looking over the mountain face in front of him, baffled at how the cracks of the door had disappeared somewhere in the cracks and imperfections of the rock face. There was no sign of an entry. It was apparent why the humans on Terran had no idea that the dwarfs existed. There was no trace of them in the world.

"This way," said Owengar leading them down a narrow trail to the right. They were high above the tree lines and all that was visible was rock and patches of dirt. Nick looked back in the direction of the watch tower where the other dwarfs should be but could not see the opening in the rocks. He did see what it was they had been watching. Off to the left down about five hundred feet was a mountain pass. There was a wide trail that wound its way up from the valleys below and crossed between these two granite peaks. Nick assumed it was the only passable road through these mountains. There seemed to be no other passable route except for through this gap between the two peaks.

Down below them, they could see the green of pine trees reaching towards them. The air was very cold this high in the mountain peaks. Nick became nervous as he looked down below and saw nothing but cliffs in every direction. His stomach tightened as he realized how high they were and that there didn't seem to be any way down from these heights.

"Stay close to me," called Owengar quietly "I don't want you to wander into their line of sight."

Nick went quickly to Owengar's side. Rhen was soon there as well. Owengar led them along one of the cliff's faces, to what looked like jagged steps. One side of these rough stairs dropped straight to the valley below. A gray granite face backed the other side. Nick kept his shoulder tight to the cool granite. With each step, he could feel a tingle shoot from his foot up through his leg and to his chest. His head was almost spinning from the unreal height of the mountain they were on.

The stairs continued down and started to curl around to the right. The sight didn't ease Nick's fear of heights as it just highlighted how high they were with the stairs outlined by the gray sky on the horizon. Just as he thought he might have to sit down for a second, the stairs curled down to a flat landing with two ornately carved stone doors.

"Here we go," said Owengar. "We should be able to move about freely in these tunnels. They are to the ancient mines of my people. We have not used them in years. We keep them locked. King Velengar started new mines that are closer to the kingdom for convenience."

Owengar pulled out his key ring again and fumbled through the five or six keys on the chain. He stopped at the roughest looking of the group. The metal was dark and rusted. He separated it from the others and placed it between his oversized finger and thumb and inserted it into the door in front of him. With the same mechanical click, as before, the door unlocked and swung into the mountain inviting them to pass into the dark tunnel before them.

Nick and Rhen stepped into the darkness as Owengar encouraged them in with the wave of his hand. The air was stale and damp. It was obvious that these caves had lain quiet for some time now. The darkness was broken by the newly lit torch Owengar now held in his hand. The floors were the rough floors of the escape tunnel. The walls were not the nice, squared or shaped tunnels of the kingdom. They resembled more the mine tunnels that Nick had worked in for the last few months. This thought brought back a memory of the Dead ones and of the misery of the mines. Nick shuddered involuntarily as the thoughts crossed his mind.

Owengar took the lead and pushed them far into the tunnels. After another hour, Nick had no idea how Owengar could possibly know where they were. They had taken so many passages that had split off from the main tunnel. It was so quiet in the mine and no one had spoken since they entered. All they could hear was the shuffling of their own feet over the cold stone floors. Soon, Owengar stopped as the tunnel opened into a very large cavern.

"This is it. This is the first mine of my people. This is where they started our mountain home. The very crown the king wears was fashioned from gold mined here," Owengar said in awe. "I have not been here many times, but each time has been on a special occasion. I find our journey to be one of these special occasions," he finished, very matter of fact.

"Nick and Rhen, we must arm you before we leave this kingdom. What is your weapon of choice?" Owengar asked.

"A long sword would be fine for me," answered Rhen.

"I am not sure," said Nick.

"Then we shall get you Rhen, a long sword, and for you Nick, I think a short sword would be best," Owengar said as he inspected Nick head to foot.

"I think a mail shirt would be smart as well. Not a mail shirt of men, but from the forges of the dwarfs. Come this way then," said Owengar leading them to a darkened archway to the left. "There should be something that will work in here." Owengar took the same key as he had used before and placed it into a large door in the archway. He unlocked it and swung it open.

As Owengar passed through the doorway with his torch, Nick took in a deep breath. There before him was the most amazing display of armor and weapons he had ever seen. Full suits of intricate plate-mail, shields, battle axes, war hammers, maces, swords, bows and helmets were all on display and neatly organized into alcoves in the large room. In the middle of the room were smooth faceless dwarven statues that had beautiful suits of armor strapped to them for display. Ornate racks were neatly organized with swords, lances, and spears. There was a table with a black, velvet covering that had a display of daggers and knives. Everything Nick looked at was made of the finest of detail and craftsmanship. Each piece was a work of art.

Everything had a hint of dust upon it, but other than that, it was all just like new. There were no signs of battle scars on the plate-mail, not a scratch on a single blade.

"It's like new," Nick said. "It is all so amazing."

"So it is," Owengar said in a choked voice.

Nick swore he saw him brush a hand past his eye.

"This is the King's Guard Armory. Only the finest of our soldiers can arm themselves here. King Velengar has ordered me to have you pick for yourselves from only the best. I want you to understand, this is the greatest of honors my people can receive. Please do it with respect and know of the respect my king has for you Keeper," Owengar said as he bowed deeply to Nick.

Once again, Nick felt undeserving of the respect that Velengar and Owengar were showing to him, but he did not want to offend them.

"Thank you for the honor," Nick said.

"Yes, we are deeply honored." Said Rhen.

There was a short silence that was broken with the ring of a metal blade being drawn from one of the racks.

"This will do nicely," Rhen said as he put his second hand to the sword he had drawn from one of the racks.

The handle was large enough for him to hold both hands comfortably on the hilt. The blade was long and thin. Rhen deftly swung it into the air and with a spin the blade whistled through the air. In several swift motions, he sliced the air into imaginary bits as he stepped, lunged and swung the blade. It was amazing to Nick. All the time the blade hissed through the air. He never imagined that someone his age could handle a sword like this.

Nick continued to look around. He followed the instruction of Owengar and finally settled with a narrower blade that allowed for only one hand on the hilt. Owengar showed him a light wooden shield that had a convenient strap that he could use to carry it on his back. It had comfortably molded leather straps on the back of it for his arm and he showed him the basics of how it could be used against an attacker to ward off their blows.

"This way you can keep yourself safe while you learn to use that sword," Owengar said after his demonstration.

Nick understood what Owengar was trying to tell him nicely. Defense would be better suited for him until he learned to fight properly. Nick could hardly imagine fighting with another person face to face. The thought didn't sit well with him at all. He knew it was a new reality in this world, but he still wasn't wired for it. How would he learn to fight like that? He just wasn't sure he could do it.

"We will stay the night here in the armory. We are safe here. As you saw when we came in, no one has been here for a long time," said Owengar.

He held the torch to the floor and waved his hand to show them their own footprints in the light dust that had gathered there. They could see only their footprints and no sign of any others.

They unraveled bed rolls that Owengar had found in another room. He also found three packs for them to load with supplies. They rolled out the bedding and arranged their things for later that night. Owengar had them open the bags they had carried all the way from the throne room. They transferred everything from the bags into the packs. Owengar showed Nick how to fasten the shield onto his pack properly so that he could easily remove it and protect himself in case of an attack. Nick smiled to himself as he realized he would look like a turtle with the shield and pack on his back. Owengar helped him to fit a belt and a proper scabbard for the sword around his waist. Nick felt a strange sense of pride once the sword hung at his side and he felt the weight tug at the thick leather belt. The scabbard was balanced just right so that as he stepped, the sword stayed out of the way and made it easy for him to move.

After he was equipped properly, Owengar brought a straw practice dummy in for Nick to learn the basic fighting strokes. At first it seemed awkward, but Nick wouldn't quit. Soon he was sweating and breathing hard as he swung the sword at the dummy. He was surprised when he began to enjoy the three steps. A short stroke to the stomach from left to right, a strong follow through from the right shoulder down to the left hip and then a quick lung and thrust into the center of the dummy's torso.

Owengar chuckled "Good, good, you are getting it."

He continued to have Nick practice but now added the shield to his arm to get him used to the movements with it in the way.

When Nick finally became too tired to continue, his arm felt like it weighed a hundred pounds. He slid the sword back into its scabbard and sat down on the cool stone floor.

"That will get you in shape," Nick said.

"Get you in the shape of what?" asked Rhen puzzled.

"Oh, never mind," Nick replied when he realized some of the sayings from home did not apply on Terran.

They cleaned up in a shower room just off the main corridor and then they had dinner from some of the food supplies they had been given. After his new sword training, all Nick wanted to do was to sleep. Not long after they had eaten, that is exactly what he did. While Rhen and Owengar discussed the roads they would be traveling, Nick's eyes grew heavy and he retreated to his bed roll. His eyelids closed and he fell fast asleep.

Chapter 18

The Slides

When Dawn came, Owengar woke Nick and Rhen. There was no bacon or eggs for breakfast, but rations from their packs. They each had thick dry cakes, that resembled short bread cookies in their packs. The cakes had a very buttery flavor. Nick thought they were pretty good. It didn't take much to make Nick start to feel full. Only half a cake seemed to be enough.

"What are these made of?" Nick asked Owengar.

"I don't know really. The cooks in the castle make them for the troops. They have been making them for as long as we have had soldiers. They don't taste too bad until you have been eating them for weeks. Then you start to dream about eating a real meal. They start to seem flavorless," Owengar pulled a face as he said this.

After eating and packing up, Owengar led them down a set of stairs that was just outside of the armory. The stairs were well worn and spiraled downward. After turning and turning around and around, they came to a landing that opened up to another intricately carved archway. Through the archway was a tunnel. The walls were not cut into flat surfaces but were the results of chipping and digging though the rock. It was raw.

As they walked through the archway Owengar announced, "The ancient mines of Anthril. He was a legendary king, the first king here in this mountain home. He was the one who decided that we would live in the earth, he taught our people to love the stone, and he showed them the treasures that lay entombed there." Owengar's eyes beamed in the light of his torch. "This is where it all began!"

As they walked down the tunnel, it started to widen into a large cavern. It reminded Nick of the mines he had been working in. Yet this mine was much cleaner and more organized. Impressive scaffolding lined the walls of the cavern. Pulley systems and buckets ran the length. There were steel tracks with carts on them that ran along the scaffolding. Nick realized that when the dwarfs mined, they were very efficient. The bucket lines and carts all seemed to be pointing in one direction, to the other end of the massive cavern, and this was the direction Owengar was taking them.

At the other side of the cavern, the buckets came down to where the carts on the tracks could be loaded. Then the carts followed a track into a small, dark tunnel that only had a couple of feet of clearance to the top of the cart. Owengar waddled up to the side of the cart in the front of the line with his short legs and threw his pack inside.

"Here is our ride!" he exclaimed with a smile.

Nick and Rhen said nothing but wandered up to the side of the cart and threw their packs in. Rhen dropped to a knee and motioned for Nick to use it as a step to climb in. Nick climbed into the large metal cart. It was just big enough that he could kneel in the bottom and hold onto both sides of the cart with his head sticking out.

After a few moments Rhen had helped Owengar climb over the side and then climbed in himself. Owengar slid his pack to the front of the cart and propped it up like a seat and sat down. There was a torch holder on the outside of the cart that he secured his torch into. When he did it projected light forward in front of the cart. Nick realized that there was a cover around the top of the torch that had some type of glass lens to keep it from blowing out and to project the light like a headlight. It was bulky but it seemed to do a really good job. It reminded Nick of the progress on Earth. First a torch, then a lantern and eventually a light bulb. It was nothing to his world, but he could see it was amazing to Rhen who was leaning over Owengar's shoulder to examine it.

Owengar was doing something to a hatch on the front of the cart but Nick couldn't see in the dark. He then heard a screech of metal and could see what he had been working at. He had released some latches on the front of the cart and half of the front panel folded on hinges back into the cart until it rested against the lower side. It made it so they could easily see out the front of the cart and gave Owengar access to a large metal lever.

"Better sit down and secure yourselves!" Owengar said with his head half turned.

Rhen settled back down in front of Nick and grabbed the sides of the cart. Nick slid his pack to the rest against the back panel and sat on it like Owengar had done. His back rested against the back panel. And smiled to himself as he settled into his newly formed seat.

Owengar pushed the lever forward and the cart began to roll toward the tunnel in front of them. It felt like a tight fit with the roof of the tunnel so close to their heads. As the cart rolled faster, Nick instinctively kept ducking his head slightly not knowing what was coming from up ahead. The torch light that projected forward helped to see but it only reached out about twenty feet to the tracks and walls in front of them.

It didn't take long for the cart to pick up speed. Nick's heart began to race a little as they plummeted deeper into the mine. The cool air was pushing into his face and was making him feel cold. Owengar must have been enjoying this because all Nick could hear was his booming laugh every time the cart dropped onto a steeper incline and Nick's stomach went into his throat. Nick could see the torch light flashing off the rough sides of the tunnel that were shooting past him. He could also see the dark shape of Rhen clinging to the sides of the cart in front of him.

Just then Nick's eyes were blinded as daylight came streaming into his eyes as the cart shot around a corner. The track had left the darkness of the mine and made a sharp left turn as it shot out along a high cliff wall. Nick just saw a flash of green below and then they turned right back into the darkness of the tunnel.

Just then Owengar started to pull back on the large lever and Nick could hear the screeching of the wheels on the track. The cart started to slow as the tunnel opened into a large cavern again. This cavern was not dark. It had a soft glow of daylight filtering up from three tunnels off to the right of the tracks. Nick could see why. There were a few of the carts in front of them with the buckets tilted to the right side to dump their loads. The carts were brought to this point and emptied down these three stone chutes.

As his eyes adjusted to the light, he could also see that the carts ahead of him were in line to turn a tight left and then be pulled up a steep straight track. There was some type of dwarven conveyor system that hooked onto the bottom of each cart and then was pulled back up the track. There were a few carts on the conveyor track, but it was not in motion for them to be pulled up.

Owengar stood up and climbed out of the front of the cart as it stopped. He let out another booming laugh and smiled ear to ear.

"That never gets old! Must be my favorite thing to do except for the slides," he chuckled.

"What are the slides?" Nick had to ask.

Owengar opened his arms in a grand gesture and waved his left hand toward the three stone chutes, that were to the side of the cart.

Nick's attention went to the chutes. He could see that they were on a good forty-five-degree angle. They reminded Nick of a waterslide carved out of stone. The surface had big marks in it and small gouges the closer he looked.

"What are they used for?" Rhen asked.

"They are used to discard all of the stone that we carve out of the mines and the mountain. Didn't you wonder how we carved the tunnels in the main city and what we did with the refuse stone?" Owengar asked.

It made sense. Even a mole or a mouse has to push the dirt from their tunnels when they dig. He didn't even think about how they were getting rid of the excess as they made the mountain city.

Owengar walked just past the chutes and opened a door that Nick hadn't noticed. He went in and when he came back out, he had a large piece of thin metal. It almost looked like a shield but was long and oval. The edges were bent up and the whole shape curved. It had a large leather pad and leather straps. Owengar placed it on the ground in front of Nick and waved to Rhen to follow him back into the room. They came back with two more of the big metal objects.

He lined all three up in front of each of the stone chutes.

"Nick, come and sit here," Owengar said as he held the straps up.

Nick realized what was going on and his stomach tightened into knots.

"Is this even safe?" Nick asked.

"Safe? We have been doing this for hundreds of years Keeper. Do you trust that I will fulfill my king's wishes?" Owengar asked Nick.

"Well, yes," said Nick.

"Then I will get you to the elves safe," he answered back.

Rhen seemed very concerned as well, as his hands clenched and unclenched. Nick walked over and sat on the leather pad as he was instructed. Owengar pulled one strap around Nick's waist. He placed his feet into two stirrups at the front of the disk and then pulled two more straps over his shoulders and connected them to the one about his waist and then tightened it up.

He did the same for Rhen and made sure the two were all secured and then walked over to the wall next to the door and pulled down on an iron lever that was next to a torch holder. When he pulled it down they could hear a mechanical clank and then a low, rumbling groan.

"That should do," Owengar mumbled and climbed onto his own disk.

"We use these in emergencies, or when we need to check the slides below. It makes things much quicker."

Owengar broke into a big smile and started to scoot his disk forward with his body weight. He stopped when he saw the other two starring at him and doing nothing.

"Well come on now, let's get going," he said gruffly.

Nick and Rhen hesitantly began to scoot their disks forward. When Nick felt his get to the edge, he hesitated a moment and then leaned forward. The metal let out a scraping noise as he started to move forward and then he started to slide rapidly down the chute. Rhen must have done the same, because he heard him let out a yelp. There was no question Owengar had started down his chute because Nick could hear his bellowing laughter over the sound of the metal sliding against the stone.

The first fifty feet were straight but as he accelerated downhill, the chute banked slightly. As Nick flew around the corner he realized that the disk was very stable and sailed straight down the center of the stone chute. A large smile worked its way over his lips, and he was actually enjoying this.

The chute banked slowly one direction and then the next. The farther he slid the lighter it became. With the growing light, Nick could see more detail as he flew down the chute. Up ahead of him, he could see what Owengar had triggered before they had left. It was a huge piece of metal, that was shaped to fit the stone tunnel. It had been switched across the chute like the switch to a train track. He could see a drop off beyond it that would have tossed him into the piles of rock below. This is where the rubble dumped from the carts exited the mountain. He couldn't even feel a bump as he hit the metal curve and rerouted to a side chute.

The chute flattened out and it was lined with a thick layer of sand that brought him to a smooth stop. To his left he saw Rhen sliding to a stop and just past Rhen came a grinning Owengar. Owengar was still laughing out loud as he unhooked himself and came over to unhook his guests.

"That is the quickest way to travel my friends," he said with a smile.

Nick and Rhen looked at each other and broke into laughter. Nick didn't know why but he couldn't stop. Rhen couldn't stop either. It felt so good to have fun. Nick had forgotten how good it felt to have fun. Since he had come to this strange land he had felt nothing but fear, hunger and pain. He realized he hadn't felt much enjoyment at all. He reveled in the feeling of joy and happiness with Rhen and Owengar as long as he could.

Chapter 19

Blacwin

After the laughing fit had passed, they worked their way down a set of stairs that were cleverly hidden in the cliff face. There was a seventy to eighty-foot drop to their right as they descended. From below there was no sign of the steps as they had been shaped to resemble the natural rock face. The steps were very wide and perfectly flat. Nick felt shaky as he worked his way down them. Owengar on the other hand, wandered down them as if they were steps at school. He turned his head and talked with Nick and Rhen as they descended. Nick just wished he would keep looking ahead.

When they reached the bottom, Nick looked back at where the slides had dumped the excess rock onto the side of the mountain. He could see an opening like a small cave, and then below just a big rockslide. It looked no different than the Mountains he had seen before. Nick felt a pang in his heart as he thought about home. It had been months since that day in the hotel. His body was much different from all of the hard work and lack of junk food. He had muscles he didn't have before and he felt much stronger. He had grown taller as well. His hair was long and shaggy, and he knew it needed to be cut.

Would they even recognize me? Nick thought to himself.

Nick was shaken from his inner thoughts as Rhen slapped him on the back, and Nick realized he had been saying something to him.

"...so high. You can come back later."

Nick just smiled in reply since he had no idea what he had just said.

The mountain sloped down into a small meadow. At the edge of the meadow, there was a sharp descent into the trees. They followed a game trail that lead them to a dry stream bed that they crossed over, and then worked their way toward the pass that Nick had seen from the lookout area. When they finally reached the pass, they stopped off in the trees so Owengar could slip on a traveling cloak. He did not want to draw attention to himself or his people.

"We travel in the open very seldom, and when we do, we travel alone. Remember, humans have not seen us for years. They are used to seeing one at a time and mistake us for smaller humans. Let's face it, we are very similar at first glance. They just aren't ready for a whole group of us walking down the road in our armor," said Owengar.

It made sense. After all these years, the humans had not known the dwarfs existed beneath the mountain. Nick was beginning to wonder about his own world. Were there dwarfs there? He definitely thought it could be a possibility.

The road was quiet, and they only ran into one traveler along their way. He seemed leery of them and led his pack mule and horse close to the other side of the road to keep away from them. He never made eye contact, just kept his head down and heading forward.

This was a relief to Nick and his party as they didn't want to draw attention to themselves on their journey. The less strangers they encountered, the better.

As they came to the peak of the mountain pass, Nick caught his first sight into the valley below. He could see miles of trees and green that ran into blue waters in the distance. What looked like rolling plains lay due north and then to their right a large valley. It was surrounded by small mountains on both sides. Nick could also hear the sound of a small mountain stream dashing off of rocks somewhere down below him.

They continued down the trail of switchbacks that led them down from the steep mountain pass. The air was cool and got much colder as the light of day started to fade. The sound of the stream grew louder and louder until the trail ran into it at a small waterfall. They sat down here to rest. They were tired from all of the hiking and hadn't said much since they had left the meadow.

As Nick was taking a drink from his water bag, he heard a loud grunt and a thud. Cursing followed and more thuds. Rhen looked towards the noise and stood drawing his sword. Nick pulled his from its scabbard as well as they moved towards the sound. Owengar swung his axe into his hands.

As they moved around a tall bush on the stream bank they could see what was making the noise. A Dead One with a club in its hand loomed over a large black scaled thin venti. He was busy beating it with the club with fury in his eyes.

"Trifle with me and you will learn your lesson child!" seethed the Dead One.

Nick was shocked to see both the venti and the Dead One. Fear bolted through him as he saw the unfeeling warrior beating the small dragon. Its small wings were folded in except the right one had been broken. The beast couldn't fold it in as the most prominent joint had been broken and the bone was partially exposed. The end of the wing hung open limply. The venti tried to fight back, but every time it did, he would club a part of its body with a sickening thud. Soon it would be dead as its strength was draining from the abuse.

Nick felt the fire building within him. No animal, evil or not should be made to suffer like this. Nick clenched his sword and went to step toward the attacker. Rhen beat him to it. Without a word Rhen slipped around the bush and swung his sword in a high arc bringing it down on the Dead One's neck. The sharp dwarven blade cleanly removed his head from his body and he toppled forward.

The venti raised its head to look at Rhen and then in exhaustion laid it back down on the ground. It let out a bleating moan that reminded Nick of an injured rabbit. It made him feel sad. He knew this was the offspring of the evil that created the Dead Ones, that abused so many and that it must be just as evil, but Nick felt a desire to help it.

"We must help it!" Nick blurted out.

"Are you mad?" replied Rhen. "This is a child of the dragon. This is what hunts for us and helps them enslave us to dig in the mines. This creature doesn't deserve to suffer, but it does deserve to die!" Rhen said as he stepped toward it.

Hearing this the venti let out another cry and tried to push itself up again but collapsed. Nick jumped in between Rhen and the creature.

"We could restrain it. It might be able to give us information that would be useful. Please, it can't hurt us in this condition," Nick pleaded.

"Nick is right," said Owengar who had been quiet until now "We might be able to learn something useful from it. Like, why was it here and how many were with this company. They could be close by and we could walk right into them, making our journey for naught," he finished.

"Fine," Rhen conceded. "Go get the rope from my pack."

Nick hurried back to Rhen's pack and returned with the rope. They quickly bound its legs and neck. It didn't even try to resist as it was too weak. Once it was bound they started to look over its injuries and tend to them the best they could. From what they could see, the broken wing was the worst of them and Owengar did his best to wrap it tight to its body. The venti cried out as he did, but it seemed to be much more comfortable when it was back in a natural position like the other one.

They decided to camp here next to the animal out of sight from the road, just in case the party that was with it came back looking for the Dead One. They drug the Dead One's body up through the trees and away from their camp. They dropped it into a crevice of rock where no one would stumble upon it.

They would not light a fire for fear that it would draw attention to them, and so they ate a cold meal of the dry dwarven travel rations. They fed the dragon a freshly killed rabbit and brought it water from the stream to drink. Then Owengar tied it to a nearby tree and bound its jaws shut. The venti seemed lethargic, but grateful for the care.

Night came on quickly and the three talked quietly for only a few minutes and then rolled out their beds and let Owengar take the first watch.

The next morning was cold and crisp. Nick woke and stretched his arms towards the sky. As he did, he could feel the cool air biting at his exposed arms. Reluctantly he got out of his bed and rolled it back up and fastened it back to his pack. He pulled his traveling cloak about him and sat down on a rock next to Rhen who had been keeping the last watch of the night.

"Morning," he said to Rhen.

Rhen just nodded back to him.

Nick looked over to the venti and noticed that it was already doing much better. It was sitting up looking back at him. Its eyes were clear and seemed to be searching him up and down. Nick couldn't help it, he slowly approached the creature to look it over in the soft morning light. As he approached, it raised its head and pulled away from him.

"Easy, I'm not going to hurt you," he said softly to it.

"Will you hurt me if I loosen the ropes around you jaw?" Nick asked the creature, not sure if it could understand him. To his surprise it shook its head back and forth.

Nick walked around behind the animal and loosened the ropes and quickly stepped away.

"What are you doing?" hissed Rhen at Nick.

"It's fine, I want to talk to it," Nick replied.

"I will watch the two," exclaimed Owengar as he wandered over from his bed "It is all right."

With that, Rhen seemed to be pacified, and Nick sat down on a rock near the venti. It had turned its head and shook itself free of the ropes that Nick had just untied. Then it watched Nick all the way to where he sat down.

"Are you feeling comfortable? Are you going to be ok?" asked Nick.

It was silent for a while and then the creature responded back in a hissing voice. "Yes, I feel much better. You saved my life. Why?" it replied.

"It was the right thing to do," answered Nick.

"Are you sure? I have been serving her since I hatched. I have done much to hurt and betray your kind. Mother forced me to do terrible things," it seemed to shudder at this last reply.

"Did you not love to serve her?" Nick asked surprised.

Owengar was also caught off guard by this. Nick could see it by the look that had crossed his face.

"I have dreaded every day in service to her. She is mean and cruel. Everything was about her and her comfort, never about us or our comfort. I have been beaten by her and her men too many times to count. I have only obeyed for my own survival. Mother said I was broken from the beginning and that I was a shame to our kind. She said I had feelings for the humans that are unnatural for a dragon. She said I had no fire for vengeance or thirst for death like a venti should. I wish never to see her again," it finished.

"Why were you being beaten by that Dead One?" Nick asked.

"I had upset her again. She had asked that I kill a young human child in a village just down the hill. I refused to hurt the youngling, and because of this she went into a fit of rage. First she killed the young girl and then broke my wing and flung me to the ground. I was lucky she didn't kill me then, but Zorig, her general, reported a disturbance in a nearby town and asked for her to come and squash it just then. Her fury left with her, but not before the instruction was given to make me suffer and then to kill me somewhere private. Lucky for me, I was receiving my punishment from Jerick when you arrived and killed him," the venti replied.

"Excuse me for asking, but are you a male or a female? You are the first dragon I have ever seen up close. I just don't know anything about dragons," Nick explained.

"I am a male. My name is Blacwin," he answered.

"Blacwin," Nick said under his breath. "That seems fitting. You do seem different than the other venti I have seen," Nick said.

"I am much different from my brothers and sisters. I never thought the way they did. I was always concerned with others and even the other races. It always made mother so angry. So eventually, I faked it to protect myself," said Blacwin.

"Don't believe it!" Rhen cried over the conversation

"They are all evil and he will kill you as soon as he gets the chance!" there was anger and hatred in Rhen's voice.

Nick immediately knew why. His mother and father had been killed by the dragon years before. Nick could understand his feelings, but felt there was something about this venti that was different.

"I am different," Blacwin said in a lowered voice. "I don't want to be like them…" he trailed off quietly.

For some reason Nick believed Blacwin. He spent the next two days tending to Blacwin's health. Rhen was not happy about the attention that Nick was giving to the creature, but Nick couldn't help it. He felt a bond with the creature he had saved from Rhen's sword. He could feel the bond and believed that Blacwin felt a debt of gratitude to him. He had shared very willingly as much information about Mortes and her army as he could. She had been with a group of fifty in the town of Errington not far from where they were when he had defied his mother. It was a lone town in the mountains that was safe, or so they had thought, from the dragon and her men. They had taken many of the men and women to work in the mine but when the leader of the town had fought back, Mortes wanted to send a message by killing his young daughter in front of all of them. She had ordered Blacwin to do it.

He had explained that the dragon had taken up residence in the old castle. She wouldn't fit through the main doors, so she had crushed a hole through the side of the main corridor that lead to the treasury on the second floor. She could just fold her wings in and squeeze down the massive hallway. She had torn down the wall that kept people out of the treasury and opened it to the hallway. Then she had the Dead Ones and slaves build a massive fireplace of stone on one wall of the treasury.

"She loves the heat," Blacwin had said. "They keep the fire blazing, so she is always warm and comfortable. The slaves have piled all the treasure in the kingdom into the treasury where she loves to lie upon the piles. It is her weakness. She is like a cat with catnip when she sits upon it in her lair. The gold and jewels drive her mad and she can't focus as she normally would," he had finished.

Rhen seemed to be even more upset than usual as Blacwin had shared all the details. He was angry that Mortes was killing and enslaving his people to glutton herself with gold and gems for her own enjoyment.

"They are no good to a dragon, she can have anything she wants. She can't even hold a coin between her claws!" he had yelled out at one point.

After Blacwin was healed enough to travel, Nick had pleaded along with Blacwin for them to release him of his bindings. Owengar and Rhen refused at first, but after Nick had studied in the Book of Secrets and found an oath spell, they had agreed to it only if Blacwin would swear an oath under the spell.

According to the book, anyone entering the oath that did not intend to keep it, would be destroyed as they spoke the oath. Nick was sure that Rhen was hoping that the venti was lying to them. He was sure he wanted to watch it disintegrate after uttering the oath.

Nick had memorized the spell and made the hand motions by brushing his hand from the left of Blacwin's head and then the right and placing his hand on Blacwin's heart.

He then cast the spell by saying "Et vien a passe."

Blacwin slowly spoke his oath "I give my life to them who have saved it. I will do all I can to protect theirs. I will gladly give my life in service to their hand and will never betray their trust."

With that said a blue shimmer of light spread over the young dragon and then passed between the members of the party. They could feel the intent of the dragon and it had spoken the truth.

All was quiet for a few minutes and then Owengar took a knee next to Blacwin. His voice was choked, and he bowed his head.

"Thank you Blacwin. I am honored by your oath. You are truly a special creature. My people have a story of a dragon like you, and they are extremely rare. Only one in millions will ever have a pure heart. It is an honor to know you." He said nothing else but turned and went back to his pack and finished packing.

Nick was astonished at the reverence in Owengar's voice and could feel something special about Blacwin, but didn't know what it was. Even Rhen looked at Blacwin differently. The hatred was gone, and he looked amazed as he looked him over.

"I guess that is that," said Nick as he walked over to Blacwin and untied the ropes.

He suddenly felt a closeness to the dragon. He slipped his arms around its neck at his shoulders and gave the creature a hug.

"Thank you, I know you meant it!" Nick said.

"It feels funny inside…. when someone treats you kindly… I like it," Blacwin said quietly as Nick stepped away.

From that moment on, Nick didn't see a ruthless venti anymore. He only saw a beautiful, black and sleek creature. He couldn't believe it. He had a dragon for a friend. He had a dragon as a protector.

Chapter 20

The Keeper

Nick and his party continued through the mountain pass. Blacwin kept to the forest and trees so that he wouldn't be seen. He kept true to his word and was serving the party. He kept hunting in the forest and bringing the fresh meat back to them to be cooked for their meals. The roads were clear, and like Blacwin had said, Mortes and the Dead Ones had moved on to another town.

Nick spent as much time with Blacwin as he could. He would walk through the forest with him when the trees were spread further apart, and the ground was clear enough to walk. The more time he spent talking with the venti, the more he liked him. The venti was full of questions and was invigorated by this new opportunity to think and live for itself. Nick was impressed by the dexterity and speed that the young dragon had.

When Nick would walk with him, he could tell that Blacwin had to hold back and walk very slow to stay next to him. He didn't seem to mind though, as the young dragon was very inquisitive and had so much to talk about.

The stories he shared of his mother and the Dead One's heinous acts were endless. They made his skin crawl to know of their evil, unfeeling character. It put dread into Nick's soul to even imagine the dragon. Village after village, she had plundered with no respect for women, children, or animal. From the stories he was hearing, she had no care for life whatsoever.

How will I ever destroy something so powerful and evil? He thought to himself.

The thought that his friends believed he was the answer weighed him down. He began to look at the ground and walk more slowly. He was feeling overwhelmed.

Eventually Nick asked Blacwin not to speak of the Dead Ones or Mortes anymore. He let him know that he could not listen to their evil acts any longer. He asked instead that Blacwin ask him questions instead.

Blacwin was happy to comply and immediately asked, "Why do humans burn their food over the fire? I prefer the beautiful taste of the raw flesh." He said.

"The flames take away the flavor of blood, so it just tastes like charcoal."

Nick smiled at the question and went on to explain that he enjoyed the smoke-filled flavor of meat cooked over a fire. This still seemed odd to Blacwin, but he accepted the fact that humans and dragons must have a different sense of taste. Blacwin had so many questions about human behavior. Nick spent hours trying to answer them.

When they drew close to Errington, Nick left the young dragon and urged him to stay deep within the trees so he would not be discovered. Nick made sure he understood that other humans would see Blacwin as a threat and would attack him to keep their people and families safe. Blacwin nodded his head as if he understood and hurried off into the forest after promising to keep watch out for the group.

They passed through Errington and saw the destruction that had been left behind. Families had been torn apart and they told of the pillaging that the Dead Ones had done to their poor town. More than half of their people had been taken to the mines and many were killed. Women were abused and those who fought back were made to suffer. Wherever the dragon and her men went, suffering and destruction and evil followed. Nick hated the dragon; he hated her men. He would put an end to this suffering, or she would put an end to him. He resolved in that moment that he would study harder, he would do whatever he had to do to keep this from happening.

Nick, Owengar, and Rhen were angered by the news. Nick noticed the town's people were taking notice of Owengar and his different build. They studied him up and down. To take away from the pain in their hearts and their suspicions, Nick suggested that they help rebuild what they could. They spent a day or two with the people there. The people were grateful for their help, but it did not take away from their sorrow and pain. It did remind them that there were still good people in the world and there still was hope if they would come together.

The nights were somber. There was a depression, a sadness that couldn't be lifted. The people were suffering for those that had died and for those that were taken. Nick and his companions, worked hard to help the people but didn't do much talking. They didn't want to be disrespectful to the people as they dealt with their tragedy. Not to mention they didn't know what to say in such a difficult time.

Owengar did become one of the people's favorite. He used his strong hands and back to mend wagons, homes and fences. He was short and stalky and extremely strong. His workmanship with wood was amazing. Some of the only smiles seen were those of children that received some of his wooden animal carvings. They were so lifelike and smooth that it looked as though a tiny animal had sprung to life in the child's hand. He didn't seem to mind the attention of the people. Nick thought he needed it after watching how the people had treated him at the feast.

After a few days, they continued up through the valley to the Northeast. According to Owengar the lands of the elves were to the East of the rolling plains that they had seen from the mountain pass. After a few more days of uneventful travel, it started to rain lightly. The roads became soft and slippery and made their journey slow.

By the next day they started to see the road covered in heavy boot prints. Owengar crouched down to look at them.

"This is the group of fifty that Blacwin had spoken of," said Owengar with certainty. "We must keep our eyes open."

"What is that smoke?" Rhen asked pointing in the direction of the northern end of the valley.

They all looked in the direction he was pointing. There were black plumes of smoke curling into the air to the north.

"I have no idea," said Owengar, "but it is coming from Darian. It is the last civilization of humans to the North. With these boot prints and the smoke, it can't be a good thing."

"It looks to only be a few days walk, so I guess we will know soon enough," Rhen answered back.

It was a day and a half walk to Darian. They were much more cautious in their travels. They kept to the edges of the road and sent Blacwin ahead to watch for trouble and to warn them if they needed to get off the road. They ran into no one and the forest was eerily silent. The light rain had stopped, and the smoke had died down the next day to just a small light curl in the sky. When they came around the road's bend into Darian, they saw the cause of the smoke.

The charred remains of a town were all that remained. There were remnants of livestock fences and trampled crops to show that there had been a town there. The people of the town had made graves for those who had been killed and then they must have left for their own safety. There were no signs of life. No livestock, no people, nothing. Rotting food that must have been taken from the homes was strewn about the streets. Animal carcasses were here and there as though they had been killed and left to rot.

It was obvious that when the looters had all they could carry they laid waste to anything else that might have value so no one else would benefit from it. It was wasteful destruction. It was an evil that Nick didn't understand. How can someone do this? Why would someone do this to an innocent farming village?

It reminded Nick of the way his life had been ruined by the move. When his father lost his job, it only took a few weeks to lose almost everything that was important to him. He knew that this was much worse, and it filled him with rage. Anger towards the dragon and anger towards the Dead Ones who had helped tear this place away from these people. The abuse in the mines, the loss of their freedom. The stories of her ruthlessness all came to reality looking at this ravaged town.

As Nick was stewing in his anger and rage, Owengar called to him to stand up and to turn around. Nick was feeling anger toward Owengar at telling him what to do, but he turned to see what it was. His rage deepened to a blurred red as he saw a group of ten Dead Ones wandering in from the trees. They were pushing a small family of four before them with their swords. They had a terrible look of evil on their faces. Nick knew that no good was in their thoughts and this family would suffer.

One called out to them in a sarcastic voice "Glad you could make it for some entertainment boys. Mortes told us some of you would return, and when you did to teach you a lesson. To start things off, you can watch this."

As he said this he grabbed the smaller daughter of the family by her hair. She must have only been five or six years old. She let out a scream and began to cry.

At this, without warning, the rage that had been boiling inside of Nick erupted. It morphed into a physical power he could feel swelling inside of his chest and spread throughout his arms. It was a feeling of true power. He lunged forward; a cry of anger came from his lips as he swung his fist through the air towards the ground. The energy surged through his body, and as he punched the ground, the power swelling inside of him surged out through his fists. A bright, white burst of energy exploded from where he punched the ground and raced towards the Dead Ones. A shock wave rippled through the ground. No one could see anything but the bright light and the sound of the massive explosion and cries of surprise from the Dead Ones and the family. They could hear the splintering of wood and the crashing of boulders.

The white light surged past where the Dead Ones had stood. Nick had his head raised. He could see all that remained of the Dead Ones. Their crumpled bodies were sizzling and smoking on the ground . The family had been knocked to the ground but seemed untouched amid their charred remains. Everything else within a one-hundred-foot circle had been destroyed. The only thing left was bare earth. No grass or vegetation- no structures or rocks. It had all been completely stripped by the explosive force. Nick had felt all his strength surge with the energy, he swayed a moment, then toppled forward onto his face in the mud, and all was black.

Rhen and Owengar stood in amazement. Without a word for the next few minutes they stood staring at the family and the newly cleared area, and back at Nick in shock. It was a massive circular area. The family stood staring at Nick's form lying in the dirt right at the leading edge of the cleared area. The mother was the first to come to her senses and ran to Nick's body and rolled him over into her lap. When she did this, Owengar and Rhen ran to her side.

Nick's head lay motionless in her lap. His skin was gray and his body lifeless. His arms hung to his sides limp. Rhen couldn't see his chest rising and falling as it should if he were breathing. He also noticed a shimmer of blue light on Nick's left hand. It soon faded and, in its place, all Rhen could see was an odd shaped scar he hadn't noticed before.

"Is he alive?" Rhen asked worried.

"Yes, he is breathing, but it is shallow… Who is he?" she said in awe.

In a reverent voice, Owengar replied, "A true Keeper."

Made in the USA
Monee, IL
04 October 2023

Bambino is an adorable puppy who lov family is shopping, Bambino gets out of ... he hears his friends swimming in the neighborhood pond, so he hurries to join them. Just as Bambino is about to jump in, he remembers his family said he's not allowed to swim there. Faced with the dilemma of having fun with his friends or obeying his family, Bambino surrenders to temptation and swims in the pond. He quickly realizes that he cannot hide his disobedience, and now he must face his family. Bambino is sorry and ashamed for disobeying, but through his family's love, he experiences mercy and forgiveness.

Bambino Gets Into Mischief is a wonderful story that demonstrates Our Heavenly Father's love and mercy when we have sinned. When we are sorry for our disobedience, God's forgiveness is greater than our offense.

For Sunday School Lessons and other inspirational readings, visit us at
successministry.net

ISBN 978-1-4984-7290-6
90000
9 781498 472906

Prelude

Mount Damavand, the symbol of Iranian resistance against foreign rule in Persian poetry, is the highest point in the Middle East and the highest volcano in all of Asia.

Images that Shocked My Soul

I am speechless. I am numb! I cannot believe what I saw a few hours ago. I am outside sitting on a bench in my garden, a place I often come to for solace. It is early afternoon, but I am still wearing my morning house suit. I have a wet handkerchief in my hand and cannot stop the tears from flowing down my cheeks. I do not know how long I have been sitting here but gradually, with great difficulty, I start to remember why I am so overcome with emotion: I would like to erase from my mind what has happened.

Today my friend Bahman, another expatriate from Iran's Imperial Navy, sent me an agonizing video. Two so-called Muslims are beheading two other Muslims. The man who was performing the violent act was using a very dull knife. Perhaps such an instrument was never developed  to facilitate such a task. Back and forth, back and forth, he was visibly struggling. Triumphantly he finished and with his left hand he raised the bloody head and yelled, "Allah o Akbar" (*"God is great."*).

I closed my eyes—I could not watch any longer. I had to escape into the sunshine. I ran out of my home office sobbing. It was almost impossible for me to gain any kind of composure. I tried to pull myself together, but I continued to ponder the horror of the video. It was during these moments that I began to reflect upon my life. Images of my own experiences flashed before me, and I realized that I could no longer remain quiet. The time had come for me to speak out!

I have gone through the Islamic revolution. I have felt fear from those who have no respect for human dignity. I have seen and experienced a great deal. I do not claim to be a scholar, a historian, and most certainly not a politician, but I have a story to tell, and perhaps I can bring awareness to those who do not want to acknowledge what is still happening.

Nostalgia

Iran is my birthplace, my home, and my heritage. The children of my time were taught about the history of our culture. Every child knew that Cyrus, son of Darius the Great, was the founder of Persia, and that during Cyrus's reign, the Persian Empire became the largest empire the world has ever seen.

Prior to 1979, there were miniskirts on our women, the latest styles from Paris in our shops, frivolity among our people, and Western music in the air. Culture and sophistication were part of my background. It was my assumption that my beautiful Iran would always be advanced in its thinking, moving toward new technology, education, and freedom of thought. However, there were those who disagreed and who were consumed with envy. They did not understand our dream because they believed in the hate and judgmental ways that their religion taught them.

In 1979, radicals led by Ayatollah Khomeini crushed the Shah's dream when Muslim extremists gained control of Iran. Khomeini stirred the envy of the poor and the uneducated, by promising them great riches in return for their support. This disaster shaped the ugly future of my great country, and led to bloodshed, hatred and the destruction of a once-dignified Persian civilization. Many of yesterday's distinguished Persians have had to bow to today's fanatics.

The Shah did not fall at the hands of the Ayatollah alone. The United States, under the Carter administration, made the questionable decision to turn their backs on the Shah, after decades of friendship between the two countries. Carter's failure to help a man who was once a great ally cemented the fate of the Shah. The resulting damage was culturally devastating. Iran, America's best friend, became America's worst enemy.

The whole world has felt the repercussions of this great mistake in human history. This was the key that unlocked the door to the fanatic barbarians who still hold the country hostage. The chaos created continues to ignite the world and contributes daily to the increasing hate against America. The Middle East remains in shambles.

My own exile has caused me sadness, but it has also given me time to reflect on all that has happened that changed the fate of my country. My words might be considered by some to be controversial. However, I feel it is time to talk about the sense of pride that I have in having been privileged to be part of the Shah's dream, to build an even greater Iran. The plan was to pave the way for democracy and to lead my country into a new era as a Middle Eastern power, encouraging regional peace and worldwide respect.

Even now, thirty years later, as I think back, I can still feel the sea breeze from the Caspian Sea. I can still hear the bustle of Tehran and smell the scents of my childhood. I often wonder who now resides in my home on the Caspian Sea, who wears my bed jacket, my clothing, and who dines on my wife's Persian china? Was it destroyed, burned, or looted, or are there Mullahs behind closed doors living a life other than the one they profess to live to their followers? I cannot help but question this, as I feel the sorrow of not being able to hold the hands of my dying parents. Yet, I remain in exile, as I have been for the past three decades, unable to go back and bring my memories to life and not having the opportunity to tell my parents goodbye.

Chapter 1

Picture Courtesy of Sinem Inkaya

The Path to Destiny

Iran Takes Its Place on the Modern World Map

In the mid-1930s, deep within the borders of a post-World War I Germany, Hitler and his National Socialist Party began to gain political clout. The night of February 27, 1933, exploded with a burst of flames from the Reichstag. The fate of Germany, and the world, was forever changed. This fire served as the catalyst of a series of events that placed the Nazi Party in charge of Germany, with Hitler at the helm.

As the Nazis began to infect the German people with their hateful message, the barriers and restrictions set forth after World War I, by the League of Nations, began to fall. Over the next few years, Germany joined forces with Mussolini in Italy, and for the first years of the war, Stalin in the USSR. Germany invaded Europe, forcing other nations to make pacts and alliances, causing a worldwide struggle for power.

In the beginning of the Nazi reign, world leaders hesitated and watched. Across the channel from Germany, Winston Churchill sat night after night in his study and waited. Churchill, as Prime Minister of Great Britain, ignored the cries of his European neighbors until he was forced to take warning for his own people.

On September 1, 1939, Germany invaded Poland and war could not wait any longer. Two days later, on September 3, 1939, France and Great Britain declared war on Germany. Within a year, France began to fall, and on June 22, 1940, France was forced to cooperate with Germany. As a result, Germany invaded France and occupied half of the country.

Across the Atlantic, America was struggling to recover from the Great Depression, and feigning blissful ignorance of the troubles plaguing Europe, until the early morning hours of December 7, 1941, when imperialist Japan, now an Axis power in league with Germany and Italy, bombed the numerous military bases at Pearl Harbor. As a result, America was forced to join Great Britain and the other allied powers in World War II.

This oft-told story clearly defines the roles of the Axis powers—Germany, Italy, and Japan—and, on the opposite side, the Allies—the United States, Great Britain, and France—but does not mention Iran.

In the 1940s, the Reza Shah, father of the well-known Mohammed Reza Shah, who later became friends of many American presidents, ruled Iran. The Reza Shah was progressive. He was responsible for building an impressive cross-country railroad and sought to give his people a country of progress and industry. In the 1930s and 1940s, as Europe's war raged, the Shah of Iran watched. While the Reza Shah did not share the ideals of Hitler, he had a long-standing admiration for German technology and military prowess. As a result, the Reza Shah wished to emulate the positive aspects of Germany and reject the bad.

In addition to his interest in Germany, the Reza Shah was also contractually bound to Great Britain. Every day Iran was pumping thousands of gallons of black gold out of the oil-rich Persian Gulf for Great Britain. Iran was obligated to produce oil for the British as part of a hundred-year deal brokered between the two nations. Consequently, Iran's place in World War II was complicated. Iran was torn between the contractual requirements of oil production and the Reza Shah's admiration of German technology, and his gratitude towards the German workers who were an integral part of building the Reza Shah's railroads. As a result, in the early stages of World War II, the Reza Shah declared his neutrality.

Iran's declaration of neutrality did not fare well with either side of the international battle. On August 25, 1941, Iran was invaded on three fronts. The Reza Shah had admiration for many German accomplishments; therefore, he did not give in to the demands to help the Allies. Meanwhile, the Molotov-Ribbentrop Pact that pledged allegiance between the Soviets and Germany fell apart and the USSR turned the table in the war by joining the Allies. Despite his outright refusal to help the German war effort, the Reza Shah still felt gratitude and loyalty toward the German railroad engineers. This loyalty led the Shah to refuse to honor the Allies' request that he exile the German people within Iran's borders and allow the Allies sole access to the crucial Iranian railroads. In order to secure this important real estate, the British joined forces with their new ally, the USSR, and together they conducted the Anglo-Soviet invasion of Iran. Consequently, Iran became a key staging area for the transfer of supplies and provisions to the battles of World War II brewing in the USSR.

The Soviets invaded from the northwest with the intention of controlling Iran's rich resources and crucial supply line for their troops, the Iranian cross-country railroad. Meanwhile, the British crossed the Iraqi frontier and entered Iran from both the west and the Iranian sea borders in the south. Suddenly, the Reza Shah was forced to give up his goal of neutrality and abdicate his throne to save his people from war.

On September 16, 1941, the Reza Shah's monarchy fell on the capable shoulders of his first son, Mohammed Reza Shah, the man henceforth known to the world as the last Shah of Iran. As the Allies forced the Reza Shah's abdication, they looked to the young prince to take on a more modern Western stance and align himself with the Allied powers. Little did they know that throughout his reign, the last Shah of Iran would be the friend, confidant, and colleague of the Western world until he, too, was forced to abdicate his kingdom.

The Young Shah

Looking back on that time, I can envision the young Shah. He was only twenty-three years old the day his father came to him and asked him to step into his place in history. Although he was well educated in Switzerland, and well prepared for this great moment of his life, in my mind's eye, I saw the look of fear and pride that must have appeared on his face as he sat in the palace overwhelmed with thoughts of the future. Like the true leader that he was, in my vision, I saw the Shah rise slowly from his chair and walk through the door, crossing the threshold to manhood in mere seconds, during this time of war.

My Parents' Marriage

While the world around my birthplace was gripped in turmoil, my story begins. In August of 1936, shortly before the war that brought the fall of Iran's Reza Shah, two families, each owners of valuable land on the outskirts of Tehran, collided in a bitter dispute over the source of life, water. Out of this conflict, through a combination of passion and wisdom, they became one family—my own.

The lands of both these families lay along the lower reaches of the soaring Elburz Mountains, which rise in close proximity to the buildings of Tehran, Iran's capital. Both of my grandparents leased their farm acreage to local villagers. The soil was fertile for cultivating fruit trees. Among them were peaches, or the term that I knew as a child, "Persian apples." The fields were also abundant with mint and wheat. On the central plains below, water from broad rivers and wells was plentiful on the higher lands. However, the families were not yet knowledgeable about converting the ancient aqueducts into newer systems that could pump crucial water back up the steep slopes for irrigation. Aside from seasonal rains, the highland farms depended completely on swift streams that flowed down the mountainsides. In the heat of summer of 1936 the streams began to ebb, and a dispute over water broke out between my two grandfathers. As the dry months grew on, the battle intensified.

In the darkest part of night, local farmers crept over to one another's hillside streams and quickly dug channels that made the water run to their own crops. Each morning, one of the patriarchs would sit up in bed, awakened by cries of sabotage from the nearby fields. The farmers felt the need to begin hiding guards at night to protect the streams. With each week, the secret water operatives grew increasingly more creative with their theft. Soon they were crossing paths and threatening one another with hoes and pitchforks. Injury and death continued to be a possibility. The owners of each land holding stepped in more than once to settle the dispute with a schedule for the farmers to take turns collecting water. But the weather was severe, the water remained scarce, and the war raged on.

In the height of the conflict, villagers from the side of the landowner named Hashim, sent a curious invitation to the other side. The offer was to meet a group of un-named horsemen from the neighboring lands in a hunt, an ancient sport in the highlands. Not wanting to refuse such an adventure, the land-owner from the invited family, Abbas, accepted for himself and four of his closest friends. What Abbas did not know, was that Hashim planned to show up for the event accompanied by secret bodyguards.

When the day arrived, Abbas and his group set out for the rendezvous point in the plains southwest of Tehran. The well-polished rifles, ready for the hunt, gleamed in the morning sun. The men rode swiftly and eagerly, anticipating a day of sport. It was a balmy summer morning, perfect for this type of frivolity. As Abbas neared the meeting place, he could see in the clear air of the plains all of the other hunters—including Hashim. He was startled to find Hashim waiting. At once, he realized the hunt was not to be a friendly pheasant shoot. He thought it might be another plot in the war of the families that no doubt had a sinister purpose. Without hesitation, Abbas rode straight to the front of the gathered hunters and faced Hashim horse-to-horse, man-to-man. He called out, so all could hear, "If you are man enough, you will kill me here in front of the others." Hashim, it is true, had painstakingly planned a fake accident that would lead to Abbas's death. The water shortage would have been solved in Hashim's favor, and he was furious to have his plan fail and be publicly exposed. In his fury, Hashim did not even acknowledge Abbas. Abbas, filled with rage and flanked by his loyal followers, wheeled his horse around, and rode home at a thundering pace.

The gravity of the situation was not lost on anyone, especially the village elders. These wise men from the lands of both Abbas and Hashim had been keeping an eye on the conflict. They gathered with the wisest leader, known as the Kad Khoda, the head of the village, and conferred. The elders had lived through many feuds. They knew at this stage that the men's fiery anger would rage on, causing increasingly dramatic challenges. The elders were determined to broker a peace. Toward the end of summer, the elders approached both of my grandfathers, Abbas and Hashim, with a plan. It was an ancient solution to unite their families. The proven wisdom of this cultural tradition was presented to them. Abbas and Hashim also realized that it was time to stop bickering. They came together for a meeting in the most senior elder's stone home, which had been built by his Persian ancestors. A proposal was presented to create a union between the two families by arranging a marriage. The feuding landowners drank their tea, as thoughtfully as they could, while carefully observing one another, and listening to the advice of those that they respected.

Hashim took the next step by calling on Abbas at the impressive manor house he had proudly constructed as a wedding gift for his wife. It was important for Abbas to impress Hashim, and tea was served with formality. It was presented in glass, encased in the filigreed silver holders that he had inherited from his family's Persian beginnings. Both men were proud of their prestigious heritage and felt the need to compete with one another. As Hashim entered the grand room, his son Ali was asked to be seated. He kept his thoughts private, as he was worried about how the meeting would progress for the families and for himself. Ali was young, with high expectations for the future.

After a moment of polite conversations about crops, Hashim came to the point. He suggested that Ali would be a good husband for Masha, Abbas's youngest daughter. Hashim diplomatically suggested that Masha, having been raised by a good family, would be the perfect match for Ali. Each man obviously kept in mind the advantages of combining a part of their land and wealth.

Later Hashim came to Abbas's home for the "Gofte gu," the arrangement meeting. He presented his son Ali to Abbas, like goods being shown to a buyer. Abbas walked around him, stared Ali in the eye, received a forthright look back, and then with a slight nod, gave his approval.

Unbeknownst to both men, someone was watching their intense exchange. The small hallway that was adjacent to the grand room was a perfect vantage point. Silently, Masha had crept behind the slightly opened door. Her quizzical hazel eyes were fixed on the scene taking place. As Ali left and was striding through the courtyard, Masha was able to catch another glimpse of him, by quickly running to a small window on the balcony. She noted his tall, slender frame, and honest features. She sighed, releasing her anxiety. At fifteen years of age, Masha knew it was time for her to be married. She was very pleased that her father had chosen a pleasant-looking young man.

A few weeks later, Masha was promised to Ali and excitedly awaited her "Band Andazi." On the morning set aside to prepare for her wedding day, all of the women came together and took her to the local Turkish bath. Masha's "Band Andazi" was a very special occasion. She was measured and fitted for several silk gowns and flowered "chadors." In accordance with Persian tradition, she was smoothed and primped. The women spent a solid day on beautification, plucking body hair, and etching elegant henna designs on Masha's feet, and the palms of her hands, so that she would look especially lovely on her wedding day. Her mother took her aside during the flurry of activity and spoke to her about her new life and duties as a wife. Once the ritual of removing Masha's body hair was completed, her eyebrows were shaped, her hair was elegantly coiffed, and she was marked as a new bride for all to see. Secretly, she looked forward to the seven days of feasting and toasting that would mark her marriage and the beginning of her new life.

When the day of the wedding arrived, the ceremony and the blessings were also traditional. The ritual began with the bride sitting in her father's home, dressed in her white organza dress and pearl-encrusted lace veil. She was placed in front of a large mirror in a ceremonial room where those dear to her gathered around her.

Good fortune was a blessing, and in order to see that it followed the young bride into her marriage, the only families allowed during this ceremony were those who had seen prosperity. According to tradition, all the widows were banished. To set the tone for good fortune, the family laid out the "Sofreh-ye-Aghd," an ancient spiritual symbolic feast for the guests to enjoy. At the top of the Sofreh was a mirror. Ornate Russian crystal candelabras flickered on each side, lighting it brilliantly. Fresh roses in front of the candles exuded color and scent. In the center rested a copy of the Koran. Around the Koran, the symbolic feast offered flowers of lavender, eggs (representing wholeness and fruitfulness), bread, grain and cheese, peaches, pears, figs, and pistachios. "Kalleh Ghand" (rock sugar) and all manner of honey, sweets, cookies, and "Esfand," a burning seed, bringing scent to rid the room of evil, were added to complete the presentation of the Sofreh-ye-Aghd.

Masha sat before the lovely feast of life with her veil covering her face and waited. Hashim then brought Ali forward. The young man took his place next to Masha. The Mullah, wearing his long flowing clerical robe, began the ceremony by asking Ali, "Do I have your consent to tie the knot with Masha as your wife?" Ali's simple reply was, "Yes."

According to custom, five happily married women with good fortune, stood up for the young couple. Each witness held a corner of a white cloth above Masha and Ali, who were sitting in front of the Sofreh-ye-Aghd. The most fortunate woman milled the Kalleh Ghand on the raised covering cloth, to bring prosperity to the newlyweds.

The Mullah then turned to Masha and asked, "Do you agree?" Masha sat silently as her family watched. The Mullah read a few passages from the Koran in response to Masha's silence. Ali's mother responded by placing a lustrous pearl necklace on the bride's lap. Again the Mullah asked, "Do you agree?" Again Masha sat cloaked under her veil and did not speak. Once more, the Mullah read from the Koran, and Ali's mother reached out and placed a handful of gold coins in front of Masha, next to the exquisite pearls. For the third time, the Mullah asked the young woman, "Do you agree?" In the carefully choreographed custom, it was the bride's turn to respond. She answered softly, "Yes." They were married, and the celebration began! Music from the Tar and Tonbak burst forth with the "Mobarak Bad Song," and Persian dancing began.

Congratulations reigned on the couple, and with the previous formality completed, Ali was allowed to lift the delicate lace veil covering Masha's head and face, by looking at her through the mirror. Ali gazed for the first time into the eyes of his bride, catching his breath as her splendor was undeniable, and he smiled.

The party continued into the night. All of the guests greeted the couple and brought gifts in honor of their union. Masha's sister stood diligently behind her and collected the coins and jewelry in a large sack. At the end of the evening, the bride and groom's closest family members crowded around them. As custom demanded, Abbas took his new son-in-law's hand and placed it over his daughter's. Family and friends cheered and followed Ali and Masha to the "Hejleh," the room made ready for the consummation of the marriage. New soft Egyptian cotton bedding was spread out, and the room was enhanced by the burning of incense to help these strangers relax as they performed their duties in the final quest to unite their families. The pair disappeared behind the door, and the family waited. A short time later, the couple emerged and presented the ceremonial unwashed handkerchief bearing the evidence of the purity of the union. The marriage was complete.

Growing Up in Grandmother's House

So, Ali and Masha—my father and mother—carried into their union important values for the rich traditions of their heritage. Nine months after their wedding, on a crisp, bright March day in 1937, I was born into what became a loving middle-class family. I held the privileged position as the first of four male children, having overcome the disagreements between my two proud grandfathers and my grandmother's reservations about giving her daughter to a family who wanted to kill her husband. All were now enjoying the productivity of their combined farmlands. The water war was settled, and they shared the joy and pride in having a new male grandson to advise and pamper.

My youth was happy, but most certainly disciplined. I lived in my grandmother's home with my parents and siblings. There was a special loving bond between my grandmother and my mother. The living arrangement was comfortable, and we were content. The home was large with brick exterior interspersed with tall white pillars. It contained twenty or more rooms and featured two melodic fountains, one welcoming us at the entry and the other gracing the inner courtyard. Since the streets were narrow, and it was unacceptable for women to be seen alone outside the walls of their homes, the family built tunnels between the adjoining dwellings of my aunts and uncles.

Grandmother was the reigning matriarch and supreme governing body in the household. She judged over family disputes, and her decisions were respected by all.

My parents, who treated us well, taught us our place in the world from different perspectives. My father was a banker and when we were young men, he was most active in our upbringing. He was liberal in his thinking and influenced us by his calm and positive behavior. My mother was a loveable woman whose kindness and sensitivity have been with me all of my life. She was the responsible parent who catered to us throughout our childhood. Although my father was not particularly religious, my mother was a devout Muslim. She knew every word of the Koran and recited verses to us. It was her devotion to her faith that gave her the support she needed to guide us all through the climaxes and pitfalls of our lives.

In 1930, religion was an integral part of the culture in Iran. There were not simply Muslims and non-Muslims. The Muslim religion had many different sects. The major divide was between the Sunni and the Shiat. The differentiation between Sunni and Shiat starts with the acceptance of the successors of Mohammad. The major difference between these two variations of believers in Islam is that the Sunnis believe Abu Bakr was the first "Caliph," or successor of Mohammad, and the Shiats accept Ali as the first Caliph.,

Abu Bakr, the man the Sunni believe to be the rightful successor of Mohammad, was the father of Mohammad's youngest wife, his nine-year-old bride, Aisha. The second Caliph according to the Sunni was Umar, father of Hafsah, Mohammad's fourth wife. The Sunnis believe that Uthman and Ali were the third and fourth Caliphs after Mohammad, who were married to Mohammad's daughters, Kulthum and Fatima, respectively.

The Shiat disagree with the Sunni version of succession. The Shiat declaration of faith states, "There is no God but Allah, Mohammad is the Messenger of Allah! Alí is the friend of Allah. Ali is the successor of the Messenger of Allah, and he is the first Caliph." Ali was a cousin of Mohammad, husband of his daughter, Fatima, the second person who accepted Islam. Ali is the central figure of the origin of the Shiat and Sunni split. This occurred in the decades immediately following the death of the Prophet Mohammad in 632 A.D. Sunnis regard Ali as the fourth and last of the Caliphs. Shiats feel that Ali should have been the first Caliph and that the caliphate should pass down only to direct descendants of Mohammed via Ali and Fatima.

My mother was a Shiat. She believed in Ali as the Caliph and in the principles of Islam. These are the beliefs that she passed on to us. Her interpretation of the Koran was based on the idea that the Koran was to serve as a guide for life. She prayed for Allah's help to give her strength and to teach us wisdom and understanding with the emphasis on love and caring. She did not take the Koran literally because she felt it had been written 1,300 years prior to her life, during a civilization when times were brutal and the sword was used to settle disputes. Nevertheless, out of respect for Allah she enjoyed practicing the ceremonies of ancient times. She considered them traditions and did not have any difficulty eliminating those that she felt were foolish. As my mother raised us, these were the beliefs that she sought to instill in me and my brothers.

Part of my mother's teachings focused on prayer several times a day. As a child, my early morning prayers, before sunrise, were carried out in a routine fashion. Each day, Mother would come to my room and rub my back until I opened my sleepy eyes. She would tell me softly, "The sun is rising Manocher, hurry, you must go." Once I was awake to her satisfaction, she would leave me to prepare for prayer. I would rise from my warm bed and cross the cold courtyard to the hand-washing room. Once there, I rolled up my sleeves and splashed my face, small hands, and elbows with icy water. During this bathing I repeated in Arabic, "I salute Mohammed and all his followers." When my hands were clean, I anointed the crown of my head with water. I remember the frigid water on my young skin much more clearly than the Arabic prayers that I diligently memorized to please my mother. I repeated this ritual each day until I was a teenager.

Once the morning prayers had been completed, I quickly ran to my room. In winters, before I was old enough to go to school, I enjoyed climbing back under the snug covers and falling peacefully asleep. In the warmth of spring and summer, it was easier to rise before dawn. I used the early morning prayers as a head start on a day full of games and mischief with my favorite cousins Misha and Hooshang.

I was eager to play in the tunnels beneath our home. I still feel the coolness of those underground hallways giving refuge on hot summer days in Tehran. Breaking watermelons on the stone floors and savoring the sweetness of the fruit was a treat that will always be special in my memory. We all experienced warm acceptance when we entered each other's home, feeling a sense of caring and congeniality. We knew that at any time we had the freedom to run through the tunnels to visit our relatives, because we were family.

On the days when my cousins were sick or failed to show up for our morning games, I would often follow my mother. As part of her faith, my mother always wore her chador, a long veil that covered her when she ventured outside the home. This is not to say that she was without vanity, but her private beauty was simply reserved for her husband and family, like all of the women who practice the Muslim faith. As a child, I remember one of the rare occasions, after my morning prayers, when I followed my mother and watched curiously as she prepared herself for the day. She applied the bright red lipstick she was so fond of to her soft lips. Smoothing the color, from top to bottom, and smiling at her reflection, she would admire the way her crimson lips complimented her young face and dark brown, shortly cropped, wavy hair. I was always proud to have such a beautiful mother.

Regardless of my morning activities, come noon it was time for the second prayer of the day. When I was old enough, I was responsible for remembering this midday pause. As I did for the Morning Prayer, I obediently walked to the washroom and cleaned my face and hands from the elbows down while chanting, "I salute Mohammed and all his followers." After anointing my head once more, I went to the grand room, where I joined my cousins to pray. We all kneeled down facing Mecca, repeating our Arabic prayers. After we finished, we smoothed our clothing, combed our hair, and looked forward to the midday meal.

Luncheon was shared at my grandmother's house with all of the families. So many people were brought together by the tunnel networks that even on a normal day, this meal became a great midday feast. The food was served in the "Sofreh Khaneh," a wall-to-wall, long, carpeted room above the large kitchen, adjoining the courtyard. We all sat together on the floor, in front of a crisp, white Sofreh, or tablecloth, that had been placed over a richly designed Persian carpet. The presentation of the meal was impressive. Fruits, sweets, and rice were presented in abundance. We all knew exactly who should be sitting to our right and to our left. The sequence of seating was mother and child on one side of the Sofreh, while the opposite side was reserved for the men.

Grandfather was always the last to enter. When he arrived, we showed our respect by standing. He was always dressed in a formal way; the white collar and cuffs of his shirt were starched to perfection. A dash of color appeared on the shawl that he wore draped around his neck, accentuating his impressive full white mustache and silver hair. After he was seated, smiling broadly while nodding, he counted his entourage and asked who was missing. In our group, we numbered thirty-two people. It was almost as if we were a small commune. My grandfather was the first to be served, and then we were allowed to begin the meal.

The adults talked together, but the children were reminded to be quiet. If we needed anything, we whispered into our mother's ear. We were never allowed to bother our fathers. As I grew older, around five, I tried being charming by emulating the adults and jumping into the luncheon conversation. To my disappointment, my mother and aunts constantly told me to sit quietly, and that I was still too young to enter into the grownup discussions. Despite the enforced silence, we children listened keenly. The result was that we learned a great deal from the adults, and we were blessed with an early maturity. There were still moments, however, when we children could not refrain from our quiet giggles and mischievous eye contact.

After we lunched with our extended family, it was time to enjoy the afternoon nap. In summer, we gathered in my grandmother's basement, which provided a cool refuge from the heat. During the winter months, as soon as the household helped clear away the meal, we brought our pillows into the Sofreh Khaneh, and the thick, intricately colored Persian carpet became our sleeping mat. Before drifting off to sleep, I enjoyed tracing the elaborate arched carpet designs with my tiny fingers, while on other days; I repetitively counted the twenty-nine horizontal wooden beams in the ceiling, which mesmerized me into sleep.

The afternoon activities brought more delectable treats, as the fragrance of Persian tea awakened me from my nap. Tea-time in grandmother's house always meant, sweets and plump, ripe dates. In adulthood, I still crave dates in the afternoon because of the love that grew from Grandmother's tea service. The household help were busy from meal to meal, and the ceremony of dining was an intricate part of our life. It was both comforting and stimulating, and I remember thinking, "I cannot ever imagine being without my family."

After tea, play time with my cousins filled up the remainder of the day. We enjoyed a robust game of hide-and-seek or hopscotch in the underground tunnels. If one of us was lucky enough to have a new toy or pair of shoes, the afternoons would include a bragging session.

Regardless of the adventures the afternoon held, at five o'clock, all of the children were called back to the grand room. This time we enjoyed fresh fruits. Depending on the season, we often had oranges, apples, watermelon, and my favorite, Persian melon, with its delicate soft pink meat. When in season, pomegranates were one of our special treats. The household help separated the kernels from the white membranes that were in the craggily, red, crusty outer coating. With the skin removed, we then all loved the ceremony of eating the succulent inner fruit, dusted with salt and coriander.

At sunset, my mother or my grandmother would call me, and I would return to the washroom to ready myself for the evening prayer. The preparation was always the same. Wash the face, wash the hands from the elbow down, and anoint the head, while chanting, "I salute Mohammed and all his followers." Facing southeast toward Mecca, I bowed and recited our Arabic prayers eight times. Once the last prayer of the day was complete, it was time for dinner.

The adults ate after eight o'clock, in the evening. Until the age of five, the children were fed earlier. I eventually graduated to the grownup's table for dinner, which was never as elaborate as our beloved family luncheon. The company varied, with cousins, aunts, and uncles retreating to their own homes to have a quiet family meal. Upon occasion we all met together for an evening celebration.

Although this was our usual routine, there was some variation throughout the week. Every Wednesday was washday, and it involved a big ceremony in our crowded household. My mother, all of my aunts, and Grandmother, gathered together to string multiple clotheslines in the courtyard. The women were dressed in loose caftan-like attire, so that they could kneel more freely as they sat on the ground with washboards and buckets, scrubbing the dirty clothing. There was always laughing, chatting, and cooking, but despite the jovial atmosphere my mother and I both dreaded Wednesdays. She was always aching and uncomfortable after the long day on the floor. I was frustrated at the loss of the courtyard that we used as our playground for the games my cousins and I created.

As part of our tradition, in addition to our thrice-daily prayers, there was fasting and worship in reverence to Allah. The fasting was tedious and required that no food be consumed during the sunlight hours, as a showing of faith. This was my mother's tradition, as my father did not observe this reverence. I remember sitting with her on fasting days while he was working at the bank.

Even as small children we were expected to follow the fast for Allah. However, my mother had a soft spot for her sons, so I knew on a day of fasting, she would hold me close as she always did, and would say, "It will be OK if you just have a few morsels of sweet cake." Although she permitted us this small indulgence, she never partook herself, waiting patiently until sunset before breaking her fast.

Even though my mother was highly spiritual and religious, she did not blindly follow every Islamic dictate. One of the practices she did not support was calling the Mullah in times of duress. Ordinarily, if stress or unhappiness came to a household, it was customary for women to call the Mullah to their home to partake in a special ceremony. This observance involved large amounts of wailing and beating of the chest. Not surprisingly, it usually became highly emotional. During the frenzy of the moment, the Mullah often reached over and joined in the pounding of the young woman's chest . . . especially, if she was pretty. As a result, what should have been comforting often turned out to be ludicrous. My mother was a wholesome woman with a good heart and a true faith, who found this practice unacceptable. We all agreed that not all Mullahs were to be trusted.

In our home, it was my grandmother, and not the Mullah, who acted as the judge. When she presided over disputes, she puffed on her water pipe as she listened to my mother and father, and my aunts and uncles, helping them handle their grievances and lover's quarrels. Whenever a problem arose, the upset relative would seek Grandmother for consultation. She allowed them to sit in front of her, and one by one, tell their story without interruption. As a child she would call me, saying, "Manocher, come, sit by me, and listen." Grandmother would look to one party and listen to their story, preventing the other side from talking. After she understood one person's complaint, she switched her attention to the other party and let them speak. When both sides were finished, Grandmother usually said, "Aren't you ashamed of yourselves? You call yourselves grownups? Manocher is just a child and even he knows the truth!" She then doled out her standard advice: "You two go home, and I don't want any quarreling. Go under the blanket tonight and then

come back tomorrow and talk to me!" Grandmother strongly believed in one marriage, one God, one husband, one wife. She felt that this was our destiny and we were to make of it what we could.

The Effects of World War II

It was largely due to my father's quiet calm and strength that I maintained stability in my daily routine as a child. I don't recall realizing that anything was ever amiss. In fact, the fears and adversities of World War II did not play a large role in my childhood. Although, I am sure that the politics of the time and the shortages of food and other essential items were worrisome to my parents, they shielded my brothers and me as much as they could from outside turmoil. My father did not speak of the trouble that he encountered daily through his job at the bank. Even as inflation increased at a rapid rate, inflicting great hardships on the lower and middle classes, he maintained a quiet confidence that somehow carried my family through the devastating conflict. My own memory of the chaos of 1941 was one of adventure. My days went on much as they did throughout my childhood, based on prayer, play, family luncheons, and lessons.

Before Iran signed the Tripartite Treaty and allied itself with Britain and the Soviet Union, there were nightly raids over the city of Tehran.

During those exciting days at sunset, my mother covered the windows with blankets. I thought of it as a game, especially sleeping on the floor of the basement with my family. What a lark for a boy of four!!! Unbeknownst to me, my parents were afraid any light that could be viewed from the air might be seen by invading planes. During the evenings, we could hear the sounds of airplanes overhead and bombs that were hitting nearby targets.

Although I can remember the blankets pulled tightly over the windows, and the roaring noise of planes flying close with the sound of exploding bombs, I have no memory of fear. I have only happy memories of a close-knit family. Early in the morning, when there seemed to be fewer of these fracases, I would toddle after my father as he scampered up the stairs to the roof, in order to view a few remaining British planes that were still bombarding the city. My father took this unique opportunity to share an adventure with his young son, instead of giving in to the terror that I am sure engulfed all the elders of my family in such turbulent times. His strength and wisdom was a solid perch for my mother to lean on, but if my memory serves me correctly, she did not appreciate our male curiosity about this type of danger, and followed us to the foot of the stairs crying, "Come down, come down." My father would heed my mother's warning and bring me back to the lower levels of our home and into her waiting arms.

When it was time for him to go to work at the bank, my father dressed for the day in a starched white shirt, fastidiously pressed by my mother on laundry day, and his perfectly tied cravat. If the pressing of his trousers was not to his satisfaction, he would remove them and repress them himself. Making his way out of the compound in a beige cashmere coat and chapeau, he pulled on his beige driving gloves and climbed into his matching Hudson. His dapper appearance made him the consummate banking professional.

After waving goodbye, my mother and I moved about our normal day, only to repeat the blanket hanging in the evening. There were, of course, food shortages to adjust to and rubble to step over as we ventured outside, but the ability of the human to adjust is quite amazing, no matter how difficult the situation. My father was always there to help us along and had the ability to maintain a calm serene attitude by taking adversity in stride. This was his special strength, and one that I have tried to emulate, but not always successfully.

Growing up, I seldom saw my father, and my memories of him are few and far between. Other than the plane adventures we shared, for a few short days in 1941, he and I had one other memorable occasion.

One evening after dinner, I heard my parents arguing. My mother was unhappy with my father, but I was too young to know why. A short time later, my mother came to me and dressed me in a clean white shirt and pants; she placed my little lamb jacket on my back, buttoning it up the front, and smoothing the shoulders. She told me that I was going to go for an outing with my father. My mother said, "I want you to look around and watch the people that you meet. When you come home, I want you to tell me exactly who you saw."

When I was ready, my mother took me to my father. He reached down and put my hand in his, lifting me into the shiny beige Hudson. We drove to the elegant Lalezar area of Tehran. My father parked the car in front of an older, brick and glass, two-story building. Lights from the window on the second floor were shining out into the fashionable, bustling street below.

My father moved me from the front of the car into the back seat and pulled a bag of candy out of his beige coat packet. He handed me the sweets, kissed the top of my head, and pointing to the lights above said, "I have a meeting up there with a few friends. They are all waiting for me. You stay here, and I will be back soon." He named the men he was meeting, and I recognized them as visitors who often came to our home. As he disappeared into the building, and the lights went out on the second floor, I began to eat the candy and wondered why I had to wait in the car.

People passed by the car, and stared into the window, trying to see the little boy in the cute lamb coat. I was very frightened.

I had no idea how long my father was gone, but at some point I fell asleep in the back of the car. The next morning, my mother quizzed me about the meeting. I repeated to her the lines my father told me, before he left me to my candy. Years later, as I recalled that feeling of fear, it occurred to me that the "business meeting" was for a kind of business with a woman. Shortly after my father's liaison in the fashion district of Tehran, the planes stopped flying overhead and my daily activities returned to normal.

The End of the British Attacks

In January 1942, Iran signed the Tripartite Treaty, bringing alliance with Britain and the Soviet Union, and ending our early morning rooftop encounters. Under the treaty, Iran agreed to extend nonmilitary assistance to the war effort and promised its neutrality. The two Allied powers, in turn, agreed to respect Iran's independence and territorial integrity, and to withdraw their troops from Iran within six months of the end of hostilities.

Sadly, the war raged on. In September 1943, Iran completely gave up its neutrality and declared war on Germany. This declaration of war was a requirement for membership in the United Nations. This must have been a difficult decision for the young Shah, who came to power based on his father's convictions that Iran should remain neutral; he, too, was facing the world conflicts head on and creating his place on the new world map.

In November of 1943, a conference was held in Iran for the Allied powers. The conference was known as the Tehran Conference and was attended by President Franklin D. Roosevelt, Prime Minister Winston Churchill, and Prime Minister Josef Stalin. Together with the Shah, these great men reaffirmed a commitment to Iran's independence and territorial integrity, and a willingness to extend economic assistance to Iran. This was the first of many joint ventures between Iran and a long list of American presidents. It served as the foundation of the strong friendship that flourished between the two countries until its ultimate demise under the Carter administration in 1979.

Education in Iran

Going back to Iran's earlier dreams to become a well respected country, in 1933, orders were issued by the Reza Shah to find a suitable location for Iran's first state-sponsored university. In the north of Tehran, a beautiful garden filled with orchids was chosen for the compound. The master plan was prepared by French and Swiss architects under the supervision of Mohsen Foroughi, one of Iran's own designers. One year later in 1934, the main building of the university was completed and was officially inaugurated by the proud Reza Shah. The first woman student was admitted in 1937. All of this was part of the Reza Shah's vision before he abdicated his throne during World War II and passed the monarchy on to his son.

During the Cold War between the United States and Russia, that marked the early years of the young Shah's reign, Iran played a key role in America's war against communism, because of its close proximity to the USSR. In 1949, President Harry S. Truman introduced the "Point Four Program," giving technical assistance to underdeveloped countries including Iran. The United States came to Iran to implement this program, by refurbishing cultural buildings in Tehran.

The Shah accepted the guidance with gratitude. This was part of the continuous friendship between the two countries. At this point, Iran already had one university and was intent on building several more. The assistance America provided allowed Iran to create libraries and other important cultural institutions that helped to educate the Iranian youth in preparedness for the highly competitive university system.

While the university was establishing itself and President Truman was bonding with the Shah, I was still living in my grandmother's home on the outskirts of Tehran. Despite my early years spent dining, playing with my cousins, and hiding in the tunnels below the house, once I was old enough to attend school, I enjoyed very little childhood frivolity.

Even as a boy, I knew that I lived in a male-dominated environment, and that I was expected to pattern myself after the men of my family, so that I could take my place amongst their ranks when I came of age. There was never a question about what my future held. For as long as I can remember, I understood that I was expected to attend the great University of Tehran.

In order to prepare for my passage, I attended the local boy's schools and set my goal to be a high achiever. Frequently, I feared my teacher's repercussions—if homework was not completed properly, the punishment was to stand in front of the classroom, wearing a foolish cone-shaped hat, while fellow classmates booed. I felt that the shame brought on by the dunce cap was so humiliating that I never wanted to experience it personally. So, I always came to school prepared.

Despite the many academic pressures, I still had a few moments of pleasurable relaxation. When I was around fifteen years of age, I spent many tranquil afternoons in a beautiful American library in the heart of Tehran. The building was furnished by the United States under the "Point Four Program." Many young people my age frequented the library to glean information about the West. We all enjoyed gazing at the handsome pictures in America's *Life* magazine. As I thumbed through the colorful pages, I was in awe. The Iranian periodicals were still in black and white. Even though I spoke only a few words of English, I lingered over the photos and hoped that if I looked up, I might catch a glimpse of one of the tall blonde American girls that graced the pages.

Next door to the library was a wonderful shop that had installed several of the first coin-operated self-serve ice cream machines. This delectable concoction came in several flavors and was called "Alaska." This sweet treat was the perfect conclusion to my languid library experience. Whenever I had the opportunity to visit my two favorite places, I walked home relaxed and contented.

As my days in high school drew to a close, I no longer dreamed of my perfect afternoons with *Life* magazine at the American library. My focus shifted to making my way into manhood by preparing to attend the university. At that time, Iran was still considered a backward country, and although modernization had started, when it came time to realize my family's vision for me to attend college, it was still almost impossible to obtain a higher education and it took many years of hard work to pass the difficult entrance exams. However, I felt my own academic achievements had prepared me for the nation's first institution of higher learning. There were few seats available in the other state universities that had been erected by the time it was my turn to sit for the entrance exams.

My upbringing brought with it not only the mandate to attend the university, but also the long-term requirement that I establish myself in one, of only a few, accepted professions. I was to become a doctor, engineer, or lawyer. These were the only recognized careers.

In my last year of high school, every university announced the time and place for their entrance exam. The students who wanted to participate in a particular curriculum would line up for hours and sometimes days. The SAT test was not yet available to filter out those who were not qualified. Our only option was to take the individual institutions exam.

I wanted to attend the University of Tehran to study medicine. This entrance exam was the toughest in the country, and the chances of being accepted were, in some cases one in 5,000. Tehran University, my first choice, was the only institution that had a respectable medical curriculum, as well as a prestigious history.

The Entrance Exam for the Navy

During the last few months of high school, my classmates and I discussed and analyzed various ways to approach passing the entry exams. Some felt that cheating might be an option, but I was horrified by that idea. One afternoon a fellow student told me that he had heard that the Imperial Iranian Navy wanted to select eighteen students to participate in Naval Science training programs in England and Italy. An entrance exam was required, and we both jumped at the opportunity to test our abilities and gain some experience.

Together my friend and I arrived at the testing location and were met with a line a few blocks long. We took our place at the end, and we waited, undaunted, with our assortment of pens and pencils. I was so eager to begin that it was difficult for me to wait my turn as the prospective students filed into the building.

Once we were inside, we were ushered into a large amphitheater. We were each given a number that appeared on every page of the exam. I will always remember my number, 1418. Not only was 1418 my testing identity, but it was also the number that led to a great change in the course of my life. When the examination papers finally arrived, I was ready. I felt very relaxed about answering the questions. As I read through the pages, I was relieved to find that I understood the material at first glance.

Later, on my way back home, I could not help but question if everyone felt as comfortable as I did about their performance. I speculated as to how my scores would compare with all of the other participants. I wondered if I would qualify for one of the top eighteen spots. Several weeks passed and I remained busy preparing for my high school final exams, as well as those I would be taking for entrance into the university.

On one weekend toward the end of the school year, my family and I were having a quiet afternoon at home, in Grandmother's grand room, when there was a knock at the door. My mother responded to the caller. When she returned, she was visibly concerned. "Manocher," she called my name, "there are two military police at the door, asking for you. I think they might want to take you for obligatory military service!" The look of concern on my mother's face was heart-wrenching and she continued, "If they are here to take you, I am afraid you may never come back." Despite her fear, this was a special moment for me, because I was able to feel and enjoy her motherly love.

As I prepared to meet my fate, I was not so much afraid as embarrassed. Since my family had no plans for the evening, I was at home in my housecoat. Without time to change, I was forced to go to greet the military police in my sleeping attire, and I was very uncomfortable.

Undaunted by my apparel, the military police asked my name. "Manocher," I replied. The officer handed me a sealed letter in response, and told me to report to Naval Headquarters as soon as possible. We exchanged formalities and then I returned to the grand room, where I found my mother shaking.

"The letter, the letter!" she shouted. "What does it say?" I opened the envelope and the first word I saw was "Congratulations!" It was as if I was suddenly in the middle of a cold shower. I started to jump up and down, shouting, "I passed the naval entrance exam!" I was in a state of euphoria, my happiness knew no bounds. My whole family was excited. This was a time for celebration. I kept saying to myself with heartwarming pride, "I am going to be in the Imperial Navy."

What none of us knew at that time was that this was going to be the beginning of a very long journey. A journey that would place me in the center of my country's great modernization movement, then bring me down to my knees at its demise. A journey that allowed me to enjoy privileges that I never dared to dream of, then took me to the depths of despair with the loss of everything but my life. A journey that has challenged me to find happiness in another land. A land that has been good to me, but is far from the country that I still hold dear to my heart.

Chapter 2

Courtesy of sarafazan.net, mighty Imperial Navy Trireme battleship (500 BC)

Joining the Imperial Navy

A Battle Royal

While I was seeking to improve myself by advancing my education and joining the Imperial Navy, changes were afoot in Iran. The oil that our country produced was beginning to play an integral role in the advancement of Iran. However, the Iranian government was locked into a 100-year oil lease with the British. Consequently, in order to bring about the necessary changes, the government had to regain control of the oil production plants.

During World War II, the export of oil from Iran significantly declined. The Reza Shah publicly denounced the profiteering affecting oil sales. Unfortunately, these protests fell on deaf ears. The monarchy tried to compensate for the loss of revenue caused by the war by demanding that Britain pay the difference in revenue, totaling 4 million pounds. The Shah threatened the British and told them that the Iranian government would take action to cancel the oil lease agreement and revise the oil concession contract unless Britain paid the difference in full. In a crucial moment for the British military, as German troops shut down access to the British mainland, England agreed to the Reza Shah's terms.

Following World War II, at the end of the British oil lease in 1951, the Iranian Parliament voted to nationalize the oil industry. The National Iranian Oil Company (NIOC), the first national oil company in the Middle East, was established to replace the old British company. However, this transition did not go smoothly. During the course of the previous lease term, the British had been making more money taxing the Iranian oil industry than Iran was making in royalties. Thus, the British were upset with the lease termination because it meant they could no longer tax the oil.

In an effort to maintain control and taxation power over Iranian oil, the British filed a lawsuit against Iran in the United Nations Security Council and the Hague International Court. Oil production came to a virtual standstill. The British technicians, who were part of the Anglo-Iranian Oil Company that controlled the oil production under the lease terms, fled the country. The British applied pressure on Iran by freezing all of their sterling assets and imposing a worldwide embargo, banning exports to Iran and any purchase of Iranian oil. The newly elected Prime Minister of Iran, Mossadegh, a Nationalist, with most of the bourgeois' support, sought to enforce the Oil Nationalization Bill and terminate British ownership and influence on the oil industry.

The Iranian Prime Minister traveled both to the United Nations in New York, and to the Hague in Holland, to face the British lawsuits. This battle royal over the billions of dollars of profit involved in Iranian oil ended with a groundbreaking victory for the Iranian people. The Hague Court voted in favor of Iran. The British Anglo-Iranian Oil Company was dissolved, and the 1933 oil agreement between the Iranian government and Great Britain was cancelled.

After his strong fight for Iran and the country's right to manage and profit from its own natural resources, Mossadegh was viewed by the bourgeois as an anti-imperialist hero. Unfortunately, Mossadegh was very eccentric. He conducted business meetings in bed in his pajamas or wearing military battle uniforms, and he continuously complained about his health. He was becoming enamored with his newly found power over the country and began to express thinly veiled desires to turn Iran into a dictatorship under his control.

When Mossadegh demanded that the control of the Imperial military be taken from the Shah and turned over to him, the Shah stood firm and refused to accept his demands. The Shah's refusal to turn the power of the military over to Mossadegh led to political chaos at the hands of the bourgeois, who supported the move.

The Shah understood that he lost the support of the bourgeois with the nationalization of the oil industry. The people expected to have plentiful jobs when the ground-breaking decision in the Hague gave control of the country's markets back to them. Unfortunately, Britain was bitter about losing control over the lucrative taxes levied on Iranian oil. As a result, Britain would place inconsistent orders for oil, often changing production requirements by large margins making it impossible to predict how many men could be safely employed.

This little game created a trend of mass hiring followed by mass layoffs in the oil industry, resulting in a sense of insecurity for the working class, and a strong sentiment of disappointment in the monarchy. Consequently, Mossadegh's popularity grew as he promised the people the consistency they needed to insure the security of their families.

With increased fame, Mossadegh's hold on the country rose to great heights, and his desire to take over was no longer shrouded. After the dispute over the military, the Shah forced Mossadegh's resignation, but the people from the Nationalist Party were furious. Riots erupted in the streets, and the Shah was forced to rehire him.

The United States and British governments felt Mossadegh's goal was to achieve a communist takeover of Iran. Both nations felt the time had come to replace Mossadegh with someone more trustworthy, so they intervened on the Shah's behalf.

In June 1953, the Eisenhower administration approved a British proposal for a joint Anglo-American operation to overthrow Mossadegh. The plot was code-named Operation Ajax. CIA agents secretly entered Iran to coordinate plans with the Shah and the Iranian military, led by General Fazlollah Zahedi. As part of the plan, on August 13, 1953, the Shah appointed his trusted general, General Zahedi, to be the new Prime Minister. However, Mossadegh refused to leave his post and used his power and influence to detain the Shah's loyal emissary. Since the appointment was unsuccessful, phase two of Operation Ajax, a military coup, was implemented.

Despite the military's best efforts, the plan did not go smoothly; for four days there were riots in the streets, the Shah temporarily fled the country, and the general was forced into hiding. On the fourth day, August 19, 1953, the Iranian military gained control of the streets and the general was finally able to take office. The Shah returned and continued his monarchy for many years to come. However, this coup served as the foundation of an attitude of hate towards the meddling Americans and British, in the minds of the Iranian bourgeois. Consequently, Mossadegh became a Nationalist hero.

Throughout the Cold War, the Shah established himself as an indispensable ally to the West. It was during this time that he hosted many American presidents, and made numerous trips abroad. The Shah learned from these experiences and continued to seek democratic reform for his country and educational programs, including reaching out for literacy of all people and seeking social equality for women.

Going to Italy

While political coups and battles over oil concerned the people of my homeland, I was an eager young man starting my naval career, as part of a quest for betterment and education. I was excited about reporting to Naval Headquarters as ordered by the letter the military police delivered to my home. My first introduction to their main building was very impressive, everything was elegantly appointed.

It was springtime and the officers were already dressed in their fresh white summer uniforms. As I looked around the spacious room, my heart swelled with pride. I could close my eyes and see myself walking briskly through the halls of this official-looking building, with my shoulders spread back and my head held high. As I entered the main foyer, I noticed a tall, well-groomed officer sitting behind a large and rather impressive desk. The Shah's photograph was hanging centered on the wall behind him. I knew he saw me but he did not call for me to immediately approach, so I sat down on a nearby bench to wait. It did not take long, because I had called ahead and I knew that the officer was expecting me. When he looked up from the official task he was occupied with, he gestured for me to come over. As I approached the desk, he graciously pulled up a chair and invited me to sit next to him.

"Manocher," he said, with a certain formality in his voice, "your score on the Naval exam was the eighth-highest score. We are selecting only eighteen students for officer training. The first six will be sent to the Naval Academy in Italy, and number seven to eighteen will be going to England for officer's training. We would like you to go with the latter group."

I was thrilled to have received such positive results from my first entrance exam. For an instant, a thought flashed through my mind about life in the Navy, and I was concerned. I wondered what the

Navy's expectations were for me. I did not even know how to swim. I quickly recovered with resolve to block out the little worries. Speculating about small things could wait. The thrill of going to England was overwhelming. I proudly thanked the officer and hurried off to share this stroke of good fortune with my parents.

When I arrived home, my family members were finishing the noon meal in Grandmother's great room. I joined them and followed the conversation, eagerly awaiting a suitable lull in the banter to tell them of my exciting news. Finally, the opportunity presented itself as the family began to enjoy their sweets and tea. I stood up as pastry was being served, and in the most regal stance I could muster, thinking of how I would be presenting myself when I was an officer; I announced the joyous news concerning my first assignment in England. Contrary to my expectations, my mother, once again, began to cry.

"Manocher, how will you manage in a country so far from home? There will be no one to take care of you." As my mother sobbed, my aunts, uncles, nieces, and nephews stood and encircled me. They had concerned looks in their eyes as they voiced their various opinions. My posture began to fall. I was very disappointed. The congratulations I had looked forward to were not forthcoming. Once my extended family began to recover from my shocking news, they sat quietly, as we began the formality of tea time.

I was silent for the remainder of the afternoon. When I learned of my accomplishments in passing the Navy's examination, I was full of pride and eager to tell my parents. I returned home to tears and fear instead of a pat on the back and congratulations. In my struggle to understand their unsupportive response, I came to the realization that my family had not ever travelled abroad. I began to understand that they were upset because they were afraid for me. The unknown lands beyond Grandmother's house and Tehran were probably very frightening to them.

I hoped for the best, a change in attitude, and ignored their lack of support. Instead I chose to focus my attention on my constant companion, the English text called *Essential English*. Although I felt quite alone without my family's well wishes, I was determined to be prepared for my education in England.

In spite of my situation, the excitement about going abroad remained with me. During this lonely time, I often retreated to a special room in my home that had been fitted with a wide variety of books of my choosing. At one time, this small space had been a storage room used for extra blankets and bedding for guests that were always welcomed to stay longer, even though their visits were usually unannounced. Grandmother knew my passion for exploring the unknown through reading. As a gift when I was growing up, Grandmother had the extra supplies removed from the tiny space and told me that it would be my special room. The unread pages that were waiting to be turned were the lure that often brought me to my little sanctuary in the corner of the house.

The only furniture in the room was a discarded garden chaise lounge. Bookcases on one side held books I had completed. The other side held reading material that I was anxious to open. Now as I flipped through my periodicals, I turned down the corners of any pages having reference to England. Whenever I had a free moment, I would retreat to my library and read each sentence on the marked pages. I loved to imagine walking down the streets on foreign soil. Anticipation was for me, the better part of life and, in that moment, was the emotion I used to travel beyond my family and the walls of Grandmother's house into the unknown. If I was not reading about England, I still found time to lay back, open my eyes, and read the profound poetry of Omar Khayyam or the thought-provoking essays written by Nicolas Copernicus regarding astronomy and the creation of the universe.

While my family was obviously struggling with thoughts of my leaving, I was not without my own concerns about saying farewell to the only environment I had ever known. I had always taken the beauty of Tehran for granted. Now, when I gazed up at the majestic Alborz Mountains, I thought of the summertime family outings when my family took picnics to the lush valleys between the jagged peaks, running through tall grasses, playing hide-and-seek with my cousins or stickball on winding country roads. Then, I would remember the bonfires at night with lamb roasting and pungent aromas of rosemary and saffron filling the air, cuddling in our blankets, leaning on each other's shoulders, happy and relaxed, after an exhausting day of play. Yes,

I thought. These images and past happenings will always be comforting to envision and bring to life again, in my memory, whenever I would so desire.

My family, my city of birth, all that I held dear to me could never be taken away. This rich background was the mold that formed my personality. It was my feeling of security that developed from this sheltered, but happy childhood and gave me the confidence to go forward into the next phase of my life.

Suddenly, after I spent a week preparing for my studies in England, I was called to the door of Grandmother's home and greeted by two naval MPs. I was in my reading room when I heard their loud knock. I hurried down the stairs, once again embarrassed by their arrival. This time I was nicely dressed. However, it was wash day and in order to reach the door the two men were forced to walk under my infamous "house suit" and assorted children's clothes, socks, and underwear hanging on one of the clotheslines that crisscrossed the courtyard.

The women of the household were shocked to see two impressively uniformed military men standing in the center of various stages of laundry. Heads not covered, they quickly fled into other doors and behind pillars. Being social was most certainly not one of their major concerns. I quickly opened the door. Undaunted and unsmiling, the MPs presented me with another sealed envelope and told me to return to Naval Headquarters the following day, for further instructions.

Again, I spent an almost sleepless night, looking forward to the meeting with curiosity and a feeling of importance. I arose early, grabbed a sweet cake off the side table, and walked hurriedly to catch the bus to the military headquarters to find out what the Imperial Navy had in store for me.

When I arrived, the same tall, and now familiar-looking, officer was sitting at his desk. He recognized me immediately and, smiling, called me over and said, "Manocher, you are now number six on our list. Two young men have dropped out, one for medical and one for political reasons. If all goes well with your physical examination, you will be going to the Naval Academy in Italy for four years."

I thanked the officer profusely. He chuckled over my enthusiastic sign of gratitude. I was even more elated than I had been about England. I was familiar with the Italian landscape of rolling hills, as well as the tiled roofs and soft stucco patina of ancient buildings. My favorite movies were made in Italy. When they were showing in theaters in Tehran, I did not miss an opportunity to see them. I also knew of the revered status of the Italian Naval Academy.

Later, I further reviewed its history at the American library in Tehran. I found an article appearing in 1893 in *The New York Times* singing the praises of the Academy and the officers who had earned the reputation of being the best posted men in the world, both in theory and the science of all naval warfare.

At the beginning of the Second World War, the British and Allied forces bombed and sank the entire Iranian Naval fleet. When the war ended, Great Britain, the United States, and Italy decided to compensate Iran for the naval losses in the Persian Gulf. The British supplied Iran with a few ships and the promise to train future Iranian Naval officers. Italy followed suit and opened its doors to their Naval Academy in Livorno.

As I made my way home, I started to romanticize about my future. I envisioned myself standing on the coast of the Mediterranean, in my own perfectly pressed white uniform, with the sea breeze blowing around me, boarding a stately ship with Italian flags flying. Although I did not speak a word of Italian, I knew that I would fit right in. I kept saying to myself, "How can I be so lucky? I will soon be living in romantic Italy." To make matters even better, I had always been fascinated with Gina Lollobrigida and Sophia Loren. Who knows, I thought, perhaps someday I might catch a glimpse of them walking by.

The change in my assignment from England to Italy did not help bolster the support of my family. My mother continued to cry when she thought about my leaving. She clung to the hope that I would still sit for the university entrance exams and somehow be persuaded to leave behind my newfound military aspirations. Even though I knew it was difficult for her, I decided to focus only on what I had already achieved.

The Imperial Navy was a profession that would allow me to receive my higher education in Europe. At that time, this was a highly coveted experience. It was extremely prestigious to study engineering or medicine abroad. A degree earned in Europe would allow me to start off in a higher category for a job search later in life. My mother's grief at the thought of my living on a different continent made it difficult to support my decision. However, rather unexpectedly, once I passed the medical exams my family, even my mother, became resigned to my imminent departure and wished me well.

I began to appreciate my last moments at home with the thirty-two members of my family. Some of my cousins were preparing for the entrance exams for the university in Iran, although we shared moments about our future, I did not have any regrets about my decision.

By the time I received my passport; two additional recruits had dropped out of the Navy, pushing my name to number four on their acceptance list.

When the day for my departure arrived, a loving group of aunts, uncles, and cousins accompanied me to the Tehran's Mehrabad Airport. My favorite, Aunt Maheen, gave me a loving farewell pat on the arm and promised to send me some of the best Iranian pistachios. It had been my daily after-school quest to hurry through the tunnel to her home to say "Hello" and pluck a handful of Persian pistachios, from a gold-edged china plate that always seemed to remain full. Aunt Maheen was a young widow and childless. The sweets that she enticed my cousins and me with, gave us all moments of delicious joy. Her comforting and sympathetic ear was always there to hear about our daily happenings. We also gave her life a special meaning. She helped me get through my recent decision making about the Navy, and I knew that she would miss me as much as I would miss her.

My younger cousin Misha came forward and gave my hand a squeeze. She was growing taller and prettier. My mind flashed back to a day many years before, when I gave her a hug while playing hide-and-seek in the underground tunnels we used as a playground. We were fourteen, and I knew she was my cousin, but I could not resist just a quick squeeze, even though it was against Islamic law. I had committed a sin; it was "Haram." She had haughtily told me that she was already promised to someone else. I wondered now, who her true love was? I thought, "She will probably be gone when I return from Italy," and for a moment I was sad.

Suddenly the gravity of my situation hit me and I felt frightened. Although I put on a brave face, I had a lump in my throat, and inside my head I was saying in a shaky voice, "What am I going to do without my parents?" This sense of bewilderment, along with the thought of leaving my rambunctious little, Ira, brought tears to my eyes. I held his hand tightly and knew that I loved him with all my heart.

My sweet mother was crying, as usual, but my father seemed composed until it was time to get on the plane. He was very quiet, and I noticed that he also had tears in his eyes. I moved close to him. I felt the distance he kept from me during my childhood fall away. I was a man now, a source of pride for my father, no longer a child for my mother to worry about. He hugged me, and I understood the love between us. As we drew apart, he handed me an envelope that he told me to open only after I was in the air. I put it in my jacket pocket and kissed everyone goodbye.

I thought about my father's composure and knew that although I felt shaky I must emulate the strength that he always seemed to have. Fortunately, I was wearing my brand-new tie and suit. Somehow the formality of my clothing became the armor that held me together as I boarded the plane.

Once inside, I looked around at the faces of my new classmates. I was reassured to see their sad looks also, indicating to me that it was an equally emotional time for them. The plane was not full. There were only a few passengers. We all scattered to find a window seat facing the airport building. We sat silently thinking of our farewells, yet nervous and excited to face the challenges of our future.

I tried to locate my family through the window. I was already missing them even though they were only a few feet away. The propellers started to turn rapidly. Although I sat motionless, I wanted to run out again and hug everyone one more time. It was too late. There was no turning back. The plane lifted into the air, and we were on our way.

As I sat in my seat, I let the hum of the engines calm me. I remembered the envelope my father had given me. I reached in my pocket and thoughtfully opened the flap. Inside was a small black-and-white photograph of my mother, myself, and my brother Ira. Attached was a note saying, "Manocher, I have nothing more worthy to give you. This is my dearest possession. I want you to cherish this gift and remember that I love you and always want the very best for you." I have always kept this photograph in a pocket next to my heart. It has travelled all over the world with me for over a half a century. After viewing my father's note, I felt calmed and finally content. I knew that I now had my family's blessings.

Arriving in Rome

The short distance from Tehran to Rome with the *Linee Aeree Italiani* took almost fifteen hours including stops in Istanbul for lunch and Athens for afternoon snacks. The plane was a four-propeller aircraft, and although we were treated very well, it still felt like a long journey.

When we descended the metal steps in Istanbul Ataturk Airport and walked toward the main building, the style of the appointments and furnishings were of a design that I had not seen before. We were too far away to view the city but there were distinct differences. There were several pictures of Ataturk on the walls, but no visible pictures or statues of the Shah. The writings were all in Turkish, and I had no idea how to read them. Fortunately, we were escorted directly to a dining hall. Even though we were only in the airport dining facility, the meal was presented with a certain formality. I thought perhaps there were instructions to serve us with ceremony. This meal marked the beginning of the reverence we continued to receive as members of Iran's Imperial Navy. Dessert at the airport was the memorable part of the meal. A

large fuzzy peach was served whole in a bowl of cold water. Later, at the Academy, I learned how to gracefully carve a piece of fruit, but at that moment, carving the peach in the water was difficult.

We left Istanbul for Athens. While in the air, approaching the landing site, we caught a brief glimpse of the Greek ruins. I had an immediate desire to walk among the elegant columns of stone architecture. I vowed to return someday and view the magnificent remains in close proximity and feel the power of the Greek empire. Once again, after we touched the ground, we were escorted to a dining room, where afternoon tea was served at the airport facility.

It was around seven p.m. and approaching dusk when we arrived at the Rome Fiumicino Airport. Only the soft-muted outline of the country and buildings could be distinguished from the sky. A young, newly graduated, Iranian officer was there to meet us. We were ushered into a military mini-bus and began our journey to the Academy. We still did not know each other's names, but after the emotional flight away from our families, we had developed a silent bond, a connection that formed in the knowledge that together, we would be sharing the same experiences.

After a short trip, the minibus delivered us to the train station. Our destination was Livorno. By now darkness had come and all we could see were a few glimmering lights as we chugged through small villages. There were several screeching, metal-to-metal stops along the way. All of us were fighting fatigue, but our curiosity kept us glued to the windows. We were out of our world—out of our realm—we were on an adventure to the unknown!

It was about three thirty in the morning when we arrived. We were met by an Italian petty officer, who spoke very rapidly. We herded together and followed him to another minibus. It was a twenty-minute drive to the Naval Academy from the train station. I was disappointed that the streets were dark and vacant. I wanted to see where I would be living for the next four years. Much to my disappointment, the sightseeing had to wait until later.

The entrance lights were on when our bus rolled through the Academy's ornate green wrought iron gates. The sentry waved us on, and I was impressed with what I saw. We finally stopped in front of an imposing three-story building. Two large anchors adorned either side of the entrance. I said to myself, "This is going to be my home for the next four years."

Our escort cordially ushered us out of the bus and into the building. I was immediately impressed with the graciousness of all the officers we had encountered. On the second floor there was a large dormitory that accommodated about thirty beds. There was a large oak cupboard between each bed with a name tag and a number. My number was 506. It remained with me for the four years I attended the Academy. As we looked around our new home, the Italian petty officer bowed slightly and politely, saying, "Goodnight." In our exhausted state there was nothing more that needed to be said. Quietly, we all prepared to end what had been a long and emotionally exhausting day. The six of us had still not conversed except for mealtime banter. We were drained after having so much to absorb. Travel had not ever been available for any of us. We were digesting everything we saw, a little at a time.

Prior to retiring, we found a spacious bathing facility at the end of our sleeping quarters. There were twelve showerheads and the water spilled out into an impressive tiled room. Each source of water was spaced about four feet apart, and every man was expected to shower, in the open, alongside the other. In the Iranian culture, it was embarrassing to look at someone without clothing. On this, our first trip away from home, we were all shy and had never seen each other nude. While we were brushing our teeth, out of embarrassment we were laughing and trying to decide how we would bathe in the morning, wondering aloud if we could take showers one at a time. The modesty issue was just another unknown to add to all the others that I tossed and turned with on that first night.

The First Days in Livorno

At 7:00 a.m., the sound of a trumpet awakened us. Yesterday's petty officer was standing at the very end of the dorm, and with great formality, gave us instructions for starting the day. We could not understand his rapid Italian, but we unanimously decided that he wanted us to leave our beds, shave, and shower. The time to tackle the first unknown was upon us. We had to shower...in front of each other! In an effort to maintain at least some form of modesty, the six of us spaced ourselves as far apart as possible. We kept our eyes trained on the tiled walls in front of us, and with some awkwardness, we managed to complete the task.

As I bathed that first morning, I washed myself quickly and efficiently. I remember thinking that this morning routine was a far cry from the predawn hours of my childhood, spent preparing for the prayers that now fell by the wayside, along with my youth. Although I no longer stopped my daily activities to face Mecca in prayer, the ways of Muslim life and its traditions that so heartily intermingled with the Persian culture were still very much a part of me. This immodest group procedure that so many of our fellow cadets, from other parts of the world, took for granted, was an enormous undertaking for me and my Muslim colleagues. It was a step that required us to turn our backs on our religion. We became acquainted very quickly, because we were all constantly adjusting to new experiences. More often than not, our confusion turned to laughter. Those first months at the Academy made for happy memories we have shared for many years.

We were six conservative and unworldly young men that were now placed in a happy "love of life" environment. The Academy was formal, but the Italians were a gracious, high-spirited society, and all of us eventually benefited by this opportunity to absorb their outgoing life style of love and laughter.

After dressing, we were escorted to the dining room. The tables were beautifully set with white linen tablecloths, napkins, and china. We sat down and enjoyed our first Italian breakfast including café latte, the beginning of an indulgence I have continued to enjoy throughout my life.

At breakfast, we finally took the time, after our emotional journey, to learn each other's names. My Persian classmates introduced themselves as Bahman, Mahmood, Syrus, Haji, and Qumars. It was a pleasure to exchange conversation and expectations with men of similar backgrounds.

Bahman had a jovial sense of humor and loved to show off, especially when he later took dancing lessons. I found his warmth delightful, and he became my closest friend.

Mahmood was the jokester of the group. His sharp wit brought him closer to Haji, who did not fret about taking things too seriously.

Syrus was the most introverted of the group; his solemn quiet attitude made it more difficult to get to know him. Syrus's love of the violin was his passion. Although he spent long hours screeching out ear-piercing notes that never seemed to show signs of improvement, the music made him happy and was a pleasant release for him after long hours of study.

We were all young and shy, but Qumars stood out as the most timid of the group. He only stayed in the Academy for a short time before he exchanged his post in the physically demanding Navy for a less regimented life as a student at a local Italian university.

After breakfast, with our introductions disposed of, our assigned petty officer accompanied us back to the dormitory and tried to give us further directions. We had difficulties understanding anything he had to say, so he resorted to international language. Off and on came his jacket, then tie and shoes. He smiled and waited a moment. We did not have any inkling about what he was trying to portray.

Qumars finally responded, "I think I might know what he is telling us. I speak a little French and it is similar to Italian. He is directing us to take another shower." We nodded to the petty officer. He seemed relieved and left with a smile.

Puzzled, we looked at each other, shrugged, and proceeded to take the second shower of the morning. I asked Bahman, "Do you suppose this is a way to help us conquer our modesty?" "I don't know," Bahman said thoughtfully. "It seems very strange."

After dressing again in fresh clothing, we sat down on our beds and waited and waited. It was almost 11:00 a.m. when an officer came by and questioned us. "Do any of you speak English?" He asked. "A little," we responded. "Did you go to the tailor for your uniform fitting?"

46

Embarrassed, we looked at each other and realized how difficult things were going to be until we could speak the language.

The second morning at the Academy, we were again awakened by the penetrating but pleasant sound of the trumpet. After enjoying our last drop of café latte, the work began.

We were ushered into our new classroom, where we were assigned to a brilliant professor who spoke seven languages, but not a word of Farsi (the main official language of Iran). Professor Dini was a young, soft-spoken Italian man. In the beginning, he invited all of his non-Italian cadets to his home for a welcoming party. Although my fellow Iranians and I wanted desperately to thank him for his hospitality and generosity, we were reduced to hand gestures as a form of communication. It was a strange feeling to look around the room and see the other groups of foreign students huddled together isolated by our language barriers. Despite the communication issues, the party was appreciated, and we all enjoyed the friendly atmosphere.

Professor Dini served delicious food that his wife brought to the table. The words for each item on the menu were spoken in each of the seven languages in Professor Dini's repertoire. After he went through the languages he knew, Professor Dini looked to us and asked for the word in Iranian. We caught on quickly and began naming the objects in Farsi. He would respond to our Farsi with Italian. Alas! A word was learned and so the game continued.

After the party at Professor Dini's, we returned to our dorm at the Academy. As I prepared for bed, I went over the evening in my mind. I realized that in order to obtain the educational credentials I longed for; I would have to master Italian. I was afraid that I would not learn the language and that I would be forced to return home in disgrace. These thoughts of home distracted me and changed my focus from Italy to Grandmother's house.

I lay in my bed with the blankets pulled tightly under my chin and reflected about home. I thought of our jovial meals around the white tablecloth and of my brother Ira. I could almost smell the pleasant aromas that would awaken me from my afternoon nap in Grandmother's grand room. I sighed as I thought about my wonderful family. They all seemed so far away.

I yearned to be back sitting beside Grandmother as she held council while smoking her water pipe. I could taste the bitterness of the tobacco as she allowed me an occasional puff. I closed my eyes as a few homesick tears rolled down my cheeks. I took a deep breath and was struck by the realization that my family would be there to embrace me upon my return. With the warmth of the knowledge that this was only a temporary stay, sleep finally came.

The next morning, I awoke with the firm resolve to succeed in the Imperial Navy. I set out to conquer my first obstacle, learning Italian. In my efforts to immerse myself in the culture, I tried to spend as much time with the Italian cadets as possible. I knew this was the best way for me to learn the beautiful language of my new home. Professor Dini was also a valuable asset in my quest. He taught us Italian for our first three months at the Academy. His careful diction enabled us to hear each letter of every word. This methodical pronunciation was the bridge between the languages that finally broke our communication barrier.

In conjunction with our Italian studies during those first months at the Academy, we were taught mathematics by Professor Tognetti. He started with a dot on the blackboard, corresponding to the Italian word "Punto." Gesturing with gusto, he asked us to pronounce the word "Punto." We all found this method very helpful and, in time, between the diligent efforts of both professors, we learned the Italian language in the Italian way. By the time we started our other classes, we were all able to communicate.

Islam and the Naval Academy

While our studies were picking up, we began very cautiously to settle into our dorm and our surroundings. This experience brought with it more stress than the average college student would find leaving home for the first time. Italy offered a culture that was drastically different from the cloistered rules required by Islam, a faith that was very much part of who I was. In the first days of the Academy, we all tried to remain good Muslims and shied away from anything that would cross our beliefs. However, from that first moment in the showers, we began to realize that our service to our country was going to require full immersion in a culture that was in direct contrast to our faith.

My first big awakening came at the end of our initial week at the Academy. With my limited skill in Italian and through some help with translation, I obeyed the command to report to the impressive green entrance gates. I was to host a tour of the campus. When I arrived, I was assigned to accompany a lovely young woman named Maria and her mother. The Academy's prestige brought many Saturday visitors.

Here I was, in charge of escorting two women around my school, and I had never even touched a girl's hand except for the women in my own family. In the Muslim religion, touching or even looking at a member of the opposite sex outside of your own family was *Haram*, a forbidden and sinful activity that leads straight to the gates of hell. As my stay in Italy progressed, I began to doubt the accuracy of the consequences of this crime. Either hell was the largest place I had ever imagined, big enough to accommodate all the men and women of Europe, or the rules were not quite as rigid as I had initially been told. On the other hand, if my teachings had been accurate, most certainly all of Italy would be going to hell.

During this first meeting with Maria, I did not question the validity of *Haram*. Consequently, I was very nervous as I tried to maintain my distance from these Academy guests, while providing a competent escort tour around the piazza. My limited Italian made conversation impossible, and I began entertaining my guests with a series of "Bon Giornos" and smiles. I decided that my duties as a tour guide were probably an essential part of my training as a cadet, so I slowly warmed to Maria. She was a kind, plump girl and laughed at my constant hellos. In an effort to expand my vocabulary, I tested the phrase I had just learned. I glanced carefully towards her and asked, "Che ore sono?" "What time is it?" I was thrilled to hear her respond to my question, but I had no idea what she was saying.

During the next few weeks, I began my required Saturday tour with Maria waiting for me at the gates. She sought me out under the pretense of discussing the time. She would smile and wave, yelling, "Che ore sono?" as I passed by. Finally, after our third meeting, Maria asked me to escort her home. We left the campus and went to the bus stop outside the gate.

I looked up with fascination as the electric bus appeared and we boarded. I had never traveled in such a vehicle before, and my eyes darted around like a child who enters a sweet shop for the first time. In my excitement, I let my guard down long enough for Maria to slip her hand on top of mine on the leather handle that hung from the ceiling to secure the passengers. The moment I felt her soft skin against mine, I pulled my hand away in shock. I had committed a sin, it was *Haram*. Heat rose up on the back of my neck, and I felt an electric current run through my body. I did not want Maria to know that my reaction was a result of her touch. I coughed and looked away, pretending to be fascinated by the workings of the bus that was transporting us.

We stopped after what seemed an eternity, and I walked Maria to her door. As soon as she was safely on the steps, I scurried back to catch a ride home.

Later that night, I lay awake in my bed, once more reflecting on the day's happenings. I could feel my old-world traditions slowly slipping away, and I made myself focus squarely on the future and the hard work that would hopefully lead to my success.

Another Test

After three months of studying Italian, a comprehensive examination was required. This provided the Academy with data to use in determining our class placement. The test was separated into two parts: the physical exam and the academic.

The first part was the physical. When it was my turn to submit to the tests, I reported to the infirmary and was met by a large, stern-looking nurse. She was a nun and was all business. She took my pulse and a blood sample as I sat calculating each touch in my head as a form of Haram. Finally, at the end of my appointment, she handed me a small jar and asked me to step behind a curtain and come out with a urine sample. I was horrified. I could not imagine doing something so personal behind such a thin curtain with a woman sentry standing so close.

After attempting for at least five minutes, I had to tell her I could not perform. "Manocher," she said, "please leave, and drink lots of water and return in three hours." I knew that this must be a common practice in the Italian Navy, and that I must overcome my embarrassment.

I obeyed by drinking at least a gallon of water. Returning to the same nurse, I found a whole tray of small containers behind the curtain. I was pleased with her faith in me, despite my apprehension. This time I could not stop, and I was thrilled with my success. After filling up at least five of the glass cups, I heard a voice quietly saying, "Manocher, we only need one." With flushed cheeks, I walked out of the room thinking, "I am nineteen years old and I have so much to learn."

After my experience with the nurse, I welcomed the scholastic tests. I was accustomed to studying, and I liked the challenge. The test was used to determine our strengths and separate us into two groups: engineers and navigators. My goal was to become an engineer. I worked hard and when the results were posted, I was proud to learn that I had earned the only position in the engineering program.

Separating from the Pack

Later on, students from Colombia, Brazil, Venezuela, Haiti, Peru, and Nicaragua joined us, and two months later, the new Italian cadets entered the Academy. After several intense months of learning Italian, we were all able to move into classes together. Shortly thereafter, I separated from my fellow Iranians and joined the engineering division.

One weekend, just after I joined the engineering students, we received a very special visit from the Deputy of the Imperial Iranian Navy, Admiral Azshirvany. While he was visiting, he met with our group of five and, in a fatherly fashion, inquired about our progress. We sat in the Academy's lounge and described our experience of learning Italian and our scholastic achievements.

The day after this meeting, the admiral returned to the Academy and called me back to the lounge. I knew that he was not only a special visitor, but that he was also the father of my former classmate Qumars. I was curious about his intentions as I entered the lounge.

The admiral said, "Hello Manocher." I responded, "Hello sir." He invited me to sit down and continued, "Manocher, I would like to give you a special job on behalf of the Imperial Navy. While you are here at the Academy, I want you to be in charge of your group as the group leader. As part of this job, you will report monthly on everyone's progress and inform me of anything that you are lacking." I thanked the admiral and left him in the lounge.

I was honored but uncomfortable about what this post would do to my newly formed friendships. I was the youngest in the group, and I was afraid that the others would not appreciate my appointment as a leader.

The admiral called my friends and informed them of my new status. As I expected, my colleagues were not pleased. During the next several days, uncertain of how I would handle my newly appointed position, they seemed distant and reluctant to interact with me. I tried my best to calm their fears by maintaining my friendly attitude and striving to avoid any type of superiority. After a few weeks passed, my new post became old news, and school became our focus once more.

For the most part, after this little episode, throughout our time in Italy, we meshed together very well. Our small Iranian group supported each other, not only as friends, but also as a link to our home and culture that was so far away.

My Daily Routine

After the tests and our special visit from the admiral, we were able to settle into a daily routine. Our classes met for eight hours a day, five and a half days a week, with Saturday afternoons and Sundays reserved for athletics. Since I was in a separate program, I saw very little of my fellow Iranian classmates, except in the evenings, when we looked forward to gathering after dinner to exchange our experiences.

Each morning the trumpet call roused us at 6:30 a.m. just in time for our morning calisthenics at 7:00 a.m. After the workout, breakfast was served in the dining hall at 7:30 a.m. We ate our meals at pre-assigned seats, and then after breakfast, I would part ways with Bahman, Mahmood, Syrus, and Haji and would head to class at the navigation school. I went on to meet my engineering classmates for our 8:15 a.m. lessons. The classes continued until lunch at noon and then reconvened in the afternoon from 2:00 p.m. to 4:00 p.m. occasionally, the 2:00 p.m. class period would be replaced with the appropriate exercise for a cadet. The Academy also required each student be proficient in elegant sports such as horseback riding, swimming, and sailing. From 4:00 p.m. to 5:00 p.m., there was another hour of free time, followed by study hall until 8:00 p.m. After study hall, we joined each other in the dining hall for dinner. At 10:00 p.m. our day would end as it began, with the trumpet call.

Scenes from those early days continue to flash through my mind. The Academy breakfast was always something to look forward to. The nights were intense and filled with study, but the traditional white table linens, along with the formality of the waiters serving us in white jackets and gloves, allowed us to catch our breath and enjoy a serene meal before our classes resumed.

At each place setting, there were small saucers filled with ten Italian cigarettes per cadet. Most of us kept them in our dresser drawer. We soon learned to smoke, but only on occasion. This turned out to be a good form of rationing the cigarettes, which became a valuable commodity during our first semester exams, when ten a day were not nearly enough for any of us.

In the beginning, the meal rituals were difficult to accept, but we soon learned to appreciate and enjoy the ceremony of dining. Luncheon and dinner were always three courses. We were served a quarter liter bottle of wine, either white or red depending on the entrée. We enjoyed both the wine and the cigarettes. We conveniently called ourselves "Modern Muslims."

Unfortunately, Wednesday evening dinner became impossible for us to accept, even for the modern men we had become. Our Italian waiters would proudly set down a tray and smile. On the first Wednesday evening at the Academy, we looked at one another and then back at our entree in disbelief. How could anyone eat these strange boiled fish with tentacles? After this experience, we were horrified to find that the Academy served the unappealing delicacy of calamari as a Wednesday night tradition.

In order to save ourselves from this feast, we decided to break the rules. In the Academy, if you broke a rule, the consequence was losing the privilege to attend dinner in the elegant dining room. Instead of going to the beautiful hall, we would be served wine and mouth-watering hot bread and cheese in a private room in the prison.

This room was really quite comfortable. There were not any jail bars, only a door. The room was furnished with a desk and chair, more like one would envision a library's private study room.

The task of escaping the sea creatures was simple after we discovered how delicious the prison meals were. Each Wednesday, we would be a little late for a class and then diligently report our misbehavior to the professor. As anticipated, we were told not to attend the evening meal. This became the Iranian Wednesday night dinner tradition.

In addition to meals, exercise was a very important part of our day. For our first two years at the Academy, our early morning calisthenics required five climbs up the 100-foot-high double mast of the *Brigantino*. The *Brigantino's* large masts rose up out of the ground of the Academy's courtyard. They were made to resemble the top deck of a sailing ship, such as the *Amerigo Vespucci*. This difficult feat was not the only physical requirement, there was also a long wire attached to the side of the tall Academy building. This wire was sixty feet high and required amazing upper body strength to reach the top. Of course, the morning wasn't the only time that these labor-intensive exercises were thrust upon us. They also served as punishment for young cadets who sought more adventure than the Academy's formality allowed.

At times, my own concerns about failing and being dismissed from the Academy became extreme. I had taken a very intensive class in design stress or "the strength of material." Professor Magini was well-known as a stickler for accuracy, and the majority of my grade was to be based on a ninety-minute oral examination. The presentation was to take place in a forum format. I was very nervous and obsessed with studying. As the day approached, I had no idea what questions I would have to answer. The professor felt we should be prepared for any or all parts of the subject. I spent the evening before pacing back and forth in front of the upstairs window of my dorm. A reoccurring thought kept crossing my mind, if I did not perform well, perhaps the only option left would be to jump. I knew that this was irrational thinking, and I could never be that foolish, but I was not alone in my feelings about needing to succeed. Other cadets had not been able to face disappointing test score results and had been responsible for their own self-inflected demise. The Academy was tough, but nothing was worth such drastic actions. However, I knew that my desire to "never fail" was what motivated me throughout my naval career. I had been selected from a small group of students to attend school in Italy, and I simply had to return to my country with honor.

The final oral exam took much longer than average, and fortunately I left the forum as a hero, with the best score in the class. My fellow students lifted me to their shoulders and carried me around the Pizzale, then greeted me with a special toast, while uncorking the Spumante. Life at that moment was joyous!

Even in my driven state, with my determination to finish at the top of my class, I was encouraged by some of my more light-hearted friends to occasionally seek adventure. In my second year at the year-round school, on a warm summer Saturday afternoon, Bahman and I decided to check out one of the school's star-class sailboats.

Together, we gathered two of our classmates and made our way to the school's dock. Bahman and I signed for the boat and agreed to the terms set forward by the school.

Outfitted like sailors, we wore our deck shoes and bathing suits and made our way to Pancaldi beach. Pancaldi was known for its beautiful assortment of young Italian university girls, especially on Saturday afternoons. We were well aware that the lovely young women chose Pancaldi because of its close proximity to the Naval Academy, with the dashing young cadets, as we liked to consider ourselves. We cruised along the beach and admired the curvaceous young girls in their colorful bikinis. By this point, we had developed a love for Italian frivolity, and as a result, our Muslim roots, once again, fell by the wayside.

We decided that the best way to attract attention would be to take turns jumping out of the boat and swimming ashore. We knew that the rules prohibited us from doing so but the draw of the sunbathers was too much. Bahman jumped first.

While he swam to shore I steered the boat around in circles for fifteen or twenty minutes and then returned to the rendezvous point. Bahman swam back and we exchanged places. When Bahman took the helm, I jumped into the ocean.

I swam toward the local coeds. About five minutes into my swim, I noticed, out of the corner of my eye, the flag flying over the Academy's signal tower had changed, signaling that all boats should return to port immediately.

As I looked back towards our small vessel, I saw Bahman frantically searching for me. I tried to yell but the roaring of the waves was too much for me to overcome. I watched as he reluctantly sailed away. With Bahman gone, forced to obey the flag's command, I was left on the shore to fend for myself in only my swimming trunks.

It was an agonizing situation. I was on the most beautiful beach, with the most delightful young women, but I was unable to enjoy even a moment of it. I knew that I was about to be in more trouble than I had ever known. I had to return to the fort-like Naval Academy and I had no means of transportation and no clothing! A cadet was required to enter the gate in full uniform, with an official salute, not bare-footed in swim trunks. I was terrified and could barely think clearly enough to plot my return, when I realized that one of my fellow cadets might be somewhere on the beach.

I began anxiously searching the shore line, and to my utter relief I found a fellow cadet who was a year ahead of me. After a day of leave, he was on his way back to the Academy. Stopping him, I explained my predicament and he agreed to return to the beach with my uniform no later than 8:00 p.m. I was grateful for his help, but I was worried about having to wait until evening.

Once I had the plan in place, I began to look around the beach. I realized that several girls I knew from dances at the Academy were there. We began to talk. For a moment, I enjoyed their attention and their sympathy. They were all very kind and expressed their concern for me. However, as the day turned to night, they all packed up their things and left the beach. They had to meet the curfews set by their own schools and families.

After everyone had gone, I sat in the dark and waited. Finally the cadet returned. Unfortunately, he had failed his mission. In his arms he carried my boots, no socks, my hat, and a uniform. I collected the mishmash of clothing and ducked into a changing cabana. As I began to dress, I realized that he had brought me my roommate's uniform, who was at least two inches taller and twenty pounds heavier! I struggled to get the clothing in order. The sleeves were down to my fingers and the pants were rolled at the waist. I was terrified that my desire for amusement would lead to my expulsion from the Academy.

As I made my way back to the school, I kept to the shadows so that I would not be seen. Once I was in front of the building, I waited in the dark next to an old church, hoping for some classmates to walk by who could provide cover for me. After a few minutes, a group of cadets appeared.

I explained my situation, and they agreed to help sneak me in through the front gates. My multiple "Grazies" more than expressed my gratitude. In response, the young men surrounded me. Pushing back my long sleeves, and hoping that my bare ankles were not showing, we walked swiftly up to the gates. I held my breath, at my place in the center of my comrades, and said a silent thank you as we made it through.

When I returned to my dorm, my heart was pounding and I lay on the bed, exhausted. Bahman was anxious to see me, and together we breathed a sigh of relief, realizing that there would not be any repercussions. We looked at my ill-fitting attire and laughed uproariously. Secretly, I vowed never to be as irresponsible again. All I could think of was how much I appreciated the opportunity to attend the Academy and how quickly I could have sacrificed my career by being so foolish.

My Cultural Education

In addition to the formal dinners, intense classes, and a few devious outings, the Academy also focused on cultural exposure. In order to become well-rounded cadets, we were required to master the refinement of ballroom dancing and the formal presentation of guests for receptions and receiving lines. Proper etiquette was expected for every occasion.

These formal settings and introductions were situations that sometimes caused humor and embarrassment. A certain rhythm was required when meeting dignitaries in a receiving line. Shake the hand of the gentlemen and kiss the hand of his lady. As nervous young cadets, much to everyone's dismay, the opposite sometimes occurred. Kiss the hand of the gentleman and shake the hand of his lady! There were many times later in my career that I was able to comfortably entertain dignitaries and attend elaborate functions because of the mandatory attention that was paid to learning proper social behavior at the Academy.

Although the etiquette was a practical lesson that I came to appreciate, the course I considered to be my favorite was ballroom dancing. The Academy did not offer instruction in dance, but highly recommended the cadets be efficient in the art.

Thanks to Maria, and the stern nurse, I had overcome my fear of touching the hand of a woman. I decided, it was time to take a step further. Following the school's advice, I enrolled in the recommended school for private dance instruction. I hoped that a lovely young female might become my dancing partner.

On the Saturday afternoon of my first class, I left the confines of the Academy and boarded the electric bus. I exited at Piazza Cavour in the center of Livorno and made my way to the second floor of the commercial building that housed the dance studio.

When I arrived, I met my teacher, Maestro Abruzzini, a stocky Italian man in a bowtie. His co-instructor was his wife, a voluptuous Italian woman. The other students were already dancing across the floor, and I was told to join in. No one was allowed to stand still. There was a constant stream of music floating up from the old gramophone in the corner. Mr. Abruzzini was always shouting out instruction. "One, two, three.... One, two, three..." were the words that formulated the ticker of rhythm in my mind as I tried to follow the steps.

On that first of many Saturdays, we began with the tango. I learned how to hold myself and my partner, and then slowly, I caught on to the complicated steps. By the end of many months of classes, I was proficient in the waltz, tango, mambo, and cha-cha. Unfortunately, I realized at some point in my lessons that in order to learn how to lead, I needed to dance with a strong male partner. As it turned out, instead of pairing off with a lovely young lady as I had envisioned, my best partner was Mr. Abruzzini. Together we would move about the room with his count of "One, two, three.... One, two, three..." as he taught me how to lead. By the time I completed my lessons, I was twirling Mr. Abruzzini around the room with all the right moves.

In addition to my newly found grace, I used my afternoons at Mr. Abruzzini's as an excuse to explore all of the best flavors of gelato on Piazza Cavour. I followed most of my lessons with a trip to one of the little cafés at the city's center, where I enjoyed my favorite flavor, Cassata. The refreshing fruity taste was the perfect end to my afternoons away from the Academy.

In the end, I learned enough steps to participate in the weekend parties hosted by the Academy. One evening, Maria visited our Saturday night dance, accompanied by a lovely young American girl named Ann. We liked each other immediately. She was dressed in light blue taffeta, and she reminded me of the pretty blonde women I enjoyed looking at in *Life* magazine.

Ann and her family became very close to me. Her father was an American officer stationed in Livorno. Ann was my first real girlfriend. I truly enjoyed her company and the time we spent together, dancing at the Academy or having dinner in her home. She had an elegant and charming mother who always made me feel like I was welcome. Ann's parents knew that I was a long way from home, and they took me under their wing as if I were a son. I rushed to tell them of my successes, as well as the obstacles I occasionally encountered along life's way.

Despite my feelings for Ann, our relationship never went into the phase of realistic courtship. I looked at her with such admiration, but I knew that the strict Muslim culture she would be exposed to, living in Tehran and Grandmother's house, would not bring my pretty little American much happiness. Even if we could bridge this cultural gap, I had many years of education and military service ahead of me that would further complicate our situation. With a pain in my heart, I left for my time at sea knowing that I would not see Ann again. I took with me the memories of her sweet gracious spirit and the knowledge that she was my first love.

Cruises around Europe and the Americas

In addition to the studies at the Academy, we were each required to complete three tours at sea. The best part of the sea voyages was the fanfare we received in every port. "Dancing around the World" was my own personal theme for our voyage, although I am sure that is not what the Navy had in mind when they sent us for our overseas education.

Dancing was supposed to complement our naval training, not be the emphasis, but during our three months at sea, dancing was just as important as our engineering and navigation skills. The lessons I learned from Mr. Abruzzini helped to prepare me for those formal evenings in officer's clubs, where we were expected to entertain the wives and daughters of officers and dignitaries by engaging them in a perfect waltz or tango.

Our first assignment was aboard the magnificent sailing ship *Amerigo Vespucci*. Her black and white hull, gold gilt trim, and billowing soft beige sails were a sight to behold.

When the *Vespucci* was at sea, we occupied our time by conquering our sea-sickness, climbing the mast, setting the sails, and learning many technicalities, but when the magnificent ship sailed into port with Italian flags flying, we were greeted with celebrity status. Keys to the city were often waiting. Orchestras were tuning up at the officer's clubs, and invited female guests were lined up to fill our dance cards. We were young, polished cadets with brass buttons shining, all of whom were eager to enjoy the evening.

Almost every night in port, I silently thanked Mr. Abruzzini for teaching me the steps to so many intricate dances. Each night that we were allowed to leave the strict confines of our ship's tiny quarters was a wonderful refresher. Although we were granted carefully guarded contact with local girls at the officer's club dances, we all enjoyed the perfumed scent of the delightful young woman in our arms. As music played, skirts flared across the dance floor. My fellow cadets and I viewed these evenings as the breath of fresh air that kept us going on the long foreign tours.

Each city that we docked in brought local dignitaries to our ship. We were often greeted by the Iranian Ambassador in the country we were visiting. He would welcome us on behalf of the Shah. In Morocco, we were privileged to meet Prince Hassan, who was later crowned as king. These moments were always a source of pride for each of us. As I think back, one memorable evening on the *Vespucci* was the night we docked in Oslo, Norway.

When we arrived in Oslo, we were eager to attend the gathering that the Norwegian Navy had graciously arranged in their officer's club in honor of our visit. The affair was on our schedules a month in advance, and we were all looking forward to the festivities. When the ship docked, we were ready. Together with several of my fellow cadets, I made my way to the officer's club.

As soon as we entered the well-appointed lounge, we were introduced to dance partners in a receiving line. I was paired with a lovely Norwegian girl. She had short blonde hair and spoke impeccable English. I whisked her onto the dance floor and did my best to impress her with my tango.

After a few turns across the floor, the dinner chime rang. We had a pleasant meal together, punctuated by friendly conversation. At the end of the evening, as I prepared to return to the *Vespucci*, I bowed to my new friend and thanked her for an unforgettable night. I was pleased when she turned to me and asked if I would have time for a tour of the city on the following day. I graciously accepted her offer and returned to my ship, where I fell asleep pleased with my good fortune. I thought to myself, "I spent the evening with the most delightful young woman, and now she is going to show me the city."

The following morning, I put on my best uniform and waited for my tour guide, just above the dock on the stairs leading up to the ship. Around the designated time for our meeting, a woman with short blonde hair approached the ship in a Norwegian Naval uniform with a lieutenant's symbol on her shoulder. I looked down twice, before I realized that last evening's gorgeous dance partner was not the local Norwegian girl I expected, she was an officer and she outranked me! Reluctantly, I joined the lieutenant for the tour and exchanged formal conversation as she pointed out the landmarks around the city.

Back at sea on the following day, I received one of my father's weekly letters. He had been thoughtful about keeping me informed of family happenings during my time at the Academy. I always looked forward to his correspondence that brought with it a taste of familiarity, allowing me to keep my home-sickness at bay.

The latest letter opened with the usual weather report, "It was cold in Tehran last week," scrawled in my father's familiar hand. He also mentioned that Grandmother's house was suffering from electrical outages from time to time. The next announcement he made was simply stated, "As you remember, Manocher, I enjoy reading every evening, but one night the lights went out early…. Now, we will soon have a new addition to our family. Your mother is expecting a baby." I chuckled as I read my father's news. I was happy that he shared this information with me, in this letter between men, and I was thrilled to be a big brother again, even at twenty years old. What a wonderful surprise!

After Norway, our next destination was the coastal city of Hamburg. There we spent the evening with a group of hearty German cadets from the training ship *Pamir*. The German Navy arranged an all-night celebration in our honor. We mingled with our counterparts over great music and dark beer. Although we were accustomed to formal affairs in every port, the jovial, frivolous atmosphere of the *Pamir's* crew made this a memorable occasion. They were a happy, robust group, and we were all grateful for the almost unheard-of opportunity to let our guard down. I distinctly remember their jabs about our double-breasted waist-length jackets and the digs we fired back at them about their black leather boots and militant attire.

As we set sail the next morning, despite the high winds, we rehashed the previous night's party and our newly found friends with fondness. Our next port was Lisbon, and as our journey progressed, the sea began to buck our handsome sailing ship, and news of a coming storm proved true. When we sailed into open water, the waves began to swell and the winds began to howl.

We soon realized we were in the middle of a wild and treacherous storm. We struggled to bring down the sails. Fortunately, our salvation was the ship's emergency diesel engine. As the waters rose to a peak, the descent down was quick and jolting. We were all frightened, but tied together with ropes; we completed our chores on the deck, secured the ship, and then retreated below to ride out the storm.

Cyclone Bertha left her calling card on our decks, and we were forced to abandon our plans and change our heading. Instead of Portugal, by order of the Ministry of the Navy in Rome, we sought safe port in France. As we pulled into dock at Brest, France, we were forced to drop anchor outside the harbor, which was full to capacity. After three long days and nights below deck, the storm passed and we continued our journey.

That fall, after we had completed our first year at sea, and were once again entrenched in life at the Academy, we heard of a ship that was a casualty of the storm we had experienced. We gathered around Bahman as he read the report in the paper. It was difficult to believe the words. I saw shock on the faces of my classmates as I felt my stomach drop when Bahman read the obituary about the cadets aboard the German ship *Pamir*.

Eighty souls were lost in the cyclone that followed our wonderful evening party with our German friends. It was a sad consequence to life at sea. It was customary at the Academy for each class to have a name of their choosing recorded at the end of their first hundred days at sea. After reading of the *Pamir* and its tragic end, my classmates and I took a vote and decided to name our class Cyclone to commemorate the class of 1956.

On our second-and third-year cruises, the *Montecuccoli* was our ship. As the longest cruiser in the world, we still commanded the respect that we enjoyed on the *Amerigo Vespucci*. However, the *Montecuccoli* was a very different ship from the *Vespucci,* and it took great concentration to learn all the nuances of this technical vessel. Despite these differences in the accommodations, our days held the same priorities.

Each morning started much like it did in the Academy: There was a wakeup call, followed by exercise and breakfast. During the day, we attended five classes presided over by one of the officers. The differences between our school on land and our time at sea arose out of the necessity to maintain and run the vessel. In order to accomplish this goal, the cadets were split into three groups. There was always one group running the cruiser, one group taking classes, and one group sleeping. This allowed us to alternate our responsibilities with the free time we enjoyed off the ship.

Despite the changing schedules, the focus of my lessons stayed constant. In the engineering program, we were taught about maintenance engineering and ship building. After our lessons, we ate lunch in the galley and took turns fulfilling our afternoon assignments by giving presentations on various subjects. By now, we had all accepted the intense curriculum and realized the responsibilities that would be bestowed upon us when we were in command in our own areas of expertise. Running a ship took exacting teamwork, and we were being prepared to be the best. In war or peace, we were responsible for each other's lives and each of us had to learn to perform our jobs well.

Throughout my time at the Academy, we had the honor of hosting visiting dignitaries, including presidents and top-ranking military personnel from around the world. One of the most memorable guests, in my young naval career, was the Shah of Iran. After all, he wanted to see how his investment in the Iranian students was progressing.

On the day he arrived, we were riddled with excitement as we prepared for the welcoming parade. Dressed in our best uniforms, marching in procession, we completed the route along the Academy's square and circled back to the entrance that led to the "Sala Visitare," the visiting room. We were all filled with anticipation as we awaited the Shah's arrival. Bahman and I chatted eagerly about how we would respond to any questions we were privileged enough to be asked.

After pulling up in a white Rolls-Royce, the Shah crossed the threshold with a regal air and smiled at all of the cadets who gathered around. I was amazed as he began to question us about our course work, our performance, and our time at sea. We were pleased to pose for a photograph with our king and even noticed his relaxed stance, signified by his uniform's open top button. After our short meeting, the Shah was escorted to the dining hall, where a private meal awaited him with the Academy's commanding officer, Admiral Barbara, and the Italian Minister of Defense.

Following luncheon, Bahman and I, along with our fellow cadets, stood guard, top coat buttons undone, as the Shah exited the dining hall and returned to his car for his departure from the Academy. The surrounding crowd had grown during the noon hour, and the noise of all of Livorno's single female population drowned out the Shah's farewell. Apparently, his status as a handsome divorcee had not been lost on the Italian women.

The school's quarter terms seemed to pass quickly, and in my third year, I was again ready to set sail on the *Montecuccoli*. Our schedule was set up ahead of time with consulates around the world, and because of the uniqueness of both Italian training ships, they were anticipated with excitement by those awaiting their arrival. Our visits were usually considered strictly entertainment, and although we studied diligently while at sea, it was important that we lived up to the expectations of our hosts and conducted ourselves like the professional celebrities we had become.

On this particular cruise, one of my third-year assignments was to be delivered after visiting the port of Beirut in Lebanon. I was to educate my fellow cadets in the history of "Musulmani", the Muslim religion. My professors thought it would be enlightening for other cadets to learn about the religion their Middle Eastern classmates observed.

To prepare for my presentation, about thirty days before our departure from Livorno, I visited the local bookshop and purchased several books about the story of Islam. I used these books to supplement the personal knowledge I had derived from my mother's teachings in my childhood.

This year, as always, we were welcomed to each foreign port with open arms and generous celebrations. I still took pleasure in evenings spent waltzing across the dance floor, and when possible, exploring the harbor towns that welcomed us. Although as cadets we were not permitted a great deal of freedom, we often enjoyed being entertained by local families, especially if they were living in Italian communities.

One beautiful afternoon while we were in the port of Beirut, I walked with my classmates among the local fishermen while returning from a planned function. We admired the Old World architecture and enjoyed the fragrant aromas wafting out of the small specialty shops that lined the streets.

I lagged slightly behind, while enjoying the colorful booths in the town square. Suddenly, the imposing ship's horn sounded to mark the end of our time on shore. When I turned to rejoin my fellow cadets, I found myself passing a charming stone chapel. As I walked by the entrance, an elderly man with a basket full of flyers reached out and placed one into my hand. I began to look down to read; when I heard my fellow cadets call my name, "Manocher, Manocher, please hurry, we must report to the ship!" Shoving the leaflet into my pocket, I quickly caught up with my group, and together we rushed back to the pier to board the *Montecuccoli*. After we returned, I could still visualize the beautiful old church, and it reminded me that it was time to buckle down and prepare for the presentation of my own religion, the ways of Islam.

Before dinner was served that evening in the ship's dining room, I used one of the solid oak tables as a desk to write my presentation. Thinking about this project brought guilt to my conscience as I thought of all the anti-Muslim activities I had participated in since leaving my homeland. Yet in my heart, I knew that I had been working hard, and doing what was expected of me, as well as learning to accept the customs and beliefs of my new Italian friends. I did not feel badly about respecting people who had accepted me and shown me love and understanding. I felt that if their religious ideas were not my own, it would still be acceptable. Perhaps, I thought, the whole world should spend time in each other's countries in order to achieve compatibility.

After contemplating for a moment, I sighed, gathered my books, and walked to the area of the study benches to spread out my work. I decided that any description of Islam should begin with the story of Mohammad, the last prophet who brought the Koran to his followers. Now, I opened the first book and began to read.

The story began with Mohammad's childhood: "He was born in the year of 570 AD in Mecca. He was orphaned by the age of six and was taken in by his uncle. In the early years of his life he was an illiterate caravan worker and camel driver." I was surprised to learn of Mohammad's illiteracy, but I did not think his childhood biography was relevant to my presentation so I skipped ahead.

The next chapter was about Mohammad's first wife. "When he was twenty-five years old, Mohammad married his employer, Khadija, a wealthy widow who owned her own caravan. She was fifteen years his senior and had three children from prior unions." I skipped ahead a little further in the book, searching for the first significant event about Islam in Mohammad's life.

Finally, I found what I was looking for. "When Mohammad was around forty years of age he frequently visited a cave located near his home for meditation. According to Muslim history, it was during one of these quiet moments that Mohammad was called upon to be a prophet. The Angel Gabriel appeared in the cave and commanded Mohammad to recite in the name of Allah. When Mohammad failed to respond, the angel grabbed him and pressed on him until he could not bear the pressure. The angel released Mohammad, and once again commanded him to recite in the name of Allah. For the second time Mohammad failed to respond, and the angel choked Mohammad. The angel then released Mohammad and again asked him to recite in the name of Allah. This time he responded, and his recitation came to be viewed as the first of the revelations that make up the Koran.

I remembered from my mother that the stories of how Mohammad acquired the Koran varied. Some said that he was given the writings and was told by the Angel Gabriel that he was the last prophet. Others told a tale of Mohammad having prophetic religious visions, and writing the Koran while he was ensconced in caves deep within the mountain. Both interpretations and several others all reached the same conclusion. Through visions and angelic interventions, Mohammad came to possess the Koran and began to preach about its message.

I decided to indulge my curiosity and my passion for knowledge. I opened the second book to read the description of how Mohammad became a prophet. The second book told a similar story but instead of the angel choking Mohammad until the revelation came to him, the revelation was brought on by the ringing of a bell. I moved on to read about the spread of my faith.

Mohammad came down from the mountain and had a difficult time finding followers outside of his friends and family. The Jews, who he had respected before becoming a prophet, would not accept him or his new faith. They continued to acknowledge their own beliefs and saw no reason to change. This infuriated Mohammad, and in response he raided and pilfered their communities.

After thirteen years of preaching and recruiting in Mecca, Mohammad and his 100 faithful supporters were forced to relocate to Medina. Mohammad took advantage of this opportunity to change his approach on how to spread Islam. He began to preach about the sword of Jihad, and encouraged his followers to take up that sword and strike down nonbelievers in the name of Allah.

It was within the introduction of the idea of Jihad that paradise became a prevalent ideal of the Muslim faith. When Mohammad's followers went into battle and were struck down, they were told that paradise awaited them. This was, supposedly, a beautiful land, and upon arrival all would be impressed by rivers of milk, and an ever-present supply of ripe, juicy dates. They should not fear, because their sacrifice would be rewarded in the name of Allah, by the entry into this fruitful utopia.

Once in paradise, the men would be presented with a reward of seventy-two virgins displayed for their pleasure. The virgins would be untouched and fair as corals sitting in rows, with soulful dark eyes. Each night in paradise, a man could select his virgin or virgins for his pleasure, and drink the constant flowing wine, that was not like the sinful intoxicating wine of that on earth. The women then awakened each morning, their virginity renewed, with the glow of eternal youth. Mohammad instilled in his followers that true life was lived in paradise.

As my despair mounted, I picked up the other texts I had in front of me and I read on. "These promises of paradise created a deep-seated belief in Islam among Mohammad's followers, enticing them to murder, loot, and ransack all who did not believe in, or could not be converted into believing, the words of the Koran."

As I digested this information, I was stunned. I quietly closed my book, and contemplated what I had just learned. I felt a deep sadness and I was numb to my surroundings. My confusion knew no bounds as I wondered, "Did my kind and peaceful mother believe in this man? How could she? How could I?"

Then I realized that Mohammad had lived 1,400 years ago, when times were very different, and most certainly barbaric. I remembered my mother's lack of trust in many of the Mullahs, especially those who were not respectful of women. I realized that she applied her faith to life in her time with a deep reverence to Allah. Obviously, she practiced only the loving and spiritual parts of Islam. (Little did I know that in a few short years, I would personally be subjected to the cruel and primitive fanatical Islam of a bygone era.)

The more I researched, the more shocked I became. The book went on to talk of Mohammad's thirteen wives. "The youngest wife was only six years old at the time of the union. Mohammad waited until she was nine years old to consummate the marriage, at which point she became his favorite wife". I was confused by this information. I closed the book more loudly than I intended. My fellow cadets turned to look at me. The formality of the Academy rules made any outburst rare at best, and I flushed with embarrassment and looked back down at my presentation notes.

It was difficult for me to digest what I was reading. Why the great reverence for Mohammad? Was he just an ordinary mortal with human frailties? A mere man whom Allah chose to use as a spokesperson to spread the word of the Koran? Or later, did Mohammad alone decide to use the power of Jihad to spread the Muslim faith?

As I shifted in the chair with a physical expression of my discomfort, I heard the sound of crinkling paper, and I remembered the pamphlet in my pocket. Without much heed, I pulled out the rumpled paper and laid it on the table beside my research materials. Still lost in thought, several moments passed before I looked down and noticed the quote on the leaflet, "Only false prophets feel the need to kill in order to spread their faith."

The irony of the quote was not lost on me. I sighed and reminded myself that the presentation was a large portion of my grade, a grade that I needed to maintain my goal of staying at the top of my class. Reluctantly, I turned the pages of the writing in front of me and continued my research. I decided to focus on the principles of Islam to allow myself time to recover from the knowledge of Mohammad's violence.

After skimming the book in front of me, I reached for another and read the section that described the five pillars of my faith. The majority of Muslims believe that there are five pillars of Islam: Prayer, Faith, the Zakat, the Fast, and Hajj. The first pillar, faith, is the belief that Allah is the only god worthy of worship and Mohammad is his messenger, the last prophet. The second pillar, prayer, tells the Muslim people that they are obligated to pray five times a day. According to this pillar, the prayers should take place at dawn, noon, mid-afternoon, sunset, and nightfall.

The third pillar of Islam is called the Zakat. The Zakat is the Islamic belief that everything belongs to Allah, and wealth is held by humans in trust for Allah. As part of that trust, each Muslim is expected to pay two and a half percent of their total wealth annually to the local Mullah. The fourth pillar of Islam is the fast. During the month of Ramadan, all Muslims fast from sunrise to sunset, refraining from food, drink, and sexual activities. The purpose of Ramadan is to increase one's Taqwa (Allah consciousness) through increased acts of worship. The fifth and final pillar is called Hajj. Hajj is an annual pilgrimage to Mecca. This pilgrimage is only obligatory for those who are physically and financially able to make the trek. While most Muslims believe there are precisely five Pillars of Islam, others believe there is a sixth pillar, Jihad."

When I saw the word Jihad on the page, I inhaled deeply. I was hoping that I would not be confronted with more violence. I read on, "Jihad is the sixth pillar of Islam. It describes the external war against those perceived to be enemies. Enemies are those who do not accept the Koran as the words of Allah."

I had read enough. With a heavy heart I thought to myself, "How could I tell my classmates about this sordid history?" It seemed that Mohammad was a cruel man, a womanizer who used copious amounts of violence and the promise of sexual promiscuity in the afterlife to achieve whatever goal he had in mind at the time. After a moment of thought, I started to write my presentation.

When it came time to explain Islam to my colleagues, I spent another sleepless night. I knew it would be awkward for me to explain all of the components of Islam to my European classmates. Finally, I fell asleep tossing and turning.

Between lessons and ship duties, the next day was as busy as all our days on the *Montecuccoli*. The morning went quickly and the afternoon approached, despite my attempts to will it away. When my turn came to present, I approached the front of the class and told the men about Islam.

My fellow cadets were fascinated, all eyes were upon me. The silence in the room justified my words as being interesting. When I completed my report, I asked if there were any questions. Immediately one of my young Italian friends spoke up. Quietly, he asked, tongue-in-cheek, "How can I become a Muslim? The virgins sound pretty great to me!" A ripple of laughter resounded throughout the room.

The comments that followed were in jest, and I had to chuckle too. How could there be a paradise of this description? It seemed as improbable as a hell that housed all of Europe. Despite the jovial and teasing atmosphere that followed my presentation, my friends were respectful of my faith, and they did not mention it again.

With my report and the last of my three sea voyages completed, I turned my focus back to my courses and prepared for my final year at the Academy. After I uncovered the history about Mohammad, I felt only sadness about rejecting some of the antiquated ideas of the religion of my youth. In my final year in Livorno, I relaxed and enjoyed the local culture, my delightful Italian friends, and the Academy's festivities that accompanied the energetic class work.

On the Job Training in Taranto

By the end of four years, I felt comfortable with my knowledge of protocol. After 300 days at sea, I had visited North Africa, Libya, Morocco, Egypt, Israel, Greece, Turkey, France, Belgium, Germany, Holland, Norway, the United States, Canada, and most ports in Italy. I was personally grateful that I had learned to live a disciplined, organized life. I now felt confident that I could face any challenge that might await me. It was naive of me to think in such a simplistic fashion, but youth has high expectations!

The Academy had been difficult but I was now fluent in Italian and had a degree in marine engineering. After I graduated in 1960, I was proud of my accomplishments, and it was hard for me to believe how much time had passed. It had been an experience that molded my life and would influence my thinking for years to come.

Prior to being allowed to return home, I was transferred to the town of Taranto in southern Italy. There, I was assigned to the *Marina Militare Arsenale*, a military shipyard for the Italian Navy. I familiarized myself with each of the facility's departments as well as the ship-building and repair operations. Being aware of a ship's every nuance was important. If anything ever went wrong while at sea, I had to understand how to correct the problem.

I was the first Iranian naval officer to go to Taranto for practical training. During the entirety of my six-month stay, I lived in a suite at the Italian Navy's officer's club. The best part of my lodging was the pool table that served as my regular evening entertainment. By the time my assignment was up, I was an ace with a pool cue. I felt that my stay in Taranto was intense, but certainly less stressful than studies at the Academy. I was included in all of the many social affairs and activities, because I was a permanent resident in the officer's club. I enjoyed having time to relax and meet many Italian Naval officers and their families. It was a wonderful finale to my four years abroad.

The Consulate in Rome

From Taranto, I travelled to Rome to pick up my orders for transfer back to Iran. When I arrived at the Iranian Embassy, I expected them to be waiting for me with my return ticket to Tehran. I walked in to the consulate, dressed in my best uniform, only to find that they did not know me and had no idea about a ticket to Tehran. Once the consulate took down my information, they told me it would probably take a week or two to receive my orders. I was asked to involve myself in clerical work while I was awaiting my transfer home.

My extended stay in Rome gave me time to walk along the worn and crumbling cobblestone streets. I felt energized to be able to visualize the remains of what was once a magnificent thriving metropolis and to contemplate about those who were responsible for the many ambitious engineering feats. The Pantheon, Coliseum, remains of ancient waterways, as well as the incredible fragments of statuary, all were still there and a marvel to enjoy. There was beauty to be seen from every vantage point.

The Roman's religious history seemed to parallel that of my own, in the Middle East. The lions in the Coliseum had created misery for the Christians. They killed and devoured, while bloodthirsty crowds watched and cheered. Not much different, I thought, than when Mohammad, with his Army, killed with their swords, beheading all who did not agree with the belief that he was the last prophet and Allah was the only God.

Of course, I knew that those barbaric days were gone forever. We had advanced in our thinking and learned from what had happened centuries ago. Little did I know that there were still those who wanted to emulate the past, controlling and killing all who dared to disagree with their desire to turn the clock back to life as it had been in more primitive times.

Besides enjoying every aspect of Rome's history, I had ample time to shop in the elegant local boutiques and spend every last penny I had saved to buy Italian souvenirs for my family. Slowly, after each outing, I filled my suitcase with soft leather gloves in brown and black, for men and women, as well as silk ties, scarves, and many other assorted items. One day while I was walking through the narrow alleyways of Rome, I looked into the window of a gun shop. A very small Beretta pistol caught my eye. It was a stately firearm, dignified yet effective, and I knew I had to have it. I entered the shop and purchased it along with a box of ammunition. I thought it would be a very special gift for my dear cousin and mentor Kazem in Tehran.

In the evenings, I continued to absorb the atmosphere on Via Veneto and the historic city. I did not want to miss a moment of the time I had left as I stopped in a sidewalk café for Campari and blissfully watched the crowds go by. Feeling a certain nostalgia, I knew that I was going to miss this marvelous country and that I would hold its memory close to my heart. Italy would always be my second home.

After filing papers for two weeks, my orders and ticket finally arrived. I said my goodbyes and I was on my way. I was going home with skills that I felt would benefit my country. I was excited about seeing my family again. Four years and six months had been a long time. I looked forward to the "Chelo Kabab" that I knew would be waiting.

Chapter 3

Artworks of Master Mamoud Farshchian

My Return to Iran

The Founding of OPEC

While I wrestled with the emotions that marked the changing times in my life, the world was also changing. In 1960, as I prepared for my return home, the United States began making new laws to regulate the sale of oil. Ever the parent in international affairs, America, led by President Eisenhower, announced quotas for the importation of Venezuelan oil purchased by the United States. The United States chose to limit the amount of Venezuelan oil that was imported in favor of promoting the purchase of Mexican and Canadian oil. As a result, Venezuela sought out its fellow petroleum producers to discuss the limitations put on them to curtail their opportunities.

Venezuela contacted representatives from the oil industry in Iran, Iraq, Saudi Arabia, and Kuwait. Together these countries represented a majority share of the world's oil supply. The men agreed to meet in September of 1960 at what became known as, the Baghdad Conference.

The meeting was a great success. The nations agreed that they would work together to set prices and coordinate policies for their nations' oil in an effort to protect their own national assets and their autonomy. The cartel these men founded became known as the Organization of Petroleum Exporting Countries (OPEC).

In 1960, I caught only a glimpse of the nuances of oil, and the effects the founding of OPEC had on Iran. I knew from the correspondence I received from my family that with or without OPEC, the newly founded National Iranian Oil Company was going to make a great deal of money. The Kayhan international newspapers, that my father regularly sent, informed me of the ambitious plans for the growth of my country's infrastructure. It was an accepted fact that because of oil, Iran would no longer remain a third world country. I was on my way home and eager to become involved in these exiting advancements.

The Return Trip Home

When I travelled to Rome to catch my flight, I carried the stately Beretta pistol next to my chest and put the ammunition in the side pocket of my jacket. I flew from this splendid city via Istanbul to Iran. It was about two o'clock in the morning when the plane finally touched down in Tehran. More than four years had passed since I had last seen Mehrabad International Airport.

I had grown from the frightened young man who had been afraid to leave his family, into an officer in the Imperial Iranian Navy. I had sailed to ports all over the world, and most certainly broadened my horizons. As I descended the steps of the plane, I immediately saw my family. They surrounded the base of the walkway. The thirty-two cousins, aunts, and uncles who had shared my childhood luncheons, at Grandmother's house, had now multiplied into almost one hundred people, and they all came to the airport to celebrate my return.

As I stepped on the ground, the crowd rushed toward me. I was lovingly pulled in different directions. Everyone, both men and women, wanted to kiss both sides of my face. From a distance I could see my father next to my mother. They looked much older in person than in the picture I held in my memory. Slowly my throng of relatives drew me across the runway towards my parents.

My little cousin Misha stepped into my path. She had grown even more beautiful in the years that had passed after our innocent rendezvous in the tunnels below Grandmother's house. Her olive skin and pure features were brilliantly complimented by the paisley scarf she had artfully wrapped around her delicate waist. As she reached up to give me her warm embrace, her dark curls fell around her face and I was struck with a feeling of pride, knowing that she had come to meet me after my long absence.

Just as we stepped forward to exchange greetings, a tall handsome man came out of the crowd that surrounded me and placed a proprietary hand on Misha's shoulder. He leaned forward and accepted my handshake. Looking up, I recognized the grown man as my cousin Dash. Instantly I realized that he must have been the fortunate suitor who Misha had been promised too. I had no idea that the connection between our homes, through the tunnels, was responsible for romantic interludes. With a slight chuckle at the thought, I looked up and into the eyes of my dear mother. After a quick hug, I left Misha and her bridegroom and stepped forward to meet my own immediate family. I fell into my mother's outstretched arms, and with tears rolling down their cheeks, both my parents held onto me tightly. My younger brother Ira had been in his teens when I left, and now he stared back at me out of the eyes of a strapping young man.

A Car Ride with My Cousin

My cousin Kazem, whom I respected a great deal, was a very bright and handsome Army officer. He had always been my mentor and the role model I had thought of before leaving Rome. Rushing through the crowd, he separated me from the others and hustled me into a parked car, where his wife was sitting in the back seat. He jumped behind the wheel and drove to a different parking spot.

We waited for the crowd to get to their cars, and when the caravan started to move, he drove behind the others, saying, "Don't be shocked. You have been gone so long, Manocher, perhaps you have forgotten that this is how your family acts when welcoming someone they love. I am going to take you home for the ceremony." I was not sure that I had ever seen quite such a welcome, but after my long absence I was honored to be greeted in such a loving fashion, and I was not about to question tradition.

While Kazem was driving through Tehran, it was very dark, the shops were closed, and I could not help but compare these quiet streets with the lively thoroughfares of Rome. I felt a moment of sadness for what I had left behind. My cousin was speaking about many subjects, but I could hardly concentrate. I was worried about not having enough gifts for everyone. I was also thinking about my cousin's graciousness, and I was happy that I had a suitable gift for him. He loved the sport of target shooting and enjoyed being a military man. I reached into my jacket pocket and with pleasure presented him with the Beretta pistol, saying, "I purchased this for you. I hope you like it." He was very pleased, and with a broad smile he said, "I love it and I am touched that you thought of me. Thank you very much."

We were close to my home when I turned back to Kazem's wife and squeezed her hand, saying, "I have a little something for you too. It is in my suitcase. I will give it to you later." I did not want anyone to feel that I had forgotten them.

Kazem drove down the street leading to the alley that was the entrance to Grandmother's home. The caravan from the airport had already arrived and there were cars parked in rows surrounding us. The family gathered together at the mouth of the alley, and as I approached they began the welcome home ceremony. I was shocked to see a live lamb being presented. The butcher and his entourage were ready to begin.

I had forgotten that at our large family gatherings, the young lamb was led in by the butcher, then slaughtered and prepared on site for our parties. Memories came back and flooded my mind about large skewers of fresh lamb meat, Grandmother's delicious dolmas and crusty rice. Half of my mind was still in Italy, but I started to relax. I sighed and felt a contented comfort coming back to me. It was good to be home with my family.

The Sacrificial Lambs

My relatives all happily continued to shower me with hugs and double-cheeked kisses. Suddenly, they let go of me and focused on the lamb. The butcher came forward and along with his crew took the lamb that had been presented to me. He laid the lamb on the ground, and with knife poised, he said loudly in Arabic, "In the name of Allah, the compassionate, the merciful." Immediately the crowd answered again in Arabic, "I salute Mohammad and his followers." Without hesitation, the knife quickly came down on to the neck of the lamb, and the butcher brought the slaughter to my feet. This was a more elaborate process than I remembered from my childhood. In horror, I quickly wondered how God, the compassionate and the merciful, could condone an act of such brutality during a joyful celebration. The Muslims were obviously anesthetized and no longer had feeling for such a barbaric act.

I knew that the fresh meat used for my homecoming was not only for substance for our guests but was ceremonial for my return. When this process was completed, we all stepped over the spilled blood and approached a second lamb.

Again the lamb was presented and as I was held back, the lamb was pinned to the ground and slaughtered. Once more, with disgust, I stepped over the spilled blood.

The third lamb was close to the entrance of my home, and I was able to enter into the familiar courtyard before the last act took place. After my time abroad, I was appalled at the brutality of this custom, but I had had no choice but to watch. This was a large gathering, and there had to be enough food for everyone in the welcoming party. This coupled with the food that I knew would be donated to the local mosque required the meat of all three lambs.

With the gruesome slaughter behind me, I began to gather my thoughts. The group outside was still viewing the carnage. I turned quickly and found myself near the familiar fountain, with a few short steps I was able to open the door and enter into the great room.

Grandmother was there, sitting in her tapestry chair, water pipe by her side. My heart skipped a beat as she held out her frail hand to grasp my own. My arms were around her in an instant. Without saying a word, we both knew what a special moment it was. Then, quickly she spoke, "Welcome home, Manocher, I have been waiting for you." There were tears in her eyes as there were in mine; the reunion was our own, before the others crowded in the door to celebrate.

As soon as I was seated in the familiar warmth of Grandmother's house, I asked to see my baby brother Behrouz. Since he had been born while I was at the Academy, I needed an introduction and I was very excited. It was almost dawn when my mother escorted me to his room. He was sleeping peacefully in his crib like a little angel. I could not resist picking Behrouz up and holding him in my arms. My heart was filled with joy as he awakened and my mother asked, "Do you know who this is?" He replied with a sleepy smile, "My brother, Manocher." In my absence my parents had given him my picture and told him that one day I would return and he would need to recognize me as his big brother. I was thrilled that he knew me, and for the next forty-eight hours, to make up for lost time, he remained on my lap.

I was touched with the feelings of love from a family that gave me such support. Life was so sweet. As I looked around the house, there were more flowers and presents than I could count. My younger brother Ira's embrace was warm and welcoming. We could not laugh enough or talk enough. My mother continued to give me loving hugs, while presenting a constant array of delicious Persian food and pastry. Aunt Maheen enjoyed the night's festivities. Her little golden dish was once again filled with the plumpest of pistachios. Conversation lasted throughout the night and into the next day. The warmth and enjoyment of home as well as a sense of belonging had never been so comforting.

Home in Iran

For two weeks after my return, guests poured into Grandmother's house to visit, enjoying succulent fruits and pastry. To this day, I can think of nothing more fragrant than the scent of freshly harvested Persian fruits mixed with pistachios. As I greeted the guests, my baby brother was always close by my side. I often thought to myself, "How could life be better?" but still, despite the joyous reunion and the warmth I felt in my heart, I did have some difficulty adjusting. I was once more forced to blend the background of two cultures and find my place in the world. I craved the steaming café latte served on a white tablecloth and the red wine during dinner. I missed all that I had left behind as much as I was enjoying all that had been waiting for me at home.

As I readjusted to my relatives and life in Iran, I started to notice some social and spiritual differences. One relative would say, "Enshallah, if Allah is willing, we will have rain," and another might comment, "Enshallah, if Allah helps me to prosper I will give the mosque more money." I was not sure if the reliance on the "Enshallah, the Will of Allah" had always been so prevalent in my family's daily conversation or if things had changed in my absence to make me more aware of it.

Either way, I was not used to hearing this type of rhetoric. I tried to justify my observations to myself, by concluding that I was just noticing the vast differences between the Catholic and the Muslim religions. I knew that I had been fortunate to experience another life and a different culture. I had returned to Iran with the ability to understand the convictions of others that might not always be my own.

It seemed to me that perhaps I had stepped out of another place in time. Even the beautiful new car and natty tweed jacket my father presented to me could not stop me from evaluating my life, my country, and wondering what mountains I would be forced to climb. I welcomed responsibility, and I was confident that I could make a mark in the world. I had never been more aware of my fifth-generation Persian heritage and wanted to learn more about that culture as well as every aspect of current life and politics in the Iran that I had returned to.

Now that I was home, I often sat next to Grandmother, in her paisley chair, as she told me of the ancient Zoroastrian religion that dated back before Christianity and was part of our family's ancestral heritage. Our origins had come from the city of Yazd, the second most ancient and historic city in the world. Because of generations of adaptations to its desert surroundings, Yazd remained an architecturally unique city, as well as pure through the generations in their beliefs in a transcendental God named "Ahura Mazda," meaning supreme wisdom. It seemed some of our family migrated to the south of Tehran, accepting Islam, while others remained in Yazd, when Umar, Mohammad's father-in-law, conquered Persia by killing those who did not want to believe in bringing Allah and the Koran into their lives as the ultimate power. It was amazing for me to realize that the vast Persian Empire, larger than that of the Roman Empire, could have been overcome by small armies. These incensed groups of Mohammad's followers, created an environment of fear and horror, and through lust and killing, persevered with their barbaric dedication to bring to Persia their beliefs in the Koran as well as the last prophet, Mohammad.

After living in Italy and experiencing my Italian friends' reverence for their religion, it was comforting for me to know of my own religious roots. Once again, education was my quest, and expanding my thinking allowed me to make thoughtful decisions about how I wanted to live my life.

The SAVAK

As I became familiar with the changes that had taken place in Iran since I had been away, I learned that in 1957 the SAVAK was established with help from American and Israeli advisors. The agency was closely molded after the CIA in the United States. It was fashioned to place opponents of the Shah's regime under surveillance and to repress the movements of dissidents. The SAVAK served to monitor potential threats to the monarchy and to respond accordingly. For their part, my friends and family took the SAVAK in stride. They felt it was there to protect the country from Islamic Marxist communists, and it did not play a role in their daily life.

The Mullahs, however, did not welcome the addition of the SAVAK, as many of their extremist supporters were seen as dissidents. The Mullahs had not been happy since the Reza Shah had come into power in 1925. His interest in acquiring industrial technology, building an army, and becoming more westernized went against their desires to turn the country back 1,300 years to the days of the last prophet. In 1960, the streets bore evidence that the Mullahs were not succeeding. In the evenings, walking through the elegant districts of Tehran, it was visible that the European dress was very popular, and not every woman wore the chador. Elegant coffee salons were filled with both men and women, sitting together, enjoying "Café Glace." My own favorite at the time was Chatanoga. They were famous for their ambiance and the presentation of their mouth-watering desserts served in tall stemmed glassware. There was a sense of freedom and frivolity, especially among the younger women.

However, in addition to the Mullahs, there were many who found reason to criticize the monarchy and their obsession with their need for a lavish life style. There were some within the royal family who took advantage of their close proximity to the king and did not have enough compassion for those who struggled to survive. I, personally, disregarded the elite, as well as the outspoken religious groups. Both spent their time criticizing. It seemed absurd to think that the radical Mullahs would be better at ruling the country than the government that we had at the time. My concentration was, instead, on my deepest passion: to bring our third world country into the twentieth century.

Chapter 4

Artworks of Master Mamoud Farshchian

A Fledgling Career

Persian Gulf Assignment

In the spring of 1960, once again, I said my goodbyes to my family. I reported to Naval Headquarters wearing my brand-new summer white uniform. My shoes were so polished they looked like mirrors. The gold stripe on my shoulder had not had time to tarnish. I was very proud, and I am sure that everyone who looked at me knew that I was a fresh new graduate.

The MP at the entrance of the naval building escorted me to the third-floor personnel office. As soon as I opened the door, I recognized the same tall officer who had interviewed me when I was selected to go to Livorno. He was now an admiral with a little grey at his temples, and he was again very cordial towards me. "Welcome back," he said. I saluted him the way I had learned in the Italian Naval Academy.

He smiled and we shook hands. It was nice to see him again. After our hellos, he escorted me to another office where there were a few enlisted men sitting by typewriters. My first assignment was to summarize my education. The admiral instructed the typists to help me draft my educational resume. This document was to serve as my entry report for the Navy. I was told to describe my four and a half years at the Academy in just two short pages. With some difficulty, I dictated my report. After stopping and starting several times, my assistants and I completed the form, and I returned to the admiral's desk.

When I turned in my educational biography, I received orders for transfer to the south of Iran. The Naval base that would be my new home was called Khorramshahr. It was located in the Kuzestan Province, situated at the confluence of the Karoon River and the Shatt al Arab River, near the Persian Gulf. Due to its prime location on the local waterways and its access to the Gulf, all of the products imported into Iran came through this port. This, coupled with the fact that Khorramshahr was only forty kilometers from Abadan, where the Iranian oil refinery, the largest refinery in the world, was located, made it a very busy harbor.

Upon my arrival in Khorramshahr, I realized that I had been spoiled by the balmy climate of the Italian coast. I soon learned that the south of Iran was plagued by the thick, sticky atmosphere of hot and humid weather, often resulting in a work day that reached temperatures in excess of 110 degrees. In the summer months, the heat forced us to sacrifice the formality of our uniforms in exchange for cool shorts, which made the oppressive heat somewhat more bearable. The fear of heatstroke and dehydration was also a concern, so our rations always included salt tablets.

My assignment in Khorramshahr was the post of chief engineer on the Imperial Iranian Ship, IIS *Mehran*, a slightly smaller ship than the PT 109 John F. Kennedy commanded during his time in the American Navy. As I tried to familiarize myself with the equipment on my new ship, I was dismayed to find all the technical manuals were in English, a language I had not as yet mastered. In Khorramshahr, the British influence from the days of the oil lease was still very prevalent, and I was forced to quickly learn the British pound and inch system. I immediately felt the pressure to perform as a leader, and I knew I had to educate myself on the British system as well as all of the other operational equipment on the ship.

There were only a few petty officers on board, and I thought that they were not experienced enough to take over my role, if there were any problems. Much to my dismay, after only two days, as I struggled to convert my metric thoughts into the pound and inch system, we were ordered to leave the port to take food and medicine to Khark Island. This was a small, thirteen-square-mile island, located in the Persian Gulf, 16 miles off of the coast of Iran and 300 miles north of the Strait of Hormuz. The Iranian government had planned to convert Khark Island into the largest off-shore crude oil terminal in the world. The project at the time was under construction.

Preceding my maiden voyage on the IIS *Mehran*, it was necessary to meet the ship's captain. The captain was about three years older than I and held the rank of junior lieutenant. He introduced himself as Shoa Majidi. He was a tall, slender man with a distinguished appearance. When he told me he had also graduated from the Italian Naval Academy, I was excited to know that we shared a common background. I immediately hoped that we would find friendship and share nostalgia about our previous experiences. This was my first night on the Iranian ship, and I was a fledgling officer looking for direction. When I introduced myself, I knew from the first moment that my hopes of friendship were misplaced. The captain looked at me coldly, contorting his features in distaste. After a brief glance, he turned his back and arrogantly ordered, "Always have the engines started in time for departure and be sure to have enough fuel and water on board at all times." He proceeded to ignore me until I left the room.

After this experience, I was concerned and apprehensive as we headed out on that first supply run to Khark Island. I knew that in order for our ship to depart, aside from fueling the tanks and obtaining fresh water, we had to disconnect from the city electricity. The port and the piers that we had to use were not equipped with electricity, water, or fuel. After the tankers came to fuel up the ship and provide water, we had to deal with the electricity. The electricity was a tricky task because of the primitive setup on the docks. The port was not equipped to supply the appropriate electricity for our ship. Instead of just plugging in, we had to use wires to rig the lights on the IIS *Mehran,* which operated on 115 volts, to the city electricity, which provided 220 volts. Once all of these preparations were complete, it was time to start the ship's engines.

I paced the deck to calm my jangled nerves. A plethora of frightening thoughts ran through my mind: "What if we had an emergency? What if we could not make it to Khark Island? What if I forget to perform one of my duties?" Just as I began to quicken my breath, the ship's chief petty officer approached me. I fired technical questions in half Farsi and half Italian at the young man.

In response to my nervous inquiries, with all of the kindness that the captain lacked, the chief petty officer smiled and said, "Sir, when the time comes you just give us the order to start the engines, and we will manage the rest. We know how to do it; we have done it all before." His calm and confident voice made the helpful young man my self-assured savior on my first short voyage to Khark Island. I took advantage of his knowledge, and after issuing the orders, I followed the chief petty officer to the engine room where I observed, firsthand, the inner workings of the IIS *Mehran.* This practical experience was far more valuable than the stacks of thick manuals I had spent my first few days poring over.

When I heard the engines turn over and we finally got under way, I breathed a sigh of relief as we peacefully navigated through the shallow waters of the Shatt al Arab River. At some of the river bends, the shoreline was only a few hundred feet wide between Iran and Iraq. On both sides there was bare land and a few dust-covered palm trees. In contrast to the clear blue of the Mediterranean Sea that I had enjoyed while sailing the Italian vessels, the water of the river was murky and muddy. We were close to Khark Island before the sea began to churn and clear in the currents of the Gulf.

As we approached the island, the waters began to rock the ship, and the winds gusting over the flat arid land picked up speed. The jetty had not yet been built to accommodate docking our vessel, so we anchored a few yards out from the shoreline and signaled the island. In response, a dingy with an outboard motor pulled a flat-bottom utility barge out to our location. The small engineless ship was attached to a rope on shore. We unloaded our supplies onto the barge and then the men onboard the ship signaled to be hauled in. Unfortunately, the wind rushing over the treeless bleak topography of Khark Island made it impossible for the rope tow to reel in the small barge.

The captain attempted to step in and adjust the delivery by attaching the rope onto the rail of the IIS *Mehran* and towing the flat-bottom barge to the opposite side of the island. The goal was to use the wind to

parlay it to the shore. I knew as an engineer that this was a risky plan, but I also realized that my commanding officer would not take kindly to my suggestions. Apparently, the captain failed to take into account that the wind created long rolling waves in the Gulf. When we released the barge into open water, the sea jostled it until it caught the starboard edge and quickly sank under the turbulent waters. The passengers were hurled into the sea and several months' worth of valuable supplies and medicines were lost.

After the first ill-fated voyage and my meeting with the chief petty officer I began to understand my leadership role as a ranking official. The vast majority of the ship's crew members were my age or younger and they were looking up to me for the guidance my rank required. Most of the young enlisted men were from the south of Iran, a mixture of both Shiat and Sunni, who spoke either Farsi or Arabic. It was very difficult for the men and I to communicate with each other about the ships business as there was not an Iranian language that contained marine terminology. It took time and patience to be able to communicate among ourselves and become productive.

The frustrations of my first assignment weighed heavily on me. I had different expectations of the Iranian Navy. I graduated from the Italian Naval Academy thinking that there would always be an organized engineering chain of command, and I would be able to learn more from my superiors. Now there was no one to ask technical questions. I envisioned that within my own engineering field I would shine and have the opportunity to be a problem solver and logically be able to climb any hurdle that confronted me. I liked organization and enjoyed hard work, but for the first time I was questioning my decision to have a Naval career.

Should I have chosen a profession where I could have moved forward without the confinements of the military chain of command? At a time like this, without any leadership to turn to, I wondered if it would be proper protocol to take the authority to try to solve problems, on my own, that needed attention in order for the ship to function.

I was disturbed about the situation I found myself in, and at night as I lay alone on my bunk, these few words came to my mind. Somehow to me it was comforting to put my thoughts into poetry:

I thought
If I opened my wings I could fly away from these abandoned lands.
I could flap my wings and go high, over the summit of the mountains.
Circle like an eagle and feel the warmth of the sun.
But when I opened my wings, my cage was my flying space.

I thought
If I opened my mouth to sing, it would resonate loud and high.
The ears of the heavenly sphere would become deaf.
I would perform a miracle and sound better than a well-beaten drum.
But when I opened my mouth, my song was my breath.

I sit in a dark corner and I cry.
This is killing me.
I don't know at this time and in this place
What I am tied to and who I am hindered by.

Gradually, I began to accept the fact that it was up to me to grasp my desire for organization and efficiency on the ship. I realized that I would have to make the necessary decisions. The majority of work that was going on in this part of the world was new and challenging for everyone. In order to shine, I had to take charge and create my own order.

As time passed, I became accustomed to my environment and my leadership role. I was pleased to finally become acquainted with my captain and his family. We warmed to each other when we played poker with our fellow officers stationed in Khorramshahr. The captain and his Italian wife frequently invited me to their home for some of her delicious pasta.

Although friendship developed, I noticed, almost immediately, that the captain made a constant effort to solicit the attention of all the officers who held more important positions than his own. He frequently wrote articles praising the Shah, and he strove to be acknowledged as one of the inner circle of officers close to the regime. In spite of his obvious need for attention and his dismissive attitude towards those who ranked below him, eventually we became friends. However, even then I had an ominous feeling about his allegiances to his fellow officers and to Iran. Later during the revolution, we were all shocked, but not really surprised, to learn that the captain had been secretly working for the Muslim Fundamentalists and had been helping to bring Khomeini to power. The captain's betrayal of his country, the Navy, and all of his friends fit perfectly with his personality. However, it was still shocking to all of those, like myself, who had served by his side with a certain camaraderie.

Khark Island Assignment

During that first year of supply runs to Khark Island, I was able to gain confidence in my leadership role. As time passed, the beginning of the second year was marked by transfer orders. I was sent to the American-built minesweeper *Shahbaz* as assistant chief engineer. The ship was also based in Khorramshahr. Our assignment was to cruise through the Persian Gulf to Karachi, Pakistan. Once we arrived in Karachi, we were the representatives of the Iranian Navy in the CENTO maneuvers.

CENTO was the organization formed between Turkey, Iran, the United Kingdom, Pakistan, and, for a brief stint, Iraq. The goal of CENTO was to provide military containment in the Persian Gulf, as well as to act as a buffer against Soviet Union aggression. This organization was modeled after NATO and was kept in place until the Iranian revolution in 1979. Despite its twenty-four-year reign, CENTO did not accomplish much more than a few joint military maneuvers and was seen as the least successful of all the Cold War alliances.

Once a year, the United States joined the CENTO organization for maneuvers in the Persian Gulf and the Sea of Oman. After participating in a few of these joint maneuvers on the *Shahbaz*, I was promoted to chief engineer of the minesweeper. In my new position, I was fully responsible for all the technical operations of the ship.

My fellow officers and I decided before returning to Khorramshahr we would celebrate my advancement by enjoying an evening in Pakistan. I was happy and carefree as we disembarked in Karachi. Everyone knew that when the Iranian ships were in the harbor, the officers were treated like kings, because there was always an abundance of money in their pockets. This evening was no exception.

As we walked the crowded streets of Karachi, dogging passenger-laden rickshaws, we tried to decide what restaurant would satisfy our taste. There were multiple small cafés, interspersed between a variety of busy shops selling silver, incense, and cloth of every color. Small braziers displayed roasting lamb, vegetables, and copper plates filled with Kuftah. All were placed out in front of the many eating establishments to entice the customer to come in, sit down, and enjoy.

We were drawn to our dining spot by the sight of golden chickens, roasting on a spit. Dressed in our white uniforms, we must have impressed the host. He immediately seated us in the inside dining room. I smiled, as I viewed the tables covered with starched white cloths. For a moment, I was remembering the Academy.

Our waiter hurriedly approached us, our status clear to him. After a brief wink and a nod from the host, he asked us for our order. We inquired about the house specialty and he seemed pleased as he responded, "Chicken Tikka." We looked at each other and nodding, we agreed, "Chicken Tikka" all around!

A few moments later, three waiters carrying large round trays on their heads proudly placed the specialty dish, along with bowls of steaming saffron rice, on our table. We began our meal and, together grasping for breath; we stood up and reached for water. The fire in our throats was unbearable. In the background, the cha-cha was playing and our jumping was in synch with the music. Nothing seemed to subdue the burning in our mouths and nostrils. We motioned to the waiter, and when we could finally speak, we asked him what was in the chicken. Displaying gold teeth, he smiled, and explained that the chicken was soaked overnight in red Savina, the hottest pepper in Indian cuisine. When we gained our composure, we graciously paid the bill and quickly left to find less exotic fare.

Later in the evening, we felt the need for more palatable food and decided to try the Metropolitan Hotel. It was the most elegant establishment in Karachi and also known for its well-recognized Western entertainment. Heads turned as we entered through a lush garden into the large foyer. Our uniforms drew the attention of the patrons who were seated around the room. They looked up and tilted their heads in quizzical inquiry. My gaze trailed across the dance floor into the eyes of a lovely young Pakistani girl in a soft pink sari. I looked away before her stare registered, and when I turned around, she was gone. We immediately tipped our way to the best set of tables in the house.

Once seated with my fellow officers, I looked up and again saw the young girl in the pink sari listening to the music from the doorway. I recognized the renewed opportunity, and I gathered myself. Rising from my seat, with encouragement from my colleagues, I walked across the room, bowed in front of her, held out my hand, and invited her to accompany me onto the dance floor. She was shy as she looked up at me. After a long moment of hesitation, she finally smiled, put her delicate hand in mine, and said, "Thank you, I would be delighted." We waltzed through several songs. Her English was impeccable, and her name was Princess Sahira. I learned that her love for Persian poetry equaled my own. We danced for the rest of the evening, until our celebration came to an end, and I had to kiss her hand in parting before returning to the ship.

In the months to come, Karachi became, for me, a very special port. Over the course of the next year, Sahira was my regular dance partner at the Metropolitan. We had a wonderful time together until my military obligations drew me away to other ports in the Persian Gulf. For a while, we enjoyed exchanging letters, but our lives were busy. Her studies occupied her time, and my own challenges seemed to consume me. Sadly, our correspondence to each other became less frequent, and our paths did not cross again. I often wonder if she still has tea at the Metropolitan hotel and remembers the love and respect we had for each other so many years ago.

After two years in the Gulf, on the *Mehran* and the *Shahbaz*, in 1963, I was given the opportunity to become the chief engineer of Khark Island. This was a fast-paced position that required working from sun-up to sundown.

The Early Days of Khark Island

There were always many unforeseeable problems that were challenging and required immediate solutions. As chief engineer, I was placed in charge of supervising several projects, including overseeing all naval developments.

There was a master plan in place to bring crude oil, via pipeline, from several locations on Iran's mainland to the small village of Gachsaran. From Gachsaran, which housed the main pumping station for all of the Iranian crude oil, the oil was pumped out to holding tanks on Khark Island. The oil travelled from a high point on the mainland to the island in pipelines that followed along the sea floor. From the sea floor, the pipeline went to the highest elevation on Khark Island. At this elevation there were huge tanks filled with crude oil. This layout enabled the super tankers to anchor a long distance from the shore. The natural topography and the difference of elevations between the mainland and the island were used in the transfer of oil. The super tankers were able to fill millions of barrels of crude oil, in a few short hours, while anchored at sea, via flexible pipes. This project was a multinational contract. Even the American contractors were involved. They were in charge of building the Khark Island main jetty that extended out into the sea, where the smaller ships could dock.

In order to begin my assignment on Khark Island I boarded the *Shahbaz*, not as the chief engineer but as a first-class passenger. Just as on the supply runs on the *Mehran*, the *Shahbaz* anchored a few yards offshore, and I was met by men in a motor boat. In my uniform attire, I stepped into the dingy and we made our way to shore. With the favorable winds we landed in a few short minutes.

Once on the island, I was greeted by Lieutenant Movaghari, the Commander of Naval Operations for Khark Island. He greeted me with a smile and a firm handshake. His affable nature and deep gravelly voice exuded self-assurance and comfort. I sighed in relief when I met him. I was having flashbacks of my ill-fated meeting with the captain of the *Mehran*, Lieutenant Majidi. After our hellos, he picked up my suitcase and tossed it into the back of his Jeep and invited me to join him for a tour, saying, "I want to show you the beauty of the island."

I was doubtful as to what we would find on this dusty barren stretch of land, but I was eager to go with him and familiarize myself with my new surroundings. Our first stop was the highest point on the island, where stadium-sized oil storage tanks were under construction.

We walked over and stood in the center of one of the tanks. I was mesmerized by the sheer size of the structure. It was an incredible sight. I immediately grasped the importance of the exciting infrastructure we were viewing and how important this project was going to ultimately be for the country. This was truly the beauty that Lieutenant Movaghari wanted me to see.

The tour continued with a drive to the National Iranian Oil Company housing facility and residence club, with its few amenities, including a billiard room, theater, and restaurant. I was pleased to hear that the club was air-conditioned and was also available for the Naval officers' enjoyment.

Next we followed the only road to the other side of the island, where we viewed the sad makeshift village that housed the local inhabitants. Their primitive buildings were without water or electricity. Men and children were the only visible islanders. Most of them were wearing the local attire, wrapping large shawls around their heads. In the open-air Jeep, I could hear their conversations as we passed by. They seemed to be speaking fluently in Arabic with a smattering of Farsi. The lieutenant related to me that we were lucky to hear them conversing because thus far they had refrained from communicating with any of the Naval personnel.

As we drove on, we caught a glimpse of some of the women and children cooking along the side of their rudimentary dwellings. I soon learned that women were seldom seen outside their home. In the center of the village, we passed a few poorly constructed stores that appeared to be stocked with basic supplies. Along our route, we also encountered some handmade wooden boats filled with patched fishing nets. Beside the craft, their inhabitants were sitting idle on the ground, legs crossed, hands clasped around their knees, gazing out to sea.

I could understand being mesmerized by the motion of the waves, but not to be so absorbed by their rise and fall that the good fishing weather we were experiencing would be ignored. The lieutenant explained to me that this was the way their days were structured, hour after hour without any productivity.

After we made our way through the rough terrain around the village, we came to our final stop on the tour, the Naval base. The base was empty land with three large trees in the center. In one of the far corners, there was a small jetty that looked to me as if it was under the first phase of construction. Scattered around the center trees were eight small homes in various stages of assembly, with a partially completed officer's club. I was shocked to find that there was not any completed housing. The lieutenant seemed to sense my surprise. He took my bag from the back of the Jeep and told me that tonight we would sleep in the open under the trees, where he had placed two cots, side by side in the center of the base, while saying, "I do not want to impose on NIOC for lodging. This is our space; we are sailors."

Despite the unbearable heat that the region was known for, I tried to make the best of my new home. Of course I also began making mental lists of necessities and a plan to rush the housing construction. That night I fell asleep under the stars. The ocean breeze had picked up, and the temperature was actually pleasant. We slept peacefully in the open until shortly before dawn, when we came under attack by large mosquitoes and other insects.

Early the next morning, I started my first day with an urgent meeting with the housing construction crews. We managed to work together and complete the first home within two weeks. We continued to work feverishly, and the remainder of the housing and officer's club was finished in short duration. This accomplishment brought further relief to our rather primitive first days on the island, and allowed me to turn my focus to the construction of the jetty and the other required naval facilities.

By the time the housing was finished, we were joined by several other officers. This was not a social time for me. My days involved long hours of hard work and were followed by an evening meal at the NIOC club. The chilled icy beer was always a welcome refresher. At night my only desire was to retire to bed early, where I immediately fell asleep.

Once the Naval base was functioning, the lieutenant brought his wife and four-year-old son to live in one of the new brick, air-conditioned homes. Occasionally, I found time in my busy schedule to stop by for afternoon tea or a pleasant evening meal. This was my only social life on the island, and I truly enjoyed seeing the lieutenant's rambunctious little boy and exchanging conversation with his petite, soft-spoken wife, Ana. She was a brave woman to bring her son to this primitive spot, and I admired the support she gave her husband. She was the first Navy wife on the island.

I was surprised to find that the majority of the local populace was very isolated. There was no means of communication with the outside world. Even the Navy lacked sophistication. We were using Morse code to keep in touch with the Khorramshahr Naval Base. The NIOC was slightly more advanced, as they used shortwave radio to stay in contact with the Abadan Oil Refinery. The only information from the mainland was received via radio. On the radio, we could pick up signals from the surrounding Arab countries to listen to the news and music. With luck, occasionally, we were able to hear Radio Tehran and the one station that was always available in English, the BBC.

In addition to the Navy's influence, the villagers were directed by the local Mullah. He was the spiritual leader and sometimes the judge. The Mullah was given a primitive house and a mosque. The people gathered around him to learn and receive direction. It was an honor for them to be able to offer their young teenage daughters to this man. Bringing the Mullah into their families gave them a sense of pride. A gift of money to the mosque could supposedly make their problems disappear, bringing happiness instead of sorrow. A few of the Mullahs were educated, and I later learned that they had come to the islands as a part of the Islamic Universal Networking System within Iran and abroad. This system was later used to spread messages from Ayatollah Khomeini.

In addition to my engineering responsibilities on Khark Island, I was also expected to visit other islands in the Persian Gulf. They were sparsely populated and inhabited by the same type of primitive people. One afternoon, a few of us were exploring Abu Musa Island, where we had to sail by rubber boat because there were not any jetties. We encountered a band of young children. They were completely naked, and when they saw me they looked horror-stricken and ran away in fright. My fellow senior officer said, "Manocher, take off your dark glasses. I think they are afraid of them."

Obviously, he was right because after removing my glasses, the children came back and stared at us with curiosity. I often wondered how this area had escaped any of the cultural advances of a 2,500-year-old Persian civilization. The primitive way these people were living without sanitary conditions or electricity was a noticeable contrast to the minimal sophistication of the project that I was witnessing. Khark Island was an ambitious program that I knew would bring a great deal of wealth to my country. Pipelines were being built to transfer inland fuel from Iran to the middle of the sea in a very short period of time, eliminating the need for a ship to come into the harbor. The engineering of this project was impressive.

National Iranian Oil Company and Sheik Abdullah

As chief engineer, I was in charge of supervising the installation of two diesel generators. This meant installing huge generators with a variety of unsophisticated tools and any unskilled personnel that I could find as crew. In spite of our lack of perfect tools and experienced help, we managed to complete our installation. Once the job was accomplished, it marked the end of the majority of my hands-on engineering work. My job then progressed into an administrative role that involved managing the development of the base and coordinating the off-loading of construction materials used by the Navy and the NIOC.

The NIOC and the Navy were working together to complete projects on the island, with the goal of starting operations as soon as possible. Each participant had various commitments in order to facilitate this goal. One of the responsibilities of the oil company was to provide a permanent source of water and electricity for the Naval base. This meant that the generators I had previously maneuvered into place were only a temporary power source. In order to facilitate the continuing projects on the island, the oil company shipped in barges of construction materials. I was the liaison between the contractors, the NIOC, and the local inhabitants to find the numerous, unskilled laborers who were needed to carry the heavy construction material, on their backs and shoulders, to the construction site.

I went to the village to search for men to unload the barges. I decided to look to the man who was responsible for building and managing the village stores. He was, in my estimation, the head of the community. The village leader was known as Sheik Abdullah.

I found the Sheik on my first visit to the village. As we sat together during our meeting, I noticed that he was a few years older than I. His dark hair and beard were neatly trimmed. He was dressed in the traditional white robes of the region, and the handsome gold ring with amber stone that he wore on his pinky finger gave him of certain flamboyance as well as the image of status. I was immediately impressed with his calm, self-assured demeanor and his willingness to listen. As I explained to him my need for laborers, he was very obliging and shook my hand, saying that everything would be taken care of and he would be delighted to work with me. I left with the arrangements for the workers in place and the confident feeling of friendship at my side.

The Sheik and I developed a good relationship and respect for one another. We spoke mainly about work, and he always rounded up the men that we needed. He was compensated by the American contractors in cash, in the Iranian Rial. He then paid the laborers what he thought would be appropriate.

At the beginning of the project, there were only a few hundred local inhabitants, but by the end of the year, people were coming in boats from surrounding areas, increasing the population to over1,000. The village expanded to include a bank and a small bazaar with lots of merchandise that was brought in from Kuwait, Bahrain, or the mainland of Iran. The local people were now using English words mixed with Farsi or Arabic. The work days were long but the villagers were happy. They were making money thanks to my coordinated efforts between Sheik Abdullah and the American contractors. I was always eager to advance the project, and in my mind, I knew that the more laborers I found, the sooner construction would be completed.

As our friendship grew by virtue of our business partnership, it was my pleasure to invite Sheik Abdullah to the Naval base officer's club for afternoon tea. He always accepted and enjoyed being with me, although I knew that he felt uncomfortable around the other officers.

One morning I went to see him to ask for another favor, and I noticed that he appeared unhappy. He seemed to be a different person. I immediately asked him what the problem was. He bowed his head and started to weep saying, "God's grace is not with my family. God is taking away my son." After questioning him, I learned that his son was ill and in terrible pain. I felt extremely sad. My heart went out to this humble man, and I knew that I had to help him. I jumped in my Jeep and rushed to the National Iranian Oil Company. I hurriedly found the director of the medical facility, and I told him about the young boy who was in pain. He responded by telling me that he did not have the authority to treat anyone other than the personnel of the oil company. I was shocked at his callous response to this young boy's pain. Finally, after insisting that the Sheik was the key figure on the island to facilitate the crucial labor for our project, the director agreed to send a message to Abadan Headquarters for permission. I left with a terrible and helpless feeling. I was worried that the child would die before I could get help.

Defeated, I drove back to the base. As I was passing the jetty, I noticed that a civilian helicopter was landing. Hope renewed, I drove as quickly as I could to the plane. The pilot was a young Italian. "What luck?" I thought. I told the pilot, in Italian, that we had an emergency on the island. I asked him to fly Sheik Abdullah and his son to the hospital on the mainland. He immediately agreed. I raced back in my Jeep, picked up my friend and his pale sick twelve-year-old son, and drove them back to the helicopter. The Italian stood true to his word and loaded them into the chopper. After a few short moments, they were in the air.

I later learned that after a quick flight, the Sheik and his son arrived at the mainland hospital. The timing had been crucial, because the boy had been suffering from appendicitis. Immediately, after landing he was taken into the hospital for emergency surgery. Fortunately, after the operation was performed, he was given a clean bill of health.

A few weeks later, the Sheik and his son returned by boat to the island. The Sheik came to see me and immediately gave me a hug, while kissing both my cheeks and right shoulder. He quickly said, "I am thankful to God for bringing you to the island in order to save my son." I was grateful myself. I had grown to care for the Sheik and his family.

It was an emotional moment for both of us, and from this experience we developed a deep friendship.

The Presentation of Khark Island to the Shah

As the Khark Island project reached completion, we knew that the Navy and the NIOC would be inviting the Shah to come for the inauguration of the base and the pipeline. My Naval group decided that before the Shah's arrival, we should make use of our two unused generators and spruce up the native village. Our idea was to help them receive electricity and, at the same time, impress the Shah.

We asked the American contractors to donate thirty poles that were left in their scrap yard. They readily agreed, and we started to place the poles, linking them to the large generators. By working many long hours, we managed to fashion a power source to carry electricity for the local villagers to enjoy. We were thrilled when we turned on the switch for the first time, lighting up their dark narrow alleyways. By the time the whole project was completed, we had cleaned, painted, and planted artificial trees in 110 degree heat, while working feverishly to provide a beautiful presentation for the Shah.

On the day the Shah arrived, the island was in perfect condition. He had several questions regarding the expansion of the Naval base and plans for the upkeep. The answer from the commanding officer was, "Yes, your majesty, we have all the plans in place, and it will be maintained as you witness it today." Several NIOC executives and a few Americans were lined up to inaugurate the pipeline. The Shah shook hands with everyone, asking what their role had been. He was very pleased with the project and seemed at ease and quite comfortable around us.

I hoped that my friend, Sheik Abdullah, was nearby to see the Imperial entourage. After all, the Sheik had gathered all of the laborers to work on this massive development, and it could not have been completed without his help. I also hoped that the Shah would visit the village and see the electrical poles that brought light to the island's inhabitants.

At that time, several million barrels of crude oil were passing through the island, bringing great wealth to the country, while these inhabitants had barely enough fresh water to survive. Unfortunately, the Shah did not attempt to drive to the center of island to observe how the people lived in misery. Later, we speculated that perhaps those who surrounded him did not want him to see the reality of how some were forced to live. Perhaps they felt it would make him feel uncomfortable to come out of the world of the **Masters** into the world of the **Peasants**. These were a few of the mistakes that probably, unintentionally, discredited the monarchy and caused the king's demise. This separation from reality saddened me.

After the inauguration, I received new orders to leave Khark Island. The news brought with it the knowledge that I would have to leave my friends and my home. When I told Sheik Abdullah about my next assignment, he wanted to give me a farewell party and asked me to seek permission for him to arrange a going-away celebration at the officer's club. I was flattered and surprised. There had been times when he felt ill at ease in this facility. Now he was excited about giving me a proper send-off.

He invited a few elders from the village as well as their Mullah. He and the Navy cook enjoyed planning the affair. They roasted a complete lamb. The meal was festive but the special part of the luncheon was when the cook filled the first plate with meat and rice, and Sheik Abdullah's son brought it to me. Bowing down, he said, "Thank you," and immediately the Mullah said, "Allah o Akbar!" Everyone repeated loudly, "*God is great!*"

My affiliation with Sheik Abdullah influenced my life. We trusted each other's word and, although our life styles were completely different, we had respect for one another. I was a young bachelor, and the Sheik was living with two wives simultaneously. He was religious and bowed in prayer to Mecca five times a day. I only occasionally still bowed to Mecca. I knew that Islam considered it a sin to shave, and yet I preferred to shave every morning while the Sheik's beard grew. Yet despite all the noticeable differences, we were friends. There were occasions when I was forced to visit his home in the middle of the night to seek more laborers. When he greeted me, he would respond graciously, saying,

"Enshallah, if God is willing we will have men for you." He always kept his commitment. I left Khark Island with many wonderful memories of what had been accomplished in a relatively short period of time.

It was now 1964, and I received orders to fly to Houston in the United States to oversee the construction of a new class of frigate being built in Orange, Texas. I had only been residing in America for a few weeks, when one evening I retired early and was suddenly awakened by a very vivid dream. When I relive this event, it still seems amazing to me, but in many ways also comforting.

In my dream, I was envisioning that I was in a very large room standing on a Persian carpet holding my grandmother's hand. Each of our free hands was grasped by the dark image of a man whose clouded face was one whom I remembered from years ago. He had been gone for a very long time. Glass windows circled the room, but only one was open. The three of us were happy as we danced several times around the carpet. Suddenly, the dark figure released my hand and flew through the open window, pulling Grandmother forcefully with him. As she began to rise, I tried with all of my own strength to hold on to her, but to no avail. She broke away quickly, peacefully floating out of the window into the black of night.

The following morning, I called Tehran and sadly learned that Grandmother had passed away. As I sat and contemplated, I was touched to have experienced a form of spirituality and an amazing connection with someone I had loved.

Upon completion and receiving the ship *Bayandor* from the United States Navy, my position became assistant chief engineer. We sailed back across the Atlantic, through the Strait of Gibraltar, the Mediterranean Sea, the Suez Canal, and ultimately to Abadan in the Persian Gulf. A few months after our arrival, I was promoted to the chief engineer position of the *Bayandor*. In that capacity, I served for three years, and during that time, I had the privilege of having the Shah on my ship, for its inauguration, and a three-hour cruise through the Shat-ol-Arab, dividing Iran and Iraq.

My new assignment allowed me to renew friendships I had known prior to Khark Island. My first commanding officer, Majidi, was now lieutenant in charge of a large battleship. Movaghari, who showed me, "the beauty of Khark Island," was now a lieutenant commander, in charge of a squadron of four minesweepers. Another officer, Lieutenant Commander Madani, who had earlier briefly crossed my path, was now stationed in Bandar Abbas as the base commander. I had often visited his port and offered my engineering skills to help him. Many times, Commander Madani had reciprocated by inviting me to dinner parties at his residence. His guests were usually townspeople who were devout Muslims, as he was.

In his home, I often heard his wife and children speaking from other rooms. I did not ever see them nor did they appear at his evening social events. It was common knowledge that he was not enamored with the monarchy, but in spite of some of our differences, I felt his respect for me, and I considered him a friend.

Upon my return to the Persian Gulf, all of our paths frequently crossed. Later, during the confusing days of the revolution, these three men played a significant role in my life. In my mind, I refer to them as the three M's that marked my destiny.

Getting Married

In 1968, I returned to Tehran on a temporary assignment to complete a manual for the Iranian Navy. It was patterned after the United States Navy's prerequisites for the promotion of enlisted personnel. At the same time in the evenings, I was teaching thermodynamics at the Polytechnic University in Tehran. I enjoyed the exchange with young students. I was young myself and we interfaced well. I also appreciated seeing the respect my Imperial Naval officer's uniform garnered in their eyes.

After a few months of working on the manual and moonlighting at the university, I received new orders. I was notified that I had been selected to attend the United States Naval Postgraduate School in Monterey, California. I was elated to be presented with an opportunity to continue my education. This was both a step in the furtherance of my career and an honor.

I returned to Grandmother's house to share my wonderful news with my family. It was difficult for me, knowing that she would not be there. As I opened the door, I glanced quickly at her empty tapestry chair. I swallowed a few times to keep my composure, as I knew she would have wanted me to do. I thought of my experience with her passing, and yes, my dream had given me comfort, and although it was unexplainable, I knew in my heart that she had been telling me goodbye.

My family was glad to see me and happy about my opportunity to study in America. However, over tea they started to question my single status, especially my mother. "Manocher," she scolded, "if you do not find a nice Persian wife before you leave for America, you will be too old when you return." I was now thirty-two years of age, and although I had had a few sweethearts along the way, I was too busy with my career to think about settling down. I sighed in agreement with my dear mother and smiled as she set about thinking of ways to find a wife for me.

One afternoon my cousin, who I knew had probably been talking to my mother, came to visit me in my office. During the course of our conversation, he suggested that I might enjoy meeting Shauna, a lovely young woman who was the daughter of a very well-respected friend. My cousin's daughter and Shauna were both graduating from the same high school. He thought that we would be a good match and wanted to know if I would accompany his driver to pick up his daughter at their school, where I might also catch a glimpse of the girl in question.

I agreed to the plan, and when the driver and I arrived at the campus, the two students were walking out of the school together. After a great deal of persuasion, Shauna accepted the invitation to be driven home. She slid into the front seat and did not turn to look to the back, where I was seated. I noticed that her hair was long and lovely, and from what I could see, she appeared to be very pretty.

When we arrived at her home, she politely said, "Thank you" and ran quickly to her front door, opening it and entering without looking back at the car. My cousin saw me a few days later and asked, "Well, what did you think?" I told him that I barely saw her. His next comment was, "What are you looking for? Do you want to marry Sophia Loren?" I said, "No," and chuckled. He continued, "Do you want me to arrange for us to have tea at her home?" "Yes!" I responded. "Most definitely."

A few weeks passed before the meeting was arranged. Upon arriving at Shauna's home, we enjoyed having tea with her parents. Unfortunately, she was out on a date. I was disappointed but pleased when she returned home before our departure. Her mother asked her to join us, and I was immediately impressed with her charm. She was wearing a miniskirt and tall black boots. She was very beautiful. I liked the way she presented herself, and I hoped that she felt the same way about me. When it was time to leave, I asked her father for permission to be able to call again. "Of course," he responded, "we would be delighted to have you any time."

When I left, I was elated and honored to have been given the opportunity to return. I quickly arranged for another tea, and after several more meetings, I was thrilled when this special young girl accepted my proposal of marriage.

It was the custom in Iran to seek the approval of the family before wedding plans could proceed. The elder member of the family must interview the prospective groom. I was nervous as my bride-to-be, her parents, and her grandmother travelled with me to the home of her eldest uncle. The family was seated in the living room, and I was ushered into the library, where her uncle asked me to sit on a chair in front of him. After a lengthy conversation, the doors were opened and I was honored when I heard the words, "Congratulations! He has a brain, you have my blessings!"

Custom dictated that the groom was responsible for the wedding expenses. My new in-laws suggested that we keep the ceremony and reception small but elegant. It was collectively determined that our money should be saved and spent for establishing our new household in the United States.

After a short courtship and a wedding of family and close friends, my mother was relieved that I was finally married. I was thirty-two years old, and after all this time, I knew that this was the woman that I had been waiting for. On our special day, Shauna was breathtaking, dressed in a gown of white silk and lace. The couture designer had been called in, bringing the latest book of European designs for her to view. After selecting one of her liking, fabric was flown in from Paris, and the gown that was created perfectly complimented her flawless cream skin and magnificent green eyes. Our cake was not only delicious, with candy nougat filling, but very appropriate. The multiple tiered layers were stacked to represent the decks of a perfect ship. The groom at the top was dressed in Naval attire, and the sugar bride was draped in white. Together we cut our cake, hand over hand, with my Academy sword. Two antique crystal candelabras graced either side of our Sofreh Aghd, lending a soft romantic glow to our ceremony. The evening was a warm and sentimental occasion. Ten days after our wedding, as husband and wife, we left Iran for America.

U.S. Naval Postgraduate School

When I entered graduate school, Richard Nixon was president of the United States, and there was a war in Vietnam. The school I attended was populated with U.S. Naval officers and Marines. It was a highly competitive environment.

The school policy required that any student with less than a B average would be reassigned to a tour of duty in Vietnam. To make matters worse, the four-month-long quarters boasted a curriculum normally reviewed in a six-month semester at other United States universities. Each subject was graded on the bell curve.

Although I was there as an Iranian officer, the B average rule applied to me as well. Instead of going to Vietnam in the event of a below-average GPA, I would be ordered to return to Iran. Even though I felt pressure at the Academy, for the first time in my life I felt the true meaning of competition. My classmates and I studied in excess of fourteen hours a day. I no longer studied diligently out of a love for education. Instead I was forced to learn out of the fear of being asked to leave America, a failure.

Life in school involved only study and research. I can recall those early days of my marriage; whenever my wife and I went out to dinner to celebrate a birthday or special occasion, we were eager to finish and hurry back home to study. We felt that every minute counted and even waiting for our entree to be delivered was a waste of time. I was always afraid that someone else who was studying during this period would be getting ahead of me.

Occasionally, in order to accommodate my beautiful bride, I spent the evening taking her dancing. When we arrived home, it was usually midnight. In order to make up for the missed study time, I sat at my desk, without sleep, until daybreak. I became so tense during finals that I continuously pulled and twisted my hair while studying. Every morning after my lessons were completed, my wife would come to clean the loose hair from my desk. Perhaps it expedited my premature baldness. To say the least, it was a stressful time.

Recalled for Duty

After four years of graduate school, I received orders to return to Iran. I had managed to complete two Bachelor's degrees and a Master's degree in Mechanical Engineering. I was taking more graduate courses and was almost finished with my PhD, but with the change of orders I was forced to stop my education midstride and return to Iran. For my efforts, the Naval Postgraduate School awarded me a special degree in Engineering. The degree was designed to be higher than a Master's degree and just under a PhD.

I was honored on graduation day when the dean informed me that, along with three of my classmates, I was nominated by the Postgraduate School to become a member of Sigma Xi. Sigma Xi was the Scientific Research Society that had fostered more than 200 winners of the Nobel Prize, including Albert Einstein, Enrico Fermi, and James Watson. As I walked down the aisle to be sworn into this very special society, I was surrounded by the school's prestigious professors wearing caps and gowns, with candles in hand. I was overwhelmed and humbled by the beauty and the honor of the occasion.

This was a bittersweet time for me. I was saddened that I could not stay and continue my studies because I was only two quarters away from completing my PhD. I made a formal request to postpone my new orders until my PhD was complete, but the request was denied by the Chief of Naval Operations in Iran. A special project was awaiting my arrival. Although I was disappointed about leaving my education unfinished, I was elated that my wife was pregnant and would soon give birth to our only son, Bob.

Since we had not had the time to experience a real vacation during my four years of schooling, we decided to order a car and drive through Europe to Turkey and then home to Tehran. We were excited when we picked up our brand-new, bright yellow Mustang in La Havre, France. We did not anticipate the commotion that the sunny yellow car would cause as we parked in small villages while travelling across the continent. After a night in a charming inn, we would emerge to find the Mustang surrounded by the townspeople. We laughed a lot and enjoyed our celebrity. The trip was a delight, driving through France, Italy, and Greece.

When we reached Turkey, we were relaxed and comfortable with our new passion for adventure. Our attitude soon changed as the roads grew rough, mountainous, and unpaved. The farther we went, the more uncomfortable we became. We were met by young children who tried to stop our bright yellow car by standing in the center of the street, begging for cigarettes. This quickly brought us out of our relaxed state back to the world of reality.

We were relieved when we passed over the border from Turkey into Iran. The contrast was overwhelming. It was evident that we were home, and our joy had no limits. Fortunately, the trip ended well, and except for one small collision with a bus, the yellow Mustang held its own!

Two months later, our baby boy was born. He was delivered by a female Iranian gynecologist in a private Jewish hospital in Tehran. Later during the revolution, this talented doctor's fingers were cut off by the militants to show their distaste for her involvement with Jews and, of course, to end her career.

Origin of Iranian Nuclear Energy

In 1972, the Iranian media were talking excitedly about many new expansion programs going on in Iran, including nuclear energy. I had been out of the country for more than four years, and it was evident that because of the Khark Island pipeline, the exportation of oil had become a very lucrative business. As a result, the country was rich. I was thrilled to know that this project was flourishing. It gave me a good feeling to have been fortunate enough to be a part of its early development.

It was hard to educate myself on all that was transpiring in my country since I had been away. I knew that in 1957, a small nuclear reactor had been purchased from America for the University of Tehran. Fifteen years later, the media announced that Iran had the intention of building the first nuclear power plant in the south. The Shah's dream was to produce 10,000 megawatts of electricity for the country, by the year 1990. In 1972, there was talk with the United States about establishing a regional uranium enrichment and reprocessing facility in Iran. It was rumored that these nuclear contracts were being imposed on Iran by the United States.

The talks between Washington and Tehran resulted in a 15 billion dollar contract for building eight nuclear power plants in Iran with a total capacity of 8,000 megawatts. The fuel for these reactors was supplied by the United States. However, Iran was to invest 2.75 billion dollars for uranium enrichment to insure that these reactors would always have the required amount of uranium.

Thirty years later, I realize that the depth of nuclear development the United States gave to Iran is being redirected against America. I always thought that the friendship between our two countries would be ever-lasting. Unfortunately, this short-sighted policy on Washington's part reminded me of an Iranian poem that was written 800 years ago:

Once upon a time a proud eagle flew high in the sky
He stretched his wings wide open, gliding in search of food.

He looked at the span of his wings and arrogantly said
Today, all the surface of the earth is under my wings.

I can fly high, see and focus my eyes on everything
I can control the smallest movement down below

If an insect moves around any bush or tree
The insect's movement will be visible in my sight

He bragged a lot with no fear from Destiny
As if this heavenly sphere was for him forever

All of a sudden, as if from nowhere, a strong arc
Released a sharp arrow right toward the eagle

The painful arrow hit the open wing of the eagle
The flying eagle started to fall down and down

He fell down hard and rolled as a fish on the ground
Then he opened his wings one at a time looking

Trying to find whether it was steel or wood
That so quickly could bring so much pain and agony

As he looked he saw his own feather in the arrow
He said who do I blame? We did this to ourselves…

Chapter 5

Artworks of Master Mamoud Farshchian

New Improved Training

Iran's Source of Revenue

Much had transpired during my hiatus away from Iran. Oil was still the main source of the country's revenue. OPEC and its members had formalized their organization, requiring a two million dollar membership fee. Production quotas and guidelines were set up to support their club. Between 1961 and 1973, the membership had grown to include countries throughout the Persian Gulf and Africa. Together, they represented over two thirds of the international oil supply.

In the year 1971, during the OPEC conference held in Tehran, the Shah spoke about his views on the newly developed OPEC organization. His words paralleled my own thoughts on the subject:

"The oil cartels are controlling the huge empire of the world's oil and I feel that this is the most anti- humanistic ruling that the world has ever seen. These cartels do not set any limits on their earnings, and they are complete strangers to the meaning of fairness. I feel the producing countries that are the owners of their underground wealth should themselves produce it, refine it, and transform it into products. The oil companies and others should come to countries, such as ours, only as buyers."

Of course, his suggestions were not considered, and the cartels continued to control the world's oil market and distribution. Personally, I agreed that if countries had to compete against each other with their sale of oil, competition would automatically keep the prices fair.

The Naval Faux Pas

Iran is a large country. Its borders encompass an area that is equal to the size of the United Kingdom, France, Spain, and Germany combined, and it is an area slightly larger than Alaska. The landscape is diversified, ranging from high plateaus to mountain ranges, with vast plains bordering the Persian Gulf and the Caspian Sea. Iran is one of the world's most mountainous countries, the elevation extremes are from almost sea level to over 18,600 feet to the top of the Damavand Mountain, in the northern part of Tehran. There are almost 3,400 miles bordering other countries and 1,500 miles of coastline in the Persian Gulf, Sea of Oman, and the Caspian Sea.

Along with the considerable range of elevations come drastic differences in temperatures. On my assignment in Khark Island, I was plagued by the oppressive heat and humidity of the southern region. However, when I returned to my country, I was pleased to be assigned to the Caspian Sea in the north, with its unique beauty and temperate climate. The weather was similar to what my wife and I had enjoyed in Monterey, California, during Postgraduate School.

Upon arriving, I was placed in charge of providing and furthering the education of all enlisted personnel in the fields of marine engineering.

My first mission in the north was to help the Navy fix a major faux pas. As part of a plan to expand the Iranian Navy, the military had ordered many sophisticated ships from the United States, England, France, Germany, and Italy. These modern vessels were to be delivered in four years' time. However, all the new, technologically advanced vessels would have been useless to Iran if they could not have been manned with properly trained personnel.

Upon arriving, I assumed the position of second in command to the team in charge of finding qualified personnel to operate the new ships. This was a very difficult task, as the Navy was unknown to the majority of the Iranian population. Many had never seen an ocean. Our quest was to educate the Iranian people about the Navy and to find personnel to staff the ships in a timely fashion, in order to operate the new Persian Gulf fleet. Training brought out my love for education, and I approached the assignment with enthusiasm.

This was the beginning of challenging work that led to my most exiting years and, as a result, earned numerous promotions, along with the unique opportunity to present our accomplishments to many dignitaries of the world, including the Shah.

Tour of the Nations

Finding enough men for the Navy in Iran, where the great majority of people had never seen the sea and were frightened of the water was difficult. Fortunately, Iran shares the longest coastline of the Persian Gulf with Iraq, Bahrain, Kuwait, Saudi Arabia, United Arab Emirates, Qatar, and Oman. My team and I thought that with a massive campaign we might be able to seduce some of the enterprising and educated people from these neighboring countries, who were familiar with seamanship, to serve as our Naval personnel. Unemployment in these countries was very high, and people from around the Gulf migrated to Iran to seek a better life. Even though we could quickly hire and train as many volunteers as we needed, the language barrier and the security issues made it very difficult. We soon found that in addition to our linguistic challenges, the most important obstacle to overcome was the lack of Naval technical training curriculum.

Creating an adequate technical training program was not an easy job. We did not have much time. The ships we had ordered would be available quickly, and we did not have the personnel to run them or to maintain them. We had thought that we could sit down with paper and pencil and create a training plan with all the curriculum and required technical aids, but we did not have the knowledge or the capabilities. Time was again a problem. As soon as we finished writing the material for an existing piece of equipment, a new one was replacing it. We finally decided that the most reasonable and logical way to proceed was to copy the training systems of the industrial countries that were building our ships and armaments.

Unlike in America, we did not have our own resources to pull from. We had to look to others in order to solve our problems. Fortunately, we had the oil money and the enthusiasm as well as a king who pushed us forward. In a very short time, we managed to arrange for an official tour of the countries that were producing for us. We visited several Naval training facilities in England, France, Germany, Italy, and the United States. We selected the programs that would be best suited for our needs. In America, Admiral Gabel was the Naval Training and Education Commander who directed us to the various facilities from east to west. During our tour in the United States, we were impressed with the functioning and appearance of the Naval Supply and Recruiting Center in Orlando, Florida, as well as the Naval Electronic Training Center in Great Lakes, Illinois, and the Naval Aviation Training Center at Miramar, in San Diego, California.

I recall our first meeting at the Pentagon with the United States Naval officials. We expressed our desire to purchase duplicates of all of the training facilities that we had selected including equipment, training aids, and a program to train our instructors. When we told them that our intention was to purchase and reproduce the exact facilities in Iran, they questioned our sanity.

At first, it seemed inconceivable to them, and they did not understand how we would be able to establish a price on purchasing a Naval training facility. It took us over two months to find the proper language to be able to express ourselves and adequately communicate as to exactly what we were looking for. We did not know what the program would cost, but we knew it would be very expensive. After careful consideration, we estimated a program implementation cost of approximately 150 million dollars. The new improved training program was approved and accepted. The ground-breaking project began in 1972.

Training Solution, the Master Plan

Our concept was to gather plans for all of the selected training facilities with detailed lists of equipment, their locations, and all the curriculum, lesson plans, and associated training aids.

We decided to adapt the United States Naval Training System and instead of having different countries in charge of advising us on their own training methodology, we asked the United States Navy to be the main contractor and coordinator. Originally, the United States Navy proposed that they be in charge of gathering all of the blueprints and the detailed equipment lists. Then, after completion, they would bring everything to Iran for construction and implementation. However, after some discussion we insisted on being involved in creating the master plan.

We wanted to have the ability to modify or expand any or all parts of the curriculum and move forward without delay. Ultimately, we agreed that the United States team would come to Iran and stay with us at the facility at the Caspian Sea for the duration of the program.

I was given the responsibility of being the only representative of the Iranian Navy who had the authority to add, delete, change, modify, or expand the curriculum. Basically, it was my job to make this project happen.

With all of our roles clearly defined, the United States agreed to our final proposal. An Iranian desk was opened at the Pentagon, and a team of ten Americans, both Naval and civilian personnel, were sent to Iran. The first step in the process was to gather the necessary data in the form of blueprints and curriculum. The estimate for completion of this initial step was six months. During this planning period, we made frequent visits to America to further witness our joint progress. Unfortunately, the United States Navy's initial time estimate for putting the documents together was not at all accurate. In reality, it took over eighteen months to complete the information gathering process.

Once we had the plans, we combined them with those we had purchased from other countries. With the help of the Iranian civil engineering contractors, we connected all the buildings into one giant compound.

U.S. Advisory Team

The head of the American advisory team was a very intelligent and likable man, Captain Lawrence D. Caney. He was a respected friend of Admiral Elmo Russell Zumwalt, the United States Chief of Naval Operations, and Admiral Stanfield Turner, who later became the Director of the United States Central Intelligence Agency. It was an honor having this distinctive officer in Iran as part of the team that was there to help us.

For the duration of the training project, we spent long hours trying to fit a lifetime of work into our four-year timetable. My social life was completely encompassed in the requirements of my position. I did, however, enjoy a warm friendship with Captain Caney as we worked closely towards our shared goal of completing this monumental project. One morning after jogging on the beach over fresh snow, the captain slipped and broke his leg. But in spite of the pain, it did not at any time deter him from his intelligent input, involving project planning, or participating, with the use of crutches, at various officer's club receptions. Together, Captain Caney and I managed our teams to develop curriculum and lesson plans for different technical rates, such as Mechanics, Electronics, Computer, Radar, Sonar, and Fire Controls. All were translated into Farsi, the main official language of Iran.

Translation Team

I was responsible for implementation of the training plans. The most important element was translating technical materials into Farsi. We did not have a Naval technical translator in the country. So I was forced to improvise. I came up with a creative method that, in another time, I would have attempted to patent, but our main goal was to expedite the project, and ultimately the system served us well.

I had over three hundred people in my organization who had been educated in different disciplines and most of whom graduated from universities in the United States and Great Britain, and a few were from France and Germany. I divided them into groups and together with other Naval personnel, they were given the task of coming up with a rough draft of the text and then a final translation. It took longer than I anticipated but the additional days were essential to ensure the accuracy of the translation.

In order to establish a uniform translation, we created a Naval Technical Terminology Bank by incorporating the terminologies used in different dialogues by the local people who lived around the Caspian Sea and in the neighboring Persian Gulf areas. Due to their close proximity to the sea, these coastal people already had words in their daily dialog for many aspects of maritime activities. Some of their terms were standard American seamen's words such as "winch," but they pronounced it "vinch." We used all of these English words, which had already been adapted into the Farsi language, as valuable tools. Within three years, the first English-Farsi Naval dictionary was published. Whenever we could not find the proper translation, we used English phonics, making it easier to sound out the words.

With the translation under way, we began to compile text after text. It was very rewarding to also be able to develop an art department to create the layout and design. They worked with the translation team in order to publish several hundred technical books, films, brochures, and tapes into Farsi. When confusion over the newly incorporated technical terms overwhelmed the reader, the accompanying dictionary was a valuable tool. Several thousand technical books were printed, while simultaneously, over a million square feet of buildings were being constructed.

The completed training facility was an exact replica of those in the United States, France, and Great Britain. The project in total was a masterpiece.

Training Facilities Development

The Iranian civil engineers had developed the overall facilities based on our master plan with the incredible cooperation of the United States Navy. The only difference between the originals and the multiple facilities on the Caspian Sea was the signage. They were engraved in both English and Farsi.

I was proud to be part of this educational project that enhanced the technical knowledge of our Iranian youth. We were on our way to becoming a country of worth. We were using our brains, and once again we were benefiting from our oil money. There was excitement over the depth of our accomplishments. Unfortunately, immediately after the revolution, this giant facility that engaged the talents of so many throughout the world, was transformed, overnight, into the country's largest prison. Later, sadly, the winds blew through the pilfered rooms as the facility lay idle beside the waters of the Caspian Sea.

Memories of the camaraderie between Iranian and American Naval personnel will not be forgotten. This was one more example of two cultures forgetting their religious preferences and enjoying the challenges of joining together for a project that momentarily cemented relationships between two great countries.

Later, the Ayatollahs and the Mullahs were claiming their successes after they destroyed many worthy projects and eliminated many intelligent Iranians in an effort to rid the country of anyone who might question their archaic mentality. The madness went on, but there are those of us who survived and are still hoping that the world will profit from lessons learned.

My Villa on the Caspian Sea

The beauty of the Caspian Sea lured many vacationers from all over Iran. A well-known developer recognized the draw of the stunning area and began construction on a large seaside vacation community. As part of project, a few of the senior Naval officers were given the opportunity to become involved in the planning of their own retirement villas.

The developer was a delightful man who shared my name, Manocher Farhangi. My wife, Shauna, and I enjoyed his friendship and respected the managerial expertise he exhibited in building the community. After two years, a few months before the revolution, Manocher completed our villa. We looked forward to enjoying the graciousness of the balconies with their sweeping views of the sea. There were large picture windows, a rounded card room, and a magnificent fireplace to light when the snow dusted the white sands of the shoreline and glistened in the winter sun.

This charming villa was to be the retirement home for Shauna and me, as well as our family vacation destination. Our second child Rammy had been born, and we were a happy family of four. We had transported our heirloom china and antiques from Tehran. They were given a special place of importance in our new dwelling. My best suits and dress uniforms, along with my wife's formal clothing, were put in place to be used for formal functions. Unfortunately, we were not given the opportunity to utilize the home of our dreams, even for a few days.

Dignitaries Visits

The news about the progress of our training facility was gradually beginning to reach the rest of the nation. Other countries began to acknowledge our progress as well. We often appeared on the National Television News with pre-rehearsed and approved interviews. During this period, I was the host of the facility. In addition to fielding the media, I had the unique opportunity of meeting and entertaining dignitaries from other counties. It was my privilege to host Admiral Elmo Russell Zumwalt and Admiral Stanfield Turner from the United States as well as the First and Second Sea Lord from Great Britain, and many others from Canada, France, Italy, and Pakistan.

I was particularly delighted and honored to receive Dr. Henry Kissinger, his wife Nancy, and his son Adam for a short visit. After welcoming them at the training center, I accompanied them to visit the Caspian Sea caviar factory and subsequently escorted them to the Shah's summer residence in NoShahr.

It was a pleasure for my family to live in such close proximity to the caviar factory. Not only was it an impressive stop for visiting officials, but we enjoyed indulging in the best caviar in the world. We were spoiled, taking for granted the availability of the little black and golden delicacies that were part of our daily consumption. Our two-year-old daughter Rammy insisted upon her morning buttered toast to be piled high with the golden eggs, the most coveted and the most expensive of the caviars in the world.

During visits from all dignitaries, there was often a representative from the SAVAK, Iran's secret service organization. It was felt, because of the importance of our visitors, they should be provided with security. At this time, it was rumored that torture was being used in our prisons against political dissidents. In the United States, President Carter was in office, and he and the American soothsayers started propaganda against torture and, ultimately, the Shah. At the time, I thought whatever tactics were being used by the SAVAK were also being used by the CIA in the United States. After all, the CIA and the SAVAK worked closely together, and the CIA was responsible for training the SAVAK. All of the senior SAVAK personnel were trained in the United States. It remains to be seen what was really happening.

It was common knowledge that, there were prisoners incarcerated due to their repeated civil disturbances. At this time, President Carter, perhaps in an effort to increase his popularity, started to campaign against the Shah's human rights violations. The Shah, having always had good relations with the previous American presidents, responded to Mr. Carter's demands and released the political prisoners, many of whom were known to be Islamic Marxist terrorists.

The release of these men endangered the Shah's life, and many of the dissidents were later responsible for murdering and torturing, educated and peace-loving military personnel. After the Shah fell, one of my admiral friends was hung by his feet out of a fourth-story window. Fortunately, he was able to escape, but not without lifelong repercussions.

I wonder if President Carter would have considered this torture. Some of my other officer friends were not as lucky, even though they cooperated with the brutal regime of Khomeini. After a short time, they were captured and executed by the firing squad. If President Carter understood the Koran, he would have known that fundamentalists' wish to kill anyone who oppose their beliefs.

At the time, my team and I were not aware of what was taking place politically. We were too busy working fourteen hours a day, seven days a week, creating the largest and most modern technical training facility in the country.

Due to the lack of professional instructors, self-paced individual study was a method we were promoting for technical training. It was multimedia, audiovisual, and we had achieved great results. Any average individual could learn and understand the most complicated technical subject matter in the shortest amount of time.

I was given the task to take all of the necessary material and go to Tehran to present the self-paced individual learning system to the late Prime Minister Amir Abbas Hoveyda. He was Iran's prime minister for fourteen years and later was executed by Khomeini's firing squad.

It was a sunny summer day when I arrived at the Prime Minister's office to present the new improved training method and to describe its benefits. The amazing part of the system was that the students were able to learn the difficult subject matter by themselves, at their own pace, without having an instructor. The prime minister said he wanted to act as a student, and he wished to try out the system. I had with me fifteen chapters of the basic electronic books. Each chapter was about a different electronic subject. He selected one of the books at random and opened it. The subject happened to be the Transistor.

Picking up the phone, the prime minister called his office manager saying, "I do not want to be disturbed." Looking at me, he said, "Now tell me what I am supposed to do?" I set up the related audio and visual parts and gave the prime minister earphones, saying to him, "You can start from here, read, listen to the tape, and view the pictures," and then I added, "Sir, you are now on your own."

Mr. Hoveyda put on his reading glasses and participated beautifully. As a good student, he read a paragraph of the book, looked to the video "slides," and listened to the tape. He continued very patiently, going back and forth a few times. After about fifteen minutes, he took the test by himself and shouted, "I scored one hundred percent, amazing, amazing, I cannot believe it." He immediately picked up the phone and told his secretary to call his Education Minister and to bring him one of his pens.

The prime minister was extremely excited about what he had experienced. When the phone rang, he shouted, "We don't have to pay millions and millions of dollars to foreign training advisors, counselors, and organizers. Let's open our eyes and take advantage of what has been developed right in our own backyard. Go to the north and see what these bright young people have done for the Navy. Even I could learn all about transistors in a few minutes, without a teacher."

As Mr. Hoveyda was in the process of finishing his telephone conversation, a middle-aged gentleman opened the door and handed him a box. After quickly checking the contents, he handed it to me, saying, "I want you to remember that you have done a great job." Upon opening the box, I was delighted to see a lovely gold pen, engraved with the prime minister's name. It was an honor for me to receive this recognition. At the time, I had no idea that in the very near future, I would be fearful to carry this gift of appreciation, and that my short association with this distinguished man could have caused complications for me with the Mullahs.

After returning to the Caspian Sea, work and achievements continued to be my joy. Looking back, perhaps it was better that I was not aware of the evil that lay ahead. It would have spoiled the euphoria that personally surrounded me. This was a small vignette in my life that I enjoyed and can never be tarnished.

A Visit from Iraq's Chief of Armed Forces

In 1978, I received orders to go to Tehran for a secret mission. I was to report to the main Naval Headquarters, where I was given the task of entertaining a group of ten high-ranking Iraqi officers. For four days, dressed in civilian clothing, I was to escort them on a tour of our country.

I had to be aware of two governing conditions. First, no one should know the country of their origin. Second, I was the only one who knew their itinerary. The secrecy of the visit was to protect General Shenshell, the Chief of the Iraqi Armed Forces, and his staff. At this time, Iran and Iraq had a respectful relationship with one another. Ahmed Hassan al-Bakr was the president and Saddam Hussein was the vice president controlling all the national affairs.

During this time, Ayatollah Khomeini was in exile living in Iraq and was recognized as being a threat to Iraq's minority Sunni government. They were concerned about a religious takeover. Of course, unfortunately, this ultimately happened to Iran. Saddam noticed that the number of common Shiat Iraqis who were following Khomeini was increasing, and he was afraid that he might have to face a violent confrontation. While General Shenshell and his team were visiting Iran, Saddam had forced Khomeini out of Iraq and was fearful of rebellion. Khomeini had already been dismissed from Iran, and the other Gulf countries did not want him on their soil, because he was known throughout the region as a trouble-maker.

In order to facilitate the national tour in conjunction with this secret itinerary, I was assigned a jet and a pilot to pick up the Iraqi general and his staff. The mission was top secret, and I was responsible for creating the itinerary. My aide carried a briefcase filled with money, and I was given a secret code to be used for any assistance that might be needed anywhere in Iran.

I managed to take the group from Tehran to several metropolitan cities in the country, enjoying lunch and noon prayers at one place, returning to the airplane, and telling the pilot to take off without any planned destination. While we were in the air, I opened the map of Iran and discussed it with General Shenshell, asking where he and his entourage wanted to have the evening prayer, dine, and spend the night. After our decision was made, I used my secret code to arrange for ground transportation and first-class accommodations. Due to the flexibility of this plan, no one knew where this distinguished Iraqi group would be travelling, and their identity remained secret.

On the last day of the four-day visit, while we were flying from the eastern city of Isfahan, I received a message directing me to accompany the general to NoShahr, the summer palace of the Shah, for a meeting. After a one-and-a-half-hour private visit with the Shah, we flew back to the Tehran Airport, where an Iraqi airplane was waiting to return the group to Baghdad.

Knowing the custom, I had prepared myself for a gift exchange. I had purchased a very fine Persian silk carpet for the occasion. At the Tehran Airport pavilion, General Shenshell gave me a suitcase filled with souvenirs from Iraq and asked me to dispense them among those who had made the tour safe and possible. At the same time, he handed me an Omega watch and said, "This is for you, with our sincere gratitude." He then opened an ornate jewelry box containing a breathtaking set of heavy 18K gold jewelry including a necklace, bracelet, and matching earrings, adding, "I hope your wife will enjoy these." We embraced, and the general and his entourage safely returned to Iraq.

Chapter 6

Courtesy of sarafrazan.net

Disastrous Revolution

Promotion to Tehran
Director of Iranian Naval Training and Education

A few days after General Shenshell's departure, I was promoted to the position of admiral and transferred to Tehran's Naval Headquarters with the approval of the Shah. I was given the full responsibility of becoming the director of the entire Iranian Naval Training program and in charge of providing training and education for all Naval personnel.

Iran's future depended on the education of our youth. My responsibilities included overseeing 1,200 students who were attending universities throughout the United States, Canada, and Europe. These collegians were studying for careers in the Iranian Navy, with majors in engineering and computer sciences.

I felt fortunate to have had the opportunity to visit many well-known universities in the United States and Europe and to be able to apply my observations to benefit our own programs. The educational system for the United States Navy was the combination of the U.S. Naval Academy in Annapolis, Maryland, and the Naval Reserve Officer Training Program (NROTC). We adapted the same system for the Iranian Naval education. We were offered and welcomed the opportunity to send some of our own qualified young students to participate in this NROTC program.

My Building and Headquarters in Tehran

The Naval Headquarters was scattered throughout Tehran in eight different locations. The Navy was in the process of constructing one large facility so that our headquarters could function under one roof. In the interim, we leased spaces around Tehran from private citizens. When I arrived in the capital, this project was partially completed. I was very excited about building a facility that could function with ease as well as becoming another jewel in Iran's enrichment program.

The six-floor building that I was headquartered in was located in the center of Tehran, on a side street off of a main thoroughfare. We did not have any major security. When entering the building, there were double doors leading into a large hall. Within the entry, there were stairs and an elevator that led to both the basement and the upper floors.

My office was located on the fourth floor of the building with a large picture window facing the street. Fortunately, I enjoyed a spectacular view of the Alborz Mountains. In the winter, they were majestic when covered with snow. Every morning when I entered my office, I paused to enjoy their picturesque beauty.

During the first few days of my new assignment, I swiftly familiarized myself with all of my officers and their responsibilities. From the beginning, I noticed that contrary to my previous position, there was no sense of urgency. Everyone seemed to be busy doing routine paperwork. I was expecting to continue to be involved in more of the stimulating challenges that I enjoyed at the Caspian Sea, and was disappointed in this slower paced environment. In an effort to become more productive, I felt it was necessary to step up the program immediately. Several times a week, I had to attend meetings in various Naval buildings throughout the city. Some of these offices were at least twenty miles apart. With the Tehran traffic, I was eager to see the completion of the new headquarters.

Naval Academy Plan

The largest project under my new command was the exciting task of taking over the plan for Iran's new Naval Academy. Although I had studied abroad and appreciated the opportunity, we now had the funds, and the knowledge, to put together a facility that would be equal to the great academies of the world. As part of the project, I was required to hire a qualified British dean. There was an assumption that the new dean would increase the prestige of the Academy due to Great Britain's long history on the seas. The search for this position was initiated by the British Royal Navy, upon the request from the Iranian Navy. My orders were to go to London to interview the prospective individual and negotiate his salary and incentive package.

Interview of Dr. Jack Levy, London City University

Upon arriving in London, the Royal Navy commander met me at Heathrow Airport. The next day we travelled to London City University. I was given an extensive tour of this very impressive facility. Upon completion of the tour, we went to the Mechanical Engineering Department to meet Professor Jack Levy, the department chairman, who was the candidate that we were considering for our Academy.

Professor Levy was a soft-spoken man of average stature; he appeared to be very cordial and gave me a private tour of his department. We then enjoyed having luncheon together in the university cafeteria. While dining, he asked me questions about the location of the new Academy. I told him that we had had discussions with the Shah and apparently he was open to the idea of using his summer palace in NoShahr, on the Caspian Sea.

Later, we adjourned to his office, where I interviewed him for about one hour. We spoke of everything but politics and his incentive package. He then graciously invited me to his home so that we could continue our conversation.

My Royal Naval liaison took me back to my hotel and then drove me to Professor Levy's home. The professor had been married for over ten years and was without children. He and his wife lived in a new three-story town home. We enjoyed a lovely dinner and my hostess, Mrs. Levy, and I discussed Iran's climate and day-to-day life. After dinner, the professor and I took our coffee to his third-floor office. I recall that the steps going upstairs were too narrow, and I was wondering how two people, one going up and one coming down, could possibly pass each other.

It was my observation that this was a typical English town house. I was sure that his villa on the Caspian Sea would be more gracious. When we were comfortably seated, I opened the conversation, saying, "Professor, you know that when you come to Iran, you will be residing in the north." He had a yellow pad of paper and was taking notes while nodding his head, reassuring me that he understood what I was saying. I continued, "We will be providing a home for you and your wife with paid utilities and telephone services." He asked me immediately, "Can I call London?"

"Yes," I said and I added, "We will provide you with a car and a driver and a full-time butler, five days a week." I did not see any change in his facial expression. His only comment was, "Sounds good," and then he immediately asked, "Do they speak any English?" "I am afraid not," I responded, "after all, you will be in Iran and some may expect you to speak Farsi."

While he was taking notes I added, "By the way, every year you are entitled to two economy class round-trip air tickets from Tehran to London." I realized that I was doing all of the talking so at this point I asked, "Will you please tell me your expectations for your salary and incentive package?"

He put away his notepad and responded, "I like the incentive package, it sounds very good. I especially like having a butler. We have never had one. In regard to the salary, I am asking for 132,000 British pounds per year." I wondered why 132,000 and not 130,000 or 140,000 pounds. Then he added, "I want three times my present salary, and presently my salary at the University is 44,000 pounds. I expect three times more than my current salary." "Why three times?" I asked. He responded very firmly, "I want my base salary plus another 44,000 pounds because I will be residing outside the Commonwealth countries. Also, I want an additional 44,000 pounds because I will be in an unstable country." He continued, "If I had children I would not consider this offer, but my wife and I have discussed your proposal and I am willing to accept the responsibility to be of help." I interrupted him immediately and I asked, "What do you mean?" He said: "The government of your country and the Shah's regime is not firm and may collapse at any time."

I could not believe what I was hearing. This was a great insult to me and to my country. Iran was well respected and was the strongest power in the Middle East. I decided to end our conversation without any commitment. I told him I would go back to Tehran and report our discussion. I thanked him and his wife for their hospitality. The Royal Navy commander drove me back to my hotel.

Learning of a Rumor
"The United States Does Not Like the Shah"

The next day, I went to our Embassy in London, where I visited with our Iranian Naval Attaché. It was a courtesy meeting. We had lunch and I told him about Professor Levy's remarks. He did not seem to be surprised. He listened quietly and said, "There are a lot of rumors here in London. The one that is currently being circulated is that the United States no longer favors the Shah."

Sheik Abdullah on the Plane

After lunch, I decided to cut my trip short and come back to Tehran. I changed my ticket to the first flight out of London. I was somewhat depressed. My trip coming to London had been filled with anticipation. The thought of Iran being able to build its own Naval Academy was, in my mind, going to be a huge step forward.

My flight was going to Tehran via Rome. As the new passengers were boarding the plane in Rome, I looked up and saw a passenger who looked familiar. Smiling, the gentleman came toward me. To my surprise, it was Sheik Abdullah from Khark Island. We were both very happy to see each other. He looked fantastic. He was wearing a handsome suit and white shirt without a tie. His beard was still groomed short in the same style he had worn when we had worked together. Now it was flecked with grey. We managed to change our seats with other passengers in order to sit next to each other. We were eager to talk.

It seemed that the Sheik had been searching for me. He had inquired at the Naval Headquarters, and they had informed him that I had been in America and was now in the Caspian Sea area. I was touched to learn that he had been trying to find me. How often I had thought of my friend and wondered what he was doing. We enjoyed a good three-hour conversation.

During our talk, he spoke of exactly what I was trying to digest after leaving London. I think that it was fate that brought him back into my life at this particular time. The Sheik told me that the Islamic movement in Iran was becoming very strong. He advised me not to annoy, and to try to maintain a good relationship with, the Mullahs. As we departed, in a bit of jest, he added, "Remember the Mullahs are worse than camels. They never forget a bad incident." I knew that my friend had been a good Muslim when he resided in Khark Island. Whatever was happening now did not meet with his approval.

Demonstrations and Strikes

The next day upon my return to Tehran, I wrote a lengthy report suggesting that Professor Jack Levy was not qualified for the job of dean for the Naval Academy because of his views regarding the stability of our government. I added my concerns that he might not be loyal to His Majesty and the Pahlavi dynasty.

In spite of my denial of the dangers of the religious changes that were taking place in Iran, I was becoming aware that the radical Muslim leaders were now opposing the Shah. I knew that for a long time they had been advocating outlawing tobacco, alcohol, movies, gambling, and foreign dress. They wanted the veil for all women, as well as, barbarian punishments for criminals such as cutting off a hand.

Even though the Shah was religious at heart, he was firmly opposing the Mullahs and religious leaders' ideals. In addition to seeking changes within the country, most of the outspoken Mullahs were opposing the presence of foreigners, especially Americans.

The majority of Iranians were in the lower income brackets, and they were following the fanatic Mullahs who did not like the Shah. On the other hand, the Shah had strong support from most of Iran's middle and upper classes; some were old-fashioned, but most were wealthy and Westernized, and they believed in the principles of Islam in a modern way. The moderate Muslim clerics were also supporting the Shah. They knew the laws of 1,400 years ago that many Mullahs were seeking to resurrect were not suited for modern life.

Iran under the Shah's vision had several great plans to modernize the country and bring the economy and social level up to European standards. He had initiated reforms in favor of the less privileged. Many clerics were outspokenly opposed to those reforms. Khomeini, in particular, was against reform and issued a "Fatwa" (religious edict) against them. The Shah, in one of his speeches, clearly said that his reforms would take Iran into the jet age while the Mullahs wanted to remain in the age of the donkey.

It had only been a week since I returned from my trip to London, and I was still digesting Professor Levy's remarks. One lovely autumn morning, I was working in my office when I heard a commotion outside my building. Quickly going to my window, I looked down into the street, and I was shocked to see many chanting demonstrators.

For the most part, they were young people, who probably had not attended school that day. There was also a sizable number of bearded peasants, dressed in disheveled fashion. They were raising their fists defiantly, while carrying posters.

Although I could not define their words, I could see their anger. Suddenly, smoke emerged from the bank that was located across the street and a little north of my building. The demonstrators were angrily breaking windows. Desks and chairs were being thrown into the center of the street and set on fire. The entire incident did not take more than five minutes. As soon as the damage was done, the crowd quickly disappeared.

By the time the police and firefighters arrived, the street was vacant. Interestingly, I realized that the bank was a branch of a very popular financial institution. The major stockholders and owners, who had obviously been the target of this destructive act, were not Muslim, they were Bahaii.

Why had I not been aware of the negative events that were happening in my country? I know now that I was in denial. I did not want to believe that all of the positive programs to build a better Iran, that I had been privileged to be a part of, could be threatened by a few ragged fanatics.

Extra Nonperishable Food

After I witnessed this incident, I immediately went to see the Naval chief of operations. I related to him the story of what happened and I told him about my deep concerns. We did not have any security in my building, and I needed to protect my staff of 200 Naval and civilian personnel.

Within a few days, he complied, and the basement was emptied with plans to transform it into a small kitchen and barracks for thirty-two soldiers who would live there and be on guard for twenty-four hours a day. I felt more comfortable knowing that this was being accomplished. Shortly after securing the building, I was informed that there were several tons of basic nonperishable food ingredients being delivered to my facility. Unfortunately, without the basement, I did not have room to store them. There were four truckloads of rice and grain, and they were not returnable. In other words, I had to receive them and find a place to accommodate them.

I called Headquarters and I asked, "What should I do with all these truckloads of food? I do not have room to store them." They told me that the foodstuffs were my responsibility. "Keep as much as you can and do whatever you wish with the rest." It was late in the afternoon, and since we did not have anywhere to unload the trucks, I kept them loaded until the next day.

That evening, when my driver Nasser was taking me home, I remembered Sheik Abdullah's advice. I asked Nasser to drive me to his store. As we approached the business, I saw the Sheik standing on the sidewalk in front of a large home appliance store. I felt fortunate to find him there. My driver stopped the car, and I lowered the window and called his name. As soon as he saw me wearing my uniform and sitting in the back seat of a dark Naval car, he looked around to see if anyone was observing him, then walked very quickly toward my car. Opening the door, the Sheik slid in next to me, saying, "What has happened? What are you doing here?" "I just wanted to see you," I replied. My military appearance seemed to be unnerving. I felt he was not comfortable having me around his office, but he immediately added;

"I enjoy seeing you anytime, anywhere. However, you know that in these days people do not like anyone in uniform."

"Why are you saying this?" I asked. "I thought the population loved us."

"Not anymore," he replied. "Please be careful. There are lots of things going on underground, and you would be considered an enemy to the movement." He took a deep breath and said, "Please tell me the real reason that you came here." He remained focused, awaiting my answer.

I responded, "You must remember the advice you gave me while we were traveling from Rome to Tehran together. You told me to be good to the Mullahs." Then I added, "There is a situation that I must handle. I have four truckloads of basic food ingredients, mostly rice, and I want to donate most of them to a mosque for charity. I do not know where to go, so I came here to ask for your assistance. Can you introduce me to a Mullah that you might know?" I could feel that he was relieved when he said, "That is great! I will call you tomorrow at 9:00 a.m. sharp and I will give you all of the information."

The next day, Sheik Abdullah called me exactly at 9:00 a.m., and as soon as I said hello, he gave me the name and address of a mosque that was in the vicinity of my office. I immediately called my driver. I was dressed in my Naval uniform and we drove to the address. As soon as I stepped out of the car in front of the mosque, I noticed about ten men standing close to the entrance. They were staring at me with rather surly expressions on their faces. One of them had a string of worry beads in his hand. As he came toward me he said, "Salaam, can I be of any assistance to you?" "I am here to see Haj Agha Sadr," I replied. "Is there anything we can do for you?" he asked. "No," I replied again. "I was told to see him about a private matter." I decided to walk closer to the entrance of the mosque. At this point another man with a beard, wearing a long tan robe, ran from inside and said, "Sir, Haj Agha Sadr is expecting you."

As soon as the men who were standing close to the door heard that Haj Agha Sadr was waiting for me, their expressions changed, and with hand gestures, they showed me the way, saying, "Please, please."

I went into the mosque where more followers directed me to go to the second floor. There were a few rooms with several men in each room, all looking at me. They came forward and opened the door to a large hall, where Haj Agha Sadr was sitting on a worn Persian carpet. Large white cotton pillows were at his back. He appeared to be in his mid-fifties. His short clipped grey beard and white folded turban complemented his long white robe and loose black half-sleeve cloak. His somber appearance commanded a certain reverence. There were two other men sitting in front of him. As soon as I entered the room, he looked up through his glasses and motioned the others away. He struggled to stand up as a sign of respect.

I took my hat off and acknowledged him by bowing my head. When I came closer to him, he gestured for me to sit down on the same carpet. I obeyed and sat on the floor in front of him. He then said, "You are welcome to the house of Allah. Sheik Abdullah has been talking to us about your decency." After a moment of nodding his head up and down, he asked, "What can we do for you?"

I replied, "Haj Agha, we have over three truckloads of rice, grain, and other nonperishable food ingredients that we would like to give to you to be distributed among the needy people." He nodded his head again and said, "That is commendable, and we thank you. Allah will safeguard you."

Our meeting did not take more than two minutes. He appeared to me to be a very nice, holy person, and I enjoyed meeting him. When I had nothing else to add, I said, "Haj Agha, with your permission, I will leave and I will send the trucks here to the mosque." I stood up, as a sign of respect, he started to rise with me, saying, "May Allah be your guardian and save you for Islam."

When I turned, I noticed the same two men were standing next to the entry door. They bowed their heads, and as soon as I passed them, they turned and followed me out of the mosque. When I reached the main entrance, the men that had been standing there earlier, now had a different expression on their faces. They were smiling and bowing down in a gesture of respect.

Upon returning to my office, I directed the trucks to the mosque to deliver the nonperishable food to Haj Agha Sadr. I assumed that our donation had been well received and of help to the needy. I did not hear anything further, good, bad, or indifferent, but I was pleased about the transaction.

I once again immersed myself in the involvement of my military responsibilities. Tehran was having more and more demonstrations, and the Mullahs' presence in society was becoming stronger. We continued to hear rumors and news about disorder and anarchy that was going on in certain parts of the country. Daily, gas stations, buses, and buildings were being set ablaze. Roads were being blocked by demonstrators, creating an atmosphere of fear among many hard-working, innocent people.

Contact with Sheik Abdullah

I continued to plan for the new Naval Academy and decided not to dwell on anything negative. I was very busy one morning when the ring of the telephone interrupted my work. I picked up the receiver, and I was pleased to hear the voice of Sheik Abdullah. He asked if he could see me. I responded immediately and questioned him as to where we should meet. He repeated the address of his home appliance store and a time when we could rendezvous. Then requested that I wear civilian clothing and not bring my Naval car. I thanked him for his call.

On the day of our meeting, I left my office after changing into civilian clothing. Since I did not have a private car, I had my driver drop me about a mile away from my destination. I walked several blocks and then flagged a taxi. At that time, this was the main form of transportation in Tehran. It was usually impossible to find a vacant taxi but there was always room to squeeze in another passenger as long as one's destination was in the same vicinity. The driver would pull over quickly, ask where you were going, and if you wanted to go in the opposite direction of those already jammed into his cab, he would screech off at breakneck speed.

On this day, I was the first to exit my crowded taxi. When I was paying the driver, I noticed Sheik Abdullah standing in front of his appliance store. We both walked toward each other, and after a warm embrace, he suggested that we keep walking. It was late in the afternoon, and the streets were busy. Fortunately, many people were strolling along the sidewalk, so we were not alone and blended in with the crowd. "It is nice seeing you," I said, "What is going on?" "Nothing really," he said, "I just wanted to chat a little."

He appeared to be nervous, and when we walked farther from his store, we turned into a secluded alley where there were fewer pedestrians. I had the feeling that Sheik Abdullah wanted to speak seriously, but as before, he did not want to be seen with me. He first looked around and then said, "I want you to be very careful. Haj Agha Sadr called me and wanted to know more about you. He found out that you had been in America for several years and that you had been working directly with the Americans. He did not like this at all. He believes that you have a very strong tie with the United States and cannot be trusted."

He looked around again and said, "I am also sure these anti-human Mullahs know, as well, about my own participation in helping the American contractors during the construction in Khark Island." He added, "There is a lot going on behind the scenes. We are going to see large-scale strikes in the entire country. These Muslim fanatics are going to start throwing acid in the faces of the women who are not wearing the Islamic chador in public. They will be creating an environment of fear among all of our citizens and promoting a holy campaign of terror and disorder."

Sheik Abdullah continued speaking very quickly; he was worried, and I could feel his compassion for me. "These fanatics do not like the present laws, in particular the one that limits them to one wife. They do not want women working in any organization, private or governmental, or in any capacity. They want them to cover themselves from head to toe and to stay inside their homes as if they were prisoners. They feel the purpose of women is only for sex, whenever and wherever a man desires. All they want is to have a male-dominated society. These Mullahs are the followers of Islamic fundamentalism, and they know in their hearts that they are misleading the people, telling them lies about the angel of death and a place in paradise where young virgin women are waiting. They control the minds of youth by promising rewards for committing Jihad in the name of Allah." He concluded by adding, "I just wanted to let you know what is really going on, and I am confident that you will keep this to yourself. I am sharing this with you because I trust you will use your own judgment concerning your safety. Please be very careful and do not go anywhere alone."

Our discussion was one sided. He kept talking, trying to inform me, and I was most certainly listening. After a few minutes, we decided that for each other's safety, it would be best if he would contact me and that I did not try to contact him. He said that he would be calling me in a few days. I was overwhelmed with sadness when we departed. After a warm embrace, each of us walked away in two different directions.

This short and sincere meeting was a real eye-opener for me. I decided that I had to be more aware about what was going on, even though I still believed that the strong armed forces of the Shah had the capability to stop any anarchy. I started to listen to the BBC on the radio.

It was interesting to hear them give the news about what had happened daily in every corner of Iran and, in addition, hint about future events such as when and where the riots and demonstrations were going to take place. They must have had excellent undercover informants. The BBC became my nightly habit.

Meanwhile, the United States was continuing to press Iran for human rights grievances and insisting that they free the political prisoners. These imprisoned Muslim militants had been setting fire to school busses, banks, cinemas, and other public offices without any regard for the occupants. They were dissidents, not political prisoners, and needed to be kept out of circulation in order to protect innocent citizens. Little did the Carter administration know how difficult things were becoming internally. It later occurred to many of us that the Mullahs, in order to cause more adverse criticism in the world, were leaking false information about atrocities that had not happened within the prisons.

One morning, I received a call from my building officer. "Sir," he said, "There is a group of demonstrators coming toward the building." I was shocked as I asked, "How many guards do we have?" He replied, "Four at the door and twenty-eight are ready on the lower level." Thinking quickly, I said, "Please make sure that the people on every floor stay away from the windows. It may increase the violence if they see us watching them." "Yes sir," he replied.

While I was talking to him, I acted against my own advice and looked out of my window. I saw at least 1,000 people chanting and walking toward our building in an unorganized fashion. I immediately called the Navy's main Headquarter security and informed them of what was happening. There were a lot of other pedestrians on the sidewalks observing. As I watched, the demonstrators were coming closer and closer. Suddenly, I saw Haj Agha Sadr. He was right in front of the demonstrators and shouting with his fist up. I called the building officer who was on duty and I told him to bring all the guards inside and lock the doors. My thought was to avoid any open confrontation.

The rebellious group was standing in the street, blocking the traffic. They were about thirty to fifty yards away from my building and chanting. You could tell which ones were the leaders by the way they took authority. Haj Agha Sadr seemed to be the instigator. I thought of going outside and facing them, trying to calm them down, but I was unsure of myself and thought I might just entice them into becoming more aggressive. I could not predict the outcome. Somehow, I hoped that they were not going to harm us, because they knew well that if they did, they would have to confront the power of the Imperial Armed Forces.

The demonstrators did not know the extent of our security or how strong our military presence was. After a short time, they became more subdued and just stood chanting. My windows were closed and I could not hear them clearly, so I did not know what they were saying, but my eyes continued to focus on Haj Agha Sadr. I could not believe that he was the same man that had appeared to be so kind and holy. My thoughts flashed back, remembering my mother's words of warning, "Don't ever trust a Mullah. They change face and become demons as soon as their will has been threatened, and if confronted, they harm without mercy and never regret it."

I did not have a plan as to what to do, and before I could consider taking any action, I heard the sirens of the police cars. The control demonstration police force, driving trucks, came along both sides of the street. As they approached, all the protesters including Haj Agha Sadr quickly ran away and dispersed in various directions.

Safe Vault and Money Transfer to United States

The next morning, I was called by the Chief of Naval Operations to immediately drive to his office. When I arrived, he was pacing back and forth behind his desk. After a quick salute, he said, "The situation is becoming difficult and we can no longer send money to our students who are studying outside of the country. The banks are not transferring any currency. Therefore, your office is responsible for sending a messenger to Washington with an attaché case filled with cash. He will deliver the money to our Iranian Naval Attaché, who is stationed there. The students need to be paid as before, twice a month. Also, unfortunately, we can no longer protect you or your family. You are going to have to look out after yourself." Then he added, "We will supply you with a Colt pistol and with enough ammunition to use whenever you think it might be necessary."

Shortly after this meeting, a huge safe was installed in my building, and I was given a Colt with four rounds of ammunition. I signed the receipt, acknowledging the engraved serial number that appeared on the pistol. I brought the Colt and ammunition home and hid them under a dresser in our bedroom. Then I selected a trustworthy officer who was charged with the responsibility of carrying the attaché case. The case was handcuffed to his wrist, and contained enough hundred-dollar bills to be distributed among our Naval students in America. Upon his arrival in Washington, D.C., our Iranian Naval Attaché would use his key to open the case and distribute the money among the students.

Pistols and Self-Protection

I recall vividly, as if it was yesterday, when Kourosh Navaii, a young junior officer who was a family friend during my tour of duty at the Caspian Sea, came into my office and closed the door behind him. He approached my desk and whispered, "It is tough out there." He reached into his pocket and pulled out a small Beretta pistol, holding it in the palm of his hand. He pressed the pistol into my hand along with two rounds of ammunition. Very sincerely he said, "I beg you, please carry this with you." I took the pistol from him and put it in my pocket along with the ammunition. It was hard for me to believe that this was happening. I thanked him for his friendship. The pistol and the ammunition became part of my daily uniform. I carried them with me, at all times, in my chest pocket over my heart.

Tehran was no longer the only city that was in the center of the news. In just a few weeks, strikes in all segments of the country were breaking the back of the government. Most of these strikes were orchestrated by the religious fanatics for political demands as well as demands for higher wages and better housing. They were occurring one after the other. Several thousand employees walked out of the steel industry, railroad facilities, petrochemical plants, and telegraph and telephone companies. The shipyard in the south and the caviar factory in the north were abandoned. The Russian-built steel plant was closed permanently, and the General Motors facility in Tehran was set on fire.

Simultaneously, it was announced that all the Iranian National Oil Company divisions were on strike. The refinery was shut down, and there was no oil pumped or shipped from Khark Island. This caused a shortage of 5 million barrels of oil per day. The strike was over a month long, and there was no longer a safe anchoring site off of Khark Island for the super tankers. My country, which had been producing millions of barrels of oil and selling them to numerous other nations, now had oil shortages. There was no longer gasoline in the gas stations, and people waited for days in long lines to fill up their tanks. During the delivery of incoming fuel the trucks were often set a blaze by Muslim militants.

There was a gloom that engulfed the city, and the number of unhappy Iranians increased daily. The fanatical Mullahs were more visible in the streets, and their empowerment was noticeable. The armed forces had the first priority to receive gasoline at the pumps, so when I travelled to work I was still able to use my Naval car and driver. The streets were empty, and there were pockets of demonstrators scattered throughout Tehran.

Most people in charge of the different segments of the government still could not accept the severity of what was happening. Many of us believed that the strong armed forces would play a role in suppressing and crushing the opposition. At the time, interestingly enough, the Mullahs thought that they could not win unless they had the support of the military. Often, to be solicitous, they would place the stem of a flower in the barrel of the guns carried by military guards.

Caught in the Middle of a Demonstration

It was January and the beginning of 1979. I was returning from a meeting held in the main Naval Headquarters building. It was around four o'clock in the afternoon. I was sitting in the back seat of the Naval car with my driver, who was in civilian clothing. I was wearing my uniform and my Navy raincoat, which covered my rank. It was not readily apparent that I was a Naval officer. My hat was on the seat next to me and not visible as my driver drove through the main streets of Tehran. I noticed that the cars were progressing very slowly and gradually we came to a complete stop.

We were close to a cross section when we heard a group chanting, coming closer and closer. We were suddenly surrounded by demonstrators who were going through the stopped cars. My poor driver was helpless. All the demonstrators were men, and the great majority of them, again, looked like peasants. They were wearing dirty clothing and most were unshaven. The crowd was divided into two groups. One group was shouting, "Armed forces personnel," and the others were responding, "Our brothers!"

Unexpectedly, one of the agitators in the crowd was walking by my side of the car; he looked through the window and saw me, quickly shouting, "Look who is here!" I had no idea how he opened the car door so rapidly and dragged me out. He and his group lifted me on to their shoulders while others were pulling my raincoat from my back. They were trying to expose the identifiable gold stripes on my sleeves and shoulders. During this struggle, part of my raincoat and uniform were torn off. The agitators continued to lift me and pass me from one hand to the other while still shouting, "Armed forces personnel," "Our brothers!"

I had no control over what was happening. I was terrified. I knew that I had the Beretta pistol in my chest pocket. I was afraid that the moving and jerking might cause it to dislodge and fall into the crowd, causing me more problems. I crossed my arms, pressing the small gun to my chest. I did not know what to do while the perspiring, agitated protesters, one after another, with wet shining faces, were grabbing me and kissing both sides of my cheeks, still smiling in a sign of friendship. After several minutes, I heard sirens and with relief, I was harshly dropped down on the street. The seemingly friendly but rough disheveled demonstrators ran away. I jumped in the car, pulling my torn uniform around me, and directed my driver to take me to the safety of my home.

Shooting into the Building

At this time, I was living in a third-floor apartment with my wife; two children; Javad, a full-time Naval servant; and a part-time nanny. The apartment complex was located in the northeast of Tehran. Most of the apartments were occupied by military personnel, including an admiral friend who resided on the second level. In the evenings, we often saw each other socially and spoke about our daily encounters. We both still believed that the armed forces would soon take care of the anarchy that we were observing.

In late January, my wife had gone shopping in the official car with my driver. It was around noon when she stopped by to see me, and we decided to order lunch and dine in my office, along with a few other high-ranking officers. We were enjoying our "Chelo Kabab" with white rice, when suddenly we heard shooting. Bullets were being dispersed all around the building. We left our delicious lunch and dove to the floor. The shooting stopped in a few seconds, and we quietly continued dining. I looked down through my window, and I could see scattered demonstrators, running and shouting. I tried to locate Haj Agha Sadr, but this time I could not find him. We were all shaken, knowing that things were becoming violent. Any one of us could have been killed by a stray bullet.

Red Car

That evening, my wife and I discussed the day's events and spoke of our concerns about not having a car of our own. We knew that we were too dependent on the military car and that it was becoming too dangerous to drive in this type of vehicle.

A few days after our conversation, I received a telephone call from Sheik Abdullah. He wanted to tell me of his concerns about my travelling in a Naval car. There had already been a few instances where high-ranking military personnel had been shot while driving. They were not shot because of their position, only because they were military. Sheik Abdullah said, "You should be driving in a vehicle that does not attract the attention of the revolutionaries. A small car would be very appropriate for you," he continued. "Don't you agree?" "As a matter of fact," I responded, "my wife and I were speaking about the same subject a few nights ago." Sheik Abdullah then continued, "I think I have the solution for you. There is brand-new two-door, hot red Renault with temporary license plates parked in front of my home appliance store. It is unlocked and the key is under the driver's seat." I was listening very carefully when he said, "Please pick the car up this afternoon; it is registered in your name."

I thanked him for being so helpful but added, "I have not paid for the car. Who must I pay?" He did not let me finish my sentence, saying, "Now is not the right time to talk about this. We will discuss it when we are together."

After so many years, I continue to remember the kind and caring tone of Sheik Abdullah's voice. It still hurts me to think about this special friend, knowing that I did not have the opportunity to shake his hand in gratitude.

That afternoon, I travelled with my driver to the vicinity of the Sheik's home appliance store. Once again, I wore civilian clothing. While walking toward the store, I immediately recognized the car. It certainly was a very hot red color and might have been more suited for teenagers. There were crowds of people in the street but it appeared that everyone was preoccupied with their own affairs. I walked briskly toward the automobile, opened the driver's door, and slid behind the wheel. I looked around to see if I could locate Sheik Abdullah, but sadly I did not see him. I reached under the driver's seat, found the car keys, started the engine, and drove home.

While driving, I tried to collect my thoughts. I realized that each segment of the country was in disarray. Khomeini was promising that Iran would use their oil money revenues for the benefit of all Iranians, and all the basic utilities and services such as water, sewer systems, electricity, gas, and oil would be free for everyone, regardless of class or income level. Khomeini continued by preaching he would promote the idea for the poor to replace the middle and upper classes in their jobs. His words could be heard everywhere as he continued to make impossible promises. Women's rights gained under the Shah would continue and there would be unity between the Sunnis and Shiat. The majority of Khomeini's supporters were uneducated poor people, and all were mesmerized. They enthusiastically organized more and more protests and demonstrations. Their slogans were changing day by day, but their main jargon was, "The Shah must go," "Death to the American Puppet," "We want independence," "Freedom," and "An Islamic republic."

Mullah Networking

I was shocked when I finally started to realize that the clergy had a very well-organized network, which had been shaped over several decades. There was at least one mosque and one mullah in every small village in the country. The worship places such as mosques were now transformed into the ammunition bunkers and combat information centers. Every House of God was now a House of War. There were over fifty Ayatollahs in Iran. Ayatollah is the highest rank given to a Shiat clergy. There were over 100,000 mullahs in Iran at that time. All were receiving daily audiotapes and pamphlets with detailed directions as to what they were supposed to do. The danger grew as the protests continued.

Social Economic Condition

It is still interesting for me to note that during this terrible time, and with the overwhelming anarchy transpiring in the country, the great majority of the people did not know what was going to happen. Most were confused and had no idea as to what method of governing would ultimately be replaced in the absence of the Shah. During the strike of the National Iranian Oil Company, the employees were opposing the formation of an Islamic Republic. They did not want this type of Islamic government, and many negative encounters occurred between the Mullahs and the workers.

The government, under the Shah, made tremendous progress, introducing free primary and secondary education for all and had started a free meal program in the elementary schools. The government had also provided financial support for all university students. The income taxes were significantly lowered, and blanket countrywide health insurance plans had been implemented. Employees of all large companies in the country enjoyed owning collectively forty-nine percent of the shares for the company that they worked for. Obviously, to those who envied all who had more than they did, this was not enough.

In 1978, there were 45,000 Americans and 15,000 Europeans assigned to a variety of industries. There were also foreign advisors to the military. Westernization was evident and quite noticeable. Differences could be seen in fashion, films, music, television programming, and the legal use of alcohol and tobacco. This growing modernized society was a huge threat to the Islamic movement.

Shah Leaves, the Fall of Iran

In response to pressure from President Carter, the Shah released the alleged political prisoners and changed the government to please the religious opposition. Martial law was enforced in Tehran and other large cities. On January 6, 1979, the Shah appointed Shahpour Bakhtiar as his last prime minister. He was one of the democratic leaders in the opposition party supported by the elite and opposing the monarchy. This party was not in favor of Ayatollah Khomeini and wanted to separate his religious rulings from their governing of the country. Khomeini at that time was still in France and was enjoying the free world propaganda. He was being supported by the French government. He declared an Islamic Council, consisting of four Mullahs and two radical modernists, to replace the falling government.

On January 16, 1979, I came to my office as usual, in the Naval car with my driver. Upon my arrival, one of my officers rushed into my office, saying, "The Shah has left and most of us also want to leave." I contacted Headquarters but I could not find anyone to consult with. It was then, that I realized I needed to give the rest of my personnel the remainder of the day off. I knew that I could not keep them by force.

Quickly, everyone left the building, and I also followed. While my driver was taking me home, I witnessed several groups in the street, blocking the traffic, asking everyone to turn on their headlights and to use their horns as a sign of celebration. I had never seen so many people dancing in the streets of Tehran.

I felt it best to pretend to wave and smile at the crowd. I was confused, my head was spinning, and upon arriving home, I released my driver, changed into civilian clothing, and decided to drive the new red car through nearby streets to see what was happening.

Again, I was shocked to see multitudes of people jumping, turning, and twisting with joy, while shouting, "Death to the King." Citizens of all ages on motorcycles, in cars, or jammed into buses and trucks were laughing and cheering in euphoric celebration. Many were wildly waving white handkerchiefs high over their heads to further show their approval.

The demonstrators continued late into the evening. When I returned home, the news was reporting Khomeini's words "Destroy the Shah's statues and everything and anything that contains his name." The film clips that followed confirmed the frenzy that continued to escalate whenever the new "Master" spoke.

Khomeini Comes to Iran

Every day, some portion of the country was on strike, and demonstrations were becoming stronger. There was violence throughout the city, and the sound of gunfire could be heard from every direction. Many people were being killed with stray bullets, and more deaths occurred during the funeral processions of others. I had never imagined that I would see this type of chaos.

The first day of the week in Iran is Saturday. Offices were closed Thursday afternoons and all day on Friday, the Iranian national holiday. It was now known that Khomeini was going to return to Iran. It was the last day of January, and all of the offices were closed. I stayed in front of the television, watching the news that made history.

On the first day of February 1979, Khomeini arrived in Tehran, with his entourage, on a chartered Air France plane. He received a very warm welcome from millions of Iranians and announced that the Bakhtiar government was illegal and called for more strikes and more demonstrations. Then he established his headquarters in the Alavi School in the heart of Tehran.

Five days after his arrival, Khomeini named Mehdi Bazargan as the prime minister of a provisional government. The Shah's government ministries and all of the very basic services were completely paralyzed. Committees were formed throughout the country, under the supervision of the local mosques. Mullahs were assuming the responsibilities for municipal functions, including the neighborhood watch and the distribution of all basic necessities including fuel oil

The citizens' joy and celebration quickly changed to overwhelming terror and fear. Many high-ranking military and civilian personnel were immediately executed by their own subordinates, such as drivers and servants. There were occasions when the military troops refused to fire on the demonstrators who were breaking the curfew.

I was still in my office when I received a call from Captain Caney. He was in Tehran and wanted to have a meeting with me regarding the continuation of the Caspian Sea Training Center. We met each other in the afternoon. He always carried a small notebook in his pocket and immediately referred to it, relating to me about the material delays coming from the United States. He was so dedicated to completing our training facility that he ignored the chaos in the streets.

I grabbed his arm, saying, "Captain, you must leave the country immediately. Where is your wife?" He calmly answered, "At the hotel with a few members of our team."

I was panicked, knowing how much danger he faced as an American. The thugs that were roaming the streets with guns were incensed with hate for the West. I feared that anything could happen. I had received word that there was an American C130 airplane on the ground at the airport. They were ready to take off as soon as they received a missing part. The captain was hesitant but finally grasped the seriousness of my concerns, as well as the realization that the environment in Iran was no longer safe. He was worried about his belongings that were still in his quarters at the Caspian Sea. I reassured him that we could manage to pack and ship everything to the United States. With my best wishes, as well as my concerns, this fine man left my office. He, his wife, and a few of his staff managed to reach the grounded plane at the airport. My last words to him were, "Do you have any cash? It might take a great deal of money to get through the angry mobs, and do not hesitate to use it for bribery. I think you are going to need it."

The Assignment that Never Came

Overwhelmingly, there was anarchy throughout the country. There was no chain of command because the people responsible within that chain could not be found. On Thursday, February 8, 1979, around eleven o'clock, I was called by our Chief of Naval Operations. He wanted to see me immediately. I stopped my work and asked my driver to take me to his office. There were not many cars on the streets, and there were pockets of demonstrations in the presence of military personnel. I arrived at Headquarters right before noon. I went directly to the chief's office. He was standing behind his desk and could not hide his nervousness.

"Our borders up north are practically open. We have no control over what might happen if the USSR learns about how vulnerable we are. Their ambition to gain access to the Persian Gulf could give them the opportunity that they have been waiting for. I am calling you because of our concerns. There is a riot in the north of Naval personnel. Most of them are your students. They are demanding more money and they want to graduate earlier." He added, "I do not know exactly what they are asking. We have reviewed the situation and we believe you are the only one who can bring them under control. The people in the Naval Training Center like and respect you, and you will be able to dialog with them."

While he was rubbing his hands together, he added, "You have total authority, on behalf of the Navy, to go to the north and raise their salaries, give them their promotions, and shorten the cycle of graduation. Do whatever is needed but stop the rioting and this mutiny."

I somehow welcomed the assignment. I thought, with all the problems in Tehran, it might be best for me and my family to leave the capital and spend a few days in our villa by the Caspian Sea. I left Headquarters and while my driver was maneuvering through the streets, there were groups of people shouting;

some had rifles in their hands. Most of the stores were closed. There were not many cars but smoke was rising from old tires burning in the middle of the streets. I came home and I released my driver, telling him that I would call within a few days. That was the last time I saw Nasser.

I asked my wife to pack and get ready to go to our villa. I first thought of flying. It was easier with the children to book an early-morning reservation. Calling the airline, I found that all flights were grounded and there were no plans to lift the ban. The only chance we had was to drive the red car to the Caspian Sea. I decided to call and find out about the road conditions. At that time of the year, snow and ice would have made the windy mountainous route very dangerous. I learned that the roads were open, and I thought if we left early the next morning, we could be at our destination within four or five hours, allowing us to partake of a late lunch together. However, we knew that it would be difficult to arrive with our two children to a cold, unheated building. I called one of my close friends, with the intention of asking him to go to our villa, to turn on the furnace. As soon as he heard about our plans, he immediately interrupted me and said, "Don't even think about coming. There are people here that are armed and looking for you." He added, "This morning a group of militants thought you might have already arrived. The demonstrators attacked your villa; broke the main door, two windows, and some of your belongings were looted."

It was amazing to learn that the militants and Mullahs followers knew, before I did, about my itinerary. "How could they?" I thought, "Unless someone high ranking in the Navy passed the information on to them."

I simply could not believe it. A chill ran up my spine. I had been the most popular person in the north up until a year ago, and now, I was the most wanted one. When I digested what was happening around me, I looked at my children and I panicked, asking myself, "Where would a safe place be for us now? How can I protect my family while I am surrounded by danger?" I felt a new fear. I had no idea about what to do or what not to do. Immediately, I decided to contact our Chief of Naval Operations, telling him that the militants at the Caspian Sea knew before I did that I was coming and had broken into my villa, looking for me. I tried several times by phone to reach him. I was never successful.

It was difficult to find rest while there were demonstrations going on outside in the street; we heard constant shouting, as well as gunshots. For the next day or so, I was glued to the television, and I decided to record the news as it came in. Every few minutes, there was a bulletin or order from Khomeini to drivers, security personnel, and servants. He demanded that they leave their posts and not perform their duties.

Military Neutrality

Early on the morning of February 10, 1979, I called for Nasser to come pick me up. I waited for over two hours. He did not appear, and I had no messages from him. I was sure that Nasser had obeyed Khomeini's orders and would not come. The promise of oil money to all citizens, regardless of position, was the power that Khomeini held that mesmerized the people and facilitated the revolution. His words still ring in my ears: "Leave your master and let your master work for you. Our country is rich with oil and the wealth belongs to you. Americans have looted our country and we will soon put an end to their aggression."

My wife and I called Jawad, our servant. We both told him that he was free to go. As a matter of fact, we both insisted that he leave our home. He replied firmly, "I am here to serve you and protect you and your family. I will never leave you, unless they kill me." It was becoming difficult. On one hand we needed him, on the other we really did not want him to get into trouble. He was absolutely convinced that he wanted to stay with us.

It was around 9:30 a.m. when I decided to drive the red car to my office. I was about a mile or two away from my home; on the way, I saw a large group of demonstrators blocking the street. There were two buses on fire, and I could hear a few gunshots. A very large, surly mob was in front of a neighborhood liquor store, and there were four or five lines of people on the sidewalk. They were removing the liquor bottles from the shelves and passing them from one to another while breaking the bottles on the side of the street, pouring the contents into a drain hole. They all were shouting, "Allah o Akbar," "God is great."

This procedure was also happening in Tehran's sophisticated hotels. The lovely lobby bars were disrespectfully being dismantled. Liquor and dirt from mud-crusted shoes was soiling and flowing over thick Persian carpets before it reached the street's gutters.

When I saw what was transpiring, I was shocked and turned my car around to come home and protect my family. On the way back, I noticed large hotel accessories being carried away. Velvet chairs, candlesticks, porcelain dishes, draperies, anything that could be transported. It was amazing for me to think that there were those who justified breaking liquor bottles in reverence to Allah. Even worse, what religious act could possibly condone stealing? I was watching emotion fired by greed, hate, and envy. I stayed home for three days, witnessing the demise of my country on television.

Martial Law Fails

A bloody battle between the militants and the Air Force continued in Tehran. All of the police stations fell, and a group of angry people started advancing to the Police Academy. A white flag was raised, and the Academy surrendered. At the same time, the commander of the Imperial Guards sent a message to Khomeini's followers, requesting a meeting with his representative, stating that the guards would not take part in any action against the people.

These were the first words that were reported by Iranian.com and many others. The course of those events have been documented and recorded for history. I, as well as others, have commented on the inept way that the Carter administration mishandled their decision making during this sensitive time. If America's lack of support for the Shah had not been as intense, perhaps the Middle East could have been saved and there would have been a possibility that Iraq would not have dared attack Kuwait.

Unfortunately sometimes, close ministers to the Shah often influenced the image that the world had about him. The monarchy in any culture and in any era has always been surrounded by those who take advantage of their status and those who become enamored with their own pomp and glory. Even then I recognized the difficulties but the alternatives to leadership were impossible for me to accept. In time, with the help of Iran's allies, perhaps there could have been solutions.

It was very interesting that in a communiqué to Washington, D.C., the United States Ambassador Sullivan reported that very soon there would be an opportune time to reconcile Khomeini's representatives with the Shah's government. He was hopeful that, prior to complete destruction of the armed forces, activities regarding transfer of power could be undertaken to preserve the cohesion of the Iranian military.

In my opinion, it was too late. Sullivan was completely out of touch. During the midmorning, a meeting of the High Council of the Armed Forces took place in the War Room of the Army High Command Headquarters. At the time of that meeting, the SAVAK headquarters were being torched, and the organization was being disbanded. The high generals of the High Council, wearing civilian clothing, were unable to communicate with their staff. It was discussed that the Shah had left, and according to the present prime minister, he was not going to return.

The prime minister wished to declare a People's Republic. Ayatollah Khomeini wanted an Islamic Republic, and his followers were supportive of him. Since the law had specified the duty of the armed forces was to safeguard the territorial integrity of the country against a foreign army, it was decided that the armed forces should pull away from any political fighting and not interfere. In the afternoon, the final communiqué of the High Council of the Iranian Armed Forces was announced on the radio and was printed in all the daily publications and read as follows:

> *"The armed forces of Iran have had the duty of defending the independence and territorial integrity of our dear Iran, and up until now have attempted to fulfill this responsibility in the best manner possible, by supporting the legal government in charge.*
>
> *Considering the recent events, the High Council of the Armed Forces met at 10:30 a.m. today, and unanimously decided to declare its neutrality in the present political*

conflicts with the aim of preventing further chaos and bloodshed. Military units have been ordered to return to their barracks.

The armed forces of Iran have always been and will always be the guardian and source of support for the noble and patriotic nation of Iran."

It was hoped that the broadcast of this communiqué would result in a peaceful transition of power and prevent further clashes between the military and the people. In some small cities, the local army commanders, clerics, and councils had agreed upon and managed to arrange for their own departure from the scene, keeping the barracks and armories closed. However, in the major cities, even repeated broadcasts of this communiqué did nothing to dampen the revolutionary fervor of those attacking virtually any place that was guarded by the military. The situation was worse in Tehran, where the large concentration of guerilla groups were relentlessly continuing their assaults.

As soon as the military announced its neutrality, Khomeini ordered his followers to attack the military bases and confiscate all the small arms, machine guns, tanks, and ammunition. Every militant was quickly armed, and in no time the peasants had looted all of the small arms. A few hours after the announcement for neutrality of the armed forces, Khomeini ordered his followers to arrest the generals and ministers. Most were captured, and after a less-than-one-hour trial by the so-called Islamic Revolutionary Council, they were condemned to death by the firing squad. The atmosphere of terror and fear had reached a new level. Khomeini now issued a statement telling all military personnel that the oath of loyalty to the Shah and his regime was now null and void. Those who had taken such an oath should now act contrary to it.

Some of the commanders did not have a chance to leave the High Council meeting and find a safe hiding place. They were captured while the people were urged by journalists and politicians to continue fighting to the last bullet. For a few hours, it appeared as if there was no one in charge.

The workers at the radio and television stations left their buildings, and the revolutionaries took their positions. After a few moments of silence in broadcasting, the voices of Khomeini supporters came on the air:

"This is the voice of the revolution of the Iranian people!"

In every corner of Tehran, a real revolution was in process. In major cities, the militants were capturing the government buildings by fighting, not by negotiations and talks. Tens of thousands of weapons were looted and distributed. Secret documents were destroyed and could be seen flying in the air. Doors to secure rooms were suddenly open. In one day of fighting, more bullets were fired than in months of a major war. All this happened at a time when there was no opportunity to rely on any form of opposition.

The doors to all the prisons were opened, and all of the criminals and murderers were set free. Part of the SAVAK office was torched, and the Senate buildings and headquarters of the police and armed forces were under Khomeini's control. Brigadier General Rahimi, the military governor of Tehran, was captured. Looters were attacking several of the palaces, and there was no interruption to the hail of flying bullets.

The Shah's last Prime Minister Bakhtiar escaped out the back door of his building while the bullets were penetrating the sand bags that were placed at the front entrance. He managed to escape to France, where he was ultimately shot by Khomeini's followers.

Members of the U.S. military personnel stationed in Iran began taking refuge in the basement of the United States Embassy building. After hearing the sound of broken glass, they frantically asked for Sullivan's help. Ambassador Sullivan was feverishly trying to find an escape route for the U.S. military personnel who were now surrounded. They informed Sullivan by phone that armed groups of militants had entered the building. Things were not any better around the U.S. Embassy, and the guards were using tear gas and threats to keep away the angry crowd.

As the day began in the United States, it was recorded by Iranian. com, that President Carter was at Camp David with his Secretary of State, Cyrus Vance. Upon hearing the news of the previous night, U.S. time, in Iran, he ordered an emergency meeting of the crisis committee.

In this meeting, Warren Christopher, Undersecretary of State, head of the CIA, deputies of the Defense Secretary, and some other military personnel were present.

The discussion was over choosing one of three solutions proposed in writing by Brzezinski, asking Iranian military leaders to either:

1. Reach a compromise with Bazargan, who had been appointed prime minister by Khomeini, instead of Bakhtiar, the last Prime Minister of the Shah
2. Declare their neutrality in the transfer of power
3. Initiate a coup

As Brzezinski was not fully aware of all that had already transpired, he was in favor of option three. By then, it was finished in Iran.

The emergency meeting of the crisis committee in Washington was abruptly adjourned after hearing news of General Rahimi's arrest, the fall of radio and television stations, and control of most army barracks. Meanwhile, Brzezinski managed to convince the White House aide, Captain Gary Sick, to report back to him if the Iranian army was ready for a coup. Brzezinski asked Sick to talk with the head of the military in Tehran, and General Huyser in Washington.

Brzezinski was trying to obtain Carter's green light for the coup, against the advice of the U.S. Secretary of States, Cyrus Vance, and the State Department. He already had Carter's tacit approval, having contacted him in Camp David's chapel, where Carter had gone minutes before for prayers. It was not a time for prayer; it was the time for action. Carter's inept handling of Iran, in my opinion, added to our difficulties. It was too little and too late. The Shah's armed forces had declared neutrality, and every ranking officer or minister was looking for a hiding place.

Finally, the United States Department of Defense prepared the text of a telex, giving permission for a coup. They were trying to contact the military officials in Tehran. However, no one was answering the phone. Finally, after several attempts, an unknown person answered in Farsi. Giving up their attempts to contact military officials, the department of defense decided to seek Sullivan's advice.

At the same moment, Mr. Sullivan, the United States Ambassador in Tehran was worried about security for the embassy. He had just begun a telephone conversation with a member of the Revolutionary Council, when a voice interrupted his conversation: "Mr. Ambassador, urgent call, White House."

Sullivan could only hear that someone was telling him, "Mr. Brzezinski would like to ask the head of the military mission, through you, whether or not the Iranian army can initiate a coup?" At that moment Sullivan was speaking to Khomeini's confidants, seeking help for the lives of United States officers who were now in danger, as their mission building had been occupied. Again, while he was on the phone with a member of the Revolution Council, he was interrupted by another call from the White House. At this point, Sullivan lost his patience and yelled into the phone: "Tell Mr. Brzezinski to cut it out—I don't know how to say this in Polish!"

It was apparent that through this telephone conversation, Dr. Yazdi, Khomeini's aide, who was educated in the United States and fluent in English, overheard about the possibility of a coup. He notified Khomeini, who immediately ordered the capture and execution of the Shah's high-ranking officers.

Members of the U.S. military mission, and some senior High Command officers who had taken refuge with them in the building, were finally rescued.

At the White House, Brzezinski asked General Huyser's viewpoint on the possibility of a coup: "Only with direct support of the U.S. military." Brzezinski asked him if he was ready to lead the coup and go to Iran. Huyser's answer was calculated: "Yes, with some conditions: I need unlimited funds at my disposal; ten to twelve U.S. generals are to be handpicked and must accompany me; I need 10,000 elite U.S. servicemen; and full authority and comprehensive national support."

Even General Huyser, U.S. special envoy to Iran, had no idea that at that very moment, when he responded to Brzezinski, General Rabiei, the Air Force commander, whom he counted on, was sitting handcuffed on a bench awaiting execution.

At Alavi School in Tehran, the supervisor of the school stood at the door and declared, "We only accept leaders of the regime." There was a certain hierarchy at the school. It was reserved for only the execution of high-ranking leaders. Hundreds of people who had been arrested were not let in by the officials. They were taken to other facilities. It appeared that some revolutionary militants wished to fit the entire collapsed regime into that one building! The same building now contained the entire political structure of Khomeini's future Islamic government. They were using the Alavi School as their temporary revolutionary headquarters. I am sure Khomeini was proud of this blood-soaked edifice, where his animalistic barbarians were enjoying seeing men of stature, they could not ever emulate, die in pain with stoic honor.

At nightfall, fighting continued in and around Tehran, and went on throughout the night. Several high-ranking officials were arrested and immediately executed. Among them were men I knew, admired, and respected. They were brilliant men who were tortured and their bodies mutilated.

General Pakravan, at age eighty-two, was brought to the Alavi School in his wheelchair. In 1964, Khomeini was condemned to death by a tribunal in Iran. General Pakravan recognized Khomeini's ambition as well as his charisma, and although not a religious man himself, he felt that the Iranian people who followed this man would cause difficulties if he were killed. The general asked the Shah to pardon him; in order to comply, he had to become an Ayatollah. Under the Iranian constitution, this was the only way he could grant a pardon. The Shah proceeded to comply before sending Khomeini to Turkey. Ironically, General Pakravan was one of the first of the Shah's officials to be executed by the man whose life he saved.

174

Amir Abbas Hovayda was prime minister of Iran for fourteen years during the Shah. He was the man who had presented me with a gold pen in gratitude for a job well done, and was also one of the first to be executed. His last request was to not be shot in the head to spare his mother from having to see him in that condition. He was granted that one request.

General Manocher Khosrodad was world renowned as a distinguished pilot. Whenever I visited him, I always enjoyed viewing his international credentials on the walls of his office. While he was piloting a small jet and a helicopter, he gave me a tour from the air of the Air Force training schools. His last words before being shot were, "Long live the king."

General Nader Jahanbani was a lovely man with an outgoing personality. I enjoyed his company several times at the Caspian Sea. He was dedicated to keeping the country fit while heading Iran's Sports Organization. He was an outstanding pilot instructor and the leader of the Golden Crown Acrojet team of Iran.

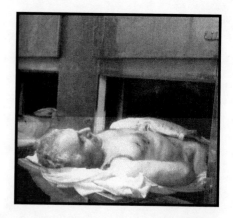

General Mehdi Rahimi was a true nationalist and good friend of my father-in-law's. He was the Shah's last hope for a coup.

The Search of My House in the Middle of the Night

Two evenings in a row, a group of militants came to our building with a portable loudspeaker. They pointed to our windows, saying, "We know who you are. We know you have a military pistol. Turn it in, or you will be executed with your own gun." I could not sleep, thinking about the two small arms and ammunition that I had hidden under the heavy dresser in our bedroom. How could I return them? After all, one of them was registered in my name.

One evening, about one-thirty in the morning, Shauna and I heard a loud knocking. We were frightened as we rushed to open the door in our pajamas. We were horrified to see a few militants wearing dirty clothing with long beards and rifles slung over their shoulders. One of them started to talk loudly. In a fraction of a second, I decided not to let him take the upper hand. Immediately, I interrupted, and with an angry voice, as if I were still in command and ordering him, I said, "You had better be quiet and speak with a very soft voice. I have two sleeping children and I do not want you to awaken them." He listened carefully and then whispering said, "We have lost one of our guards. He was a sentinel at this complex. We are going to search your home to make sure that you have not captured him."

I felt a little better, but I doubted about their truthfulness. I thought they may want to come in and capture me. I responded, "We have not seen a guard here and I am positive that he is not in our home." The militant in charge came forward a little and closer to the door jam, saying, "We must search anyway, and make sure you have not hidden him."

I agreed and told him to be very quiet. The lead militant and two others came inside. My wife closed the door, not allowing the others to enter. She moved across the room and leaned her back against a small bar so that it would not be noticed. The militant looked around and then started to open the doors of the bathrooms, closets, and children's rooms. When he started to look inside the kitchen cabinets and my dresser and desk drawers, I immediately sensed that these men were not looking for a lost guard, they were trying to find small guns. I moved closer to the intruders as I said, "I don't think your guard would fit in the drawers." At this time, Rammy, our daughter, woke up, and I used that as an excuse to speak in a very disturbed tone of voice, saying, "You awakened our daughter. You had better go somewhere else and search for your guard." I could see the disappointment on their faces while the lead militant gestured to the other two to leave.

I realized that the small guns hidden under the dresser were a large problem, especially the Colt that was registered in my name. It could be the end of me if they had the sophistication to trace the Colt serial number back to me. I knew now that I had to find a way to safely return them.

It was announced on the radio and television that all military and civilian governmental offices were closed until further notice. I did not return to my office for three days and constantly watched the news, witnessing high-ranking generals and ministers being executed in Khomeini's Headquarters.

The revolutionaries' tactics were fully at work. It was an environment of fear for those of us who did not participate in their bloody conquest. History records the overthrow of other countries that happened in similar fashion. First, killing the educated and empowering the masses, then later, only to be controlled by the instigators, the few, with their own agenda. Now, I along with many innocent citizens was the victim of this type of backward aggression.

Called in to Report to the Main Naval Headquarters

At least ten times on Thursday and Friday, February 15 and 16, 1979, there were announcements on television and radio, calling the names of senior officers of the Navy. They were being directed to report to the main Naval Headquarters at 8:30 a.m. on Saturday, February 17, 1979. Unfortunately, my name was among those called.

It was a very difficult time. All of us in high positions were living in horror and waiting for something to happen. We were apprehensive after viewing the execution of many high-ranking blameless citizens. We knew that something alarming was about to take place. Personally, I felt completely helpless.

I had been summoned to attend the gathering at the main Naval Headquarters. There was no other alternative, I decided to take the red car and wear civilian clothing. My son was awake and partially aware of what was happening. He kept holding onto my leg. When I was ready to leave the house, he ran in front of the door and opened his arms, as wide as he could, to block my passage. As I left, he was crying and begging me to stay. But I knew that if I did not attend the meeting, I would be giving the militants an excuse to come and arrest me. Although I tried to reassure him with my warm embrace, I had no other choice but to leave.

I stepped into the red car and drove, with fear, toward the Navy's main Headquarters, leaving the pistols hidden at home. When I was close, I saw several militants with guns in the vicinity of the entrance. I decided to park some distance away and walk. It was about thirty yards to the gate. This was where I had always entered with my driver in the Naval car. One of the militants with a gun on his shoulder came close to me, saying, "Where are you going?" I told him who I was and that I was supposed to report for the gathering at 8:30 a.m.

He escorted me toward the gate while saying to another militant, who began to give me a body search, "He is one of them." The revolutionary was still searching my pockets when a third man carrying a gun pulled me away and escorted me inside the huge courtyard that was so familiar to me.

The main Naval Headquarters was built in a C shape, with an enormous assembly area between the buildings. There were several hundred officers and Naval personnel, all standing facing the balcony of the middle building. Most were in civilian clothing, only a few officers were in uniform, with their shoulder ranks torn off. The majority of the people were petty officers and civilians employed by the Navy. Some were shouting, calling others by names. Others angrily were bad-mouthing their superiors.

These were very uncomfortable moments. I was standing among a few junior officers and civilians, trying to be invisible. It was around 8:30 a.m. when all of the sudden a machine gun started firing from the balcony. A tall man of large stature with unkempt beard and disheveled clothing came behind the microphone and said, "I am the commander in charge of the main Naval Headquarters. I have not slept for three nights, and if any of you do not follow my orders, I will respond to you with this!" He lifted his machine gun and fired at least fifty rounds of ammunition into the air. When he stopped firing, the silence was deafening.

There were several other people on the balcony, and to my surprise, one of them was Admiral Majidi, my first captain out of the Academy. I recalled the days that we had worked closely together in the Persian Gulf and then later at the Naval Headquarters in Tehran. I thought back over the course of our relationship and how I had never trusted him, even though, over time, we had become friends.

When Admiral Majidi came to the microphone, he made an amazing announcement. "I have been part of Khomeini's underground group and I have been in contact with our leader, long before he went to France." The assembly of the Naval personnel were stunned by his acknowledgment and started to boo him, shouting, "You are Bahaii." "You are not even a Muslim."

In response, the quiet assembly turned into a shouting match. Once again the sound of the machine gun filled the air, followed by the same voice saying, "I have to remind you again, I am the commander and you will all do as I say. Quiet now!" In spite of the danger that I faced, I took a moment to reflect on the many poker games I had played with Admiral Majidi. Thinking back again, I realized that he had always affiliated himself with whoever was the shining star of the moment and shifted his alliances in order to better his own position.

Taken Hostage in the Naval Headquarters

Admiral Majidi was trying hard to continue his speech when one of my subordinates, in uniform with his ranks torn off, came toward me. He did not salute me. He had always called me by my rank or "Sir." This time, he took my arm, calling me by my first name and saying, "Mr. Manocher, your time is over. Come with me."

I was alarmed but I tried not to show my fear. I smiled and with composure started to walk in the direction that he was leading me toward the north wing of the building. On one end was the Chief of Naval Operations office and on the other end was the office of the Deputy to the Chief of Naval Operations. These were magnificently beautiful offices with impressive mahogany bookcases. We stopped near the deputy's office, where several other militants were assembled.

Once again, I was subjected to a body search and then ushered into the office of the Deputy of the Chief of Naval Operations. The beautiful mahogany bookshelves were brutally smashed, and the contents were strewn across the floor. The deputy's desk chair and sofas were ripped apart. Obviously, they were suspected of containing hidden pistols.

Upon entering the room, I immediately saw ten of my admiral friends and other senior officers. Two admirals and one of my classmates were sitting on the sofa. As soon as they saw me, they moved over to create space for me. I sat next to my dear friend Admiral Movaghari, who had been my commanding officer and showed me the beauty of Khark Island.

No one was talking and none of us knew what was going to happen. We could hear the sounds of the machine guns outside in the assembly area. Gradually more senior officers were brought into the room. We soon numbered twenty-one people, all hostages of the militants that armed the door.

Outside, speeches continued and there was cheering between the rounds of machine gun fire. Later, we learned that Admiral Majidi had contacted Khomeini's son-in-law, telling him that he captured twenty-one of the top Iranian Naval officers. He asked for permission to take all of us to the Alavi School, handcuffed, and blind folded, to be sentenced.

Khomeini, and the revolutionary council, were at that chaotic moment in a frenzy, executing anyone that they felt was of potential danger to them. The firing squad on the roof was barbarically carrying out the orders. When Khomeini's son-in-law conveyed Admiral Majidi's request asking for Khomeini's approval to take us to the Alavi School, Khomeini responded by saying, "I have appointed Admiral Madani to be the man in charge of the Navy. Admiral Majidi needs to get Admiral Madani's approval." At that moment, Admiral Madani was in the south, in the Persian Gulf, where he had been making speeches to calm riots that had broken out. Admiral Madani always seemed to be a down-to-earth commander, he had been my dinner host on many occasions, and I thought, we had had mutual respect for one another.

While still confined in the deputy's office, Admiral Majidi, with many difficulties, contacted Admiral Madani, and asked for approval to send us to the Alavi School. Fortunately Admiral Madani did not approve the request. He claimed that the Alavi School was overcrowded. We later learned that his hesitation was personal. He knew all of us, as well as our children, who called him "Uncle." Because of the closeness of our relationships, he needed time to think and temporarily suggested our temporary release. We knew nothing about what our fate would be or what was being discussed between the power-hungry Majidi and Khomeini's new Naval Commander Madani, who had no respect for the monarchy.

It was around one o'clock in the afternoon, when a few militants brought in a large tray, with a plate full of dates and a few pots of tea. One militant looked at one of the admirals and said, "Take any pot of tea and pour it into a cup." The admiral did exactly as the militant ordered. The militant then picked up the teacup and drank the tea, saying, "The tea and dates are for you. I wanted to prove to you that it was not poisoned." The revolutionaries obviously had respect for Admiral Madani and now did not know exactly what to do with us. Admiral Majidi must have been annoyed that the senior in command had given us a temporary reprieve.

We drank our tea as we slowly whispered to each other. We were all concerned about what was going to happen. The militants were watching us while we were sitting and waiting for the unknown. I reached over and took a newspaper that had been lying on the floor. Very carefully, I tore the edge of the paper into pieces, about one and one half inches wide. I wrote my father's phone number backward and rolled one of the strips as small as possible. Passing it to Admiral Movaghari, I asked him to call the number that I had written, if anything happened to me. I repeated the procedure a few more times and quickly passed the telephone numbers to the others in the room.

The time crept by and about five o'clock in the afternoon, the sound of the machine guns began quieting down. Admiral Majidi came in with a few revolutionaries following him. He pretended to act in a friendly fashion, as if nothing had happened. He opened the dialogue by stating, "It was my decision to separate you from the rest. After all, you are the leaders of the Navy." He added, "The people are emotionally charged, and I did not want anyone to harm you."

When we heard this from Admiral Majidi, we wanted to believe that he was saving us, and for a moment he became our hero. We spoke together and started to feel that perhaps there was hope and that we could immediately return to our families. However, he soon turned to us and, dashing our ill-founded hopes, he said, "In a few minutes every one of you will be interrogated individually, and after the interrogation, you can go to your homes."

My Lucky Release

It was around eight o'clock in the evening when one of the militants called my name; leaving my friends behind, I was escorted out into the room, passing through the corridors that I had proudly walked so many times. Unbelievably, a part of me still felt at home even though now I was terrified as I was being escorted by armed militants. I hoped that the wild thumping in my chest would not give me away. I was overcome with fear, but I dared not panic. These are moments that I will not ever forget.

In the next office, there was a Mullah and one of my subordinate officers. The Mullah was sitting behind a desk. He appeared to be stern and angry. In front of him was an empty chair and very bitterly he told me to sit down, while asking my name and my most recent position in the Navy. He wrote down my answers, and defiantly started the conversation by saying, "Whatever you have been doing has been against Islam." He encouraged me to admit, for my own welfare, that I had been acting against Islam and had been working for the benefit of the United States. I refused to accept these words, and I kept telling him that what I had been working on was in the best interest of my country.

I strongly believed my response to him, and when he started to raise his voice, I decided to reply by taking a commanding posture. "Don't shout at me," I said. "I know what I have done and I am proud of helping to educate our young people and introduce them to today's technology." Speaking firmly, I continued, saying, "I did not know that learning and education were non-Islamic."

Even though I was concerned about what the reactions would be to my strong words, it seemed that showing my strength worked. He immediately lowered his voice, and finally, he reached over and put a Koran in front of me. He asked me to put my right hand on the Koran and swear that I would return whenever they called me for further interrogations. As soon as I responded to his command, he called a militant over and said, "He can leave." A surly armed man came forward and escorted me to the outside of the building and handed me to another armed guard, who escorted me to the gate.

As I left, I could not see the blood, but I could smell the scent of death and feel the agony that had taken place that day. There was an ominous cloud that engulfed and sickened me. It was more than fear—it was the questioning of human existence, of survival, of power, of so many things.

I looked down the street and saw my shiny red car. I walked as quickly as possible, trying not to show my panic, in order to reach my sanctuary. Somehow, I managed to open the door and slide into the seat but my relief was short-lived. The sobering fact was that my family and I had to hide, and immediately would not be soon enough.

Chapter 7

Courtesy sarafrazan.net

Our Escape

Only an Hour at Home

I drove home much faster than usual. Various scenarios kept running through my mind. I did not want to face reality, but I knew that I had to hide or leave the country. "Who could I trust? Who could I go to for help?" As I made my way back to my home, I was in a state of shock; I could hear the uproar going on around me. I did not look left or right. I knew there were riotous crowds of radical Khomeini loyalists all over the city. I drove as if I was in a dark tunnel, relying on blind instinct to find my way. I feared death at any moment. It was difficult to control my terror. My body was damp with perspiration. I could not get a grip on the steering wheel; it slipped through my fingers as I was turning into the main thoroughfare that led to my home.

I was trembling slightly and realized that I had to calm down. What if someone noticed my erratic driving? I could be picked up and taken away for an unknown destiny. In my mind, I went back over the day's events concerning Admiral Majidi and his betrayal to his country. Was he disappointed when Admiral Madani gave us a temporary reprieve? We had all become friends. I kept re-evaluating the relationships and trust that our children had enjoyed with these men. I knew now that I dare not be lulled into thinking that I was safe. Their cause was greater to them than my life. It was evident now that this would not be a permanent truce.

I hoped that embracing my family would clear my mind. They were my life and my substance, and for them, I had to find a way. As soon as I arrived at my building and opened the door, I found Shauna in the position that she had been in when I had left her that morning. She was still in bed, and beside her was an ashtray filled with partially smoked cigarettes. Bob was awake and sitting next to her. When he saw me, he ran to me. Picking him up, I kissed his soft cheek, and for a moment we both relaxed.

"What happened?" Shauna asked. "I will tell you later," I replied, "just hurry and select some clothing for the children. We must go now, it is not safe here, and I only know that they are going to call me back for further interrogation."

Jawad—The Loyal Butler

Jawad, our butler overheard our conversation. He entered the room, saying, "I cannot let you go alone. I would like to come with you and protect you. At least," he pleaded, "I can protect the children. Thank you." I replied, "But you really must leave and report to the committee. The longer you stay with us, the more trouble you will face for yourself."

Jawad refused to go to his barracks and kept saying, "I cannot leave you alone. I have to protect you and your family." He was very upset, and we finally agreed to allow him to stay.

A Plan to Escape Is Born

It was around ten in the evening when we left our home. The anxiety we felt did not allow us to become emotional. As I glanced at our cherished belongings, a feeling of nostalgia suddenly overwhelmed me. Our life in Tehran, our goals, our dreams, everything we felt comfortable with was fading from my view and from my grasp. I picked up baby Rammy and wrapped her in a pink blanket. With my family walking ahead of me, I did not look back as I closed the door.

We drove directly to the home of Shauna's parents, with continuous furtive looks in the rear-view mirror. I was concerned that we were being followed.

The tension we both felt was an emotion that we could not discard. Even though we longed for tranquility, any reprieve we might enjoy, we knew, would be in the distant future. Fortunately, the streets were relatively clear, except for a few checkpoints that we encountered along the way. Twice we were stopped by some angry militants. We held our breath while the two small valises in our trunk and our sleeping children in the back of the red car were evaluated. Nothing seemed to cause alarm, apparently the revolutionaries were looking for small arms, and our mundane cargo did not alarm them. I continued to think of the pistols I had hidden at home, and again, I knew that they had to be eliminated, but for the moment I dismissed those thoughts and tried to come up with a logical plan.

It had been an exhausting day. Arriving at Shauna's parents' home, we were greeted by her youngest sister. The family were all there and happy to see us. After being warmly embraced, they tried to make us feel comfortable with their gracious conversation. Our son Bob was awake, and it was important to us not to concern him with talk of our despair. We all knew of the dangers that we were faced with. Despite the fear, that night, as we pulled our down comforters around us, for the moment, sleep came.

The following morning was bright and sunny. It was difficult to accept the situation that we were in. I wanted to stay in bed, sleep for a while, and then enjoy a leisurely breakfast of sweets and tea. This type of relaxation was unfortunately, a long way from reality. After a short discussion, Shauna and I decided that we would stay together at all times. It was too difficult for her to wonder about my safety if we became separated.

My commitment to education influenced our decision to keep young Bob in school. I needed time to think and felt that continuing our son's daily routine would give him a more secure feeling. Our plan was to drop Bob off at the American School, where he was registered as a first-year student. His classes were only for the morning session. During this time, Shauna and I decided that we would drive repeatedly around the block, with our young daughter, until Bob was dismissed at midday. After a few days had passed, we became concerned that we did not have enough of our personal essentials. One afternoon, after picking Bob up, we decided to take the risk and drive to our home. As soon as we opened the door, Jawad was stationed in the living room, wearing civilian clothing with a rifle slung over his shoulder.

"Jawad," I asked, "Where did you get the gun? Where did it come from?" With a broad grin, he happily replied, "I went to the nearby mosque and I told the Mullah that I wanted to be a solder of Allah. They asked my name and they gave me this rifle and lots of ammunition. Sir," he said very bravely, "now I can really protect you and your family." In a fraction of a second, I realized I already possessed two hidden pistols, and now a rifle had been added. I swallowed hard, composed myself, and sincerely thanked Jawad, saying, "I am sure you can be of great help." I was impressed by this kind man's loyalty.

Quickly we gathered a few more articles of clothing. We were eager to leave and fearful that, at any moment, we would hear a knock at the door. I thought of the hate on the faces of those who were standing on the balcony of the Naval Headquarters and I knew, if they came, this time, there would not be a reprieve.

Driving back to our temporary home, I stopped at a public telephone and called Kourosh Navaii. Something had to be done about returning the guns, especially the one that was registered in my name. It seemed ironic to me that Jawad could obtain a rifle so easily, when I would quickly be eliminated if found with any firearms in my possession. I had now become an obstacle to the new regime. The more I thought about how dedicated I had been about helping my country, the more depressed I became. Kourosh answered the phone himself. After the usual formalities, I asked him if I could return the pistol he had given me. He agreed that it would be prudent to do so, and suggested that I wrap it in a towel, put it under the car seat, and meet him the following afternoon.

After picking up Bob at school, we retrieved the Beretta as well as the Colt. Fortunately, we were not stopped by roadblocks. We met with Kourosh for less than an hour, and it was apparent that he was nervous about having us as guests in his home. He was surprised that I also had a Colt, but took both guns from me, promising that my name would be eliminated from the registration lists. I insisted that he obtain the receipt and watch closely as they crossed out my name. He honored my request, saying, "This is the least I can do for you." During the last few minutes of our visit, my friend gave me a full report on the latest arrests. Our feelings that it was definitely a necessity to leave the country were reaffirmed. The noose seemed to be getting smaller and closer.

The following morning, after driving Bob to school, I stopped at a few public telephone booths and made a notation of their numbers. I wanted to talk to Sheik Abdullah and thought that if Jawad could go to his appliance store with a note from me, we could set up a telephone rendezvous. Being very discreet, my trusted servant made the contact and told me that the Sheik would be calling me according to plan.

The selected telephone rang promptly at 5:00 p.m. The Sheik's opening words were, "How are you getting along? I hope you are being very careful." "Yes," I replied. "But I cannot be in hiding forever. Do you know of any ships or small vessels that might be sailing anywhere in the Persian Gulf, So that, we could be dropped off in another country?" With concern, the Sheik responded, "No. No—that is not advisable. There have been several incidents of those trying to escape being shot at the pier. Also, all of the borders are closed and under tight control."

Once again, I was disappointed. Not giving up, I said, "How about Pakistan or the Soviet Union?" "Forget about the Soviet Union," he replied. "The Russians will handcuff the escapees and return them to the committees." "Another dead end," I thought. We decided to speak daily at the same time. Hopefully something would open up.

Passports

Shauna and I both had valid passports, but in the photos, I was dressed in my Naval uniform. It was also filled with visa stamps from England, America, and the Soviet Union. I knew this would not be acceptable. The children were not included on my wife's passport. If we were going to manage to leave the country, it was mandatory that we try to amend both passports. I decided to keep my real name on my own and only select a new address and occupation.

A large stadium had been converted into the new passport office in order to facilitate the several thousand people who were trying to leave the country. We picked up two applications without any incident. After filling them out with our information, we returned in two days to receive legitimate identification. Militants with machine guns were wearing ski masks, herding groups into lines. Two frightening openings disclosing the eyes of the occupants added to the terror that we felt. It was later rumored that Khomeini had brought these men from Palestine to add muscle to the revolution.

I recognized the exhausted faces of diplomats and high-ranking military officers who had not, as yet, been executed. None of us spoke; the silence of such a large crowd gave a surreal feeling to this somber mass of citizens.

Fortunately, the lines moved quickly. When my turn came, I gave my new information to the proper official. He looked me over closely, then stepped back to confer with a fellow cohort. For a moment, I felt as though I could not breathe. Then without hesitation, he came forward and looked through a stack of passports, picked mine out, and handed it to me, saying, "Next." I was delighted to have new identification. When I turned, I looked at Shauna, winked with a smile, and flashed the new passport in front of her.

I stepped back to watch her move forward while digesting my own good luck. Any feelings of relief were short-lived as, within minutes, two attendants ushered Shauna out of my line of vision. "What could possibly be wrong?" I thought. "Should I go after her?" After what seemed like an eternity, my pale and shaking wife reappeared. My relief was apparent, as she told me that they had thought that she had been in the Navy. "Oh no," she had replied. "That was my first husband. We were divorced several years ago." Showing me her passport, including the children's names, my next words were, "Thank God, let's get out of here."

While having dinner that evening, my father-in-law told me of a news bulletin that he had heard. It seemed that Khomeini would consider the request of any military personnel who would like to seek early retirement.

Early Retirement from the Navy

The room was crowded as I filled out the necessary paperwork at the armed forces retirement agency. It was necessary to include my bank account number in order to receive direct monetary deposits. In a matter of a few seconds, the young major who was helping me handed me my retirement documents. After twenty-six years, my career was over. I had not been able to participate in the formal ceremony to celebrate my promotion to admiral, and I had not been allowed to stay in the United States long enough to complete my PhD, the degree I had worked hard to obtain. I did not dwell on the bittersweet, as I ran to the car to show my wife my official papers. "At least," I told her, "I will be paid monthly compensation." At the time I was in denial. I wanted so badly to still believe in the goodness of humanity.

Militants in Bob's School

Taking Bob to school one morning, I felt a certain sense of composure. For a moment, I allowed myself to relax and reflect about my situation. Perhaps, I could find a civilian job as an engineer and take my family to a new city, where, once again, we would find tranquility.

Shauna had stayed home with Rammy and her sisters that morning to rest, while her mother chose to be my companion. Kissing us goodbye, Bob ran into the school building. We continued our sentry by driving repeatedly around the block.

After about one hour, as we were approaching the rear of the school, my mother-in-law noticed Bob standing in the open back door that looked out into the street. "Manocher," she said with alarm in her voice. "Why is Bob out of class?" We knew immediately that something was wrong.

Leaving the car, I quickly ran to Bob, saying, "Why are you out here?" "Dad," he responded, "some militants, with guns, are inside waiting for you. They questioned me, and I ran back here to see if I could find you."

In seconds, I gathered my six year old son, up into my arms, ran to the car, and sped off. My earlier fantasy about staying in the country was over. This was the last day that Bob would attend school in Iran.

The Black Book

That afternoon, after my narrow miss with the militants, I waited anxiously at the telephone booth for Sheik Abdullah's call. He was pleased about my news relating to the passports but concerned that the new regime had decided to bring me in. After a long pause, he started to speak with despair in his voice, "I think you should know something of a serious nature. Have you heard of the black book?" "No," I replied. "What black book?" He explained to me that there were alphabetical books with the first letter of the last name of those who were forbidden to exit the country. They were being updated daily and kept at the airport. If a passenger's name matches the one in the book, they are arrested immediately. After taking a deep breath, he continued, "Unfortunately, your name is in the 'B' book."

It was a long time before I could speak. I had risked my life and my family's to obtain new passports, and now I faced another dead end. Sensing my disappointment, the Sheik whispered softly, "Please don't worry, we will find a way." Continuing, he tried to comfort me by saying, "I have a relative who is assigned to airport security. I am going to talk with him this evening. He told me of an oil company plane that was scheduled to go to Turkey in a week. Perhaps, with his help, we can get you and your family on board." Again we agreed to speak at eight-thirty the following evening.

I did not discuss the black book with my family. I could not bear to further worry my wife with this heavy burden. I was beginning to feel that it was just a matter of time before I would be arrested and taken to the Alavi School to be executed. One thing was very clear to me, as I had suspected, Admiral Majidi had decided that his new position with Khomeini was more important to him than my life. Someone put my name in the black book, and I knew that I had once been considered one of the "Six million dollar men" in the Shah's Imperial Navy. My dedication to the Navy and my affiliation with the United States would never be excused.

Wednesday 9 to 11

Arriving at the phone booth promptly at 8:00 p.m., I was upset to see a woman occupying the telephone. The more I paced up and down the sidewalk, the more she talked. I was smoking continuously as I glared into the booth. She turned her back and I am sure continued speaking, only to annoy me. Finally, as she stepped away, the phone rang quickly and I was relieved to hear the Sheik's voice. "My relative will be at the airport, the following Wednesday, between nine and eleven in the morning. If you can manage to leave from Tehran within this time frame, he will hide the 'B' black book." For a moment, I felt my desperation waning until the Sheik added, "By the way, the oil company plane is grounded until further notice." Another blow, but I thanked my friend and told him we would speak the next day. The hiding of the "B" book was hopeful; perhaps I could find other passage. Maybe, I thought, if I could obtain a commercial airline flight during those few designated hours, I could take my family and we would be able to work our way to America.

The first travel agency, as well as others, dashed my hopes. All tickets for all planes leaving Iran were sold out for three months. Still, giving up was not an option. I was willing to take any risk to ensure the safety of those I loved. Suddenly, I remembered that my younger brother Ira had a very good friend who lived in his apartment building and owned a travel agency. I called Ira immediately, and there was a certain feeling of relief, for me, as I told him my story; I knew that he would need all of the information in order to help me. He was shocked to hear the seriousness of my situation and immediately called his friend Amir.

Shauna and I met my brother at the agency and told Amir that we needed four airline tickets for the following Wednesday. The plane had to leave between nine and eleven in the morning, in order to comply with our plan. "Where do you want to go?" he asked. "Anywhere," I responded. "Japan, India, Pakistan, anywhere." The agent stood up and paced around his office, saying, "I must leave now, but I will talk to you tonight." I told him we were not in our home, we were not safe, and that it was imperative that we leave the country.

Dining that evening at Shauna's parents' was difficult. I knew that if today's events did not prove to be of help, there was no place else to turn. At nine o'clock the telephone rang. It was Ira. Speaking excitedly, he told me to meet him at the travel agency at nine-thirty the following morning. It was difficult to finish my meal; the stress of not knowing, if this would finally be our way to escape, was overwhelming. I retired early and in the morning, I was dressed and ready long before my family had arisen. My wife as well as the children all accompanied me to Amir's office. Ira's car was already at the curb when we pulled up in front of the agency. As I glanced at my brother, I could feel the compassion that he felt for me. I was fortunate to have him to share my concerns.

Together we all walked into the agency, only to be handed an envelope containing a note. It was obvious that Amir did not have time to talk; the room was filled with people. Back outside on the sidewalk, we quickly read the contents, telling us to return promptly at five o'clock that evening.

A long day stretched ahead of us. Ira suggested that we all go to his home, so the children could play and we could relax and enjoy luncheon. Somehow, the hours passed. I constantly looked at my watch, knowing that at noon, I had a scheduled telephone meeting with Sheik Abdullah. During the morning, I managed to break away, and when the call came through, his first words were "Did you have any luck finding tickets?" "I don't know yet," I said. "My brother's friend, a travel agent, might be able to help us." "I will talk with you on Monday," he said. Wishing me luck, we ended our conversation. The minutes continued to tick by in slow motion. Finally, it was close to five o'clock and time to report back to the agency.

Amir greeted us at the door. He invited us in while moving a few chairs to the front of his desk. I was holding my breath during the time we were being seated. Finally, he spoke. There was a British Overseas Airways Corporation (BOAC) plane leaving Tehran on Wednesday at ten-thirty in the morning. The destination was London. The look on his face was grim as he glanced down, opened a heavy drawer, and with a trembling hand, brought forth a sealed white envelope. When he spoke, his voice was strained. "These tickets are for someone else, but I am giving them to you." I looked over at Shauna; Rammy had fallen sleep on her lap. Bob's head was resting on my brother's shoulder. I thought of my family; for a minute I hesitated, then quickly said, "Thank you; will we be getting into trouble by using them?" With head down he responded, "No, if anyone gets into trouble it would be me." Pushing his chair aside, he stood. "May I please have your passports?" he said. Taking them from me, he disappeared into the next room. We all sat quietly. Who were the people whose tickets we would be using? Hopefully, I thought, they would be able to find another way out. It was too late to have regrets; the tickets were in my pocket. We had found a way, but would we be able to get past the black book?

Amir walked back into the room. We were waiting for further instructions. For an instant my heart dropped as I listened to his words. "The present system calls for the passenger's passports to be delivered to the service office at the airport for security checks, two days prior to the departure date. One hour before the flight, passengers must go to this office, with tickets in hand, in order to obtain their passports. Unfortunately, the airport messenger has already left." "Oh no," I thought. "What now?" Amir quickly continued. "Don't worry; I am sure I can arrange to have the tickets delivered tomorrow. You can make your payment now and even though it is Monday, we know what to do." With relief, I quickly pulled out my wallet and paid what I knew was a very inflated price. It did not matter; my spirits had lifted, although I was still apprehensive. I could not help but speculate. What if there was further money waiting for the travel agent if he turned us in to the authorities who were trying to locate me?

When we walked outside, night had fallen. Shauna put the children in the car and my brother and I embraced. We were both drained after the day's happenings. I knew that his help had given us the slim possibility to escape. Ira's hand remained on my shoulder as he asked me about seeing our parents. "Manocher, you do not have much time left, but I know you will want to say goodbye." "Of course, of course," I responded. "We will be there tomorrow morning and Ira, thank you." My voice broke. "I know, I know," he said and with a handshake we parted.

Thus far, I had only trusted two people with our plight: my good friend Sheik Abdullah and my beloved brother Ira. Now, we were on our way to tell our family that we were leaving. The circle of those knowing about our plans would be expanding, but there was no other way. I had to say farewell.

We arrived before lunch and the family had gathered. My youngest uncle greeted us at the door. He was a businessman, one of the largest exporters of lamb casings in the country. He was glad to see me and told me he was having trouble shipping his product to his customers in Europe, because most of the cargo planes had been grounded. He had never been involved in government or political affairs and fortunately was removed from the ongoing slaughter that was continuing throughout the country.

My younger brother Behrouz ran to us and took little Bob's hand; he had just turned nineteen, and I was concerned about leaving him. I wanted to have a presence in his life, now that I was living in Tehran. For a moment, I had forgotten that I had retired from the Navy and I was running away. Reality quickly returned, as my mother approached with her loving smile. My father, following her, stopped to pick up Rammy and kissed her on the top of the head. She was the first girl in our family in three generations, and he enjoyed treating her like a little princess. Mother moved forward and slowly asked me, "Are you going on a trip, Manocher?" "Yes," I responded. "How did you know?" She replied softly, "My dear son, you must be a mother to know these things. Please, Manocher, take your family someplace safe and for now don't think of coming back." I appreciated her wise words, and thanking her, I turned to the family group and told them that Shauna, the children, and I were going on a trip and we would return when things in the country were calmer. "It is important," I said, "that we keep our parting date a secret due to a slight element of danger."

Immediately, all in the room wanted to know the date of our departure. They were shocked to learn how quickly we were leaving, but assured me that they would be there to see us off. This was another poignant moment for me. After all, we had numbered thirty-two around Grandmother's Sofreh, and I knew that our bond could never be broken.

I had endangered all of our lives further by including so many in our plans. I hoped that in case I was captured it would not be in the middle of the airport for all my family to view.

As we were leaving, my mother and father kissed us all goodbye and wished us well. I held them tightly, and as I broke away, there was a lump in my throat and sadness in my heart that did not disappear for many hours.

After our short visit, it was almost time to rendezvous with Sheik Abdullah. He was pleased to know about our tickets and reassured me that his relative was taking care of the black book. We agreed to meet at the BOAC ticket counter on the morning of our departure for a discreet goodbye. I owed this man so much and looked forward to seeing him one more time.

Shauna's parents were our last audience. We proceeded to tell them that in two days we would be going away for a while. My father-in-law did not push us into leaving as my mother had. "Look," he said, "the danger has possibly passed, don't be hasty, the majority of the executives of the government and military are in hiding or have been executed. There will be room in the new regime of the private sector for people with your background and talent. Perhaps, the misfortune of others has created an opportunity for you." He continued to insist that if I took my family and left, I would be making a big mistake.

I reminded him that I had already filed for and been granted early retirement from the Navy. He told me that my retirement placed me in an ideal position, saying, "That is better. You can occupy some post within the government in the civilian sector." Even this lovely man could not believe how brutal and overpowering the Ayatollah's regime was going to be.

After announcing our plan to "visit America" to our parents, everyone in each of our extended families quickly knew our secret. Each well-meaning family member told the next, "It is very confidential. Don't let anybody know about it."

Once again, I could not sleep during the two short nights before our journey. My mind raced in many different directions. On one hand, I was frightened about the decision I had made to escape; on the other hand, I knew if I could get out of the country I would have to protect my family someplace in the world without any income. I decided to set aside my concerns and focus on safely escaping Iran.

Collecting Our Money

Since we had left our home in the middle of the night to stay in the temporary safety of my father-in-law's home, we had returned several times, but not gathered many of our belongings. Early in the morning, we drove to our home for the last time. As soon as I put the key into the door, my trusted butler Jawad was standing in the living room with his rifle. "Hello sir," he said. While smiling affectionately, he said, "Everything is just fine." I answered him with appreciation in my voice, "We just came to take some clothing and prevail upon you to leave for the Naval base." Again, he gave the same heroic answer, "I cannot go. I must protect you and your home." "Jawad," I said in a worried tone, "it may become a problem for you, everyone else is there but you." "There is no problem. I am sure about it," he answered. Unshaken, he continued to stand guard.

Within a few minutes, my wife and I gathered a few pieces of our clothing. I decided to take my long beige ankle-length raincoat and wear it to the airport. We picked up a few of our antiques. Shauna gave some money to Jawad, thanking him for his kindness, but allowing him to think that we had just decided to stay elsewhere for the time being. My beautiful wife was in a state of shock, and as we closed the door of our home for the last time, I noticed that her black lace negligee was draped on our bed, ready for a night together. In a fleeting moment I thought, will there ever be normalcy in our lives again?

We drove into downtown Tehran, stopping at a good-size antique shop. Collecting the few family heirlooms we had salvaged, we approached the shop's owner, asking if he would be interested in purchasing our precious possessions. Without speaking, he motioned for us to follow him. Stopping in the back of the store, he revealed to us a large pile of Persian carpets, magnificent silver trays, and candelabras.

Finally pausing, he spoke. "These days, people are looting palaces and wealthy homes. They are selling everything for very little money. Please, I know these lovely artifacts are yours, but don't sell them now. None of us in the antique business can buy them from you at anywhere near the fair price."

We were very disappointed. We needed the cash, but another wall had been thrust in our path. After a few moments of hesitation, we drove to our bank. My wife stayed in the car and I went inside. I managed to cash out our savings account, and I was happy with the transaction. With our life savings in hand, we drove to a nearby money exchange and bought a few thousand British pounds and U.S. dollars on the black market. We both felt that something positive had been accomplished.

During our last evening with Shauna's family, everyone was sad about our imminent departure, and the air hung heavily around us. As I tossed and turned on that last night, I suddenly remembered that I had the telephone number of Manocher in England, the affluent gentleman who was building villas at the Caspian Sea. I knew that he had an apartment in Kensington, London. Immediately, I picked up the phone and called him in the middle of the night. After two rings, his wife said, "Hello?"

The realization that I could still connect with someone outside of Iran was so overwhelming that I could barely contain myself. I managed to talk to Manocher and explain that my family had a short window of opportunity to escape from Iran and that if we were successful, we would soon be in London. He was happy for us and hoped that we would prevail. He graciously invited us to stay in his home. It had been such a long journey in such a short time, and now we had a place to rest if we managed the escape. I was so relieved and exhausted that I could not remember the flight number or our arrival time to give to Manocher, so we agreed that I would call him the following day, once we arrived in London. Slowly I drifted off into a troubled sleep.

Chapter 8

Artworks of Master Mamoud Farshchian

Goodbye Iran

Airport Scenario, Looking for Sheik Abdullah

On the morning of our departure, we dressed ourselves in modest clothing, nothing flamboyant or colorful that would attract the attention of the dissidents at the airport. Shauna filled our two suitcases with diapers and a few articles of clothing. I divided our cash into small quantities and put packets in the different compartments of my jacket and raincoat. Shauna tucked some of the money into her purse, knowing that there might be a possibility that we would become separated.

Together, we all descended the stairs and walked into the dining room. My in-laws had already finished their breakfast and were sipping their tea. Fruit and sweets were awaiting us, along with warm toasted bread and Persian cheese for the children. The thought crossed my mind, "When will we be able to dine again?" The table that could accommodate eighteen now seemed long and lonely, as the six of us sat quietly at one end. We were remembering happier occasions when the chairs were filled with elegantly dressed guests and the banter was stimulating.

We finished the morning fare and, gathering our few meager travelling necessities, asked Shauna's parents if we could speak to them privately. Leaving the children to finish their breakfast, we stepped into the foyer. After a lingering embrace, we explained to them how we hoped our affairs would be handled while we were out of the country. I had already signed fifty blank checks. I handed them to my mother-in-law, along with the two keys for our homes in Tehran and our villa at the Caspian Sea. We had had this discussion previously, and again, we asked her if we could prevail upon her to periodically cash a check for us from my account, and send the money to us. I explained that all my savings and retirement funds had been transferred to this one account. "Well," I said sadly, "thank you, it appears that you are in charge now."

While my wife was hugging her mother again, she said, "I know it is a lot of trouble for you, but please sell anything you possibly can." Interrupting, my father-in-law said reassuringly, "First, I am sure you will be back soon. I will buy your Persian carpets myself. Don't worry, we hope that you have a safe trip."

For the last time we drove the red car to the airport. Everyone followed in their own automobiles. The streets of Tehran were rather quiet. There were not that many people on the sidewalks but the cars were rushing as usual and blowing their horns as they passed. It was around seven-thirty in the morning, and we were only a few miles from the Tehran International Airport. The traffic had picked up, but now had started to slow into two lanes that were designated by the placement of sandbags, eventually feeding into one. Several militants with a few police patrol cars were stopping the traffic. While following their directions, my wife and I had rehearsed how we would respond if questioned. Our story was going to be very simple, "We are going to England for a few weeks and we intend to come back as soon as things settle down." Two Islamic militants both wearing Army battle dress approached us and positioned themselves on either side of our car. We lowered the windows while they looked inside. One of them asked me, "Where are you going?"

I replied: "To the airport."

The other militant asked: "What do you have in your trunk?" "Two suitcases and my raincoat," I replied. Brusquely, one militant said, "Open your trunk." I obeyed and walked to the back of the car. "This might be the end," I thought. "Perhaps they wanted me standing so I could be captured more easily." My only choice was to do exactly what I was told. Finally, after moving the suitcases from one side to the other, the one militant looked at the other, nodded, and said, "Okay, you can go."

We had passed our first obstacle and continued driving. As we approached the main terminal, everything appeared to be normal, except that the airport was over-run with militants. "It will be a miracle," I thought, "if we manage to get through this chaos." I parked the car next to a light post and put on my long beige raincoat, hoping that it would act as some sort of disguise. Even the children sensed our fear as we walked toward the terminal building. Their small hands gripped ours tightly and they did not make a sound.

Inside the Terminal

During the course of the morning, I repeatedly told Shauna to take the children and continue the trip if something happened to me. She responded, as usual, by saying, "No, Manocher, I will not leave the country if you are detained." We were both very frightened as we made our way to the BOAC counter in the center of the terminal. As we walked, I recognized other government employees. When our eyes met, we quickly turned away. None of us dared to acknowledge the other. Many, I am sure, were travelling with new false names. I had been in the same terminal many times for the Navy, travelling on commercial airlines, as well as receiving and sending off visiting dignitaries, but I had never felt such feelings of anxiety. I continued to look for Sheik Abdullah. He was to meet me at the BOAC counter, and I desperately wanted to thank him for all he had done for me as well as to give him back the red car.

From a distance, I could see my parents and my uncle. I knew that they were also filled with fear. In a matter of minutes, we were surrounded by my parents, my brothers, my wife's parents, and siblings. Everyone wanted to be with our children, embracing Bob and lifting little Rammy up into their arms. I could see the sadness on their faces but I decided to try to be cheerful, speaking to everyone as if everything were normal.

Passport Tracking System

It was around eight-thirty in the morning, and we were scheduled to go one by one, with our tickets, to the passenger security room and introduce ourselves. Beneath my outward calm, I was terrified. When my turn came, I quickly turned to Shauna and said again, "If I do not come out from this door, take the children and go." Smiling at the crowd, I turned and walked with confidence into the room, where a few armed militants were dealing with the travelers. Behind the counter, there were civilians, as well as a few men in police uniforms accepting the passengers' tickets. After reviewing the ticket, it was taken to another room for scrutiny. There was a middle-aged gentleman in front of me. When the security representative returned from the back room, he loudly said, "Your passport is stamped Debarred Exit." Immediately one of the armed militants came over to him, grabbed his arm, and escorted him out.

My heart was beating so fast that I reached up and loosened my collar button. There were moments when the room started to spin, but I was trying hard to keep my head up, showing that I was confident about my situation. Now, it was my turn. I said, "Salaam," to the security representative and handed him my airline ticket. Reading it, he walked back into the next room. It seemed to me that time had stopped. "What if they stamped my passport no exit? What is going to happen to me and to my family?" After a few moments, the security representative came back through the door, holding my passport and ticket. He looked at me, paused, then giving them back to me, miraculously said, "Have a nice trip."

I could not believe his words. I emerged from the passenger security room, victoriously holding my passport. I could see the relief in the eyes of my relatives, who had been patiently waiting for me to reappear. We could not rejoice, as yet, because now it was Shauna's turn. I winked at my wife reassuringly, telling her, "Good luck." I remained with the children and my parents while she went through the same process. Fortunately, her procedure was also successful. She received her passport and came out of the security room smiling.

I was still searching for Sheik Abdullah, hoping to see him at any minute. While we were chatting with our relatives, I continuously looked past the crowd to the far corners of the room. I wanted desperately to hug my friend who had gone out of his way to help me. Armed militants continued to move around the terminal. They were very intimidating, and it occurred to me that perhaps the Sheik had not wanted to jeopardize my escape.

Luggage Search

It was now around nine in the morning, and we had to proceed to the BOAC counter to check in. After showing our tickets, we took our luggage to be searched. My father-in-law and uncle were standing next to me while I put our two suitcases on a long table. The official in charge, looking down, said, "I am sorry, but I must touch your belongings." He barely looked into the first bag and began sifting through the second one. After only a few moments, he very quietly said, "You may take your luggage now and may God be with you, Captain." I was stunned that I had been recognized. "Was it over after all we had been through?" Quickly, I turned to my uncle, who nodded his head, smiled, and softly touched my shoulder. It was then that I realized that he had taken care of this man monetarily.

We turned our luggage into the airline and with relief joined our relatives. I was still searching for Sheik Abdullah. I had no way to contact him. My elder brother-in-law loved cars. In desperation, I took him aside and I handed him the key to the red car while asking him for a favor. "Daryoush, I need your help. This is the key to my car." I told him where it was parked. "Please," I said, "go to my home and ask Jawad my butler to accompany you to Sheik Abdullah's appliance store. He will be able to identify him for you. Please give him the key and thank him for me." Then I added, "Tell Jawad that we have gone and that he must return to the Naval base, but be sure that he knows that we will never forget his loyalty."

As soon as my conversation with Daryoush was finished, my uncle, with tears in his eyes, whispered to me, "Do you have enough money to take care of your family?" I replied, "Not really, but I hope we can manage."

While he was wiping his eyes, he referred to the suitcases, saying, "Is this all you are taking with you after twenty-six years of dedicated service and twenty years of education?" Frowning, he opened the attaché case that he was carrying and pulled out a few pages of his stationery with his company's letterhead. Giving them to me, he said, "This is my business information and my telex number in Switzerland. If for any reason you need money, please send me a telex."

I took the papers from him and thanked him from the bottom of my heart as we embraced. I was filled with emotion and the realization that I was leaving my family and all of my dreams for the future.

Sheik Abdullah on the Balcony

BOAC announced that it was now time to board. The airplane was a few hundred feet away from the terminal, and only the passengers with their tickets and passports could pass through the door going to the outside. The visitors were told to proceed to the second-floor balcony in order to see the passengers off. We kissed and hugged everyone. My mother was crying again, and my father was hiding his tears. My father-in-law had smoked a pack of cigarettes during the period of time that we spent in the terminal.

We left everyone and passed through the crowd, out into the open air toward the airplane. I turned back, one last time, to see if I could catch a glimpse of my relatives. There, standing next to the guard rail on the balcony, right in front of my eyes, was Sheik Abdullah. He was wearing his long white robe. As soon as he saw me, he raised both of his hands to the sky as a Muslim's sign of thanking Allah. I waved happily to him, and he responded with a smile.

In that moment, tears came into my eyes and flowed down my cheeks. A great sadness that still haunts me is the realization that I did not have the opportunity to personally embrace this lovely man and to tell him of my deep appreciation for his loyalty. Later on I was saddened by the news that the Sheik had been executed by the brutal regime of Khomeini. After so many years, I can still see the image of my dear friend bravely waving to me.

Plane Remains on the Ground

On our approach to the airplane, there were scattered armed militants. We boarded with only one carry-on. Our four seats were in the middle of the economy class section. There were two opposite each other, on either side of the aisle. My son and I were together and my wife sat with our three-year-old, Rammy. We anticipated we would be leaving very quickly, because we boarded half an hour late. Unfortunately, that was not the case.

The armed militants boarded the plane and walked up and down the aisles. They paused at each seat and looked intently into our faces. The plane became very quiet. Once we were seated, the militants left, only to be replaced by a harsher group who were calling out the names of certain passengers. Before they approached me, I leaned across the aisle and took my wife's hand, saying slowly, "If they call my name, I am not going to answer." I could see that she was very frightened but she replied, "Of course." The passengers, who responded when their names were called, were immediately escorted out of the plane and replaced by new passengers.

Rifles were being pointed randomly into the faces of those of us who were praying that this interrogation would soon be over. The words "Where are you going?" were spoken over and over again. The air inside the plane was becoming very warm, and the air-conditioning was not cooling down. Everyone, especially the children, were restless. I held my breath in anticipation that something horrific might happen. Now, at the last minute, I was afraid that these men might find that our tickets belonged to someone else and we would be escorted off the plane.

Plane Leaves Two Hours Late

It was almost twelve noon, and we had been in our seats for nearly two hours. The plane was still on the ground with the engines turned off. The majority of the passengers around me were mature men, and some of their faces looked familiar. Most had not shaved for a few days, and their clothing emulated the peasant look. I felt at the time that the presence of our children helped us in not being interrogated. It was around one o'clock in the afternoon, when over the loudspeaker we heard the voice of our Iranian captain. He was announcing that we had received permission to proceed. The armed militants left the plane. As soon as they moved the stairs away, we all felt the joy of relief and gratefully looked at each other. The plane started to move down the runway. This happiness, however, was short-lived, as a police car pulled out to block us. Apparently, someone in the car was giving a message to the pilot. It was still completely quiet in the cabin. Finally, the engines once again began to roll, and we started to pick up speed, getting ready for takeoff.

From a distance, we could see the airport balcony, but we were traveling farther and farther away. I still wanted to catch one last glimpse of Sheik Abdullah, as well as my family, but they were not distinguishable. Never in my life had I felt such emotion.

As we were lifted into the air, the joyful passengers, showing their happiness, started to cheer. After a few seconds, the captain once again came over the loudspeaker, saying, "Wait, we are still in Iranian air space. I will let you know as soon as we leave Iran's territory." It was a big relief for all of us. I leaned over across the aisle and, smiling, said to my wife, "I guess we made it." There was a sudden feeling of euphoria, the peasant clothing came off, and women were pulling on their pretty blouses, taking scarves off their heads, and were engaged in applying colorful new makeup. Men were lining up for the bathrooms in order to shave. The aroma of fresh perfume and aftershave lotion filled the air. The look of joy and happiness was visible on everyone's faces. We were humbled and grateful to leave the dangerous situation behind even though our future destiny was unknown.

Seeking an American Visa

It was a great moment for my wife and I when the plane landed at Heathrow Airport in London. At that time, Iranian citizens did not need an entry visa for Europe. The immigration personnel stamped the passports, and we were welcomed into England. As soon as we finished going through immigration, I made my way to a public telephone and called my friend Manocher. He answered immediately, and as soon as I said hello, he screamed, "Stay where you are. I will see you in thirty minutes."

We picked up our luggage. It was hard to believe that today at noon we were being tormented by militants and now at sunset we were ecstatically happy to be in a free country. As soon as we stepped out of the terminal, we saw Manocher running toward us. "Glad you made it," he said, smiling, and added, "It is a miracle. We have to celebrate."

He drove us to his beautiful apartment in Kensington, where he was living with his wife and two teenage sons. He parked his car in the lower level and carried one of the suitcases to his third-floor apartment. His wife opened the door, smiling, and hugged all of us, saying, "Our home is your home, you are welcome."

They had a large apartment by English standards. There were four graciously appointed bedrooms with private bath and balcony, a lovely sitting room, kitchen, and living room that enjoyed a magnificent view of Kensington's lush green park. We were delighted to be given such comfortable accommodations. We quickly changed and joined Manocher and his wife on the terrace, where he opened champagne. We toasted to our victory. Manocher suggested that we leave the children home with his teenagers. He was eager to take us to dinner. It was around eight in the evening London time when he asked, "Are you tired?"

"Are you kidding?" I replied. "We have had many sleepless nights. We are used to it."

Soon the four of us were in his car driving to the Ritz Hotel and Casino in London. We had a very nice dinner with wine and then decided to go to the lower level casino to gamble. We could not get over our happiness. We were wildly drinking and gambling as if there was no tomorrow. It was not until after we had lost a few hundred pounds that I suddenly came to my senses.

I whispered to my wife, "Do you realize what we are doing? We are refugees with no future, and we are gambling with the little money that we have left." I added, referring to Manocher, "He has his home and wealth. He can gamble. You and I with our children must find our future." We immediately stopped and just watched the others. When we returned to the apartment, we were happy to find our dear children asleep. That night, rest was blissful. I felt that there would be time to worry later. Early the next morning, my wife and I, with our children, went to the American Embassy in London. We showed our passports to the consulate officer and asked for entry visas that would allow us to travel to the United States.

"Why are you going to America?" the clerk asked. I replied firmly, "We want to permanently make the United States our home." "Sorry," the clerk said. "We cannot issue you or your family a visa." I said emphatically, "I am Captain Bakh from the Imperial Iranian Navy. There are Naval personnel in the Pentagon who know me. I have escaped from Iran, and I find it imperative that I take my family to the United States." Nothing that I could say influenced the clerk. He said, "Sir, we have strict orders from the State Department that Iranians cannot travel to America, unless they have proof that they will be returning to Iran." Then he added, "Unfortunately, you admitted that you have no intention of going back to your country; therefore, we cannot issue you a visa."

It was a shock for me to think that we had come so far, but we still had a long way to go. We all sadly returned to Manocher's apartment. I was numb. I kept hearing the clerk's voice denying us our visas. I left my wife and children and took a taxi to the Iranian Embassy. I hoped that some of my old friends might help me influence the people at the American consulate to issue me a visa.

When I arrived at the Embassy, a young man was standing at the closed door. I announced myself and asked to see the Naval Attaché. He was not in but I was allowed to speak with his assistant, who was a commander and knew me very well. He received me cordially and when I told him my story, he repeated that the U.S. State Department would not allow Iranians entrance to America. While I was in the office, other officers gathered around me and wanted to hear the details of what was happening in Iran. Unfortunately, I felt as though my back was against a wall, and although I tried to be cordial, I was in no mood to chat.

It came to my mind that if the U.S. State Department issued an order, it would be the same for all the consulates. Since this consulate knew of my request, I thought it might be worth it to try to apply in another country. This time I would have to have proof that I planned to return to Iran.

Prior to leaving the Embassy, I asked one of the officers if they would grant me access to their Farsi and English typewriters. They graciously took me to an office where English and Farsi IBM typewriters were available.

I reached into my pocket and pulled out the stationery with my uncle's printed letterhead. I quickly typed in English and Farsi the following memorandum.

To: All managers
CC: Board of directors

During this difficult time, I have to take a short trip to the United States to attend the wedding of my brother-in-law. I will be gone a maximum of one week.

While I am in California, I will attend the Bank of America's meeting regarding the properties in Rolling Hills.

This letter authorizes, in my absence, Mr. Mehdi Karami, the Chairman, to decide on all ongoing matters, and act on my behalf.

I am sure you will give him your full support.

Best Regards
Signed Manocher
Chief Executive Officer

After preparing the letter, I went directly to the Air France office and purchased a round-trip ticket to Paris for the next day. Very early the following morning, I wore a white shirt with my only suit. I flew to Paris to visit the American consulate. That morning, I was the first person in line asking for a visa. There was a nice woman behind the window. I handed her my passport with the bogus letter folded inside. I had conveniently displayed my uncle's letterhead that would be visible to anyone who opened it. Very politely I said, "I need a visa to go to America to attend a wedding for one week."

She looked at my Iranian passport briefly and looked at me, then asked, "Do you have any proof that you are returning to Iran?" I immediately responded, "I have to return as soon as possible to protect my business. I cannot be away with all that is happening in Iran." She repeated the same thing that I was told in the American Embassy in London: "We have strict orders from the State Department that Iranians cannot travel to America, unless they have proof that they will be returning to Iran." Then she added, "Sir, you have to have proof"; while speaking, she glanced at the letter folded in my passport. As I started to speak, she interrupted me, saying, "Just a minute sir; oh, this is good, this is good. Can I make a copy of this letter?"

"Yes please," I replied.

She left to make a copy and returned in a minute with my passport and a stamped tourist visa that was valid for four weeks. I immediately reached into my jacket pocket and handed her the passport for my wife and children. As a matter of fact, I said, "As long as I am here, would you mind issuing me a visa for my family?" She took the passport in one hand with the stamp in the other. Flipping through the pages, she said, "Sir, they are not here in France. We cannot issue them a visa while they are in England." I took the passport, thanking her, and happily hailed a taxi that took me back to the airport. I returned the same afternoon to London.

Immediately, I rushed to share my joy and success with my friends and family. My first plan was to accompany my wife and children back to the American Embassy in London and, based on the new evidence, request a visa from a different window. My alternative plan was if for any reason the visa could not be obtained in London, we would fly together to Paris and approach the consulate there. The next morning, we all went back to the American Embassy in London. Luckily, within a few minutes, the visas were ours.

We spent our last evening in London with Manocher and his family. He told us that he was planning to return to Iran to take care of his properties. He was feeling some resistance but he did not feel any danger. I asked him if, in my absence, he could sell my villa. I gave him full power of attorney, and he thought that it would not be difficult to market the property on my behalf.

U.S. Navy's Help in Washington, D.C.

The next day we booked our flight directly from London to Los Angeles. We had jumped over some very large hurdles. I was happy to think that I had made the impossible possible. One of my cousins was a psychiatrist working for the Veteran's Hospital in Long Beach, California. I had contacted him before we left London regarding our plans. He immediately invited us to stay with his family.

We were happy flying over the Atlantic Ocean on our way to America. It is hard to explain the extent of our relief. We were going to call the United States our home. My wife and children were looking forward to a new life. I knew that I could not let them down but my concerns over how I was going to make a living haunted me. A different kind of fear continued to engulf me. What if I could not succeed in being able to support them? Starting life all over again in a new country was very difficult. I knew that I would have to use all the ingenuity I could muster in order to obtain employment and find housing. I did not want to convey my negative thoughts to my family. Flying allowed me a moment of peace that I hoped would never end; exhausted, sleep finally came.

My cousin was waiting for us at the Los Angeles Airport. He had been our guest in Monterey when I was attending the Naval Postgraduate School. It was wonderful to see him again. He was married to an American girl, and they also had two children almost the same age as ours. Their large, beautiful home in the Los Feliz district of Los Angeles had been occupied by a well-known movie celebrity and was located on a small hill with eighty steps to the street. The bathroom floors and walls were enhanced with magnificent Art Deco-style marble. They had prepared two adjoining rooms for us and since they knew that we had left everything behind in Iran, they were gracious enough to suggest that we stay with them for a while. Our children were eager to play with their cousins, even though they were not able to communicate in each other's languages.

After a day of rest, I called the man who was my counterpart in the U.S. Navy, Captain Lawrence Caney, in Washington, D.C. He was ecstatic to hear my voice. "Captain, I need your help," I said. "It has not been easy for us to get here. I jeopardized my family's life and I had to lie, cheat, and forge in order to receive a visa that is only good for four weeks." He said emphatically, "Don't worry. The U.S. Navy is behind you. You must travel to Washington." We agreed that I would come as quickly as possible.

I packed once more and left my family with my cousin, flying to Washington, D.C., where Captain Caney awaited my arrival. I reminisced about the four years I had spent working with him. We had been very close to achieving our goal to create the ultimate training center for the Iranian Navy.

I remembered the last day that the captain was in my office in Tehran, and had reluctantly accepted my advice to leave the country. I had always wondered what had become of him and his wife. There was no doubt in my mind that my American counterpart would have been added to the list of fifty-two hostages that were later captured at the American Embassy in Tehran. The irony would have been sad, if Captain Caney had been captured. He probably would have been transferred to our magnificent new training center that was immediately transformed, by Khomeini, into the largest prison in Iran.

I often think of the halls we walked, of the dreams we had, and of the suffering of those who were later taken to this giant establishment. We had built this large Mecca as one of the projects that was intended to bring Iran to the forefront of the world. Instead, it became the center of despair for anyone who had been involved in the Shah's regime. Islam clearly won this battle in the war of progress.

When I finally arrived in Washington, Captain Caney looked at me fondly and, with true caring in his voice, said, "Thank God you're alive!" When we arrived at his condo, his wife Ann received me with open arms. We were all delighted with our good fortune; we were alive and safe in the United States. They were as curious to hear how my family and I had escaped from Iran as I was to hear their story. I eagerly asked them if they made it to Turkey on the C-130 flight that I had counseled them to take.

During our conversation, I learned that after the last day we had seen each other in Iran, the captain, his wife, and a few of his team members had been able to make it to the American C-130 aircraft that was flying to Turkey. In order to get to the airport, the captain was forced to bribe his way through the streets of Tehran in exchange for safe passage. Once they finally made it onto the tarmac and safely into the plane, they thought their wait was over. Sadly, he described the fear and frustration they felt when the plane's captain announced that they could not take off because a vital part was needed. Over the next eighteen hours, my friend and his team waited and waited. Finally, the plane's captain came to the harsh realization that the part was never going to arrive. With few choices left, the pilot decided he needed to try and get his passengers to Turkey. Secretly, a part was pirated off another C-130, and after an agonizing wait, they lifted off and safely made it to Turkey, and freedom. Captain Caney described the ordeal to me as, "the shortest but longest flight" he had ever taken in his life.

The next morning, Captain Caney and I travelled to the Pentagon to see Admiral Boyd and Admiral Frank Collins. They were delighted to know that I was alive. Admiral Collins was very helpful and scheduled a meeting with Mr. Waxx, who was the immigration advisor to President Carter.

I told them the truth regarding the lies that I had had to invent in order to come to America. A private meeting was arranged for me to go to the immigration office and fill out the proper forms. Captain Caney accompanied me, and within a few minutes, all of our passports were stamped under a very special visa called "Under Doc Control." The benefits allowed us to have working permits and the ability to stay in the United States indefinitely or, as long as Iran was not safe.

We were among the fortunate that had managed to escape from our country. Unexpectedly, a few brave acquaintances, people we did not know well, were there to help us. I had always been good to them, and they were there for me. Later, I learned the one that helped me the most had been executed. It was a bloodbath, and the pain will always remain with me.

I wonder now what kind of betterment the elimination of those precious lives brought to my country? We lost the king, a man who devoted his life to his people, and now there was another type of control. Was it religion? Or was it the need for power? I do not know.

Within a few weeks after being in America, we received information from Manocher. He had successfully sold my villa and transferred the money to my account at the bank in Tehran. The money in that account represented my twenty-six years of retirement savings as well as the money derived from the sale of my villa. Unfortunately, before I could have my funds transferred to the United States, they were confiscated by the order of Khomeini. The regime did not have the pleasure of capturing me, but they had found away to enjoy their revenge. Now, as a family of four, we faced unforgettable difficulties.

Starting Our New Lives in Exile

At times, my anxiety was overwhelming. I was concerned that I might disappoint my wife's expectations. This was an enormous learning experience for her, but she supported my endeavors. I knew in my heart that if all else failed, I would be forced to seek employment, even at the local gasoline station. Above all, I had to feed my family! I lost count of the number of employment applications that I filled out. Because of my international experience and education, I was always overqualified; people did not seem to understand that, despite my credentials, I was willing to take whatever work I could find. Finally, I received a phone call from a company that had faith in my ability and hired me as their industrial engineer.

My new position was very challenging. Fortunately, my experience and my knowledge of common-sense engineering allowed me rapid advancement. I was thankful to accomplish the success that enabled me to educate my two beautiful children.

When Shauna and I escaped from Iran and established ourselves in the United States of America, the one thing that no one could take away from us was our deep Persian Principles. We still struggle with the transition between American behavior, in a capitalist environment, and our Old World cultural customs. Our deep gratitude toward the magnificent country that accepted us will always remain in our hearts.

Another Life Ends

In 1981, Manocher Farhangi left Iran for Spain after the Mullah's forced him to leave his magnificent complex at the Caspian Sea. His departure and exile were a result of Manocher Farhangi's refusal to build a wall into the sea to separate the male and female bathing areas. His outright defiance of the new regime's antiquated rules necessitated his escape, shortly after he helped sell my Villa on the Caspian Sea.

Like many Iranian expatriates, Farhangi found a place for himself in Spain. He purchased an old Spanish palace and converted it into a school for Iranian students. Farhangi's teachings were not Islamic, however, he continued to be pursued because he openly disagreed with the fanatical religious views that permeate today's Islamic environment.

In the early spring of 2008 as I compiled these memoirs I was saddened to hear that Farhangi was murdered. On a peaceful morning in the affluent residential section of La Moreleja, Spain, Farhangi responded to a seemingly innocent knock on his front door. He was confronted by a cloaked woman who lunged at him with a knife. The stab wounds the unknown assailant inflicted, in his abdomen, proved too much for my dear friend and he died from his injuries at 82 years of age.

In the days before the murder, reports of the investigation detail an argument between Mr. Farhangi and a woman intruder, at a Nowruz, Persian New Years celebration. The young woman was posting pro-Islamic Republic announcements, and Mr. Farhangi confronted her about the provocative placement of the propaganda during the joyous celebration. When I think of his death following such a telling event I ask myself, "could it be, that after so many years, hate and revenge lives on in the minds of those who believe in Mohammed's chilling words, "convert or die"? "

My Reflections

Artworks of Master Mamoud Farshchian

by Mano Bakh

The Big Question

Twenty-nine years have passed since our plane landed on United States soil. Those difficult days after our arrival seem like a dream. Now, out of the thirty-two members of my family that sat around the white Sofreh, on Grandmother's Persian carpet, only my brother Ira, Misha, and I are still alive. While I am writing these reflections, Misha is living in London and courageously fighting cancer.

Fortunately, my family and I have integrated into another way of life. Our young children are grown, and they have been educated in the finest universities in the United States. Shauna and I consider it an achievement that we have been able to provide the opportunity for them to become productive American citizens.

It seems as though it has been an eternity since I viewed the horrific act of two Muslims beheading two other Muslims. It was after that somber glimpse of this barbaric deed that I was shocked into facing the reality of what had happened to Iran. I now know the "why." I realize that there was a plan that was carefully executed and became a reality. This occurred because of the patience and perseverance of those extremists who quietly, at first, gained momentum, working behind the scenes to seduce the innocent, brainwash the youth, and then, when their army was strong, attack those of us who discounted their ranting and their ragged clothing, and underestimated their evil Islamic power.

As I shuffle back through the pages of my life, it now seems so clear to me that we, the educated and the hard working, did not take heed of those who were devious in soliciting the weak to carry out their horrific deeds. They were conniving enough to preach their religious furor, but were clever enough to also engage the elite who remained powerless when, too late, they became aware that they had been used, had been misled, and had become only a lonely voice. I recall vividly, at sunset, the eerie sounds of "Allah o Akbar" echoing throughout the city. The crying was not coming from the followers of Khomeini, but from those who wanted to be considered, and to remain, as part of the new government. They anticipated that their display of support might give them this opportunity, but their shouting fell on deaf ears. Within a few months, most of these intellectuals were executed or had found a way to escape Khomeini. The victor continued to bribe the poor to be the "militant," whose rage and envy were against the intellectuals and hard-working people, especially those who did not encompass their fanatical beliefs. In the weak mind of the militant, this level of society had to be eliminated.

I am searching for the answer. "What has happened?"

The power of oil brings money to a government that can be used for the betterment of their people—or the power of oil can be used by a government to control its people. Oil is money, and the amount of money that oil brings is power.

Why did the people of Iran who loved the Shah turn against him? And why did a country like Iran with great relations in the world become the axis of evil? When the Shah was in power, oil money was used to improve the infrastructure of the country. Roads were constructed, communication systems were put in place, and there were educational programs for the poor, as well as scholarships that sent young people to institutions of higher learning around the world. Oil money paid for this financial burden. The ultimate goal was to be able to emulate a modern Western-style country that would set an example within the Middle East and become a prosperous place in which to live. The thirst for knowledge was in the eyes of those of us who also dared to dream the dream, who knew that help from the West was needed in order to quickly expedite this vast undertaking. It was also necessary to utilize all of the brain power that we could muster within the country and elsewhere. This was a key factor in order to quickly build a foundation that could grow and be successfully maintained for years to come. With the emergence of President Carter and his administration's unrelenting agenda against the Shah's alleged human rights violations, the support of the West was diminished and the opposition gained power.

It was true that the king and monarchy seemed to be, for some, frivolous by following tradition with money spent for their pomp and ceremony. *It was true* that some surrounding the monarchy used their positions for self-gratification. *It was true* that some intellectuals thought that they and their counterparts could better spend the oil money in a more democratic way without bowing to the imperial power. *It was true* that the modernizing was, in some cases, proceeding too quickly and at times money was wasted. But, *it was also true* that the Shah's goal was the hope that the country, in a very short time, through education, would be ready for democracy. At the time the level of social and political education was very low, and the poor were not realistic in their demands. They did not have the patience to support plans for the gradual growth in infrastructure that would allow them, through hard work and education, to participate in their own future betterment and ultimately democracy.

Unfortunately, it was true that the Shah raised the ire of the Muslim fundamentalists, those who wanted no part of the West and threatened his life daily with bomb throwing, fires, strikes, and sabotaging anything that would stop the implementation of the "Master Plan." Because of the SAVAK, the organization that was created by the CIA, the domestic terrorists were captured and placed in jail for committing treason. In the eyes of the West, their incarceration was not clearly understood because they were categorized as political prisoners.

At the time, most of these prisoners were tried as Marxist Communist dissidents. The United States, who was in a Cold War with the USSR, was concerned about their aggressions toward encroaching on and occupying the Persian Gulf. The Shah, sharing the same concerns, appreciated the vision of the United States. His diligence kept these agitators at bay. President Carter, with his naiveté and lack of knowledge about the brutality of Islam and Muslim Marxist Communists, continued to criticize, not understanding that it was crucial to keep these fanatics out of circulation. Unfortunately, as the American press increased its crescendo against the Shah, giving credence to other factions that had different agendas, the monarchy started to crumble.

When President Carter's approach forced the Shah to leave the country, a vacuum was created and filled by the return of Ayatollah Khomeini. A rebellious, angry army was ready! They had been well coached, and those of us who had discounted their surly ways were not prepared. They were everywhere. Ayatollah had no intention of being a quiet religious leader.

Shame on Carter's administration for not taking the time to understand what the consequences of supporting Khomeini would be for the world. Shame on Carter for not protecting Iran, and not realizing that radical Islam only accepts those who believe literally in Mohammad and the basic pillars of the Muslim religion, including the pillar of Jihad.

The fall of the Shah had a domino effect that empowered Muslims around the world, and unfortunately, the United States government indirectly unified their movement against imperialism.

Beware! History seems to repeat itself, or is it really history? I do not believe that for the last twenty-nine years, the momentum has stopped. The scenario is very simple. The majority of the world's oil is controlled by Muslim countries, which financially benefits their religious leaders. Oil revenue supplements the Mullahs' flourishing businesses. They further invest on propaganda used to brainwash their people about the evils of a materialistic life. The purpose of the Muslim fanatics is to influence the minds of their followers to become martyrs with the promise of a beautiful life in paradise. Jihad, the suicide bomber, is the ultimate form of Islam. Iran is the center of support and planning for turmoil in the Middle East. There could come a time when their conquests could be large and very devastating. There is radical Muslim infiltration occurring around the world, and we in the United States are the number one target. Their growth is insidious, and as before, in Iran, the evil might not be realized until it is too late. They are Muslims with no mercy. They are the fastest-growing religion in the world, and they cannot be stopped with conventional armies.

What Did Happen?

Why did several million Iranians escape to unknown destinies?

Why were several thousand people in Iran executed without any legitimate reason?

Why will Jews never see peace?

Why is a well-respected America now hated?

Why is the Muslim religion expanding?

Why is the oil revenue from Iran being spent outside of Iran for Hezbollah?

Why are the human rights activists in America deaf and blind?

Why are there so many suicide bombers killing innocent people?

Why are there so many violent acts committed by Muslims?

How did Al Qaeda, Bin Laden, and the Taliban come to power?

Why do we differentiate between Fundamentalist, Conservative, Moderate, Fanatical, and Radical Muslim extremists?

Why does America suddenly have so many enemies?

Why does the West think that it can reason with Muslims?

There are many more "whys." How can we find the answers? It is clear that at this time with all the complexities, there is not an easy solution. There is no silver bullet. We first have to be aware of the dangers around us in order to protect ourselves.

Rundown

I hope that through my personal experiences I have created awareness about the evil of radical Islam and the magnitude of danger that still exists in the world today. I have personally witnessed a moderate Muslim country's transition into a barbaric society. This country believed that Allah was a peaceful God, cared for its people, had respect for women, and was working for a brighter future while enjoying a wonderful degree of trust with the civilized world. When the fanatic religious leaders replaced the political governing bodies, the country changed. They destroyed all that had been accomplished, while murdering those who did not want to return to life as it was in the barbaric days of Mohammad! It reads like fiction to think that such a story could have happened. The well-planned riptide of hate that swept through Iran, promoted by Khomeini, was so devastating that we were powerless to defend ourselves.

The religious fanatics, some intellectuals, as well as the United States and the BBC media, unknowingly worked together to fan the flames against the monarchy. President Carter's relentless human rights agenda to release Iran's political prisoners was heard around the world. These things combined were overwhelmingly responsible for the creation of another backward, brutal regime. The bungling and disagreements that went on in the State Department under Cyrus Vance as well as Ambassador Sullivan (with Carter's knowledge), influenced the United States government to withdraw their support at a very crucial time. This was all that was necessary to give the fanatical opposition the opportunity to take over. In order to please President Carter, the Shah had ordered the release of the "political prisoners," who then joined Khomeini's followers to murder and plunder. While President Carter prayed in the church at Camp David, blood flowed in Iran.

I have lived in a country that was diligently trying to utilize their oil money for progress until I had to flee for my life, leaving behind a country that quickly turned into an "Axis of Evil." Today in 2009, in spite of the embargo to boycott Iran, they are still an active member of OPEC, producing around 4 million barrels of oil per day, and selling it to countries other than the United States. Money flows from the Mullahs' coffers into the building of Hezbollah's armies.

OPEC is an international organization of eleven oil-exporting countries that rely heavily on oil revenues for their income. OPEC members collectively supply about forty percent of the world's oil output and possess over three quarters of the world's total proven crude oil reserves. OPEC oil and energy ministers meet twice a year, or more if required, to decide on the organization's output level and to consider whether any action to adjust output is necessary, based on current and anticipated oil market developments.

Recently, Ayatollah Ali Khamenei, the religious leader of Iran, has publicly asked all oil-producing countries to unite and use oil as a "weapon" to shock America and Israel. Oil is the only thing that the

Muslim countries have in abundance, and their revenues have increased twenty times in the last thirty years. Therefore, if they ever decide to carry out their threat to cease selling oil to the West for one month, and if other anti-American oil-rich countries follow suit, it would be devastating for the free world.

Situation Today

In writing about the happenings that have taken place in my life, I realize how special it is to live in the United States, where one can speak freely. In trying to portray my story, I have criticized Muslims who try to control the minds of others, and through brutality force them to accept their way of thinking. I have personally been subjected to this type of behavior. It is part of my story and why I am in exile. Had my own life not been threatened, I would not have questioned another's religion or the personal choices that they made as to how they wished to live, as long as they gave me the freedom to do the same. I am now speaking brutally about Islam because of what I have personally witnessed. I "cry out" to warn my fellow man to remain informed and not to trust easily. There are those who will not be happy until their own religious beliefs and way of life control the world.

Since the Iranian revolution in 1979, the strength of the Islamic movement around the world has increased significantly. Muslims in seventy countries have given strength to the Iranian Mullahs to promote the "anti-American" movement in other countries.

All other opposition parties during the Shah's reign became puppets, as they supported the Mullahs while hoping to promote their own programs. In the end, the extent of their efforts became nothing more than the shouting of "Allah o Akbar" ("*God is Great*")!

Not until after Khomeini's Fundamental Islamic government was empowered in Iran, catching the whole world by surprise, did the West, very slowly, become aware of the religious turmoil in the Middle East. Islamic groups from all around the world have now turned the clock back to the days of Mohammad. They operate in different degrees of severity according to their interpretation of the Koran.

They adapt themselves to the environment in which they live, having their own leaders and languages, but always strongly supporting each other in principle. A variety of Muslim groups are known in the United States, but each has originated according to their own circumstances.

Al Qaeda

Al Qaeda was created in 1979. This was the same year that Iran fell into the hands of Ayatollah Khomeini. Al Qaeda is an international Islamic terror organization and was founded by Osama Bin Laden. The group dislikes any country that is associated with the West. Al Qaeda would like to have a single Muslim nation that operates according to Islamic laws.

Taliban

The Taliban originated in the refugee camps of Pakistan during the Soviet occupation of Afghanistan. The war against the Soviet Union was supported by Muslims all around the world. The Taliban implemented a very strict type of Islamic government that was inhumane to women. They were also the originators of Madressah Schools, which recruit young children to become suicide bombers.

The United States supplied over 10 billion dollars worth of weapons to Afghan Freedom Fighters in an effort to force the Soviet Union out of Afghanistan. When the Soviets left, there was anarchy everywhere. In 1996, the Taliban took control of Afghanistan. They ruled from 1996 until 2001. After September 11, 2001, Bin Laden was hiding in Afghanistan. The Taliban refused to deliver him to the United States. Together with Great Britain the U. S. invaded Afghanistan and Taliban followers were dispersed throughout Afghanistan and the borders of Pakistan.

After the terrible destruction of the World Trade Center Twin Towers in New York on September 11, 2001, America responded with honor, and felt that if they did not react these devastating types of attacks would have continued. I will not debate the pros and cons of this decision, but I do agree that the fanatical Muslim group that planned this event would have continued to show their hatred toward America. I still believe that the free world has not done enough to change their evil intentions.

Hamas

Hamas is a well-organized force in Palestine acting as the main opposition to the Israeli occupation of 1967. Very much like the Islamic Republic in Iran, Hamas wants to create an Islamic State within Palestine that is under the rule of Islam. Hamas recruiting systems are focused on low-income families, although they try to create the image of being liberators of the poor. Messages to Hamas members are spread through mosques and Islamic religious organizations.

Hezbollah

Syria as well as Iran's Islamic Republic backs the Lebanese National Party Hezbollah. This group is the number one enemy of Israel. Hezbollah is completely supported by the Iranian Islamic Republic and is very well equipped with abundant amounts of money from Iran. They have a large arsenal that includes missiles and night vision technology. They are leaders in youth training, and they train teenagers in military tactics while brainwashing them with radical Shiat Muslim beliefs. This organization is similar to the others and has the common objective of wanting all Muslim countries to unite without any boundaries.

The Hezbollah selects children to become part of the army, but only if they are willing to become martyrs.

Revolutionary Guard

The Iranian Revolutionary Guard was formed right after the 1979 revolution. It operates independently from the regular armed forces.

They have their own Navy, Air Force, and ground forces. They originally were established to defend and protect the Islamic revolution in Iran. They report to the ruling clerics. The guard has over 300,000 troops. They were seen outside of Iran in the 2006 war against Israel, providing missiles to Lebanon's Hezbollah.

The Revolutionary Guard is involved in many industries such as refineries, oil pipelines, banks, telecommunications, and pharmaceuticals. They are also engaged in procuring nuclear technology.

Conventional War in Iraq

As I struggle to write down my thoughts, I know that to some, they will be controversial. The United States has been fighting a war in Iraq, and at this time they are engaged in finding solutions. There is great pressure to bring the soldiers home. The death toll among the American and Iraqi forces continues to rise, as well as the destruction of the militant insurgents who value death more than life. Their suicide bombers are a difficult enemy to detect and to attack in conventional ways. They have become an endless succession of human armament.

It is suspected that arms and insurgents are being sent into Iraq from Iran. There have also been reports that Iran continues their development of nuclear weapons. In my opinion, these reports are accurate. In spite of these occurrences, there is pressure for the United States to withdraw its troops from Iraq and normalize their relationship with Iran.

The new government and the majority of people in Iraq are Shiat. Iran is also Shiat. Although shaky, the United States has provided a roof of protection over Iraq, and if they leave now, I feel the pillars that hold up that roof are hollow and would quickly crumble, endangering the lives of many innocent people. With the absence of the American forces, Iran would definitely expand its fundamentalist Islamic government into Iraq. The Sunnis and the Kurds who are in the minority would fight the Shiat's domination, possibly leading to a full-blown civil war.

It is again my opinion that the United States must have some presence in Iraq for a long period of time in order to weaken the presence of Al Qaeda. Since 9-11, America has become a target and it can never again become complacent. A line has been drawn in the sand.

Muslims

My total environment influenced and immersed me!!!
When I left my mother's home for the first time, the words of my
childhood were always in my mind...
I am nobody; I am only the obedient servant of Allah...
I have no rights to question or to analyze Allah's will...
I have to obey anything and everything that Mighty Allah said through
Mohammad...
If I obey fully, I might come close to paradise but if I do not follow Allah's
will, it is certain that I will go to Hell
I do not want to do anything in this temporary life that will jeopardize
my beautiful eternal life in paradise.

As I reflect back in history, remembering my ancestry, I ask, who defeated the Persian Empire, the largest empire the world has ever known? Without dispute, it was Islam. For several centuries, the majority of true Iranians have been reluctant to accept the brutal and barbaric Muslim religion as their true faith. True Iranians are Persians, and they differentiate themselves from Arabs. Their dissatisfaction with the Islamic brutality has been recorded in history, and many times through the centuries, they have risen up against Islamic rule. In my opinion, the day will come when Iranians will act as Persians and reject injustice, discrimination, and intolerance from any tyrannical government that oppresses its citizens rather than protecting them.

Historical facts demonstrate that during the 700 years after Mohammad, most of the cities and regions that were conquered by the sword accepted the last of the three options that were enforced by the Muslim Crusaders:

(1) *I will bring against you tribes of people who are more eager for death than you are for life*, fight, and die.

(2) Convert and pay the Zakat (Only a small tax.)

235

(3) Keep your Biblical faith and pay the Jizyah (A large tax.)

Most preferred to remain in their own religion and pay Jizyah.

The expansion of Islam in the Middle East and North Africa was accomplished by intimidation, fear, and force. Today, the growth of Islam in the world is financed by the vast amount of Middle Eastern oil money. These revenues are used in sinister ways to buy nuclear weapons and ballistic missile arsenals, as well as the financing of terrorist armies. Most Islamic governments have allocated massive funding for the marketing of Islam propaganda in Western countries as well as China, Australia, and South Africa.

It is very difficult for me to understand the reasons why the West avoids dealing directly with Islamic problems. It seems that they are hidden behind an invisible curtain. Is it because Muslim countries control the oil that the West vitally needs? Or is it because the West needs oil money to maintain their economic liquidity?

Interestingly, the West continues, for unknown reasons, to define the terrorist Muslim as a Jihadist and the insurgent Muslim as a militant. These different titles have caused confusion. Whenever there is a Muslim uprising, the West invents a new terminology to fragment the source of the problem. The Western media differentiates the moderate Muslims from the extremists and the fanatics from the fundamentalist. In reality, they are all Muslims. They all believe in Mohammad, and they all follow the writings of the Koran. The Islamic culture has created violence and fear among all non-Muslims for the last 1,400 years. Islam is a violent religion!

I sympathize with the Muslim people who have not had the opportunity to be exposed to other ways of life. They live in a controlled environment filled with the bombardment of Islamic propaganda. Many in the world today are harassed and persecuted for their religious beliefs against Islam. Free speech is silenced with brutality and imprisonment. Women and children are denied their dignity. I feel pain for the Muslim youth and women. Censorship has kept the majority in the dark and has not given them the opportunity to experience the feelings of joy, love, and happiness. They are brainwashed into continuously mourning for Mohammad and his followers who were killed over 1,400 years ago. They believe by mourning and crying they will become closer to their promised paradise. Music, fun, and laughter are banned. Even dressing in colorful attire is considered anti-Islamic. The Muslim philosophy of life is to celebrate death and to look forward to an eternal life in paradise.

How can we emulate Mohammad, the founder of Islam, who consummated a marriage with a child nine years of age? How can we condone today's followers, who now encourage young innocent children to attend Madressahs, where they are brainwashed into thinking that it is evil if they do not spend many hours a day praying while bowing their heads in constant motion? They are the youth that are often recruited to be used for human armament and motivated by the promise of the ultimate life after death.

It is important for me to clearly emphasize that I am not against the Muslim people. I realize that they are constantly under pressure to abide by the rules that are spelled out in the Koran. The Muslim religion is considered by some to be a powerful cult. It is Islam, and when it is interpreted literally, its barbaric rules are inhumane. I personally have problems with such interpretations. In today's world, I feel that there is no room for backward barbarian laws and religious Fatwa.

Killing Is the Name of the Game

Terrorists are fighting an ideological and spiritual war. Their intolerant mission is to kill anyone who does not believe in Islam and does not follow their interpretation of the Koran. The terrorists have no value for life on earth because they believe the eternal life is in paradise. To become a suicide bomber is considered an honor, and there are always monetary rewards for the family that is left behind. Male terrorists are further motivated by the promise of the unlimited sexual pleasure that awaits them with seventy-two virgins in paradise.

Paradise is a land of bountiful streams, ripe fruit, wine that is not intoxicating, and peaceful serenity. When Mohammad led his men into battle against the Jews, they were convinced that they need not fear because, if they were killed themselves, this euphoric land would await them.

Today, women are also motivated to kill Jews. These women are enticed into self-sacrifice, knowing that their children will be taken care of financially by the Mullahs' oil money and that they themselves will be rewarded with a worry-free utopia.

In the twenty-first century, the brutality of the sword has returned and, combined with bombs and bullets, is a sanctioned mission of killing. The ancient hate for the Jewish religion still remains in the hearts of all Muslim followers. As long as Muslims exist, it is my opinion that there will always be hatred against the Jews.

It is difficult to fight a conventional type of war with this kind of elusive enemy. Killing becomes a game. As more terrorists are killed, others are being brainwashed and prepared spiritually for the next attack.

Training to Become a Killer

Training to become terrorists and suicide bombers continues to grow. It is suspected that even in the West, and especially in Great Britain, there are youth training facilities associated with certain mosques. Evidence has been found that some Islamic schools are teaching anti-Jewish and anti-Christian sentiments. Enjoying the advantages of freedom allows Western schooling, within the mosques, to operate without scrutiny. It is rumored that some of these schools promote discussion that portrays Osama Bin Laden as "simply the victim."

Once again, I am evaluating some of the frightening experiences that I was subjected to, which have given me the courage to be very candid about my conclusions regarding fanatical Islam.

What would have happened if Iran, with America's support, had remained a governing power in the Middle East? Obviously, we would not have seen the power and cruelty of Saddam Hussein. Kuwait would have never been attacked by Iraq. Iran with its ten percent of the world's oil would have maintained a power within OPEC that would have influenced the price and the volume of production, making it more competitive.

If we had not seen the power of Khomeini's religious ideas, which gave credence to the barbaric practices of the Taliban, Hezbollah, Hamas, and other fanatical Muslim groups, the civilized world would be a better place today.

As children, my brothers and I laughed and played with our modern Muslim friends. We were Muslims, but not fanatics or extremists. We were encouraged to attend school and learn to study in order to be able to choose a profession that would allow us to better our lives. We were not forced to pray at the mosque on Fridays or to leave school to gather for a demonstration. We prayed to Allah at the proper time, but we were not taught to kill others who did not believe in our religion. If we missed a prayer, we felt no guilt because, after all, a prayer was our own personal reverence to a "just" God, and we knew that he would be lenient if we were engaged in a worthy project. My mother passed the Muslim religion on to me, but adapted it to a contemporary society. She eliminated aspects of the religion, which no longer made sense, such as, total obedience to those Mullahs whose personal interpretation reflected a religion that was 1,400 years old. While continuing to educate myself in the Navy, the emphasis was always on defending and protecting the Muslim country of Iran. It would have been appalling to think of training our young cadets to kill those who did not believe in following Mohammad's teachings. We were respectful of all religions.

While living in Iran, my acquaintances were fine, decent Muslim men and women. Many from my era are gone now. They were murdered or fled and are now scattered throughout the world. Many of us, including my brothers, as well as our children, are no longer practicing Islam. In 1979, when Ayatollah Khomeini returned to Iran, it became difficult to justify his radical religious views that dated back to a barbaric society that existed 1,400 years ago.

What can I do to make the world aware of this insidious growth of Islam? What can I do to stop this madness? How can the innocent, hard-working people in the world become aware of the objectives of Muslims defined as "radicals"?

For the remainder of my life, I will extend a helping hand to the youth in Muslim countries. I was born a Muslim, and I have escaped Islam by discarding a religion that plays with the minds of all who embrace its evil teachings. My passion and quest is to educate the youth and, through constant exposure, teach them that they have the right to think for themselves and to break away from their controlled religious environment.

The ability to counteract daily brainwashing that teaches hate and self-sacrifice is difficult, but with the growth of Internet users around the world, powerful messages can be observed. Exposure to youth from other cultures can be positive and words of hope can be encouraging.

The Islamic government of Iran restricts Internet communication. However, younger generations have managed to avoid regulations by communicating and networking above the restricted grid through digital audio and video media.

In this highly controlled environment, Iranian youth have come up with their own solutions for expressing themselves and communicating with each other. They use a secret language and increasingly use the Internet to communicate. This has changed the way the Iranian youth think and can be a great opportunity in order to exchange ideas.

I have founded a website, www.lsbinternational.org, for educating youth to appreciate **life** not **death**. A nonprofit organization has been formed with the emphasis on eliminating the motivation of the suicide bomber. To me, it will be a constant piercing needle that penetrates the darkness of evil and encourages youth to realize that they have the ability to think freely, to question and achieve feelings of self-worth by becoming productive members within their own society.

I will not be satisfied until radical Islam recruiters see a significant slowdown in the availability of their young candidates for human armament. I hope that the day will come when the world will know that they have seen the last suicide bomber.

At the beginning of 2009, as I turn off my computer and put down my pen, the United States has completed a national election. By the time that this manuscript is published, there will be a new president in the White House. The American people are concerned about a shrinking economy and a volatile stock market. Oil prices continue to be unpredictable. Hopefully, America will remain informed and aware of what could happen if their need for oil, and an unrealistic peace, forces them into making concessions with countries who hate us. There are those who might, at first, hold out an olive branch, but then, at a later date, attack aggressively when the time is right. The whole world watches as America struggles with these important decisions. It is my hope that world negotiators concur with my family's wise advice: "Mullahs are not to be trusted."

Mano Bakh

Kelli McIntyre's Note

Three years ago, I stepped into my grandparents' Southern California home and my life changed. I was introduced to a warm, friendly man wearing an adorable beret, Mano Bakh. He had just presented a matching hat to my grandfather, who laughed in his deep chuckle of pure amusement and promptly placed it on his bald head. My grandfather was in the late stages of pancreatic cancer, and it was a difficult situation for our entire family. We were pleased to share our afternoon luncheon with Mano and his wife. During this meal, I first heard bits and pieces of the harrowing adventure that led Mano to Southern California. Even in his ill health, as the story was told, my grandfather recognized the potential for a fascinating biography and together with my grandmother began to encourage his good friend, Mano Bakh, to write about his life.

Sadly, over the next several months my grandfather's health began to fail until, he passed on Easter Sunday 2007. After the difficult loss, we were all left at loose ends. In honor of his memory and in support of his great friend, my grandmother, Jacqueline Le Beau, dedicated the next two years to the editing and translation of Mano Bakh's story.

While my grandfather was alive, my grandparents had many amazing adventures. His engineering skills coupled with my grandmother's amazing penchant for design made them a creative powerhouse and a force to be reckoned with. After his passing, as my grandmother delved into the incredible adventures that led to her powerful friendship with Mano, it was an honor to work with her.

Since that first luncheon, I knew that Mano had a marvelous adventure to be told and an important message that the lessons of his life left with him. Although I could never dream to fill my grandfather's large shoes as a creative partner to my grandmother, my involvement with her in this project has truly changed my life. It is seldom that a grandchild has the opportunity to partake in such a project with a grandparent. This journey could not have been possible without the frantic hours of editing, note taking, and research, which kept her awake late into the night. This living story would never have come to fruition, without the time I spent with Mano and my grandmother at the long oval table in her dining room, writing, rewriting, reading, and rereading this book.

This note is my opportunity to thank both my grandmother and Mano for pushing me to finish this project and providing all of the research, editing, and contributions that made it possible. Thank you.

References

The Islamization of America: The Islamic Strategy and the Christian Response.
By: Abdullah Al-Araby

On the road to a new world, published in the Islam Review (Islamreview.com).
By: Abdullah Al-Araby

Carter sold out Iran - 1977 – 1978, written by Chuck Morse, published in www.chuckmorse.com

Ruhollah ibn Mustafa Musawi Khomeini Hindi, published in September 2005 in www.dictatorofthemonth.com.

The United States and the Iran-Iraq War 1980-1988, written by Stephen R. Shalom and published in the Iran Chamber society, / www.iranchamber.com

Defying the Iranian Revolution, By Manouchehr Ganji

Articles from Iranian.com / history.

Personal memoir and notes.

Glossary

Abbas	Mano Bakh's grandfather (*mother's side*).
Abu Bakr	Aisha's father. The Sunni believe he is the successor of Mohammad.
Aisha	Mohammad's second wife. She was 6 years old when she was married to Mohammad.
Ali	Mano Bakh's father's first name. Also the name of Mohammad's son in law.
Allah o Akbar	Expression used by Muslims around the world. Meaning *"God is great"* in Arabic.
Amerigo Vespucci	A three steel mast sailing ship named after the explorer Amerigo Vespucci.
Axis of power	During World War II Germany, Italy and Japan opposed the Allies.
Ayatollah	Means 'the sign of Allah. (*Those who carry the title are experts in Islamic studies.*)
Ayatollah Ali Khamenei	The Ayatollah replaced Khomeini as the supreme leader of Islamic Republic of Iran
Ayatollah Khomeini	Shiat Muslin leader of the 1979 Iranian Islamic revolution.

Band Andazi	A form of hair removal. Using a thread (*the band*).
Brigantino	A training sailing ship built on land, at the Italian Naval Academy in Livorno.
Café' Glace	Hot coffe mixed with ice cream.
Caliph	Caliph, referred to as Commander of the Faithful, or leader of the Muslims.
Caspian Sea	The largest enclosed body of water on Earth by area. (*A full-fledged sea north of Iran*).
CENTO	The Central Treaty Organization was adopted in 1955 and was dissolved in 1979.
Chelo Kabab	The national dish of Iran. (*Steamed, saffroned Persian rice and scewed meet*).
Chicke Tikka	Chicken cubes marinated in Indian spices and cooked in clayoven called tandoor.
Cyrus	Cyrus the great, the founder of the Persian Empire (*c. 600BC*)
Damavand	Mount Damāvand is a dormant volcano and the highest peak in Iran.
Farsi	The official language of Iran. (*Also spoken in Afghanistan, and Tajikistan*).
Fatima	Mohammad's daughter who was married to Mohammad's cousin, Ali..

Fatwa	A religious opinion on Islamic law, issued by an Islamic scholar.
Gofte gu	Or Goftegu is the arrangement meeting to discuss and agree on details of a wedding.
Hafsah	Umar's daughter. (*The forth wife of Mohammad*).
Halal	An Arabic word referring to what is permissible under Islam.
Haram	An Arabic word referring to what is prohibited by Islamic faith.
Hashim	Mano Bakh's grandfather (*father's side*)
Hejleh	Room prepared fro Bride and Groom to consumate a marriage.
Jihad	Is he duty of Muslims for expansion and defense of the Islamic state.
Jizyah	Per capita tax levied on Islamic state's non-Muslim citizens, who meet certain criteria.
Kad Khoda	Or Kadkhoda is the headman of an Iranian village.
Kayhan	One of the most influential newspapers in Iran. (Published by the Kayhan Institute).
Khadija	Mohammad's first wife, the wealthy widow fifteen years his senior. (*555-619*)

Khark Island	A small island in the Persian Gulf, once the world's largest offshore crude oil terminal.
Khorramshahr	A port city in southwestern Iran. (*The city extends to the right bank of the Shatt al-Arab*).
Koran	Muslims believe the Koran or Qur'an is the book of divine guidance for mankind.
Kulthum	Mohammad's daughter who was married to Uthman.
Madressah	Or Madrasah, madarasaa, medresa, madrassa, etc. is an Arabic word for school.
Masha	Mother of Mano Bakh.
Montecuccoli	An Italian Cruiser, built in 1935. (*almost 600 feet long, used for cadet training*).
Mullah	The title for some Islamic clergymen.
Musulmani	Italian word for Muslims.
Nazi	Established as a totalitarian dictatorship that existed from 1933 to 1945.
NIOC	The National Iranian Oil Company.

Nowruz	Nowruz, "Iranian New Year," is the first day of spring.
Omar Khayyam	A Persian poet, mathematician, philosopher and astronomer, (*1048 – 1122*).
OPEC	Organization of Petroleum Exporting Countries.
Pamir	A training German sailing ship. (*Built in Hamburg in 1905*).
Punto	Italian word meaning point.
Reichatag fire	Was an arson attack on the Reichstag building in Berlin on 27 February 1933.
Reza Shah	Founder of Pahlavi Dynesty, king of Iran (*1925-1941*).
SAVAK	The domestic security and intelligence service of Iran from 1957 to 1979.
Shah	The title of Iranian kings, commonly referred to as the Last Shah of Iran.
Shiat	those who Believe that Ali, Muhammad's cousin and son in law was the first Imam.
Sofreh	A Persian word for cloth. (*Spread on the floor on top of the carpet, on which food is served*).
Sofreh Khaneh	A room where Sofreh is spread, such as diningroom.

Sofreh-ye-Aghd	A Sofreh addorned with food, is placed on the floor, facing east for the wedding ceremony.
Stalin	Was General Secretary of the Communist Party of the Soviet Union's (*1922-1953*)
Sunni	Almost 85% of the world's muslims are Sunni, believing that Abu Bakr was the first Imam.
Tar	A long-necked, small waisted Iranian/ Persian musical instrument
Tonbak	A goblet drum from Persia. (*The principal percussion instrument of Persian music*).
Tripartite treaty	Signed in Berlin on September 27, 1940 between Nazi Germany, Fascist Italy and Japan.
Umar	Father of Mohammad's fouth wife. The second Caliph according to the Sunni
USSR	Union of Soviet Socialist Republics
Uthman	Mohammad's son in law. (*The Sunni believe he is the third Caliph*).
Winston Churchill	British Prime Minister during World War II and again from 1951 to 1955.
Zakat	The Islamic principle of giving a percentage of one's income to charity.
Zoroastrian	The religion and philosophy based on the teachings ascribed to the prophet Zoroaster.